# NIGHTINGALE

## By the Author

Ladyfish

Clean Slate

Nightingale

Visit us at www.boldstrokesbooks.com

# NIGHTINGALE

*by*
Andrea Bramhall

2014

# NIGHTINGALE

ISBN 13: 978-1-62639-059-1

THIS TRADE PAPERBACK ORIGINAL IS PUBLISHED BY
BOLD STROKES BOOKS, INC.
P.O. BOX 249
VALLEY FALLS, NY 12185

FIRST EDITION: MAY 2014

**CREDITS**
EDITORS: VICTORIA OLDHAM AND CINDY CRESAP
PRODUCTION DESIGN: STACIA SEAMAN
COVER DESIGN BY SHERI (GRAPHICARTIST2020@HOTMAIL.COM)

# Acknowledgments

*Nightingale* is a work of fiction. But behind the fiction is a reality that is lived by millions of women and girls across the world, every single day. Not because of religion, but because of ignorance, illiteracy, and the abuse of religion by those in power, no matter who they are or where they are in the world. Education is the key to reducing this imbalance, but it is a gift taken lightly by the few and beyond the reach of so many—despite all they would suffer for it. At the age of fifteen, Malala Yousafzai was shot in the head by the Taliban because she refused to stay home from school. She survived and spoke at the UN on her sixteenth birthday. She told delegates of how her injury and her struggle made her stronger and more determined to gain her education and help her country toward peace in any way she could. If only there were a few more like Malala, maybe then stories like *Nightingale* would belong only in the realm of fiction.

There is a tireless group working behind the scenes at Bold Strokes Books, and without them this book wouldn't be what it is. Rad, Vic, Cindy, Sheri, and Sandy are but a few who make the magic of books look so much easier than it really is. Thank you for your help and your expertise and yet another fabulous book cover.

My merry band of beta readers, Louise, Amy, Kim, and Dawn. Thank you really isn't enough. Your help and encouragement are appreciated more than I can ever tell you. And thank you to Nicki Hastie, for naming Steph MacKenzie at the Bold Strokes Books UK festival in Nottingham in 2013.

To the love of my life, always...Galaxy chocolate...LOL, just kidding, of course I meant Louise.

And also to the woman who taught me the most about acceptance and tolerance. My Auntie Wendy. Your acceptance and your lack of judgment in all things have been one of the biggest influences of my life and I hope—I truly hope—you see that within these pages.

# CHAPTER ONE

*Pakistan, today*

Charlie took a deep breath. The aroma of sun-scorched earth, spices, and small farm animals filled the air. Goats bleated their greetings to anyone who passed, and chickens pecked at the ground. It never ceased to amaze her. She was less than an hour from Islamabad—a bustling metropolis—and yet she felt she had stepped into a different world. The small Pakistani village was home to no more than a hundred people on the edge of the Peshawar plain where the desert encroached on one side and the mountains loomed on the other, and Charlie had the feeling that the village had stolen the land it was sitting on. Everything had a temporary feel to it, as though mountains or desert would soon reclaim it and cast the villagers out in search of another place to settle.

She climbed out of the Jeep in front of her destination and pulled the scarf closer to her face. She hated wearing it because of the way her sweat seeped into the fabric in the heat of the fast-fading sun. But as much as she hated it, she knew it was a small price to pay to be able to accomplish her work.

The house was made of thick clay walls. It had a straw roof, and a rickety fence enclosed a dusty, rocky yard with a chicken coop in the corner. It was typical of the village, and she knew that inside there would be no plumbing, no electricity, and the only heating in the surprisingly chilly Pakistani winter would come from a fire in the hearth. She knocked on the door and waited. She could hear voices inside, a child sniffling, and the soft shuffle of slippered feet across the floor. The hinges creaked as the door swung open and a bearded man appeared.

"Yes?" His English was thickly accented, and he looked at her curiously. It had been a long time since Charlie had questioned why people never addressed her in Arabic, since her blue eyes and blond hair visible under the headscarf were a definite giveaway to her Western roots.

"Mr. Malik, I'm Charlie Porter. We've spoken on the phone several times over the past few weeks."

"The woman from the embassy?" A frown marred his face, the deep-set eyes turned wary, and the crinkles at the corners deepened. The white linen tunic of his traditional clothing stood out starkly against the roughhewn wooden door, and the loose-fitting pants rustled as he moved.

Charlie prepared herself. "Yes."

"I have nothing to say to you." He began to close the door, and she quickly held out her hand to halt its progress.

"Sir, I have a proposition for you. Would you allow me to speak with you? Please." Charlie looked him in the eye as he stopped pushing, determined to make him listen. She knew that this was the final resolution for this case, and a child's future rested in her hands.

"You want to take my daughter from me." His voice was gruff, scratchy almost.

"No, sir, I want to make your life a little easier." She held up a newspaper folded into quarters and a paragraph was circled in red. "I can give you the fresh start your family wants you to have." The circled piece was a notification of his new wife's pregnancy. It had been placed in the newspaper by Mr. Malik's father and father-in-law, and it was obvious not only how proud they were of the impending birth, but also that the child of his first failed marriage, to an English woman they hadn't approved of, was something of an inconvenience for the family—a reminder of his failure and a block to them all moving on. She was sure that both families must be putting him under enormous pressure to do something about the little girl. She hoped that the option she was offering him was somewhat more palatable than it had been before.

"She is my daughter. She should be with me."

"A little girl needs her mother too."

"She has a mother." He started to raise his voice, then caught himself. "I have remarried. She has a good mother."

"I understand that." Charlie hated the way she had to appease the man, playing to his ego to get what she needed from him. But this wasn't her first negotiation, and she knew how to play the game. As a child, she had been fascinated by the game of chess. She'd read about the strategies, and the defences, opening gambits, and sacrifices. She loved the nuances and the variations, and she loved the dichotomy of the aggression and subtlety that incorporated the game. And the patience she had learned had always been one of her greatest assets. She put every lesson she'd learned into play now. "I also understand that it must be difficult for her."

"My wife is a proper Muslim woman. She will do her duty."

"I'm sure she will. But wouldn't it be easier for you both to be able to start your new family with just the two of you, instead of having the reminder of your failed marriage living beneath your roof?" Charlie loathed the way she had to make the little girl sound like an inconvenience for her father. She hoped that the child was far enough away or unable to understand English after three years in Pakistan.

"She is my daughter." His voice cracked, and Charlie knew she was making headway.

"I know. But wouldn't your wife appreciate you thinking of her needs at this time? Her first baby, your first baby together, is due soon."

"My wife will do as I tell her. She is a good Muslim woman."

"Mr. Malik, do you know much about the cuckoo bird?"

"What are you talking about?"

"The cuckoo bird, Mr. Malik. Do you know anything about it?"

"What does that have to do with this?"

"If you would indulge me a moment." She waited for some sign of acknowledgment before she continued. "The cuckoo bird doesn't make a nest of its own. It's a parasite in the bird world. It lays eggs in the nest of another bird and leaves the host to raise the chick. The cuckoo chick grows so fast it will often kill the host bird's chicks by pushing them out of the nest or squashing the eggs." Charlie watched to make sure that he was following her. "The host bird will continue to feed and raise the cuckoo chick until it flies from the nest, and it will do so to the detriment of her own chicks."

Mr. Malik leaned back from the door and stared off to his right, seemingly into space.

Charlie smiled. "The cuckoo chick isn't evil. It's not even wrong. It's merely trying to survive." She could see the effect her words were having on the man. His shoulders slumped and his brow furrowed as he seemed to consider everything she was saying. Perhaps everything his family had been saying too. "It's the nature of the bird. It cannot help that it's in the wrong place."

He slowly raised his eyes to meet her hers. She could see the glimmer of tears, and she knew he'd made his decision. "She will be taken care of properly?"

"You have my word."

"It will be best for everyone."

"Of course." Charlie felt the thrill of victory surge through her, the adrenaline making her hands shake as she pushed the newspaper into her bag. She tempered her excitement, not wanting to say or do anything that would make him backtrack on his decision. All she wanted was for him to hand over the little girl and for the two of them to leave, get back to the British Embassy, and get the child back to her mother.

"Horia." He shouted into the house and turned his back on her. He spoke in Urdu before pushing the door open wide. He had his hand on the little girl's back as he pushed her toward the door. Charlie knew from the file that she was five years old and had been in Pakistan for three years. Her clothes were well kept, if a little dirt-smeared at the end of the day. She looked healthy, whole, but not very happy.

"What did you tell her?" Charlie held her hand out to the child and waited for her to take it.

"I told her that she was to go with you. That is all."

Charlie nodded and bit back the angry retort she wanted to yell at him and reminded herself that it wasn't her place to judge. She was here to reunite a mother and her daughter, not decide who was the better parent—the one who hadn't stopped searching for Horia, or the parent who had taken her as a way to punish her mother. And, conceivably, based on the tears in his eyes, because he actually wanted her as well. It saddened her how common it was that children were used as weapons by their parents. The damage done to them in the process was immeasurable.

She waved and beckoned the child to her. The girl's eyes were wide open, and fat tears clung to her lashes as she tugged on the thin cotton shirt she wore. Mr. Malik pushed her out the door toward Charlie, muttering after her. The child's lower lip trembled, and the first tears ran down her cheeks. Charlie lifted the child into her arms, settling her against her hip, and reached into her bag again with her free hand.

"I need you to sign this document, Mr. Malik." She waved a sheaf of papers at him.

"What is it?" He took hold of the pages without glancing at the content.

"It gives me custody of Horia and will enable me to get her a passport. It says that you give up your legal responsibilities and rights over her." Charlie held out a pen to him. "I need you to sign it."

"And if I don't?"

Charlie shrugged. "You'll make it difficult for me, but not impossible." She played down the difficulties she would face if he didn't sign, knowing it would be damn near impossible to get the child a new British passport quickly without his signature, especially as she was leaving without any legal documents for the child. The girl's mother had already explained that he had burned the child's original passport and birth certificate, which meant things were far more complicated.

He looked at the little girl, then down at the papers in his hand. Charlie could hear a soft voice behind him, but she couldn't make out what was being said. It seemed whatever it was helped her cause, though, because he grunted and held the papers against the wall as he signed them.

Charlie stuffed them into her bag when he handed them back to her and walked as quickly as she could to the Jeep. She slid the child across the bench seat and climbed in after her. A woman's cry from behind her made Charlie wind down the window.

The woman had her hair covered and was holding the scarf over the lower half of her face. Only her eyes were visible, and tears gathered, growing fat behind rapidly blinking lids. She reached through the open window and held a stuffed bear out to the little girl and wiped the tears from her cheeks. She whispered softly to her words that Charlie couldn't understand, but the little girl nodded and stuck her thumb into her mouth as she cuddled the bear tightly against her chest.

"She good girl. You take care good?"

Charlie smiled. "I promise."

The woman nodded and waddled back to the house, her heavily pregnant body obviously struggling.

Charlie pressed on the accelerator and gripped the steering wheel tighter as she drove over the hard, rocky ground. She glanced in her rearview mirror, pleased and saddened in the same instant that the little girl's father had already closed the door. She was happy the fight was over and that mother and daughter were to be reunited, but the feeling of disillusionment was always strong when a parent so readily gave up their child.

"My name's Charlie, and I'm going to take you back to your mother."

The little girl trembled but didn't say anything, her little arms wrapped tightly around the stuffed bear. Charlie shook her head and tried to block out the surge of sorrow that always accompanied moments such as this. As many times as she saw it happen, it never ceased to amaze her how much pain people were willing to inflict upon others. Especially those they were supposed to care for.

"It's going to be okay." Charlie risked a quick glance and smiled at her, and wondered if she remembered how to speak English, or even understood anything she was saying, but Charlie doubted it. She brushed her hand over the little girl's head, soothing her.

They had about an hour's drive to the British Embassy from the small village on the outskirts of Taxila on the Peshawar Plain, and soon the rutted dirt roads gave way to smooth tarmac and the growing lights of the city on the horizon as dusk began to descend.

She clipped her Bluetooth earpiece into place and dialled. She tapped her fingers on the steering wheel while she waited.

"Goddamn it, Porter, where the hell are you?" Jasper Jackson's voice shook as he clearly tried to control his anger.

Charlie flinched at the volume directly in her ear. "I'm about an hour out. I've got the kid with me, so you can get the mother on standby."

"What the hell did you do?"

"Nothing. I just talked to the guy."

"We've been talking to the guy for weeks. What the hell did you have to say that was any different this time? Why did you have to go in person? Why did you go alone? You know the rules. Damn it, Charlie! What the hell—"

"Sorry, JJ, you're breaking up." She hung up quickly, knowing she'd pay for that later, but at least not while she was driving.

Charlie ran her fingers through her short curls and rubbed the back of her neck in a useless attempt to ease the tension that caused a headache behind her eyes.

She turned off the Grand Trunk Road onto the Kashmir Highway, keeping up a litany of useless information for the child. She told her about the High Court building as they passed it, the Pakistani flag flying proud and true as the lights shone and the gentle breeze stirred the air. In the distance, she could make out the illuminated pillars of the Shah Faisal Mosque with its ornate marble façade reflecting the light into the sky, a siren's call to the faithful. She exited the highway and made a couple of turns before she was driving down Embassy Road into the heart of the diplomatic conclave.

It had always surprised her how drab and ugly the British Embassy building was next to the other ornate buildings within the diplomatic heart of Pakistan—utilitarian, box-like, and beige. But it was safety. It was British soil and protection in a land that was foreign and rarely forgiving.

Armed guards swung the gate open and let her inside as she flashed her ID. She had barely pulled the car to a stop when a small group hustled to the car and pulled open the doors. The child startled and began to cry as hands she no longer recognized pulled her out of the vehicle.

"Horia." The woman cradled the child to her breast and fell to her knees. "My baby." Tears rained down her face as she looked over the little girl's head at Charlie. "Thank you. Thank you. You've brought me back my angel."

Charlie smiled, choking back her own tears. "I don't know how much English she still knows. I don't think she understood me at all."

The woman waved her hand. "It doesn't matter." She cupped Horia's face in her hands and kissed her forehead. "She'll learn."

Charlie felt a meaty hand on her shoulder. "Another maverick stunt, Porter? What am I going to do with you?"

Charlie turned and grinned up at her tall, redheaded boss. "Give me a raise?"

Jasper Jackson shook his head and tried to hide his smile beneath a scowl. "I should put you on some sort of probation or something. You can't keep going off and pulling stunts like this. Every time you go out there on your own, you're in danger."

"JJ, I know what I'm doing." She watched the woman and child as they were led into the building.

"Yes, but even you can't control everything out there, Charlie. What if you'd shown up at his house and he'd pulled a gun?"

Charlie rapped her knuckles on her chest and the unmistakable metallic sound of a bulletproof vest sounded.

"That doesn't protect that pretty blond head of yours."

Charlie laughed. From anyone else she might have taken offence at the comment, but they had worked together for almost three years now. She knew the giant of a man had nothing but the utmost respect for her professionally and cared for her deeply as a friend. "I'd spoken to this guy for weeks, JJ. He wasn't going to pull anything like that. He wanted the kid off his hands. He wanted to make life a bit easier with the new wife now that she has a baby on the way. This was convenient and allowed him to save face. He wasn't going to do anything to me."

"He never mentioned anything about any of that in the calls."

"No, but his father and father-in-law posted an advert in the local paper announcing the happy news that his son and new wife were expecting their first child." She buffed her fingernails against her shirt.

Jasper shook his head. "And you didn't think it would be a good idea to tell me this?"

"I just did."

"Before. As you damn well know you should have done."

"Look, the info came in. I saw an opportunity, and it paid off. We got the result we wanted, and a mother and daughter are back together and will soon head safely back to the UK. What more do we need, JJ?"

"Come with me." Jasper led her into the building, not stopping until they were in his office. He stepped behind his desk and reached for a file, flipping it open before he held it out to her. "We have a new recruit coming on board."

Charlie took the file and glanced over the photograph and basic info. There were six members of the task force, including the two of them. They all had different areas of expertise to aid in their mission, which was to return British nationals who had been forcibly relocated to Pakistan back to the families and loved ones waiting for them in Britain. "Okay. And?"

"I want you to train her."

Charlie dropped the file back onto his desk. "JJ, no. You know I can't do that."

"No, I know you don't like to. But you can and you will train her, and I want you to do it by the book."

"I'm not cut out to teach. I don't have the patience."

"Charlie, you have all the patience in the world when it comes to a negotiation, and you have more than enough to train someone."

"Don't do this. It won't be good for her."

JJ laughed. "I think it'll be perfect for her. And for you."

Charlie scowled.

"Look, Charlie, you are by far the best negotiator I have ever worked with. You get more results, faster, with less intervention than anyone else on this task force. And this list"—he held up a stack of A4 paper filled with names—"only gets longer every day. We need to be able to give more families the result you just did tonight."

"Did I not just get a dressing down for that?"

"I need you to keep me in the loop more and I need you to follow protocol, but I need you to be effective too." He ran his hand over his face. "Next time call me en route, okay?"

"I did."

"I mean on the way there. Not the way back."

"All right, all right." She picked up the file again and glanced at the picture of the woman. "You're really gonna make me train her?"

"Yes."

"Why?"

"I need more people who can do what you do, Charlie. Walk in there without a gun and bring people home." JJ pointed at the file in her hand. "Read it. I think you'll find it interesting. But if you think she can't do it, then…"

Charlie rolled her eyes and turned to leave. "See you in the morning."

The streets were quiet as she drove home to her empty apartment. She left the lights off and dropped the file onto the coffee table in her lounge. The bright city lights that shone on the other side of the glass were more than enough for her to see by. She poured herself a glass of locally brewed vodka, grateful she'd had the foresight to purchase the permit that allowed non-Muslims to drink liquor. The alcohol warmed her throat as she sipped and stared out the window, and the question that never stopped plaguing her rose again. *Are you still out there, Hazaar?*

# CHAPTER TWO

*The North of England, then*

Charlie stared out the window and drummed her fingers nervously against her bag as she neared her destination. She glanced at her watch before dragging her hand through her curls and scratching absently at her scalp. She opened her bag again to check that the music she needed was still inside and hadn't escaped, just to finish off her morning from hell.

She'd set off for her audition an hour early to be sure she wouldn't be late. She waited for her first bus, not concerned when it arrived ten minutes late because she had fifty to spare. While she waited for the next bus, the rain began. Not heavy rain that's over in a few minutes, but rather a fine drizzle that was barely perceptible to the skin and had her drenched to the core in about thirty seconds flat. She'd rummaged through her bag but couldn't find her umbrella, and with no shelter close by, all she could do was wait in the rain. She held her bag over her head, trying to stave off the explosion of frizz that would soon attack her hair and create an untamable mass. Her crisp white shirt was quickly heading into the realms of indecent, and her black pants were stuck to her legs. The truck that sped quickly through the large puddle that had formed at lightning speed in front of her made everything so much the worse.

She needed to get to the Royal Northern College of Music and try to dry off a little before her audition, and precious time she should use to practice would be wasted in front of a hand dryer in the ladies' bathroom. She began to softly hum the melody of her piece, going over the trickier parts in her head, hoping her voice would hold on the top note, right at the height of her range. Music calmed her, and right now, she needed to stay calm.

The bus finally approached her stop, and she made her way to the front, her shirt and trousers stuck to her slim body and pulling uncomfortably with each move. The bus driver's gaze raked over her, and when he eventually met her eyes and raised his eyebrows suggestively, she rolled her eyes and shook her head. Not even if she were desperate. She spent the journey staring out the window and ignoring the way he stared at her in his rearview mirror. When they arrived, she hurried down the steps before he could speak and ran for cover under the college awning.

She made her way to the front desk and waited patiently as the receptionist held up her hand and answered the phone. Her nasal voice grated as she spoke into the mouthpiece.

"Hello, Royal Northern College of Music, please hold." She looked up and smiled at Charlie as she spoke. "How can I help you?"

"I have an audition with Mr. Swallen."

"Of course, your name?"

"Charlie. Charlie Porter." The woman trailed her finger down the computer screen in front of her.

"Ah, yes. Charlotte Porter. If you'll take a seat, he'll be ready for you in a few minutes."

"Can you tell me where the ladies' room is, please?" Charlie motioned at her clothes, and the receptionist looked her up and down. She smiled slightly and nodded toward the far corner as she answered another call.

Charlie turned around and made her way across the reception area, pushed open the door, and went straight to the dryer. She tried to angle the nozzle to dry off the front of her shirt, but it didn't do any good. She looked over her shoulder and checked all the stalls were empty before she slid off her shirt. She held it under the dryer and kept listening for the door to open, not wanting to be caught topless. She jumped when she heard a creak outside and froze till the hot air started to burn her skin. No one came in, and she relaxed. The old building must be creaky in general. She drew in a breath quickly and moved her fingers, trying to speed up the drying as the fabric creased in her hands. She didn't react to the next creak, sure it was nothing, just like before.

She screamed and jumped when she looked in the mirror and saw someone moving behind her.

The young woman's eyes widened. "I'm sorry."

Charlie glanced at herself in the mirror. Her curls were somewhat wild, her trousers were stuck to her legs, and she clutched her shirt to her chest, dismayed that it wasn't covering her bra. She shook her head. "No, I'm sorry. I got caught in the rain and I have an audition and I can't go to it like this. I was just trying to dry off a bit, and it's not going very well." She tried to adjust her shirt to afford herself some modesty, with little success. "I'm rambling. I'm sorry if I've embarrassed you."

"You'll find the second one along is quicker." She pointed to the next dryer. "It happens all the time. I've no idea why, but the second one always gets things dry quicker."

Charlie moved over and pressed the button. She kept her eyes focused on the task in hand and hoped the stranger would just move away and let her carry on.

"Who's your audition with?"

"Mr. Swallen." Charlie caught a glimpse of amused eyes watching her in the mirror as the young woman washed her hands and moved to the dryer next to her. Her arm brushed against Charlie's as she reached out, and she shivered under the jolt of electricity that coursed through her, and her shirt flittered to the ground. They both squatted to pick it up. Charlie's fingers trembled as she picked it up off the floor, and she couldn't help but stare into the young woman's eyes. They were chocolate brown with flecks of honey gathered around the pupils, and she licked her full lips with a deft flick of her tongue. They looked so soft Charlie wanted to reach out and touch them, to run her fingertips over their soft fullness, perhaps even taste them with her own.

She shook her head to clear the fog, unable to recall anything the young woman had said as Charlie stared at her mouth. "I'm sorry. What did you say?"

She smiled, those beautiful lips pulling back to reveal a row of even, white teeth. "I said, that must mean you're a singer. He's a good teacher. Hates people who sing show tunes at the auditions, though. He gets inundated with people singing songs from musicals. Anything else gets in without any problem. What are you singing?"

Charlie wanted to groan as they stood up together, and she took in the full exotic Arabic beauty that stood in front of her. Mahogany dark hair hung in soft waves around her shoulders. Long, graceful fingers were still wrapped about her blouse, and Charlie could make out the full womanly curves beneath the flowing gypsy style skirt and blouse. "'I Dreamed A Dream' from *Les Misérables*."

The woman laughed and pointed to the shirt. "Might be best to leave it wet then." She laughed harder, and her hair swayed as her head moved. "I'm just kidding. But your bra is just going to wet the shirt straight through again anyway."

Charlie sighed, knowing the woman was right. As soon she left, with a cheerful "good luck," Charlie removed her sodden bra and tucked it into her bag before quickly redressing. She couldn't get the woman's face from her mind. The striking beauty she assumed to be Middle Eastern played on her mind as she went over and over each detail of the brief encounter, and she was shocked to find herself more turned on than she could remember being in a long, long time.

The reception area was quiet when she left the bathroom, and she looked for the woman who had spoken to her, relieved when there was no sign of her. She let out the breath she was holding and made her way toward the chairs.

"Miss Porter, Mr. Swallen is ready for you now." The receptionist pointed to the door next to the reception desk that led to the main auditorium. Charlie paused before she walked through the doors, just long enough to push away the butterflies gathered in her stomach.

"Make your way to the stage, please." The deep male voice rumbled toward her from the front of the seating bank, disembodied from the person that never glanced in her direction. She walked slowly to the front of the huge room and up the steps onto the stage.

"Thank you. Miss…?"

"Porter. Charlie Porter."

"Thank you, Miss Porter. Now what have you prepared for us today?" Charlie stuck her hand into her bag and pulled out her sheet music, the number from *Les Misérables* lying on the top. The words of the young woman in the bathroom echoed in her head, and she quickly shuffled the piece to the back and held on to the stack with trembling hands.

"It's a song called 'Nightingale' by Norah Jones." She heard papers rustling and the creak of a chair.

"Very well, an unusual choice of song, I must say. May I ask why you have chosen this piece?"

"It's a favourite of mine, a simple song with a beautiful melody. I just love to sing it." She smiled as she spoke and gained confidence in her snap decision as she did so.

"Give your music to the pianist, and when you're ready, please begin."

She walked slowly toward the piano, and her hand shook as she neared. The woman from the bathroom grinned at her from her seat on the piano bench.

"Do you want me to play it in the key it's written?"

Charlie nodded, then cleared her throat. "Yes, please."

"No problem, and don't worry. Your secret is safe with me. I'm very good at keeping secrets." The woman winked and took the shaking pages from her hand. She laid them out quickly as Charlie returned to centre stage. The first chord rang from the piano and held in the air, twisting on the breeze of the air-conditioning unit. Her eyes closed as her lips formed the first sounds of the song and gave life to the simple words.

The piano followed her effortlessly; the chords danced about the auditorium, and her voice caressed every note.

It was over much too quickly. The piano's notes faded as her voice drifted to a whisper, and she let her head fall to her chest. A small applause sounded from the seating bank.

"Very refreshing, Miss Porter, thank you very much. I'll have an answer for you quickly, I'm sure."

She could make out the faint scratching of a pencil against paper as she walked to the piano to collect her music.

"Beautiful." The woman smiled, and those full lips taunted her again. The woman's eyes met hers without a hint of amusement or teasing this time.

Charlie smiled back, again surprised at how nervous and excited she made her feel. "Yeah, well, thanks for the tip."

"I meant you." Their fingers touched as Charlie took the papers back and the electricity shot along Charlie's arm. "Meet me in the cafeteria in half an hour. You can get me a coffee as thanks."

Charlie knew she was staring, but she couldn't stop herself. She'd never responded to anyone so quickly before, and her reaction scared her as much as it excited her. She quickly stuffed the papers back into her bag and tried to hide her shaking hands. "Why on earth should I wait for you?"

"Because you're curious."

Charlie spluttered a laugh. "About what?"

The woman's gaze never faltered. "About me." She turned back to her music with a mischievous smile.

Charlie was stunned as she backed away from her and left the auditorium. She was through reception and on the college steps before she stopped to think about what the hell had just happened. Adrenaline coursed through her body, and she knew it was her reaction to the woman just as much as from her performance. She stood under the concrete awning and looked out at the street. The rain was still falling, heavier than before, and the raindrops rippled in the puddles created by the uneven paving stones. Cars, bikes, and busses all drove past her, people walked by, and Charlie closed her eyes.

Running away. Not from the woman behind the piano and her laughing eyes, but from herself. She'd decided to make a fresh start. That's what coming to university was supposed to be all about. Starting over, taking chances, learning, experiencing, and growing. And here at the first chance she had to meet someone new—someone she found extraordinarily attractive—she was running away. Again.

*What am I so scared of?* She didn't need to ask the question. Not really. She already knew the answer. She was afraid to feel again. Terrified to give her heart and lose it to another woman. The image of Gail filled her mind. *No! I'm only twenty-four years old. I can't live in those painful memories for the rest of my life. I can't stand by her grave forever.* She pushed the vision away and turned back. She found the cafeteria with little problem.

This was a new beginning, new people in her life, new experiences. Now wasn't the time to hide behind the memories and fears she had lived with for the past three years. Now was for moving on.

She was halfway through her second cup when she felt a hand on her shoulder and a voice whispered near her ear.

"You can hardly tell you aren't wearing your bra."

Charlie's face burned as the woman sat down opposite her with an amused smile. "Hazaar Alim." The woman held out her hand and Charlie shook it gently.

"Charlie Porter."

"I know."

Charlie knew she was blushing and hoped she wouldn't regret the impulse to meet with the beautiful pianist as she held the warm, soft hand within her own. It wasn't until she felt Hazaar's thumb caress the back of her hand that she realized she was still holding it and quickly let go. "You said you wanted coffee. Do you want milk, sugar?" Charlie started to stand up.

"I don't want coffee. I just wanted to talk to you."

Charlie's brow creased. "Why?"

"Because you sang about me." She smiled as she sat down. "Hazaar means nightingale in Arabic."

"Ah. It was a personal tribute to thank you."

Hazaar raised her eyebrow questioningly.

"For the tip."

Her smile returned in full force, and Charlie felt her breath catch in her throat. Hazaar's flawless mocha-coloured skin glowed, accenting her dark eyes and long lashes. Charlie crossed her arms over her chest and looked down at the table to avoid Hazaar's searching gaze that made her feel naked and raw. Hazaar reached forward and gently touched her hand, waiting to speak until Charlie looked up.

"I won't bite, you know?"

Charlie laughed nervously and tried to shrug off the anxiety. "So you work here?"

Hazaar leaned back comfortably in her chair. "Kind of. I finish my degree this year, and I'm hoping to start work on my master's at the beginning of the coming term."

Charlie nodded her head. "Have you picked a topic for your thesis?"

"Yes. The theory that musical education creates division within our society while other, supposedly less advanced cultures, have no such division."

"How can you possibly say that? Music can create unity and solidarity just as easily as division within any society, probably. Just look at football grounds. A group of complete strangers singing songs that their fathers sang before them, supporting people they don't know, who don't know them, to do the best that they can."

"And trash the opposition. Also singing their songs. And supporting strangers—"

"But it isn't the music that creates the division there. It would exist without the music. It's the nature of the competition that creates the conflict. That builds the tension, not the…" Charlie noticed the smile growing on Hazaar's face. "You're making fun of me."

"No." She shook her head. "Not at all. I'm simply gathering information."

"Opinions for your paper?"

"No."

Charlie tilted her head as she waited for Hazaar to continue.

"Information about you."

"And why do you want to know about me?" The desire in Hazaar's eyes burned hot and left Charlie with no doubt about what she wanted—or why.

Hazaar stood up slowly and gathered her bag. She moved around the table and then bent low, whispering in Charlie's ear. "Because I want to see you without your shirt on again."

She walked away from the table and pushed open the doors before Charlie managed to shake herself back to reality and looked over her shoulder. Seeing Hazaar walk out the door propelled her into action. She quickly grabbed her bag and ran after her.

"You can't just say something like that and then walk off!"

"Why not?"

"Because you can't."

"Sure I can."

"But—"

"Look at it this way. If you'd been offended, it would have saved us both a lot of awkwardness and possibly me getting a slap for being cheeky." Hazaar laughed.

"Why do I keep feeling like you're making fun of me?" Charlie shook her head and followed Hazaar out the main doors.

"Oh no, I'm not making fun." She stroked her fingers down Charlie's cheek, and her knees went weak. "I'm not making fun of you, Charlie. I just like to see the funny side of everything."

"Really?"

"Oh yes." Hazaar's voice was husky, laced with desire.

"And that makes everything easier to cope with, does it?"

"Among other things."

"What else makes life easier to cope with?"

Hazaar picked up Charlie's hand and brought it to her lips. "The touch of a beautiful woman."

Charlie's head spun and every nerve in her body tingled. Hazaar stroked the inside of her wrist, and her heart beat faster, suffusing her body with pure desire.

She needed to clear her head a little. She needed to think before she pulled Hazaar into her arms and kissed her where they stood, a girl she'd only just met and didn't know at all. Charlie cleared her throat and held her hand out, catching raindrops. "So how would you cope with this frizz ball I have on my head now?"

"I'd get a car." She pushed the button on the key and Charlie grinned as the lights flashed on a red Beetle in front of her. She watched

Hazaar run across the car park and yank open the driver's door, her long skirt billowing around her ankles. Charlie didn't move until the passenger door was pushed open and Hazaar leaned across the seat and looked at her through the wet windscreen. The smile on her lips turned seductive and her eyes sparkled.

It had been a long time since a woman had smiled at her like that. A smile filled with promise, passion, and pleasure. And Charlie found herself running toward the car before remembering she wasn't wearing her bra. She checked her speed and made her way quickly, slamming the door firmly closed behind her. Her mind reeled. *I can't believe I'm doing this. I'm in a car with a complete stranger. A beautiful stranger. But a stranger, nonetheless. Who's already seen me without my shirt on!* She twisted the strap of her bag between her fingers. *This isn't my imagination. This is really happening. Right?*

"So, Charlie Porter, tell me something about yourself." Hazaar started the engine and laughed as she pulled out of the car park. "God, that sounds like an interview question, doesn't it?"

Charlie chuckled, glad that Hazaar didn't seem to have any problem with the situation. But then, why would she? She was the one who had instigated everything from the moment they'd met. "What would you like to know?"

"Everything, I think. But I'll start with the bits you want to tell me." Charlie stared at her and Hazaar laughed again. "You're so young."

"I'm not that young."

"No? How old are you?"

"Twenty-four."

Hazaar's eyes widened in shock. "Really?"

Charlie grinned. "Yes, really. I know I look about twelve. Damn freckles. But the good news is I'll still get asked for ID when I'm forty and I won't feel so bad about being really old. What about you?"

"Twenty-six."

"Have you done all your studying at RNCM?"

"Yes. It was a good way to evade the family obligations for a while."

Charlie didn't ask what the family obligations might be, because the scowl that passed over Hazaar's face made it clear that the topic wasn't a happy one for her. "Where is your family from?"

"Bradford."

Charlie knew she'd given away her naivety when Hazaar laughed again. She was expecting Pakistan, or Egypt, or somewhere exotic and warm.

"I travelled a long way to get to Manchester." She exaggerated a Middle Eastern accent and had them both laughing. "What about you?"

"I live in Stockport. Born there. Raised there. Bored there."

"Still with your parents?"

"Until I find out what's going on with my audition, then I can get my student loan applied for and get everything sorted out and get my own place."

"You're in. The letter should get to you by tomorrow or the day after."

"Really?"

Hazaar stopped at a set of traffic lights and turned to look at her. "Really. He loved your audition."

Charlie squealed and waved her arms in the air while she danced in her seat, then squealed again as she wrapped her arms around Hazaar's neck and kissed her on the cheek before she realized what she had done. She pulled back, still wiggling in her seat, then froze. Suddenly, she realized what she was doing, and she could feel the growing heat in her face as her embarrassment peaked. "I'm sorry. I wasn't thinking…I didn't…oh shit…I'm really sorry…"

Hazaar leaned over and kissed her on the lips slowly, gently increasing the pressure until Charlie's lips parted. Her tongue slid slowly across Charlie's bottom lip and slipped inside her mouth. Charlie moaned at the soft exploration. Goose bumps broke out across her flesh as Hazaar's finger's wound their way into her hair and caressed her scalp, the back of her neck, and down her throat.

Then it was gone. Charlie's eyes were still closed as Hazaar pulled away.

"Should I say I'm sorry?"

Charlie opened her eyes slowly. Hazaar's fingers were soft on her skin, and her eyes changed in the light, like honey and cinnamon and chocolate, and Charlie was caught fast. She no longer cared that she knew nothing about this woman. She wanted her. She wanted to touch and be touched. She wanted to feel alive. She felt reckless and impulsive, and that turned her on as much as the woman in front of her. "Only if you don't do it again."

Hazaar's mouth was on hers, hungrily searching, tasting, and teasing her. Her hands cupped Charlie's face, holding her firmly as the kiss deepened before one hand slipped into her hair, sending shivers down her spine.

The blast of a car horn behind them stunned them both from their passion.

Hazaar threw the car into gear and laughed as she pulled away, and the sound caused a jolt through Charlie's stomach. The deep, melodic laugh that had attracted her earlier was now mixed with the blatant huskiness of desire and sent ripples through her being.

*I can't believe I'm doing this! I'm in a car with a stranger going God knows where, with every intention of making love to her. What the hell am I thinking?*

"So what's going on in that pretty head of yours?"

Charlie laughed. "You'd probably think I was crazy."

"Try me."

Charlie leaned her head against the headrest and took a deep breath. "I was thinking that I must be crazy. I'm in a car with a complete stranger who's taking me God knows where, knowing that when I get there, wherever there is, all I want to do is rip your clothes off and make love to you. I think I've lost my mind."

Hazaar laughed again. "I'm glad it's not just me thinking all that." Hazaar reached across and held Charlie's hand. "We don't have to, though."

Charlie waved her other hand at Hazaar. "I know. I'm a big girl. I can say no if I want to." Charlie stroked her thumb across the back of Hazaar's hand as she spoke. "Just because I think I might be going crazy doesn't mean I don't want to be exactly where I am right now."

Hazaar retrieved her hand as she manoeuvred into a parking space. She turned to Charlie. "Well, if you want to stay here, you can. But I'm heading up there." She pointed to an apartment block and grabbed her bag from the backseat. They both jumped out and ran for the foyer. Hazaar clicked the car locked as she fished her house keys from her bag and opened the door.

"Where are we, by the way?"

Hazaar chuckled again. "Didsbury."

"Very nice." Charlie mimicked a mock posh accent as she followed Hazaar to the lift. The tension grew between them as they waited side by side for the lift to stop. The air was thick and heavy, and the scent of Hazaar's perfume clung to the edges of her senses, a heady mixture of jasmine, spice, and desire. Charlie watched the sway of Hazaar's hips as she followed her blindly down the hall. She barely registered Hazaar toss her bag onto the chair by the door. She dropped her own as Hazaar's hands found her waist, pushed her backward, and pinned her against the door. Her lips parted under Hazaar's hungry kiss, sucking her tongue into her mouth. They moaned together as Hazaar's fingers began to explore under Charlie's shirt and raked against her skin. Her lips left Charlie's and burned a trail across her cheek until Hazaar's teeth nipped gently at her earlobe. She pressed her head against the door, exposing her throat. Tender kisses followed the opening of each button of her blouse, and she entwined her hands into Hazaar's hair, eliciting small groans of pleasure from the mouth suckling at her breast. Charlie groaned and pressed her chest forward. She wanted Hazaar's hands on her, needed to feel her lips and tongue.

Charlie opened her eyes long enough to see the hunger on Hazaar's face as she pulled away and lifted her top over her head. All she could see were Hazaar's full breasts, her nipples straining against the lace fabric that held them captive. She barely noticed as Hazaar removed the rest of her clothing and the delicious pressure of Hazaar's body fuelled the need building inside her.

Hazaar pressed her knee between Charlie's legs and ground hard against her centre as her lips closed over one swollen nipple. Charlie cried out and her hands skittered across Hazaar's back and down her sides. She felt her trousers loosen and slide down her hips, along with her underwear.

Hazaar's thigh ground into her again, and she could feel her desire coat Hazaar's leg. Charlie's breath caught as Hazaar's fingers stroked over her belly, then dipped lower into the drenched folds of her sex. She clutched at her shoulders and let her head fall back as Hazaar's hand moved into her faster, and the energy coiled in her core, amplified by every press of Hazaar's lips until she cried out her release.

Charlie clung to Hazaar as her breathing returned to normal.

"Welcome to my home."

Charlie laughed sheepishly. "You're a very gracious hostess." She kissed Hazaar's lips gently, her hands finding the clasp of her bra and releasing it. "Do I get the tour?" Hazaar led her through the apartment in a straight line, pointing as she went.

"Kitchen's that way. Bathroom over there. TV over there. This is the bedroom." Charlie pretended to look in the directions Hazaar had pointed, but she couldn't take her eyes off the gorgeous body in front her.

"Beautiful. Now let me see if I can properly thank you for that very warm welcome." She pushed Hazaar back against the bed and eased soft black panties over her hips. "Lie down." She watched as Hazaar stretched out on the bed, her arms reaching for her.

She lay down next to her and traced the line of Hazaar's lips with lazy fingers, down the line of her throat, between her breasts and slowly across the soft flesh of her stomach. She watched as Hazaar's pupils dilated and turned her eyes so dark they looked black. She caressed Hazaar's hips and the outside of her thigh as she leaned in to kiss the full lips waiting for her.

She took her time, enjoying herself and Hazaar's reaction as she slowly traced her lips with her tongue. Her hands mimicked the achingly slow speed as she completed a fingertip survey of Hazaar's hips, waist, and ribs, but stopped below her breast. Hazaar tried to twist beneath her in an attempt to make contact where she needed it.

"No you don't." Charlie pulled back slightly. "It's my turn now." She dipped her head to blow cold air across her sensitive nipples, eliciting a sharp intake of breath from Hazaar.

"Are you trying to drive me mad?"

Charlie flicked her tongue across the hard tip, then blew gently again. Hazaar cried out as the nipple contracted further against the cold air that teased the wet, pebbled flesh. "Yes, I am." Charlie pushed her tongue deep into her Hazaar's mouth, and she eagerly devoured every moan that escaped her. "How am I doing?" Hazaar was panting and writhing as Charlie drew lazy circles around her breast, still avoiding the aching tips.

"Better bring in the straitjacket."

Charlie's mouth closed over the nipple. Hazaar pressed her fingers into Charlie's hair and tried to pull her closer. She opened her mouth wider and pulled in more of the pliant flesh. Her tongue raked across the swollen tip as her fingers skated across the goose-bumped flesh of her stomach and thigh. Hazaar opened her legs and twisted her body in an attempt to gain contact with Charlie at her centre. Charlie lifted her head and grinned at her.

"Why so impatient?" She blew across the soaked nipple, and her smile widened as Hazaar jumped, her hips thrusting off the bed.

Her voice was thick with her desire as she opened her eyes. "I don't think I can take anymore."

Charlie slowly inched her way up Hazaar's inner thigh.

Hazaar immediately opened her legs wider. "Please."

The word, a whispered plea between them, brought Hazaar's desire into sharp focus. The scent of her arousal reached Charlie and she was lost.

She moved quickly and her mouth watered as she neared her goal. She glanced up to see Hazaar watching her, her chest heaving as she tried to pull enough air into her lungs. She watched as Charlie licked her lips, then her head fell back against the pillow with a guttural cry as Charlie's mouth covered her.

Charlie felt her own excitement spreading down her thighs as she took her first taste of Hazaar's sweetness. She closed her eyes after she saw Hazaar wrap her fingers around the spindle of the headboard. She held Hazaar's hips to hold her still as she feasted, too aroused to go slowly and too hungry to be gentle. She sucked and licked the velvet flesh as though she had starved for it all her life, barely able to hear Hazaar's cries as ecstasy claimed her again and again.

When the tremors finally subsided, Hazaar stroked her fingers down the soft, pale cheek and placed a kiss against her lips.

"Wow." Charlie grinned.

"I'll second that." Hazaar's smile was gentle, warming the deep chocolate brown of her eyes.

"Does Hazaar really mean 'nightingale' in Arabic?"

"Yes." She smiled. "Did you think it was just a chat-up line?"

Charlie felt her cheeks burning, and Hazaar laughed. "Maybe."

"Maybe I should remember that in future." She turned Charlie's hand over and kissed her wrist where her pulse began to increase the tattoo it was beating.

"Maybe," she whispered as she captured Hazaar's lips with her own.

# CHAPTER THREE

*The North of England, then*

Charlie stretched her arms above her head and winced slightly at the ache of her muscles, then smiled as she recalled the reason why they ached. She opened her eyes slowly and looked around. The room was silent and the bed empty. She listened intently for sounds in the other rooms, then turned to look at the clock. Nine forty-five. She closed her eyes again and let her head sink back against the pillow.

It took another ten minutes before nature roused her from the bed. She flung the covers from her body and glanced around to find something to wear. Her clothes had been neatly folded and placed on the dresser on the other side of the room. She quickly plucked her shirt from the pile and wrapped it around her shoulders, taking in the details of the room for the first time. Tasteful, neutral colours decorated the walls and carpet, and the bold swatches of red and gold curtains, wall art, and cushions that would normally have adorned the bed now lay exiled upon the carpet.

She slipped from the room hoping to find Hazaar sitting on the couch or drinking coffee in the kitchen, but the apartment was empty, and Charlie felt a swift stab of disappointment. She made her way to the bathroom, taking the time to look around as she crossed the room. Neutral walls again, this time accented by a rich seascape at sunset painting which hung above the fireplace. The reds, purples, and oranges were so vibrant that the ocean seemed alive, the waves appeared to crash against the canvas, and it held Charlie enthralled. She felt slightly subdued until she reached the bathroom and saw the note stuck on the mirror.

*Morning Charlie,*

*Hope you slept well. You looked so peaceful this morning that I couldn't wake you. Please feel free to use whatever you like, shower, bath, breakfast, whatever. I won't be home until about seven this evening. You can hang around if you have no plans, if you like. If not, I hope you'll call. My mobile is 07876641652.*

*I really hope I hear from you.*

*Soon.*

*Hazaar*

*XO*

A fresh towel was folded neatly over the radiator for her. Shampoo, conditioner, and shower gel were on the tiled windowsill, which acted as a shelf for the bath and shower. She showered quickly and headed back to the bedroom.

Twenty minutes later, she was dressed and pulling the covers straight on the bed. She smiled again as she checked that the note was in her bag and headed back into the living room. She looked for a piece of paper but couldn't see anything, and unwilling to search through draws and cupboards, she pulled sheet music and a pencil from her bag and wrote across the top of the page.

*Call to arrange returning my music, 07799114430 x*

She left the pages on top of the piano, then slung her bag across her shoulder and left.

The bus journey home passed quickly for Charlie, her mind on the amazing night with Hazaar. It was almost lunchtime when she arrived home to find her younger sister, Beth, draped over the sofa watching TV. Lights shone throughout the house, but she knew that Beth was the only one in. She tossed her bag over the banister and hung up her coat, flicking off the lightswitch as she passed on her way to the kitchen, ruffling her sister's spiked hair as she went.

"All right, Flipper?" All she got in return was a muted grunt.

Charlie put the kettle on to boil and spooned coffee granules and sugar into two mugs before Beth appeared in the doorway.

"Can you stop calling me Flipper?" Beth hopped up onto the kitchen counter.

"Probably not." The nickname had been formed even before Beth had been born. Charlie was eight when their mum had found out she was pregnant with Beth. At the twelve-week scan, Charlie had looked at the picture and decided that it looked like a little dolphin jumping in the water, probably as her favourite program had been *Flipper*. Charlie had used the name ever since for her little sister. It was something they argued about but both secretly loved, a special bond between them.

"How did the audition go?"

"Okay, I guess."

"Did you do the *Les Misérables* piece?"

Charlie shook her head as she poured water into the mugs. "Can you get the milk? No, I did the Norah Jones piece. 'Nightingale.'"

"Why?"

"I heard the guy doing the auditions was sick of show tunes, so I thought something different might go down better."

"Did it?"

"He certainly seemed pleased." She shrugged. "Just have to wait and see."

"When will you know?"

"Soon, I hope." She poured milk into the cups, then handed the bottle back to Beth. They took their mugs back to the living room, where they sat on the same sofa and Beth stretched her legs across Charlie's lap. A slow grin spread across Beth's face, her blue eyes twinkling mischievously.

"And why weren't you home last night to tell me all this?" Her grin widened as Charlie started to blush. "Mum and Dad were really worried. They tried your mobile and everything, but apparently, it was off." Charlie's blush turned crimson as she recalled running naked across Hazaar's living room, grabbing her phone out of her bag and turning it off, then being greeted by Hazaar's hands turning her around, pulling her down to the floor, and ravishing her again.

Beth was laughing. "Worth it then, was it?" She tried to look nonchalant as she sipped her coffee. "So who was it? Not the redhead you went out with a couple of weeks ago. Please not her. She was freaky. Please tell me it wasn't her."

"Paula?" Charlie smiled as Beth nodded. "No, not her. That was a single blind date. That's all."

Beth waited, her eyebrows raised expectantly. "Aw, come on. You gotta tell me."

"Why?"

"'Cos I'm sixteen and I've got no life of my own."

"You're sixteen. You aren't supposed to have a life of your own."

"Aw, Charlie, please. Dearest. Bestest. Kindest. Wisest big sister ever." Beth shifted and leaned her head against Charlie's shoulder, looking up at her with big sad eyes. "Please take pity on your little Flipper." Her grin turned mischievous again. "Go on. Give us a thrill!"

Charlie started laughing. "It's no one you know. She's someone I just met."

"How just met?" Beth's eyes were twinkling. "Like just met yesterday? Like that just met?"

Beth howled with laughter, and Charlie could feel the heat in her cheeks. "Beth!"

"I'm just teasing. It's about time you let your hair down." Beth smiled sincerely. "So tell me all about her."

Charlie sipped her coffee. "She's called Hazaar. She's in the final year of her degree, and she was the pianist for the auditions."

"So were there like, sparks flying while you were on the stage?"

"Do you want to hear this or not?"

Beth pretended to zip her lips closed and settled back against the sofa.

"I got drenched on my way there, so I was in the ladies' trying to dry off my shirt and—"

"She came in while you were naked and you did it in the loos—" Charlie slapped her arm. "Ow!"

"Behave. No, but she did see me without my shirt on. She's the one who gave me the advice about the song choice. Anyway, at the end of the song she asked me to meet her for a coffee in the cafeteria. I don't know why, but I did. Then before I knew what was happening we were at her apartment. And…"

"Yeah. And…?"

"And I'm telling you nothing else, you little perv!" She was laughing at the stricken look on Beth's face.

"You can't do that."

"Yes, I can."

"No, you can't."

Charlie shook her head. "No more."

"Just one thing?"

Charlie waited, making no promises.

"Is she a good kisser?"

Charlie's grin widened, and she leaned closer to Beth's ear. "Better than you could ever imagine."

It had always been easy between them. The age gap made it easy for the older Charlie to dote on the real-life baby doll her parents had thoughtfully provided for her, and Beth had an older sibling who didn't try to beat her to a pulp, like her friends had, which was a major respect earner. As they had gotten older, Charlie had begun to realize her sexuality, and it had been Beth who had comforted her and given her the strength and unconditional love she had needed to be honest with herself about her true feelings. When she had told Beth years earlier, it had been easy, even with the avalanche of questions that were Beth's trademark.

*"So who's prettier? Me, Angelina Jolie, or Cameron Diaz?"*

*"Easy. You're the prettiest, but the most fanciable for me has to be Angelina."*

*"I can live with that. Okay, house rules are, no trogs..."*

*"What's a trog?"*

*"Like, someone who totally doesn't deserve you, ugly inside and out."* Her expression was totally serious, and Charlie wondered at the youth who thought such things and wondered, not for the first time, just what Beth would become when she grew up.

*"Point taken."*

*"Number two. No one prettier than me."*

*"Not possible to find anyone prettier than you."*

*"Number three."* Beth paused. *"I want to be there when you tell Mum and Dad."* She jumped off the bed and raced out the door. Charlie caught her just as she called for their parents.

"Hello! Earth to space cadet!"

Charlie shook her head as she tried to focus again on what Beth was saying to her.

"Where did you go then? Memories from last night perhaps?" She wiggled her eyebrows wickedly.

"No, of you, actually."

Beth rolled her eyes. "Boring! So anyway, I was saying, are you going to see her again?"

"I hope so." She ruffled Beth's black spikes again and took another sip of her coffee.

"Oh, post came earlier. There's some for you." Beth leaned forward and tossed several envelopes into her lap. The first three were junk that she tore into pieces and set aside for the bin. The fourth one caught her eye as Beth picked up the remote control and began flicking through channels. She turned it in her palms several times before she tore it open. It was postmarked from the day before. It was here already. She couldn't believe it. Beth was looking at her.

Charlie held it out to her. "Read it to me."

Beth took the folded page from her shaking hands. "What is—oh." She saw the letterhead paper. "Bloody hell, that's fast. It got home before you did." She giggled nervously. "You sure?" Charlie nodded. "Okay. 'Dear Miss Porter. I would like to take this opportunity to thank you for your audition. Your choice of audition piece was extremely refreshing, and your love for the piece shone through in your performance. I would, however, have liked a more complete example of your full range.' Jesus, why doesn't he just get to the point?"

Charlie frowned. "Just read it."

"Sorry." She cleared her throat. "'Even so, I am delighted to offer you a place in September's class. All details and necessary paperwork will be sent to you in due course. I look forward to seeing you in September and thank you again for a very refreshing break in an otherwise tedious day. Yours, Professor Swallen.'"

Charlie jumped to her feet and danced around the room.

Beth bounced on the sofa. "How cool is that?"

Charlie couldn't speak. She couldn't find the words. She grabbed Beth and they jumped around together until they ended in a heap on the floor.

"You know what this means?"

Beth's grin widened as she nodded. "Party?"

Charlie shook her head. "Nope."

Beth's grin shrank. "Pizza?"

"Nope."

Beth's grin slid to a smile. "Pub?"

"Nope. You get the big bedroom in September."

Now it was Beth's turn to be speechless, for a second, anyway. "Any chance you can start next week?"

Charlie swiped her hand across the back of Beth's head.

"Watch it. I'll get brain damage!"

"Too late."

"Bitch!"

"Language, Elizabeth Porter." They both started and stared at the open door and the scowling figure of their mother.

"Sorry, Mum!" Beth dropped her head and looked sheepish.

"So, what's with Tigger over there?" She peeled her gloves off and tossed them on the table with her keys as she looked at Charlie.

Charlie held the letter out to her mother and watched as her head dipped while she read. Tears sprung to her mum's eyes as she pulled her into a tight embrace. "I'm so proud of you. I can't believe how quick this got here." She stroked Charlie's back and kissed her cheeks. "I'm so proud of you."

"Mum, can I paint the room black when she goes?" Beth asked.

"No!" They looked at her as they answered in chorus.

"So why didn't you ring me when the post came?"

Charlie felt her cheeks redden slightly. "I only just opened it, just before you got in."

"Yeah, she made me read it 'cos she was too chicken."

Her mother's eyebrows were raised. "Was the post late?"

Charlie closed her eyes and cursed the fair complexion that she knew was beet red.

"No, Charlie was." Beth was practically skipping around the room. Charlie tried to think of something to say through her embarrassment, but her mouth kept opening and closing with nothing coming out.

"You look like a fish doing that. Have you had something to eat?" Her mother smiled easily, and Charlie was grateful to her for trying to ease her discomfort. Charlie shook her head. "Why don't you go and get changed and I'll make something? Bacon sandwich?"

Charlie nodded and made her way to the stairs, as her mother grabbed hold of Beth's hand.

"It wasn't the weird redhead, was it?" her mother whispered perfectly audibly. Charlie groaned and made her way up the stairs two at a time, knowing full well that Beth would tell her mother everything, and that her mother would never say a word to her. She began humming as she walked to her room, unfastening her shirt and tossing it into the laundry basket next to the pine dresser her grandmother had given her a few years ago, adamant that it was an antique. Charlie hadn't the heart to tell her that she could see the sticker for IKEA on the underside. Her Gran was a huge fan of car boot sales and flea markets, convinced that she was going to find something that would be worth millions. Her usual finds were IKEA "antiques" and fifth-run "first editions" with pages missing.

Charlie changed quickly into a pale blue jumper and jeans and reached the top of the stairs when her phone rang. She looked at the caller display, frowning when it said number unknown. She flipped the top and held it to her ear.

"Hello."

"Congratulations."

"Thank you." Charlie gripped the phone tighter and her stomach did a flip.

"You don't recognize my voice, do you?"

"Well, you do sound a little different when you're not out of breath or chanting my name, but I knew it was you."

Hazaar laughed.

"I wasn't expecting to hear from you so soon. I thought you were going to be out all day."

"Me too, but Swallen got through all the singers by twelve. Half of them didn't even get to finish their songs. The man was on a mission. So I got free early. I was hoping you'd still be here when I got back." Her voice dropped suggestively. "I was hoping to congratulate you in person."

"Hm, that would have been nice. Sorry to spoil the surprise." Charlie could feel herself blushing again.

"Nice?" Hazaar's voice slid over her like honey. "Oh, I think it would have been more than nice."

Charlie's reaction was immediate. Heat flooded between her legs, her nipples stood to attention, and every inch of her body felt sensitized.

"Much, much more than nice. And you know you agree, Charlie."

"Charlie," Charlie's mother called from downstairs.

"One second, Hazaar." Charlie cleared her throat. "Yeah, Mum?"

"Lunch is ready."

"I'll be right down. Sorry, I have to go."

Hazaar laughed again. "Okay. When can I see you? To return your music."

"When did you have in mind?"

"Now."

Charlie laughed. "How about tomorrow night? My family will want to celebrate the good news with me tonight."

"Sounds good. Do you want me to pick you up or meet you somewhere?"

"How about meeting in town?"

"Sure. Coyote's? About nine?"

"Sounds perfect. I'll see you then." Charlie knew she was grinning like an idiot, but she couldn't stop.

"Charlie?"

"Yeah?"

"Wear something that comes off easily."

Her breath caught again as the phone went dead, and she crossed her legs to stop the throbbing.

Beth was at the foot of the stairs, grinning. "Was that her?"

"What?"

"Hazaar? Was that her?" They both knew exactly what she was talking about, but Charlie eased past her and into the kitchen. Her sandwich was waiting on the table alongside a fresh coffee, and her mother smiling sweetly at her.

"You both have big mouths," Charlie grumbled as she sat and took her first bite.

"That means it's tomorrow night, Mum." Beth slid into her chair. "Pay up." She held out her hand, but their mother shook her head.

"Not until we get confirmation."

Beth scowled. "When are you seeing her? Mum bet the last bar of chocolate that it would be tonight. I said tomorrow 'cos you wouldn't want to look desperate. So who gets it?"

Charlie glanced from one to the other while she quickly finished her sandwich. "Put the chocolate on the table." Her voice was low and quiet. Her mother clearly worked hard to hide the smile that tugged at the corner of her lips as she slid the chocolate bar into the middle of the table. Charlie slowly picked it up and twisted it in her hands.

"So who wins?" Beth's pleaded with her, but Charlie was up and out of her chair like a shot. She was at the foot of the stairs before they had a chance to react.

"Neither of you. It's all mine." She giggled as she reached her room. "Serves you right for betting on my love life!" Heavy footsteps thumped up the stairs, and Beth complained loudly every step of the way. The door swung open as her mother and Beth crashed into the room.

"Where's my chocolate?" Beth was insistent.

"Mine!" Her mother was doing her best to keep a straight face, but failing miserably.

"Mum, it's not funny. It's, like, theft or something." Beth dropped onto the bed.

"It's gone, Flipper."

"No way. Not even you can eat chocolate that fast."

Charlie held her stare.

"Seriously? No way."

Charlie didn't even flinch.

"Damn." Beth looked crestfallen. "At least let me know if it should have been mine?"

Charlie grinned and started to laugh.

"That's evil. Mum, tell her she owes me a chocolate bar."

Her mother broke out laughing too. Charlie loved times like this, when she could let go of the pain and anger that she carried and just enjoy the laughter and love of her family. The days when she could almost forget Gail. Almost, but not quite.

# CHAPTER FOUR

*Pakistan, today*

Hazaar held her hand up to shade her eyes from the brutal midday sun. The heat beat down on her as she moved, and she was still uncomfortable in the *shalwar kameez* and *dupatta* she was expected to wear daily, the robes and head scarf that covered her completely. She watched Afia play on the tiled floor of the courtyard. The chunky wooden blocks shaped like animals were bashed into place with a triumphant smile, before they were tipped back onto the floor for the game to begin again. Always in the same pattern, first the giraffe, then the bear, the elephant, and finally, the lion. The bear and lion were put in with accompanying roars, and the two-year-old squealed with laughter.

The mustard yellow paint on the clay-covered walls of the aging house was peeled and chipped, as was the deep green paint on the wooden window frames. It frustrated her every time she washed the windows that she would inevitably end up picking paint chips out of her nails. The heat was stifling, and she wished she could open the windows more than a few inches. She craved the gentle breeze and the illusion of freedom it gave, but the security bars on the outside prevented it. The house sat in the heart of Peshawar's old city, tucked away amidst a maze of tea shops, bazaars, and the many gates that had once protected the walled ancient city. They'd been built to halt invaders, to protect those inside the walls, and now they were attractions for tourists, monuments to the past.

Hazaar had only seen one of those gates. Once. The day Yasar had brought her to his home and told her that she would learn to be a good wife and mother. She could see it so clearly in her mind. The red brick structure shaped like a proscenium archway had pedestrian walkways on each side and the flag flying proudly in the breeze. She dreamed of seeing that gate again. Just once.

Hazaar ran her hand over her chest and enjoyed the feeling of comfort she got from the pendant underneath her clothes. She wore the silver nightingale to remind herself of the life she really wanted—the life she'd had. The life she continually worked to get back to in every way she could. No matter how long it took, she would find a way. She shifted her head covering and continued hanging out the laundry, cursing herself and how awkward the shawl made her movements when she dropped the peg.

"Here, Mama."

"Thank you, Afia." She smiled and took it from Afia's chubby hand and squatted down beside her. "Have you finished playing with your puzzle?"

Solemn brown eyes stared at her as she nodded.

"Good girl, then you should put it away." She tickled Afia's belly, making her giggle and squirm. "Quickly now, Afia, before Baba and Abu come home for lunch."

"I'll help her." Amira bent beside Afia and helped her pack the blocks into the handwoven basket she used to move her toys around the house.

"Thank you, Ami." She smiled at her sister-in-law. "I don't know what I'd do without you."

"Well, you'd probably have more arguments with Abu."

"Very true." She dropped another pair of linen pants into the laundry basket. "He hates me."

Amira laughed. "The feeling is entirely mutual, Hazaar, and don't you even try to pretend it isn't."

"Yeah, but I didn't come here hating him."

"Of course you did."

"I didn't—"

"And I don't blame you. The way they brought you here, the way they have kept you here—I understand."

Hazaar looked down at Amira as she scooped the last of the jigsaw pieces into the basket and then held out her hand for Afia. "I always thought you agreed with them. That I was wrong."

"I don't think you were right. He is your husband, and you should not have tried to do that. But I do not think he was right either. He was scared and reacted badly. Now," she said, "well, Abu is the way he is."

"Why do you stay, Ami? He treats you just as badly, and you could go and stay with other relatives."

Amira shook her head. "No, they will not have me. My mother's shame haunts me still, and they were glad I was no longer a burden to them when I was married to Rafi. They will not accept responsibility for me again."

"What happened to your mother? You've never mentioned her before."

"It does not matter. I was a young girl, just eleven years old. My uncle arranged for me to marry Rafi three years later."

"At fourteen? They made you get married at fourteen?"

"Yes. I thought you knew this."

"No." Hazaar shook her head and dropped the last of the clothes into her basket while Amira picked up Afia and settled her on her hip.

"My uncle did not wish to be reminded of the shame she had brought to the family. The quicker he could send me to a respectable situation, the better it would be for everyone."

"But you were fourteen."

"Yes." She smiled a little sadly. "It is not so unusual, Hazaar, and Rafi was good to me. He was kind and mostly left me alone."

"How old was Rafi when you married?"

"He was just a young man. Twenty-five years only."

"That's wrong, Ami." The image of her fourteen-year-old daughter being married off to an older man seared itself into her brain. She couldn't let it happen. She just couldn't.

"No, he was nice to me. He treated me very well. When we first married, he would bring me home little gifts from the market sometimes. He brought me a music box one day that played me a lullaby to go to sleep to on nights when he was out late. He knew I did not like to be in the house alone. The quiet made me nervous, so he brought me the music box. He was sweet."

Hazaar wanted to say that she didn't care how sweet he was, that he was abusing a child, but she knew it would only alienate Amira. That Amira considered the situation to be normal and acceptable wasn't a shock for Hazaar, nor was the fact that Amira considered her husband to have been a good man because of a small kindness shown her. The amazing fact was that they had lived together for more than three years, and Hazaar had known so little about the shy young woman who had helped her through the early days of her new life in Pakistan. Her sister-in-law had helped her through the morning sickness, the headaches, and dizzy spells that had accompanied the late stages, and the difficult home birth, and she just now realized that she didn't even know how old she was.

"Ami, how old are you?"

"This next birthday I will be twenty-five. They will be home soon. We should take Afia inside." Amira picked her up and swung her in her arms.

"You're right."

"Do you want me to take her? I could put her to bed if you like."

"No, thank you. I miss it if I can't read her a story before she goes for her nap." She leaned forward and kissed Afia's cheek and laughed as Afia wrapped her arms about her neck and placed sloppy baby kisses on her face.

"Here, you take her." Amira passed Afia over. "I'll get the laundry."

"Thank you." Amira finished the chore and opened the door with one hand to lead them both inside as the wrought iron gate to the courtyard swung open. Hazaar forced a smile and turned to face her husband and father-in-law. The resounding click of the gate behind him assured her that the lock was firmly in place. It was a sound that haunted her dreams.

"She should be sleeping." Tazim Siddiqi kicked off his sandals at the doorway and crossed the room. "I don't want to come home at lunch time to hear your brat squalling."

"Abu, she is not a brat." Yasar closed the distance to Hazaar and bent to kiss Afia's cheek. "Are you, *Beti*? You are a very good little girl for your Baba, aren't you?" Afia giggled and jumped into Yasar's arms.

"I was just about to put her to bed. I'll do it now." She reached out to Afia, but Yasar spun her around above his head.

"I'll do it." Yasar beamed while Afia kicked her legs excitedly. "Do you want Baba to take you for your nap?" He blew a raspberry on her tummy. "Do you?" Afia squealed and clapped her hands.

"You should probably stop doing that or she'll never go to sleep," Hazaar said.

"I don't have time for this nonsense. I have meetings this afternoon. Where's my lunch?" Tazim scowled at her.

"Very well, I'll get it for you." She kissed Afia's cheek. "Be good, and Baba will read you a story, okay?" Afia nodded, and Yasar smiled as he walked out of the room with Afia cradled in his arms.

Amira quickly prepared a simple meal of dhal and chapatti while Hazaar set the tea to boil. The *khawa* tea that Tazim and Yasar both loved was a tradition among the Pashtun tribe. Both men were so fiercely loyal to their tribal heritage that she had spent time perfecting the mix of Chinese-style green tea flavoured with cardamom and spices in an attempt to gain favour with them. She sighed as she poured the tea and mixed in milk and sugar. It had given her something to concentrate on, as she had very little else to do with her time anymore. She looked down at her hands and ran her fingers along the edge of the counter as though it were a piano, and for a second, she let herself believe that she still had the life she had chosen, rather than the one she lived.

She carried the food and tea into the dining room and set it down for him. Yasar was still upstairs. She could hear his voice as he told Afia her favourite bedtime story about a zebra who wanted spots instead of stripes. Hazaar pictured her clapping her little hands when the zebra finally got her wish and her stripes were changed for spots, only to decide that she didn't like the spots after all.

She waited patiently until Tazim had finished eating to reload the tray, and gathered her courage to ask a question she was certain she already knew the answer to. "Abu, we need more food from the market. I know you're busy, so I can go this afternoon."

"No." He wiped his hands on a napkin and tossed it on top of the tray. "You do not know your way around. You will get lost. You stay here and take care of Afia. I will arrange for the shopping. Give me a list."

She wanted to remind him that she would never learn her way around because he never let her leave the house. The courtyard in the centre of the high-walled garden was the only outside space she ever saw, and she ached to taste the air somewhere else. "I know you are a very busy man. Amira can show me the—"

Tazim slammed his hand down on the table. "I said no."

Hazaar jumped and stepped away from him. The look in his eyes was cold, hard, and unforgiving. She knew there was no point in arguing further. He was the man of the house, and his word was law. She ducked her head and went to the kitchen to make out the list. The picture of the Peshawar gate flashed in her mind—then it was gone.

# CHAPTER FIVE

*The North of England, then*

Hazaar twisted the strap of her bag around her fingers, her palms sweaty as she chewed on her lower lip throughout the taxi ride. She still couldn't believe she was doing this. Hell, she still couldn't believe she'd seduced Charlie in the first place, and seeing her again was asking for trouble. But she couldn't stop herself. She didn't want to stop herself. She only had a little time left to call her own, and she intended to make the most of it.

Hazaar paid the taxi driver and slipped her wallet back into her bag. She smiled as the blond bouncer with a crew cut pulled open the door of the nightclub, and the music hit her like a wave, the bass pumping in her chest as though it was trying to force her heart to beat to its own rhythm. She climbed the stairs and looked around.

It was easy to spot Charlie. She was sitting on the edge of a brown leather sofa against the far wall with a drink in one hand, and a young woman trying to keep hold of the other. Charlie was shaking her head at whatever the other woman was saying to her, and Hazaar couldn't help but smile. It was obvious the woman was trying to pick Charlie up, and equally clear that Charlie didn't want to be picked up by the leather-clad woman with short, spiky hair and tattoos up both arms.

Hazaar walked across the room, wondering if Charlie would notice her before she got to them, or if she would be able to hear the conversation first. Her smile widened as she homed in on Charlie's voice.

"No, really, I'm here to meet someone." Charlie put her hand on the brunette's shoulders in an obvious attempt to push her back.

"Who says that someone can't be me?" The woman leaned toward her again.

"I do."

They both looked up, startled. Charlie's eyes met Hazaar's, and her smile lit up her face. The brunette was still leaning toward Charlie, and Hazaar held out her hand and helped her up.

"You look beautiful." She leaned in to kiss the lips she'd been dreaming about for the past two days. The kiss was gentle, her hands gliding softly over Charlie's back and down to her waist. Suddenly, she didn't want to be in the club anymore. She wanted Charlie to herself. "Let's go somewhere else."

"Where do you have in mind?" Charlie smiled against her lips.

Hazaar tossed the young woman a look that told her exactly where she had in mind and led Charlie to the door. Their fingers entwined as they made their way quickly down the steep steps.

"Good night, ladies." The bouncer smiled at them as they left. Hazaar caught the look of disappointment she cast in Charlie's direction.

"Do you always cause this much trouble when you're down here?" she asked as they rounded the corner.

"What?" Charlie blushed.

"Between Spike in there and the look the bouncer was giving you, I thought I was going to have to fight to get you out of there."

"Don't be silly." Charlie squeezed her hand. "They were just being friendly."

"Friendly? Spike?"

"Well, maybe a bit over friendly."

"Be honest. You thought she was about to rip your clothes off."

Charlie flushed brighter. "I'm not full of myself or anything."

"You don't have to be, darlin'. She *was* about to rip your clothes off." Hazaar looked her up and down. The form-fitting black pants clung low on her hips, and the black sleeveless top with plunging neckline was cropped to show a tantalizing amount of soft, creamy flesh. "If we don't head somewhere soon, I might just do the same." She grabbed Charlie's waist and pulled her into her body for a fierce kiss. "You're a dangerous woman, Charlie Porter." They kissed again, deep and hungry, and raw passion surged between them. Hazaar felt her skin crackle where Charlie's fingers touched her, sending electricity through every nerve in her body.

"I bet you say that to all the girls."

Hazaar pulled back and laughed. "No, I don't." She pulled Charlie's hand to her lips and brushed gently across her knuckles. "I definitely don't." She stared into Charlie's eyes and felt more than the rush of desire. There was a shadow there that spoke of a deep sorrow, of regrets that she was too young to own, that gave a colour and texture to her voice when she sang, and Hazaar wanted to know what was behind it. She wanted to know her in every way possible. Hazaar shook her head. "Come on. Let's get out of here before I ravish you on the street." They both laughed as Hazaar led them down the street. "Have you eaten?"

Charlie shook her head. "I was too nervous."

"Fancy something to eat now?"

Charlie smiled seductively at her. "Yes, but what I'm hungry for won't be on any menu."

Hazaar grinned as the fire hit low in her belly. "Oh, I don't know. I'm sure something can be arranged." She pulled Charlie closer to her as they walked, twining their fingers together. "In the meantime, how about we build up our strength? Chinese?" They were on the outskirts of Manchester's Chinatown, surrounded by neon lights blazing out names and Chinese characters. One restaurant had ducks hanging in the window. Hazaar steered them toward her favourite restaurant and watched Charlie as she climbed the stairs in front of her, admiring the sway of her hips, and the perfectly shaped arse.

She leaned in and whispered into Charlie's ear. "Nobody should have an arse that good." She caressed her backside gently, shocked at her own brazen behaviour. She wasn't usually so forward, especially in public, and she felt exhilarated. The waiter led them to a table in the far corner of the room, then left, returning quickly with their drinks and a basket of prawn crackers. Once they had ordered food, they sat staring at each other.

"Have you been here before?"

Hazaar nodded. "Yup. I play with the jazz band here every Wednesday night." She pointed out the tiny stage with a piano lodged at the back against the wall.

"Cool. You're an amazing pianist," Charlie said, gingerly lifting her hand, turning Hazaar's fingers gently in her own. "You have amazing hands. Such long, beautiful fingers." Hazaar smiled as Charlie flushed crimson. "I can't believe I just said that."

"Why? I'm glad you like them." The waiter arrived with their starters. Charlie reached over for the soy sauce and splashed liberal amounts into her chicken and noodle soup as the man leaned over and whispered to Hazaar. She smiled at him. "Maybe, after I've eaten." Charlie looked up, one eyebrow raised. "They want me to play."

"Will you?"

She shrugged. "Later. If you want me to."

"Definitely." Charlie sipped her soup. "How long have you been playing?"

"Forever." Her mouth twisted into a wry smile. "My mother made me take it up when I was six. I hated it."

"Why did she make you play if you hated it?"

"Well, school was pretty easy for me, and when I was bored I used to get on her nerves. It was her way of keeping me out of her hair, I suppose. Or from bothering my dad." She shrugged at Charlie's frowned question. "Dad was away a lot when we were young, building up the business, but when he was here he spent more time with me than any of the others. Taking me to and from recitals, exams, and stuff like that. She thought he was spoiling me or something."

"Was he?"

Hazaar grinned. "Yeah, probably. I guess you could say I'm a daddy's girl." She laughed. "I used to complain for hours at first. I stopped doing that after a little while. I mean, I still hated it—even years later—but by that time I'd spotted my opportunity." She slid a forkful of crisp seaweed into her mouth. "If I was good enough, I might just escape the family obligations and be able to decide my own life."

"Do you enjoy playing now?"

"Yes. Those keys are the keys to my freedom." She nodded in the direction of the piano. "Each note I play perfectly is another minute where my decisions are my own." She continued to eat slowly, her stomach slightly queasy as she uttered the words she didn't really believe.

"Is your family strict Muslim?"

Hazaar smiled around another forkful of seaweed. "Yes and no." She smiled at the look of confusion on Charlie's face. "Well, they are in most ways. They eat only halal meat and observe all the religious traditions for the main part, but they not only allow me to play piano, they encouraged me to do so. Traditionally, Islamic music is restricted to voice and a drum. Very occasionally, you can find guitars similar to a sitar. But not the piano."

"So they're, erm…progressive? Is that the right word? Because you don't seem to wear the traditional clothes or anything."

Hazaar laughed. "In some ways. My mother was born in England. My father was born in Pakistan. It's kind of a mixture. There are some things that he won't give in on, and some that he will. In some ways my mother is worse. Trying to live up to the expectations she *thinks* my dad has instead of ones he really does."

"Tell me about it."

"About my religion? Well, as you can probably guess, I don't really follow it religiously, so to speak. My family is pretty devout, though. Ramadan, Eid, every religious holiday is followed, every practice. No pork, all halal. Much of my family is in Pakistan. My older sister is married with four children, and her husband took her to Pakistan when they married."

"Do you miss her?"

Hazaar shrugged. "We were never close. I was always different, playing my music and practicing all the time, or studying. Anything I could to try to keep in my father's good books and out of the family's customs. My sister's wedding was arranged. Her husband's family are wealthy, and it gave my father good contacts for his business."

"What does he do?"

"He's an importer. Does a lot of business with companies in Pakistan, importing and exporting goods."

"And what about you? Are you expected to marry to enhance the family business?"

Hazaar laughed. "Oh, it does sound so seedy when you say it like that. At this point in time, I think it's still open to negotiation. I'm bringing honour and prestige to my father with my career in music so far, so no, he won't expect me to marry yet. He will eventually, I suppose, but who knows where I may be able to take the piano to keep me out of the marital curse."

"You see marriage as a curse?"

"For me, yes." She placed her fork onto her plate. "I see marriage as a prison. I would be stuck in a house, a life, a bed, with a man I haven't even met, who I don't know, and I certainly couldn't find attractive. I would be expected to bear his children, clean his house, cook his meals. I would be a glorified slave. If he cheated on me, I would be expected to bear it silently. If I cheated on him, I could be divorced, dishonoured, and disowned. Even killed." She didn't want to think about what could happen if, like her sister, she was also taken to live in Pakistan, but she couldn't stop the thoughts from running through her mind. Images of her in prison without bars gnawed at the edges of her mind. She shook her head. "I couldn't live like that. I know myself too well. I know I couldn't bear it."

Charlie's eyes were wide. "What if you refused?"

"I would shame my father as well as the family of the man I was supposed to marry. I would be, at the very least, shunned within the community, and maybe disowned by my family." She laughed wryly. "Definitely disowned by my family."

"How do you accept it?"

Hazaar laughed. "I don't. I keep my head down and hope they'll forget about me. I'll be the pianist daughter and nothing more. I pray that they'll stay on the outskirts of my life so that I can be myself as much as possible." She cringed inwardly, knowing that every word she spoke was a wish, and something she could only hope for. "I love them. And they love the person they think I am."

"They don't know you're gay." It wasn't a question. It was a statement, but Hazaar shook her head anyway. "What would happen if they found out?"

"I would be disowned. It would be as though I never existed. I'd lose everyone I love."

Charlie's eyes were the size of saucers. "Like the film *East Is East*." Hazaar stared at her. "Sorry. I was just thinking that it was a bit like the film, where the oldest brother refuses the wedding and turns out to be gay. The dad takes down all the pictures of him and everything." Charlie stared down at the tablecloth. "Sorry."

"Don't be. Yes, it would probably be a little like that." Hazaar smiled sadly, knowing that was the best she could hope for.

Charlie squeezed her hand gently. "You're very brave."

"Why do you say that?"

"You're living your life, being who you are, knowing that there would be consequences if they found out." She finished off her soup. "That takes guts."

Hazaar wanted to deny it, to tell Charlie that it wasn't bravery that allowed her to do any such thing. It was fear. She feared not experiencing everything life had to offer her as much as she feared what those experiences could cost her. And she lived in the shadow of that fear, too scared to stand still in case they caught her, too scared to run away in case they found her. She felt like she was treading water. Some days, there was a small part of her that wished she would be caught, that her father or her brother would see her in the arms of a woman and it would be all over. She wouldn't have to make the decisions then. They would take care of it for her. That was her cowardice talking, and she knew she could never go that far, but some days she wished for the easy escape.

The waiter came to remove their plates. "Can I get you more drinks?"

"Vodka and cranberry juice and an OJ please," Hazaar said, as he nodded and moved away. "So what about you?"

"Oh, I'm not religious at all." Charlie grinned and Hazaar started to laugh. "I am close to my family, though. I have one younger sister, Beth. She's sixteen, and we get on really well. She loves to tease me, and I tend to call her Flipper."

Hazaar laughed. "Flipper? Why?"

"When Mum went for her twelve-week scan, I thought the picture looked like a little dolphin. So I've always called her Flipper."

"Cute." She waited while the waiter returned with their new drinks. "How does she like it?"

"She pretends she hates it, but she loves it really." Charlie sipped on her drink. "How come you're not drinking?"

"I am." She sipped on her orange juice as Charlie cocked her head to the side. "I don't drink."

Charlie raised a questioning eyebrow. "Why? Do you have a problem with alcohol?"

Hazaar laughed. "Yeah. It's against our religion."

"Oh. Right. Sorry. I guess I should've known that."

"Why?" Hazaar frowned as Charlie blushed.

"I Googled it."

Hazaar burst out laughing. "Really?"

Charlie nodded, seemingly unable to raise her eyes from the tablecloth as she twisted a napkin between her fingers.

She looked so uncomfortable that Hazaar couldn't help herself. "You Googled alcohol?"

Charlie lifted her head quickly, her eyes wide and her jaw slightly slack. "No. Muslims and Islam."

Hazaar leaned back in her chair as Charlie threw the napkin at her when she realized she was being teased.

"You're such a shit."

"Me?"

"Yes, you. Teasing me like that."

Hazaar tried to school her face into an innocent look, but Charlie's laughter convinced her it was less than successful so she smiled instead. "Sorry."

Charlie shrugged. "It's okay."

"So what did you learn?"

"Not a lot, apparently."

Hazaar reached over the table and entwined their fingers, again shocked by how demonstrative she felt toward Charlie. "I'm sure you learned a lot, and I really appreciate you trying." Charlie blushed again and Hazaar had to fight the urge to kiss her again. "You're adorable when you do that."

Charlie cleared her throat. "You said you'd play for me?" Her lips curled into a tantalizing smile as she lifted her glass and watched Hazaar above the rim. Hazaar squeezed her fingers and leaned back in her chair.

"Okay. On one condition."

"What's that?"

"You sing."

"What? With you?" Hazaar's smile spread as she nodded. Charlie took a long drink, her hands shaking.

"Does the thought of singing make you nervous?"

"No." Charlie shook her head and rubbed her hands over the tablecloth, clearly uncomfortable, but an explanation didn't look forthcoming.

"Then…" Hazaar waved her hand in the direction of the stage.

Charlie looked at her. Hazaar shuddered under the weight of her stare, the cornflower blue eyes pierced into hers, and Hazaar felt they examined her to the very core of her soul. And she expected to be found wanting.

"Okay," Charlie whispered softly.

Hazaar stood slowly and wandered over to the stage. Charlie took another drink and then followed her.

"So, what do you want to sing?"

Charlie shrugged. "You choose."

"What if you don't know it?"

Charlie grinned. "Then I'll just have to sit it out."

Hazaar frowned and let her fingers begin to dance across the keys. The first notes of the Roberta Flack classic "The First Time Ever I Saw Your Face" swept through the room. Charlie smiled as she reached for the microphone and let the soft yet powerful lyrics fill the air.

Her voice rang sweet and true through the room, her eyes closed as she offered the song like a prayer. Hazaar felt every note in her belly, every harmony with the piano struck a chord in her soul, and she knew without question that Charlie would change everything for her. She knew she should run. She knew she should walk away from Ms. Charlie Porter and never look back, for both of their sakes. Instead, she played the song to its finish, and as applause drifted into the private world she and Charlie had created for them, she realized that it was already too late. In the space of a day, because of one chance meeting and a leap of faith, Charlie had already changed her.

She had walked away from her previous affairs without so much as a backward glance, knowing as she'd gotten involved that they were temporary, just a dalliance to pass the time and create a few fantasies that would help make the days in her future easier for her to bear; the tender caress of a woman's hand to replace the indifferent touch of her unknown and unwanted husband.

Her head said "run away" just as surely as her heart drew her toward Charlie, and her fear immobilized her.

Charlie held out her hand, her smile soft and gentle, eyes shining with desire. "Shall we get out of here?"

Hazaar stared at her hand knowing that it meant so much more than Charlie realized. Should she, could she, accept it? Take what Charlie was innocently offering and let the chips fall as they may? Hazaar tried to remember where she'd heard the saying, but the soft kiss of Charlie's palm against her own startled her from her reverie. She didn't recall making the decision to move, but her body had done so. She couldn't remember standing, or putting one foot in front of the other, but she was walking beside Charlie, out the door.

Neither of them spoke. They didn't have to.

# CHAPTER SIX

*The North of England, then*

Hazaar slid her hands across the cotton sheet and smiled when she found soft, warm skin. "Good morning." She smiled lazily and stretched her arms above her head, easing out some of the ache in her shoulders.

"Morning." Charlie yawned before covering Hazaar's forehead with soft kisses and jumping out of the bed. "So what are your plans for today?" Charlie called from the bathroom.

"Not a thing. I was hoping I could entice you into staying in bed."

"Sounds great. I just have one problem."

"Oh yeah. What's that?"

"I'm hungry."

Hazaar laughed as her own stomach rumbled. "I think I can do something about that. What would you like?"

Charlie poked her head out of the bathroom, toothbrush in hand and a mischievous smile on her face. "Bacon sandwich?"

"Wow. Google really does need to up their game."

Charlie laughed. "I'm just teasing. I know you don't eat pork."

"Very true—" The phone beside the bed rang and Hazaar stretched over to answer it. "Hello."

"Hazaar, we will be with you in a few minutes. Put the tea on." Her father's voice echoed down the line, and the look of concern on Charlie's face confirmed her suspicion that the colour had drained from her face.

"Of course." She replaced the receiver, the dial tone ringing in her ear before she finished speaking. "Shit. Fuck." Hazaar threw the covers off and started to gather up the discarded clothes, tossing Charlie's at her as she found them.

"You okay?" Charlie asked.

"Fuck." She barely recognized the shrill sound that came out of her own mouth, and her hands shook as she grabbed at everything, trying to straighten the room. *This can't be happening.*

"Hazaar, what's wrong?"

"Fuck, fuck, fuck, fuck, fuck." She pulled the duvet straight over the bed and pushed open a window, beads of sweat forming on her forehead, and every noise off the street made her flinch. "Hurry. You have to go."

"What?"

Hazaar ran through the apartment to the kitchen and quickly put the kettle on to boil. She looked about her quickly as she went back through the house, trying to spot anything that would rouse suspicions. Other than Charlie, she couldn't see any. Charlie was standing in the bedroom pulling her jeans up and scowling.

"What the fuck's going on?"

"I don't have time to explain. You have to go." She ran into the bathroom, hurrying through the necessities and pulling on her clothes before Charlie was fully dressed.

"Please, we don't have time. You have to go."

"Why? Who was that on the phone?" Charlie pulled on her heeled boots as she leaned against the doorframe.

"I'm sorry, Charlie. I don't have time to explain."

"Fine." Charlie's jaw was clenched as she pulled up the zip on her boot.

"I'm sorry." Hazaar could feel tears welling in her eyes. She didn't want Charlie to be angry with her, but she couldn't be there when Hazaar's family arrived. She just couldn't. "It's my family."

"They're coming here?"

Hazaar nodded.

"Why didn't you just say that? Christ, I thought—hell, I didn't know what to think."

"I'm sorry."

"No need to be. It's fine." Charlie grabbed her jacket and pulled open the door as Hazaar followed her. "Will you call me?"

"Yes. When they go."

Charlie smiled, kissed her chastely on the cheek, and pushed the button for the lift. "Then go and get ready."

Hazaar closed the door behind her and grabbed a head scarf to cover her hair. Everything was as it should be when the intercom sounded seconds later. She pushed the button to release the security door in the lobby as she tried to calm her racing heart and shaking hands. She hated the way she felt. They were her family, but every visit increased her sense of impending doom.

The knock at the door startled her out of her maudlin thoughts. Her heart jumped in her chest, and her breath caught in her throat. *Shit.* Her hand shook as she reached for the lock and pulled open the door.

"Baba." She leaned forward and accepted the kiss on her forehead before Isam Alim walked into the house.

"*Jugnu.*" He shrugged off his coat and handed it to her; she smiled at the term of endearment. *Jugnu,* Urdu for firefly, was her father's way of showing he cared for her. "Has the tea boiled?"

"I was just going to check, Baba."

Her mother walked in and followed her into the kitchen, clicking her tongue behind her teeth. "You've lost weight again, Hazaar. We need to get some food into you before you disappear. No man wants a wife who is all sharp elbows and knees."

Hazaar looked down at her full breasts and hips and noted that she was far from skinny, but nodded to appease her mother. She had learned over the years that it was far easier to keep the peace than it was to weather the arguments. "Yes, Maa Jee."

"You are a good girl, *Beti.*" The term of endearment always made her smile, even though her mother had used it for all four girls, since the word simply meant daughter. Nisrin patted her cheek. "You make your father and me so proud."

Hazaar bit her lip and let her gaze fall to the floor. She felt the weight of her mother's stare, those knowing eyes that had followed Hazaar her whole life, and she prayed to Allah that her secrets weren't written all over her face. "The tea should be ready."

Hazaar took her time preparing the tray with cups and saucers, sugar, milk, and the beautifully painted teapot her mother had given her when she moved into her apartment. She needed the time to compose herself as her mother recounted the latest community gossip. Who was getting married, and more importantly, who wasn't. Her sister, Badra, was expecting another baby, her fourth child in six years of marriage. Hazaar shuddered, making the pottery on the tray rattle noisily as she carried it into the room. Her father was staring out the window, apparently looking down onto the street, a distasteful curl on his lips.

"I'm not sure about you living here, *Jugnu*. There are too many bad influences around."

Hazaar crossed the room and looked out. Charlie was crossing the road and heading toward the bus stop. She swallowed and looked at her father. Her stomach felt leaden, and her tongue felt thick in her mouth. "Come and have some tea, Baba," she said with difficulty.

He grunted and sat down, sipping on his tea when she handed it to him. "So tell me about the university."

"I've been accepted onto the master's program, Baba. The course is two years."

Her mother clicked her tongue. "Two more years of schooling. It is not necessary. Why do you need so much education?"

"It is a great honour, Maa Jee, and when I finish, I can study for my doctorate in music."

Her father grinned. "My little *jungu*, a doctor. Dr. Hazaar Erina Alim. I like the sound of that." He scratched his head and resettled the prayer cap atop his head. "Tell me more about this course."

Hazaar took a deep breath and began to explain the master's program and the further doctorate studies that she wanted to pursue.

"So it will be three more years before you finish?" Her mother fidgeted on the sofa, sipping her tea and inching closer to the edge of her seat.

"Yes, Maa Jee."

"And what of finding you a husband? A good man to give you babies."

"There is still plenty of time for all of that. Hazaar is still a young woman." Her father put his tea cup on the small table beside his chair.

Her mother waved her hands in the air. "Already she is twenty-six. People talk."

"Yes, they talk. They say how accomplished my *beti* has become, how proud she must make me, and how she is a good girl."

"How she is an old maid."

"Enough, *Zoujah!*"

Hazaar flinched. Her father rarely addressed her mother as *Zoujah*—wife—and did so only ever to remind her that he was the man of the household, and he didn't like to be questioned. Her mother ducked her head and melted back into her chair, her eyes downcast, knees pressed tightly together, and her hands clasped around them. She appeared so still Hazaar wondered if she was even breathing.

Her father cleared his throat. "You work very hard, *Beti*, and whilst your mother does make a valid point that you aren't getting any younger, you continue to bring honour to our family with your accomplishments." He leaned forward and rested his elbows on his knees, looking her in the eye. "Tell me why you want to continue with this so much. Why should I not find you a suitable husband?"

Hazaar's breath caught in her throat and her heart raced. She hated lying to her father. He was a good man, he loved her, and she knew that he had tried to give her and her sisters the best lives he could. His own marriage had been arranged, and she believed that her parents genuinely cared for each other, even loved each other. Arranging the marriages of his own children wasn't something he took lightly. He saw it as his gravest responsibility to protect his children's futures, placing their care into safe hands, as he had watched his father do, and his father before him, and back generation after generation. It was his privilege to do it for them. He saw it as his final-child rearing duty, and he was determined to do the best he could for them. It hadn't even occurred to him that it might not be what his children wanted.

Her palms were sweaty as she tried to focus her thoughts. *Focus? Hell, I can't even hear them over my bloody heartbeat.* She squeezed her hands between her knees, zeroing in on the pressure, and forced the image of the executioner from her mind. "Baba, you've been a wonderful father. You've provided us all with everything we could wish for, and you've taught us how to be good Muslims, good children, and good people. At your knee I've learned pride too. Pride in you, in my family, and in myself. I know that you wished you had been granted more sons, to carry your name to Allah and into the future. I can't do that for you, Baba, but I can bring your name honour in a different way."

She looked up and smiled when she saw the look of rapt attention on her father's face. "Allah has granted me with a gift, Baba. To not use it—to not allow it to bring you honour—would be a sin."

He nodded his head slowly, his eyes never leaving hers. "Come here."

She stood and walked to him, dropping to her knees at his feet. He took hold of her hand, and she dropped a sweet kiss to the back of his hand, then rested her forehead against it, determined to do everything she could to convince him to let her stay.

"When the time comes, I'll find an honourable man for you, one who will appreciate all you have accomplished and who will treasure your gifts. You're very special to me, *Beti*. You may continue your studies."

"Thank you, Baba." She kept her head bowed as she whispered the words, afraid he would see her look of relief. The executioner moved back into the shadows of her brain, his axe still raised above his head, blade glinting in the light. She'd bought herself some time, but was it enough?

# CHAPTER SEVEN

*Pakistan, today*

Charlie spun her pen on the desk, watching it travel across the scarred and battered wood through the slatted light caused by the wooden blinds at each of the windows. Ceiling fans rotated, stirring the air, making the dust motes dance in and out of the shadows. Stilted coughs bounced from one end of the conference table to the other, neckties were loosened, straightened, and then loosened again. Charlie brushed away the drip of sweat trailing down her neck and felt sorry for the guys sitting in long-sleeved shirts and pants. It was too stifling for conversation, so they all waited for the boss in silence.

The door burst open, and JJ strode into the room, a stack of files tucked under one arm, a mug cradled in the other hand. "So last night we had a result in the Malik case." He dumped the files on the desk and looked at each person around the desk. "Horia is now with her mother, and they will be heading back to the UK before the end of the week."

Applause went around the room, and Charlie smiled. It was days like this she loved her job. She loved making a difference in the lives of the children and women she helped to bring home. The degradation she felt at bartering for the lives and futures of children who deserved nothing but the best tore at her soul and reminded her of past promises she couldn't keep. But right now another little girl was safely returned to her family, and for today, it kept her demons at bay.

"How did that happen?" Liam slapped his left hand on the table—his right having been lost when a bullet severed the artery just above the elbow a year ago. He'd been trying to prevent a woman from being stoned to death, the penalty she was to pay for what they called adultery and Charlie called rape. Delayed health care and an infection cost him dearly, but it was the memories of the woman dying that haunted him and kept him in the office chasing paperwork rather than operating in the field. "I thought he was in it for the long haul. Stubborn bastard."

Charlie slapped him on the back. "You pointed me in the direction of those local newspapers. I did a search on his name, and I found an announcement of an upcoming birth."

"Ah." He nodded knowingly. "You go with the 'new start for everyone' angle?"

"It's an oldie but a goodie."

"I taught you well, young Padawan." He patted her on the head.

Charlie laughed. "If you say so." It was good to see Liam in a good mood. The past year had been difficult for him. He'd been her mentor, her advisor, and her friend, and now she was technically his boss and he rarely left the office.

"You all done down in the cheap seats?" Jasper slid a file across the desk, and it stopped right in front of Charlie.

"Cheap seats." Liam scoffed. "Bloody cheek. Who is it that makes him look good?"

Charlie sniggered and opened the file in front of her.

"Before we get to the paperwork," Jasper said. "We have a new recruit." He motioned to the young woman beside him. Charlie guessed her to be around six feet, and jet black hair hung in a long, sleek ponytail down her back. She lifted a pair of dark sunglasses away from her face, perching them atop her head, and scanned the room with the most piercing blue eyes Charlie could ever remember seeing. "This is Steph MacKenzie."

"Please, everyone calls me Kenzie."

"Okay. Well then, Kenzie, this is the team. We got Luke Odoze." Luke waved and leaned back in his chair, crossing his legs to rest one ankle on his knee and the chair on its back two legs only. "Luke's our communications and IT specialist."

"How're you doing?" He tipped his head back as he spoke, the movement causing the precariously balanced chair to tip, and he landed on his back with a hard thump. Laughter erupted around the room. Luke jumped up and scowled at those nearest to him. "Who pushed me?"

"No one did, numb nuts." JJ shook his head. "I swear if you weren't so good at your job I'd pay your airfare out of here myself." He turned back to Kenzie. "He's harmless to everyone but himself. Next to Luke is—"

"Hillary Arthur, research and analysis." She stood and held out her hand. "Welcome to the team."

"Thanks, it's good to be here."

"Let's hope you think so later," JJ said. "Down at the bottom we have our two reprobates, Liam Evans and Charlie Porter." They both waved. "Charlie is the negotiator responsible for bringing the Malik case to a close. Liam's her backup and our logistics man. And finally, we have Albert Garrett."

He held out his hand. "Al. I'm in charge of field operations and security. When you're heading out there, please follow my lead." He cast a pointed look at Charlie. "Not like some people, who fly off half-cocked." Charlie pointed at her chest and threw him her best *Who, me?* look.

"Don't know what you're talking about," she mumbled under her breath as a chorus of chuckles went round the room.

"All right, people, settle down." JJ turned to Kenzie. "Why don't you give us a little of your background, then we'll get started."

"Sure." She nodded and Charlie studied her as she spoke, looking for signs that gave away nervousness, trepidation, or indecision. She smiled when she saw none. "I have a master's degree in psychology, and I spent the last seven years in the military. Most of that based in Afghanistan. Just the other side of the Khyber Pass for the most part."

"So this must feel like home for you," Luke said.

Kenzie shrugged. "Something like that."

"What did you do in the military?" Liam homed in on the question burning in Charlie's mind.

"Military Intelligence, debriefing and interrogation corps." Kenzie cast a quick glance at JJ, and Charlie caught the subtle nod out of the corner of her eye and guessed that Kenzie was ascertaining the level of security clearance in the room. Charlie wasn't worried. She knew they all had top secret clearance.

"I was working with the Afghanistan ISI training their troops and interrogating high-level Taliban and terrorist suspects."

Charlie did a quick calculation, and given the timing, she had to ask the question on everyone's mind. "Were you at Abu Ghraib?"

Kenzie turned, and her eyes locked on to Charlie, her face still as stone. "I was there after the atrocities became public knowledge. I was part of the cleanup operation, and the team who brought in new techniques to retrieve information."

"Forgive me for saying, Kenzie, but you still seem very young. Abu Ghraib was 2006," Liam said.

"Was there a question in there?" Kenzie's gaze never left Charlie.

Liam chuckled. "Well, my mum warned me never to ask a woman her age, but I guess I'm wondering how someone so young got to be involved in cleaning up a cluster fuck like that. Timing? Or are you that good?"

Kenzie smiled and turned to look at Liam. "I guess we'll see."

"Okay, if we're quite done, should we get to work?" JJ pointed at the files spread across the desk. "Kenzie, Charlie is gonna be your mentor. She'll help bring you up to speed and show you the ropes."

Charlie kicked the chair next to her away from the desk and smiled at Kenzie as she patted the seat. "Come and join the A-team."

Kenzie laughed and made her way across the room.

"Word to the wise though, Kenzie," JJ said. "We call her Maverick behind her back, and it isn't always a good thing."

"That was behind my back?" Charlie pulled her face to adopt a look of mock outrage. "JJ, you suck at keeping secrets, mate."

"Yeah, yeah, bite me." He flopped down into his chair. "Shall we get to work, people? We've got a lot of women and children to find."

# CHAPTER EIGHT

*The North of England, then*

The TV blared noise at Charlie as she starred into space. Beth was draped over the sofa with her head resting in Charlie's lap, her feet over the arm. Her chatter drifted over Charlie's head until a sharp elbow to the ribs quickly brought her focus back to earth.

"Hey, what was that for?" She rubbed her midsection absently as she scowled down at Beth.

"I'm talking to you and you're doing a very poor job of paying any attention to me."

"Aw, is the poor little baby feeling all neglected?" Charlie reached down to tickle Beth mercilessly.

"Hey, why am I being tortured, just because she hasn't called you yet?" Beth managed to sputter between fits of laughter.

"That was cruel, and uncalled for, and demands an exacting price!" Charlie grasped both of her wrists in one hand and dragged her across her lap and planted a loud, wet raspberry against her skin.

"Ew, you're disgusting! Let me go! Let me go!" Beth twisted free of her grasp and ran for cover.

"Come 'ere, Flipper, and take your punishment like a man!"

Beth giggled as she ran for the kitchen. "But I'm not a man and you really need to retake biology if you think I am." She stuck her tongue out as Charlie rounded the doorway and entered the kitchen. Charlie's phone rang in the front room. "Bet that's her."

Charlie ran back into the living room to grab the handset. "Hello." Charlie turned her back on Beth as she skipped into the room.

"I'm so sorry. My family descended and I've literally just escorted them from the building."

"I think I saw them arrive. Two days ago." Beth danced around the room, her arms wrapped around herself as she made kissy faces at her. Charlie scowled at her and turned her back.

"I'm really sorry. They turned up unannounced and uninvited. The only reason my father called was to tell me to put the kettle on because he wanted tea. It's a good job, as it would have been so very difficult to get them to believe that we were just friends if they had found us both naked in the bedroom."

"It's okay." Charlie smiled, and the image of Hazaar's naked body made her heart beat a little faster.

"It was a good visit, though. My father and I agreed on some stuff about me staying here in school for a while yet, so it was definitely worthwhile."

"Well that's good then, right?"

"Yeah, it is. I'm just sorry it took so long."

"Honestly, it's okay."

"I can't stop thinking about you. I've barely been able to hold a conversation all the time they have been here...I'm babbling, aren't I?"

"Yes. It's cute."

"I'm sorry. I do that when I'm nervous. Right now I'm really nervous. Please say something."

"Hazaar, it's okay. You'd already told me that your family doesn't know you're gay. There's really no need for a big explanation. I understand that part."

"Wow. You do?"

"Yes. What I don't get is why couldn't you just tell me that your family was on the way?"

"Usually people don't understand about my family, and it's really difficult to get them to see it from my side of the equation. You know the 'I'm not ashamed of you, or them,' kind of thing. It's just a very difficult conversation."

"I get it."

"They caught me off guard and I didn't react very well. I guess I expected a reaction I didn't have time to deal with. Please forgive me?"

"Nothing to forgive." Charlie looked over at the mantel shelf and the picture of her with her arm around a petite redhead, and memories of Gail bombarded her. Images of the two of them when they first fell in love filled her mind. The innocence of that first love had filled their hearts and made them believe that nothing and no one would ever come between them. They had been so wrong. Tears filled her eyes as she remembered the last time she'd seen Gail. The day they had buried her had been the worst day of her life. Charlie still felt the pang of guilt just as sharply as she had the day she'd cradled Gail's cold body, and she knew it wasn't in her to ever try to push someone to come out to their family. The price for some people was far too high.

"Next time, just be honest with me. I'm not like everybody else. I don't intend to make life difficult for you, or judge you. Just be honest with me."

"There's going to be a next time?" Hazaar's voice sounded so hopeful that Charlie just wanted to hold her.

"If you still want one?"

"Yes." Hazaar's voice was little more than a whisper.

"Then just tell me what's going on in future, and we can deal with it. Like I said, I won't judge or push. If you don't want to drink because of your religion, that's fine. No worries. If you need me to leave in a hurry because your family is coming round, tell me the truth so I at least know why I'm hiding in the wardrobe or shimmying down the drainpipe. I can handle it." Charlie's face was flushed as she spoke. There was silence on the other end of the phone. "Hello, are you still there?"

"Wow. I think I could fall in love with you!"

Charlie laughed. "Oh, so we're going to have a typical lesbian relationship then, are we? When should I sterilize the turkey baster?"

Hazaar laughed. "Maybe we should try a slightly atypical one."

"Probably a good idea." She paused, debating whether or not to say what she wanted to, but she knew it would irk her if she didn't. "You could have sent a text, though."

"I know. I should have done a lot of things differently. I'm sorry. I really didn't think you'd be this cool about it. I guess I was expecting drama and didn't want to try to explain it in a crappy text." Hazaar's voice dropped. "Are you really this cool with it or am I being lulled into a false sense of security and you're planning to pounce on me any second?"

"Well, if you were here, I may very well be about to pounce on you, but I don't think you'd mind, sweetheart." Charlie felt her breath catch in her throat as the endearment slipped past her lips, completely bypassing her thought processes.

"Well, maybe we can rectify that problem, babe." She could hear the smile in Hazaar's voice.

"Oh yeah? And what did you have in mind?" She tucked one leg underneath her as she sat on the couch.

"How about a night in front of the telly? You pick the DVDs you want. I'll organise food. Do you like Mexican, Indian, Italian?" The question hung in the air.

"Well, if you're cooking, the choice should be yours."

Hazaar's laughter echoed down the line. "Who mentioned cooking? I'm trying to get you to forgive me, not kill you!"

"You're that good a cook?" Charlie teased her.

"Better. So what's it to be, gorgeous?"

Charlie could feel the heat creep up her neck and colour her cheeks. "How about Mexican?"

"Perfect. Anything in particular, or rather, anything to avoid?"

"Nope, I'm easy."

"I already know that. That's why I'm keeping you around."

Charlie nearly choked as she spluttered down the phone. "Hey, I thought you were begging forgiveness. You can't be casting those sorts of aspersions on my character! I might have to make you suffer now."

"Promises, promises."

Charlie laughed again. "What kinds of films do you like?"

"Thrillers. Comedy. Not a big fan of scream fests, or weepy chick flicks. But as I already said, the choice, my lady, is all yours."

"Such gallantry. Okay, *Friday the Thirteenth* and *Titanic* it is. What time do you want me?"

"A loaded question if ever I heard one. Right now would be my favourite answer to that, but then we would never eat, as I have nothing in. The locusts cleared me out. It was the deciding factor on when they were leaving me in peace. How about six? Gives me time to run out and pick up some stuff for us."

Charlie smiled as she whispered into the mouthpiece. "And is formal attire required at this dinner party?"

"Darling, attire is entirely optional. It won't stay on long enough for me to really see it. Now go, before I can't walk anymore. Thinking has already stopped being a possibility. There's no blood left in my head. See you at six."

Charlie grinned as she hung up the phone, grabbed the cushion next to her, and tossed it at Beth before running for the stairs.

"Hey, what was that for?" The cushion sailed after her and landed with a dull thump against the banister rail.

"Just for being your usual charming self, Flipper." She mounted the stairs two at a time, already planning what she would wear. She wanted it to be a night Hazaar wouldn't forget.

# CHAPTER NINE

*The North of England, then*

Charlie hitched the backpack higher on her shoulder as she stepped out of the lift and crossed the landing to Hazaar's door. She raised her hand to knock, but the door opened before she made contact and she was tugged inside. Hazaar gripped her waist and pulled her close until their lips met in a searing kiss, leaving her breathless and wet.

"Hi."

"Hi." Hazaar's fingers slid across her back and down to grip her backside. "I missed you." She leaned in for another kiss and Charlie twisted her fingers into the ebony locks that tumbled around Hazaar's shoulders before she found the back of her neck and pushed the other hand under her shirt. Charlie eased away from the kiss and trailed her lips along Hazaar's jaw, up behind her ear, then down the length of her throat. She ran her fingers over the soft, smooth skin of Hazaar's belly and palmed her firm breast when she reached it. But it wasn't enough. She was hungry, eager to reacquaint herself with her new lover, and she pulled the lacy fabric away from her breast and pinched the pebbled nipple between her fingers. She rolled the turgid flesh between her finger and thumb until it reached a tantalizing peak, before tugging it hard and covering it with her mouth. Hazaar's moan was music to her ears.

Charlie walked them backward toward the breakfast bar as she sucked and caressed Hazaar's breasts, not stopping until her buttocks hit the bench. She quickly lifted her onto the table and skimmed her hands down the long, colourful skirt. She gripped the hem and flipped it above Hazaar's knees, her lips and tongue still working at the stiff, puckered nipples.

She pressed Hazaar's knees apart and eased the skirt higher. Inch by delicious inch, smooth thighs were revealed to her questing fingers, and the scent of desire filled the air with the tantalizing undertones of spice, jasmine, and musk. As she worked the skirt up to her hips, she groaned and licked her lips at the sight of Hazaar's sex, naked, wet, and waiting for her. Charlie dropped to her knees and buried her face between her thighs. The need to taste, to please, was overwhelming, and Hazaar's obvious desire only made Charlie wetter. Her clit throbbed, pulsing in time to every beat of her heart.

Hazaar leaned back, supporting herself with one hand as the other covered Charlie's head, fingers laced through her curls, as her tongue dipped inside her. Charlie used her thumbs to part the folds of her sex and feathered her lips along the stiff bundle of nerves, gently pushing back the protective hood and using the tip of her tongue to tease the sensitive flesh quivering between her lips. She released it and blew across the overheated tissue before she pulled it between her lips and sucked. Hard.

Hazaar was close; she could feel it in every breath as she chanted Charlie's name like a prayer. She slid two fingers inside her, filling her, and she pumped slowly at first as she licked at her clit. She wished she had the patience to draw out their pleasure, to push Hazaar further, higher, to bring her more pleasure than she had ever known. But she knew neither of them would last much longer as she rocked her hips, creating a delicious friction against her jeans. She stroked in time to her own hip thrusts, slowly driving deeper and faster as she began to suck again, and pulling her clit between her lips, she created pressure in her mouth, then used her tongue to flick her clit in time with each thrust. Hazaar came hard, bucking against her mouth as her arm gave way and she collapsed back against the table.

Charlie released the pressure of her mouth and eased her tongue to lap gently at the tender flesh, waiting for the after tremors to subside before she slowly removed her fingers and eased her way up Hazaar's body. She gently drew her into her arms and held her while her breathing returned to normal.

"I missed you too."

Hazaar smiled into her shoulder. "So I gather." She stroked her hands up Charlie's back and her grin widened as shivers followed in her wake. Hazaar pulled out of her arms a little, a playful smile upon her lips. "So what film did you bring?"

"*Red.*"

"And what's that?"

"Action comedy with Bruce Willis, Helen Mirren, Morgan Freeman, and a few others. Retired spies getting pulled back into the game for a deadly mission. Sounds quite entertaining, and it's a good cast." She shrugged and began to move away. Hazaar held on to her tight and leaned up to kiss her.

"Sounds like it should be fun. Would you like to eat now or later?"

Charlie grinned wickedly.

Hazaar laughed. "Food, you pervert. I went out and got perfectly good take-away that's probably spoiled while you've been manhandling me."

"Are you complaining?"

Hazaar grinned and kissed her lightly. "No, baby, not at all. But we have all night." She kissed her neck. "And I did have a plan." She pulled her in for another long kiss.

"Really?" Hazaar nodded. "Tell me about your plan then." She bent to kiss her again, but Hazaar stopped her and gently pushed her away. Her skirt fell back to her ankles as she climbed down from the breakfast bar and walked around to the kitchen. She passed a stack of plates and cutlery to Charlie.

"Go and put those in the living room? Then I promise to tell you all about my plan."

Charlie did as she was told and set the places on the low table in the front room. Hazaar entered with a bag and two wine glasses in one hand, a bottle of wine tucked under one arm, a jug of ice water in her other hand, and a bottle opener sticking out of her mouth.

"Here, let me help you." She removed the bottle opener and kissed her before she could divest herself of any of her burdens.

"How kind. Thank you." They settled before the table, and Hazaar slowly unpacked the bag of goodies. "I wasn't sure what you would like, so I got one of everything and I thought we could share."

"Sounds good. Now tell me about your plan." She plucked a nacho from the bowl and stuffed it into her mouth, grinning as the cheese and sour cream ran across her taste buds.

"Well, this is stage one. Feed my beautiful girlfriend while I slip copious amounts of alcohol into her—"

"Did you just say girlfriend?"

Hazaar blushed as she poured a glass of wine for Charlie and a glass of water for herself. "Yes." She looked over at Charlie. "Is that okay?"

Charlie stared into Hazaar's beautiful chocolate brown eyes as they danced with a mixture of excitement and trepidation. *She's as nervous as I am.* Charlie saw a glimmer of the hesitation that lay beneath the surface, and suddenly the confident seductress seemed a little bit unsure of herself. Uncertain of what, Charlie didn't know. But she wanted to. She wanted to ease the anxiety, the fear. She wanted to soothe the turbulent soul she could see peeking out at her so tentatively. She reached across and stroked Hazaar's cheek gently. "Most definitely, sweetheart."

Hazaar grinned too before spooning spiced rice onto her plate, and Charlie was glad to see some of the tension leave her shoulders.

Charlie waved her hand and signalled for her to carry on as she loaded her plate with rice, salad, and fajitas.

"The plan is to feed my beautiful girlfriend while I try to get her drunk so that I'm sure she has fully forgiven me for being stupid and I can take her to bed without any problems."

"It's a good plan. I only see three small problems with it."

"Problems?"

"Well, details more than problems."

"And those would be?"

"Well, number one, if I drank a whole bottle of wine, I would definitely be going to bed. Unconscious."

"Okay. I can handle that. The top goes back on after the next glass." Hazaar tapped her forehead. "Note to self, got me a cheap date."

"Ha ha."

"Next detail?"

"There was nothing to forgive. I told you I understand. I'm not the kind of person who tries to make people do something against their will. I won't push you to come out to your family, your friends. That decision is entirely personal. As long as you understand that I'm out to my family and friends, and that I won't lie about myself, it's fine. I can be discreet. And I totally understand that it's difficult for you. All I need is for you to be honest with me about what you need from me. And I'll do the same. Then we figure it out between us." She fished around for another nacho. "It might not always be easy, but as long as we're honest with each other, we should be able to work it out."

"And this is the Charlie Porter School of Relationships?"

"No. It just makes sense to me."

Hazaar studied her plate, her expression thoughtful as she played with her food. "And the third detail?"

"Who says we need a bed?"

Hazaar looked up and laughed as Charlie quirked one eyebrow. "Very true, baby. Very true." She leaned across the table and kissed Charlie softly on the lips. "So tell me, where did you come to all this wisdom about relationships? Do you have a cupboard full of exes hiding somewhere?"

Charlie laughed. "Not hardly. I just really don't think your need for me to leave because your family arrived is anything to get all bent out of shape about." Hazaar kept watching her, one eyebrow arched. "What?"

"Exes?"

"What about them?"

"So it is them, as in plural?"

"Why so interested?"

"I'm interested in everything about you."

"And will you answer the same questions?"

"Sure."

"Okay. Then you can start. How many exes of yours do I need to avoid?"

"Avoid?"

"Well, based upon demonstrated form, the music school is your hunting ground." Charlie curled her fingers in the air imitating quote marks around the word hunting, but softened the words with a quirky smile. "So how many of my fellow students do I need to avoid?" She was grinning as the flush began to creep up Hazaar's neck and cheeks. "I wouldn't want to make any of your jilted lovers jealous, after all."

"And if I told you there were no others?"

"I would be very surprised."

"Why?"

"Firstly, a naïve, innocent young woman wouldn't have come on to me like you did at the audition. Second, an inexperienced, virtuous young woman wouldn't have brought me back here and fucked me against the door."

Hazaar put her fingers against Charlie's lips. "Such language from such beautiful lips." The twinkle in her eyes gave her away as she leaned in and kissed her again.

"So?"

"Okay, there have been a few lovers in my past. But you won't have to worry about them being jealous or anything like that."

"Why?"

"My first lover was actually an older student when I first started my undergraduate degree. She was in her final year and giving extra tutoring for part of her credit. We started sleeping together in January, knowing full well that she would be leaving in May. She works with an orchestra in London now. My second lover was a cellist. We worked together for many hours on duets for part of our final concerts. She was called Melissa. She graduated last year. I'm afraid we didn't part on very good terms." Hazaar sipped her water.

"How so?"

She shrugged. "She wanted more than I could give her."

"How do you mean?"

"She wanted to meet my family. Said that she would tell them we were friends. Melissa wasn't subtle or discreet. She fit the stereotypical lesbian profile, and as much as I cared about her, I didn't love her enough to risk my parents finding out." She hung her head. "I know I sound like a complete bitch saying that. I knew Melissa wasn't going to be in my life forever. I knew that it was fleeting. I didn't see the point in rocking the boat for no reason."

"Did she love you?"

Hazaar shook her head. "No, I don't think so. I think what she loved was the idea of me. The exotic girlfriend." She laughed. "Bradford really isn't that exotic, but whatever." She grinned. "Since Melissa, there have been a few very brief affairs. Musicians giving concerts and so on. No one important." She looked deeply into Charlie's eyes, and again the fear radiated from within and made Charlie wonder at its cause. "Till you." They kissed again, a soft, tender kiss, a promise.

"Hazaar, how do you think your life will end up? Do you think if you found the right relationship you would tell your family, or do you think you'll always be looking for a fleeting relationship until you're forced to toe the line?"

Hazaar was silent for a long time, toying with her fork, chasing rice around her plate. "I guess I'm torn. In one way, I think maybe I'm waiting to find the right person to walk into my life. The one I can love with all my heart." She smiled a little sadly. "Someone who will fill me up so much that I'll find it possible to walk away from my family, my friends, my culture, everything that I've known and been a part of since I was born. Because that's what I would have to do." She put her fork down and pushed the plate away. "In another way, I think I'm trying to fit as much living—as much life—as I possibly can into the tiny amount of free time I have left before I have to comply with the customs of my people, and the wishes of my family. I don't know from one day to the next which way I'll go when the time comes. I think it will depend entirely on who is in my life when the time comes to make the decision. I know that isn't a good answer. I know that people want guarantees in a relationship."

"There are no guarantees in a relationship. I'll say again, just be honest with me and keep me in the loop. Teach me about your religion, your customs, your culture. Help me to understand."

"What do you get out of that?"

"I get to spend time with you. I get to know you, and vice versa. If that helps you with your decisions one day, great. If not, I'll have learned a lot along the way. I'll be honest, Hazaar. Like everyone else, I would love to find the woman I'll spend the rest of my life with, but I also know that I'm twenty-four years old, and I don't need to find that yet. That doesn't mean I should sit around and just wait for her to fall out of the sky. It could be that you and I are meant to be together. Or it could be that we aren't. We'll never know if we don't spend time together and see. Everything you've told me suggests that you're as uncertain of your future as anyone else is. If that changes, as your girlfriend, I would expect you to tell me that, but that's a bridge to cross some other time."

"You're an amazing woman, Charlie Porter." They kissed again, Hazaar's lips brushing hers as softly as a butterfly's wing, her tongue barely wetting her lips as it sought entrance to her mouth. The passion burned beneath the kiss laced with devotion, and Charlie's head spun as Hazaar slowly eased away. "So, it's your turn, beautiful."

Charlie frowned, her eyes still closed. "My turn what?"

"Exes."

"Oh, sure. Just one."

"Oh my God, really?"

Charlie nodded.

"Wow." Hazaar popped the last nacho in her mouth. "She must have been very special. Tell me about her."

Charlie took a deep breath and steeled herself. If Hazaar could open up about her fears, it was only fair she do so too. "Well, Gail and I met at school. We were best friends, practically inseparable. She had some problems with her parents. A lot of the stuff she wouldn't talk about, but she would come into school during the first few years in school with some awful bruises on her. She forged notes to get out of sports so that the teachers and other kids wouldn't see them. She'd stay over at my house as much as possible, but we really didn't know how bad it was. I still didn't, until it was too late. Anyway, we finished school and went out to celebrate finishing our exams. Gail was always really outgoing and vivacious, the life and soul of the party. She was always looking out for me, like my protector or something." Charlie laughed a little sadly at the bittersweet memories. "We got absolutely smashed that night and ended up kissing. I'd never been kissed like that before. I mean, I'd kissed some of the boys who had asked me out when I was in school. Played spin the bottle and all that. But when Gail kissed me, it was like coming home at the same time as being the most scared and excited I had ever been." She ran her fingers through her hair. "We spent the whole summer together, mostly at my house. Kissing whenever we could get time alone. Learning each other. Exploring. We became lovers before the end of the summer, and when we started college, we decided it was time to tell our parents. My parents were actually amazingly cool with it. They loved Gail. My mum was forever telling her that she was like another daughter to her. It was really very easy for us at my house. My parents did take a little time getting used to the idea of us sharing a room together when she stayed over, but they got there in the end."

"Your parents sound amazing."

Charlie grinned. "I know. I was—am—so lucky to have them. They've been so supportive. When Gail came out to her family it was a very different story. She didn't want to. She was scared of how they would react. So we waited a while. Another two years, actually." She laughed humourlessly. "Her mother threw up when we told her, and her father…" Charlie scrubbed her hand over her face, wishing she could scrub the memories from her brain.

"He took his belt off and started to beat her. I was trying to get it off him, to stop him, but he pushed me back and slammed me into a wall. I passed out. When I came around, I was on the pavement outside the house. I looked around for Gail, but I couldn't see her anywhere. I could hear sirens getting closer, but my eyes wouldn't open properly. When the ambulance got to me, they took me to the hospital and I had a really bad concussion. I was in hospital for three days. No one would tell me where Gail was, or what had happened when I was knocked out. One of Gail's neighbours had seen her dad dump me on the pavement unconscious, and called for an ambulance." She sipped her drink before looking directly at Hazaar. "Are you really sure you want to hear all this?"

"Yes. I think I need to know. It makes up a big part of you, doesn't it?"

Charlie nodded. "It was the second day that I was in the hospital that Gail's mother finally called the ambulance after her dad went to work. He had beaten her nearly to death. Four ribs were broken, her right arm was fractured, and both her hands were crushed where he had stomped on them. Her knee and shoulder were both dislocated, she had a hairline fracture of her skull, and her cheekbone was broken. There were sixty-eight puncture wounds across her back, shoulders, bum, and legs from the buckle of his belt, and her skin was just this bloody pulp. They didn't think she'd survive. It was then that a lifetime of fractures and injuries were discovered as well." Charlie rattled off the catalogue of injuries she would never forget as long as she lived, the horror of them still nearly as fresh as the day she'd been told.

Hazaar picked up her glass and took a sip of water while Charlie pulled a deep breath into her lungs. She hated how much each memory still sliced her to the core. "The bastard used her as a punching bag from the time she was just a kid. Just a fucking kid, and he beat her so many times." Her throat felt dry and scratchy. She pointed to Hazaar's water glass. "Can I have a sip?"

"Sure." Hazaar handed her the glass. "Finish it if you like."

"Thanks." Charlie swallowed down half the contents and rolled the glass between her palms as she rested her elbows on her knees. "He raped her when she was thirteen. Over and over again." She wiped the tears from the corner of her eye as she sipped her drink again. "She survived that last beating, but had to have loads of surgeries. The therapy was agonizing. My parents insisted that she come and live with us. I talked to them, and we all agreed that I would take some time out of college to be with her, to help her with her therapy for her hands, the hospital appointments, counsellors, police interviews." Charlie's voice cracked. "Then there was the trial. It was…" She brushed away tears as they streaked down her cheeks. "It was almost two years later when she took her own life."

Hazaar pulled Charlie close to her. Her head rested on her shoulder as she closed her eyes, memories assailing her.

"I found her in the garden. It was a lovely sunny day. First one that year. March. She'd told me she was going to lie in the garden and read. She spread the blanket out and took her whole prescription of pain meds and antidepressants." She took the tissue Hazaar passed her. "She just went to sleep. She left a note saying that she was sorry. That she didn't deserve me. She didn't deserve to be a part of my family and that I should forget all about her and move on with my life. That I deserved someone beautiful and unspoiled. She said she couldn't take the pain anymore." Charlie sniffed and wiped at her eyes. "I never saw her like that. To me she was always beautiful. She was so strong to have survived all she did. Everything he did to her. I wish so much that she had believed me when I told her I loved her. No matter what she thought, to me she was special and beautiful and wonderful. She wasn't just my lover or my friend. She was so much more to me." The tears fell silently down her cheeks, and Hazaar rocked her slowly. "I wish I'd known when we were still children. I wish I could have helped her more."

"I'm sure she knows that, baby."

Charlie sniffed and wiped the tears from her cheeks. "Sorry. I'm sure that wasn't part of your plan for the evening."

Hazaar pressed her fingers against her lips. "My plan for the evening was to get to know you. Please don't trivialize everything you've told me. You're a very special woman, Charlie. I'm honoured that you shared it with me." She pulled Charlie's hand to her lips and kissed the back of her knuckles. "I'm so sorry that you had to go through it all. And I'm even sorrier that Gail suffered so and lost her way." She placed a tender, chaste kiss against Charlie's lips. "Thank you." She wrapped her arms around her and held her close.

Charlie slowly pulled herself out of the morose memories and back to the present. She smiled as she eased away from Hazaar's hold.

"Do you want to watch that movie I brought?" Charlie dug out the DVD, handed it to Hazaar, and settled against the dark leather couch.

"Is that why you're a more mature student?"

"Yeah. It took me a while to straighten myself out after Gail died."

"And there hasn't been anyone since?"

"I went on a couple of dates, but I haven't found anyone I clicked with. Certainly no one that I wanted to sleep with. Till now, anyway."

"Then I'm even luckier than I thought."

Charlie frowned in confusion as Hazaar put the DVD in the machine and walked back to the sofa. "I have a wonderful girlfriend, and I'm the only one who knows how amazing she is in bed." Hazaar laughed and Charlie knew she was blushing. "You're adorable."

"Shut up and watch the film." She grumbled playfully as she settled her head against Hazaar's shoulder and wrapped an arm across her stomach. She felt the kiss Hazaar placed against the top of her head as the credits scrolled across the screen. She hadn't talked to anyone about Gail in a long time, and certainly no one outside her family. But talking about it with Hazaar made her realize it hurt a bit less than it had. For the first time in what felt like forever, the thought of being in love again didn't seem quite so terrifying.

# CHAPTER TEN

*The North of England, then*

Charlie leafed through the pages of the *TV Guide*, well aware that she hadn't read any of the articles or even seen any of the pictures. She glanced up at the clock—again—and noticed that the one in the living room was three minutes slower than the one in the kitchen. *No wonder I'm always burning my pizza!*

"Charlie?"

"Yeah?" She twisted to look over her shoulder as Beth walked into the room.

"Mum wants you in the kitchen."

She practically ran into the kitchen. "What is it? What's wrong?"

Her mother looked up and grinned at her. "Nothing's wrong, Charlie. Relax. I just wanted you to taste the casserole and make sure it's all right."

Charlie nodded and headed for the stove. "What kind of stew is it?"

"Pork and cider."

Charlie whirled on her mother. "Mum, I told you—"

"I'm teasing, Charlie, relax. It's lamb casserole. I went to a halal butcher to get it, and there's no alcohol in the recipe." She rubbed her hands across Charlie's upper arms. "Please, sweetheart, relax before you burst. Flipper has promised not to ask any embarrassing questions while Hazaar is here, and I promise I won't embarrass you either."

"Mum, I'm twenty-four. You don't embarrass me anymore. I just really want you to like her. She's...I...I really like her and I'm just nervous." Charlie shrugged.

Her mother wrapped her arms tightly around Charlie's shoulders.

"I'm sure she's lovely. If you like her so much, she must be very special. Just try to relax and it will probably be easier for her to relax too."

Charlie sighed and wrapped her arms about her mother. "Thanks, Mum. It really means a lot to me that you've gone to so much trouble."

"You are my daughter. This is not trouble. The first time I met your father's mother—oh my God—that was a nightmare." She pulled away and went to stir the casserole.

"What happened?"

"Well, your gran was already on her own by the time I met your dad. Your granddad had died about three years before that. So I actually thought it would be a bit easier." She shook her head. "I was running late coming home from work. I was working at the solicitor's then, typing letters and filing mostly. I was supposed to meet your dad in Stockport, at the bus station, and then we'd get the bus to his house for tea. But me being late out of work meant I missed the bus and so wasn't there to meet your dad on time. He waited for me, though, and when I got off the bus, we just carried on. Well, your gran had gotten tea ready for when we should have been there. She'd set it all out and dished it up, so it was waiting for us on the table when we walked in. Your dad was serving his apprenticeship to be an electrician so he got cleaned up and left me with your gran, waiting for him. With the food in front of us. She'd tried something a little different, she said. She'd done a salad. Well, this was a new thing for your gran. We each had a lettuce leaf. One each. A tomato cut into quarters, three slices of cucumber, a radish, some cress, a stick of celery, and a slice of this pink, pretend meat. Spam. Foul, disgusting, slimy, gelatinous, horrible-tasting stuff. She didn't say a word the whole time we waited for your dad, and when he came in, he sat down and she started telling him off for being late. He looked at me and sorta smiled, shook his head, and just said, 'Sorry, Mum. The bus was late.' Then he starts tucking in to his plate. She still hadn't said anything to me. Your dad, bless him, kept trying to bring me into the conversation, but your gran was having none of it. A couple of hours later, your dad was taking me home, and we stopped for fish and chips because we were both starving, and while we were waiting for the bus he said, 'Well, Sarah, tonight's about as bad as it gets. What do ya say? Will ya marry me?' And he pulled this ring out of his pocket." Her mother wiggled her left hand at her. "I still think he did it just to get away from the old bat."

"Mum!"

"Charlie, you've met your dad's mother." She pointed at her with a ladle. "You know it's true."

Charlie giggled and let go of some of the tension that had built up inside her. "I know." She started to head for the kitchen door before she stopped and turned round. "Mum?"

"Yeah?"

"You did say we were having lamb, not Spam, right?" She ducked and skipped out of the room giggling as a tea towel flew toward her head. She was almost in the living room when she heard voices from the hallway.

"Hi, I'm Beth."

"Nice to meet you. Charlie's told me a lot about you."

"Yeah? Was it good?"

"Flipper!" Charlie stepped behind Beth and slapped her lightly across the back of her head.

"Ow. You're gonna damage the merchandise if you keep doing that." Beth rubbed the back of her head.

"Not possible to do any more damage than you've already got."

"Be nice, Charlie. Remember, I know embarrassing stuff about you."

"Yeah, yeah." She playfully pushed Beth aside and reached for Hazaar's hand. "Come in."

"Charlotte Porter, don't leave the poor girl on the doorstep. Bring her in," her mother said.

Charlie blushed furiously and closed her eyes resignedly. "And so it begins." She opened her eyes and looked at Hazaar. "Are you sure about this? It could be pretty awful."

"Only for you, darlin'."

"Why, thank you so much." She quickly tugged Hazaar over the threshold and led her into the kitchen. "Mum, this is Hazaar. Hazaar, this is my mum, Sarah."

Her mother dried her hands off and held one out to Hazaar. "It's lovely to meet you."

"Thank you for inviting me, Mrs. Porter."

"Oh no. I'm Sarah. Mrs. Porter is my mother-in-law, and as I was explaining to Charlie just a few minutes ago, I'll not be serving Spam salad." She giggled at the look of confusion on Hazaar's face. "Charlie will explain, I'm sure. Can I get you something to drink?"

"I've got it, Mum." She grabbed a glass from the cupboard and poured ice water from a jug in the fridge before handing it to Hazaar. Their fingers brushed as Hazaar took the glass and smiled. "Shall we go and sit down?"

Hazaar nodded and followed her out of the kitchen as Beth stepped in and headed straight for her mother. The door hadn't even fully closed behind them before Beth started firing questions at her mother. Charlie grinned and pulled Hazaar to a stop as they eavesdropped on the conversation.

"So what do you think?"

"I've barely spoken to her yet, Beth."

"But you think she's pretty, right?" She didn't wait for a response. "I think she's pretty. She can't stop smiling at Charlie. And they keep holding hands. It's really quite cute when old people hold hands with each other."

Charlie stroked Hazaar's blushing cheek. "Who knew my sister would have such good taste?" She leaned forward and kissed Hazaar gently.

"Beth, your sister hardly counts as an old person," her mother said.

"I know, but you and Dad hold hands a lot too."

"Elizabeth Porter!"

"Oops. Sorry, Mum. You're not old either. But Dad is."

Charlie deepened the kiss, dragging her hands down the length of Hazaar's back.

"Charlie, wait." Hazaar pulled back and turned to face Beth, who stood in the doorway.

"Sorry." Beth was blushing as deeply as Charlie was. "I was trying to be quiet and just go."

"It's okay." Charlie smiled at her, despite her flaming cheeks. "I'll get my own back when you finally bring your boyfriend home."

"No chance."

"Ashamed of him?"

"Nope."

"Ashamed of us?"

"Occasionally, but not the reason."

Hazaar muffled her laughter with her hand as Charlie frowned.

"Then what is it?"

"I'm a sadist, not a masochist."

"Swallowed a dictionary, have you?"

"Very funny. I just don't want to suffer the embarrassment, pain, and fear that you'll go through tonight. I'd much rather dish it out." She stuck her tongue out and ran back into the kitchen.

Charlie shook her head. "I swear sometimes I think she's thirty, and the rest of the time I think she's three!"

"She's much more fun than any of my three sisters ever were."

"Maybe that's because all your sisters were older than you, so you can relate to Beth easier."

Hazaar kissed her again. "I'd much rather relate to you." Her fingers slipped into Charlie's hair, and she pulled her into a deep kiss, swallowing the moan that slipped out, but breaking off before they became oblivious again.

"Lucky me."

"When does your dad get home?"

"Anytime now. He's usually here by this time, actually." She sat on the sofa and pulled Hazaar next to her. "Are you okay? Nervous?"

"I'm fine, baby. Your mum and sister seem really nice. You are amazing. I'm sure your dad will be equally nice. What's to be nervous about?"

Charlie smiled a knowing smile and quirked her eyebrow.

"Okay, I'm terrified. What if they don't like me? What if they think I'm too old for you or that my religion is a problem?"

"Sweetheart, my parents aren't racist. They wouldn't care if you were bright blue with polka dots. And you're only three years older than me. That isn't an age difference. There are ten years between my mum and dad."

"Really?"

"Really. So don't worry about that. What matters to them is how you are to me. How you treat me. When I first came out to them, all they said they wanted was for me to be happy. If you make me happy, they will love you." Hazaar didn't look convinced. "Okay, remember what my mum was saying about Spam salad?"

"Yeah, what the hell was that all about?"

"She was telling me about the first time she met my dad's mum. He took her around for tea and she served Spam salad."

"What is Spam salad?"

"Salad with Spam. Spam is this kinda canned meat made up of all the leftovers and covered in this sort of jelly. It's really disgusting stuff. Anyway, she served that and didn't speak to my mum the whole evening. Knowing my gran, that is totally what happened." She trailed her fingers down Hazaar's cheek and made her look in her eyes. "So far, my mum has spoken to you. My sister has walked in on us kissing, and still talked to you. My mum has made a lamb casserole, after going to a halal butcher to get the meat, and is making every effort to put you at ease. My family is really lovely. They will tease me mercilessly, and you'll find out all kinds of embarrassing information about me. You may even get to see naked baby pictures, though if Flipper pulls out the one with me in a sheepskin rug with a colander on my head, I will probably die of shame. But they will be nothing but nice to you."

"Are you naked on this sheepskin rug?"

Charlie shook her head. "Worse. I was naked on the floor and using it as my superhero cape."

"I have got to see that picture." They heard the key in the front door, and Hazaar tensed.

"If you relax I might be persuaded to give you your own private re-creation."

Hazaar's head whipped around. "Is that a promise?"

"You'll have to wait and see." Charlie was already making her way to the door and opened it just as her dad reached for the handle. "Hey, Pops." She wrapped her arms around his neck and hugged him close.

"Hey, baby girl."

"Busy day?"

"They all are, honey."

She stepped back from him. "Dad, this is Hazaar. Hazaar, this is my dad, Andrew Porter."

"I'm very please to meet you, Mr. Porter." They shook hands.

"Please call me Andy." He smiled warmly at her, then winked at Charlie. "I'm going to go and get cleaned up, but can I get you a drink first?"

"No thank you, I have one."

"Okay, then if you'll excuse me a few minutes." He backed out of the room and went into the kitchen before they heard his footsteps on the stairs.

"You okay?"

"Yeah. Should we go and talk to your mum?"

"Yeah. Probably best not to leave Flipper with her for too long." They stood, and Charlie started to lead the way back into the kitchen.

"Why?"

"She'll be giving a running commentary on your technique."

She felt her arm pulled behind her as Hazaar stopped. "I'm kidding, sweetheart. Totally kidding." She kissed her gently. "Shall we?"

Hazaar didn't say anything but allowed herself to be tugged into the kitchen just in time to hear Charlie's mother chastising Beth.

"Elizabeth Porter, you will not tease your sister like that. Put the picture album back in the drawer, or I swear to God, I will go and find that young man you're pining after on Facebook and send him your baby pictures. Just because you won't bring him here doesn't mean you're safe. Do you understand me, young lady?"

Charlie was barely able to contain her laughter as Beth walked out, mumbling under her breath.

"I never should have explained the damn Internet to her."

"I hate to burst your bubble, kiddo, but I work with the damn Internet."

"Damn it." Her mother's eyes met Charlie's, and the two of them burst out laughing, with Hazaar smiling as she looked on.

"I'm sorry about that, Hazaar. She has a slightly wicked sense of humour." Her mother laughed. "I'll rephrase. She has a totally evil sense of humour, and occasionally, I have to rein her in. I still find blackmail and threats are by far the most efficient, and she hasn't figured out when I'm bluffing."

"Not a problem, but I might actually want to see those pictures."

"Hey!"

"I'll bring them back in later. It's not acceptable for Beth to embarrass Charlie like that, but I'm her mother. It's in the manual."

"See, I told you they would tease me mercilessly."

"I'm not teasing, honey."

Charlie rolled her eyes and sighed. Taking pity on her, Hazaar squeezed her hand and spoke to her mother.

"Mrs. Port—"

"Sarah. If you call me Mrs. Porter I'll be looking for his mother."

"Sorry. Sarah. Is there anything I can do to help you?"

"No, thank you. My kitchen is my castle, for want of a better phrase. I let the girls in from time to time, mostly to ensure they don't starve when I kick the bucket, but I enjoy cooking, and they're pretty bad in the kitchen."

"Hey!" Charlie said.

"It's probably my fault. I should have let them do more than peel potatoes and lick the chocolate bowl as children, but I do know Charlie is very good with tins. Soup, beans, anything like that."

"I'm right here, Mother."

"I know, dear. She's pretty good with toast too."

"I'll have to remember that," Hazaar said.

Charlie's mother ushered them into chairs at the breakfast bar and continued pottering around the kitchen.

"Do you cook, Hazaar?"

"When I'm at my parents' I do. I don't cook that much at home. It's a lot of trouble for one person."

"So your mum taught you to cook?"

Hazaar laughed. "Not so much taught as demanded. All of us girls had to learn how to cook. Not my brother though. He just had to learn how to eat it all."

"Sounds like the better end of the deal. Do you enjoy cooking?"

"Nope. I'm afraid not. It bores me to tears. In my culture, the kitchen is the main focal point for the women. Gossip, recipes, and more gossip is swapped, elaborated on, and swapped again just for good measure."

"Sounds like every kitchen I've ever been in," Charlie's mother said with a broad smile. "So what did you prefer to do then, if not cook?"

"I always resented not being able to practice when I had to be in the kitchen."

"Piano?"

"Yes."

"Charlie said you're very talented. I would love to hear you play sometime." She turned back to the stove and stirred the large pot, the delicious meaty aroma filling the kitchen as she did so.

"Something smells good." Charlie's father walked in, slipped his arm around her mother's waist, and leaned in to kiss her cheek.

"Hungry, love?"

"Starving."

"It's ready now. Will you put the bread on the table for me?"

"I've got it, Mum." Charlie grabbed the huge bowl and led Hazaar into the dining room. Her mother followed close behind holding a dish of rice and held the door open for her father as he carried the heavy casserole dish.

"Beth!" her mother shouted. "Dinner's ready." The heavy sound of a teenaged elephant thundered down the stairs before she burst through the door. Her mother grinned wickedly. "You can come in, but you can leave the herd outside."

"Huh? Oh. Very funny. I'll see you doing stand-up next."

They all found seats and Charlie gently squeezed Hazaar's knee and winked at her when she jumped slightly.

"So, Mum, what is this?"

"It's a recipe I got off the Internet. Pakistani mutton stew with rice. I hope it's all right. I haven't made this before." She smiled shyly.

"You made this for me?" Hazaar's hand flew to her mouth. "I'm sorry. That was terribly presumptuous."

"It's fine. Yes, I did. I know this lot of mine will eat anything I put in front of them, but I wasn't so sure I would be allowed to bully you into the same deal, so I thought I would do a little surfing. I hope this is okay?" Beth was already spooning rice onto her plate, and then ladled a generous helping of stew over the grains.

"Looks good, Mum."

"It's my favourite." Hazaar began to fill her plate. "This is really wonderful." She looked directly at Charlie's mother. "Thank you for going to so much trouble."

"Nonsense." Charlie's mother blushed slightly under the praise. "It's about time these heathens broadened their horizons, and it gave me a new challenge."

"It's wonderful. Thank you." She pulled her spoon through the stew before plopping it into her mouth, a huge satisfied grin spreading across her lips.

"So, Hazaar, Charlie said you're doing your master's degree." Charlie's father quickly filled his own plate.

"Yes. I start in September."

"What do you plan to do after that?"

"I'm not sure yet. I would love to be a concert pianist or join an orchestra."

"The Halle?"

"If they would have me."

"I'm sure they would, Hazaar. You play so beautifully," Charlie said.

Hazaar smiled at her. "Not as beautifully as you sing." Charlie felt herself being pulled toward Hazaar. The tantalizing shine to her moist lips called to her, and she ached to run her tongue over them.

Beth cleared her throat loudly, breaking the spell. "Have you taught lots of people to play the piano?"

"A few. I wouldn't say lots."

"Is it hard?"

"It can be. It depends what you want to learn to play. If it's just basics, then it can be quite easy. Jazz and classical are the hardest forms to master."

"Why?"

"Well, classical music has an incredible amount of discipline involved. Scales, techniques, chords. They're all very difficult, and the notation is sometimes archaic and difficult to follow. The pieces also tend to be quite long, so learning them can be very tricky. Jazz is very difficult, for very different reasons. The chords structures and forms are different and so much of it is improvised that some people have real problems getting to grips with the idea of there being form without form."

"That doesn't make sense."

"That's the problem. With jazz you kinda have to leave all preconceived notions at the door. When you play a song, your only constraints are the notes in the chord that is backing you. But even then the rules are meant to be broken."

"So you can just play anything, have it sound all kinds of awful, and just say it's jazz?"

"Well, you could. But the really great jazz musicians can make the broken rules and the improvisation sound magical."

"Like who?"

"Dizzy Gillespie, Courtney Pine, Charlie Parker, Thelonius Monk, Duke Ellington—oh, there are so many."

"I like Dave Brubeck and Fats Waller myself, but as a sax player, I think John Coltrane is totally the mutt's nuts!" Beth spoke around a mouthful of food and her mother looked at her reprovingly. She grinned and swallowed.

"You play sax?"

Beth nodded. "Wanna jam?"

"Anytime, Flipper. Anytime."

Beth's face fell, and everyone laughed. "Does everyone get to call me Flipper now?"

Charlie's mother reached over and ruffled Beth's hair. "No, baby. Just family."

The laughter continued until Charlie sensed Hazaar's unease and covered her hand, leaning close to whisper. "Are you okay?"

Hazaar nodded her head, but her expression still seemed distant.

"Are you sure? Beth wasn't meaning to be hurtful."

"I know. She wasn't. It just seems a little surreal." She shook her head. "It's fine." She turned her hand in Charlie's and laced their fingers together. "I promise." She pulled her hand away and reached for some of the roti bread on the table as Charlie leaned back in her seat, throwing a pointed look at Beth.

"You said earlier that you worked with the Internet, Sarah. What is it that you do?" Hazaar asked.

Beth groaned, to be met by a light slap across the back of her head. "That's child abuse!"

"I design websites." Charlie's mother ignored Beth and answered the question.

"Really? How did you get into that?"

"After I had Charlie, I needed something for myself while I stayed at home with her. I went to classes for graphic design. I always loved drawing and design and such, so I got qualified to do all kinds of design work and then I got a job part-time for the local paper. I did layouts for adverts and things in the magazines and inserts. I started to discover the Internet then. I really loved it. When I was at home with Beth, I decided to train some more and got into all of the technology side of the design. I loved it even more. I'm freelance now, so I get to stay home and pester my kids as much as I want. It's worked out really well for me."

"Did you study art at college?"

"God, no. I left school at sixteen and started work in a solicitor's office. I was training to be a secretary from the bottom up. Office junior, filing, making tea, typing letters, that sort of thing."

"Did you enjoy it?"

"Nope. Not in the least." Sputtered laughter fluttered about the table. "It was a job that led to a decent career for a young woman, and it was just kind of expected. I'd finished school, and my parents thought that my fancy drawings and arty-farty ideas were a sure way to starvation. So I did what I had to do. I liked the people I worked with well enough, and I didn't mind the work too much. It could have been much worse. So I stayed with it until I had Charlie. Andy was doing well and already a foreman by then, so we were doing well enough that I could give up work and stay home with the baby." Charlie's mother smiled fondly at her.

"How did you become an electrician?"

Charlie's dad told Hazaar the story of his decision to become an electrician, mostly because he didn't want to be anything else, and about his father, who was less than paternal. Banter flew across the table between her mother and father and left them all laughing. Hazaar listened and joined in occasionally, but with everyone laughing and talking over one another, she mostly just laughed along with everyone else.

Charlie's mother collected the empty plates before making her way to the kitchen. "Last one in here with a dish gets to wash up." The scramble to grab dishes and head for the kitchen left Charlie feeling dizzy and staring at an empty table. They had a brief moment alone.

Charlie leaned back in her chair and studied Hazaar's serious face. "Are you sure you're okay? You look so serious."

"I'm fine. It's wonderful to see. It's so obvious how much you all love each other. Family meals for us are a constant competition. Honour and pride are served as condiments with every meal, and for me, the fear of stepping out of line, saying the wrong thing, letting my feelings slip…" Hazaar whispered. "It drips into your soul with the water in your glass. Every accomplishment is documented and detailed, paraded before guests like a pony in the pasture." She smiled sadly. "My father loves me. I don't doubt it for a second. But it feels so different from what I feel and what I've seen here tonight. Your parents know you. They know Flipper. My parents don't. They love the person they think I am. The one I pretend to be when I'm with them. Me, the real me, would only bring them shame."

Charlie cupped her cheek, searching desperately for something to say. "I think we can probably negotiate a deal to share them."

Hazaar chuckled softly. "Really?"

"Really."

"And what kind of deal did you have in mind?"

"Well, I was thinking, if you take Flipper off my hands, I'll share Mum and Dad with you. How does that sound?"

Hazaar leaned forward and kissed her, a slow smile spreading across her lips. "Like you're getting the better part of that deal." She pressed her lips to Charlie's and slowly deepened the kiss. "How about you share all three of them and I'll make it up to you in sexual favours?"

Charlie's breath caught in her throat. "I think that would more than suffice, sweetheart." Their lips met in a kiss that scorched Charlie to her very soul.

"Dessert." They broke apart as Beth placed a stack of small plates, forks, and spoons on the table with a noisy clatter. Charlie reddened as she broke away from the kiss but stared deeply into Hazaar's eyes before she moved away.

"So what do we have, Flipper?"

"Some stuff I can't pronounce. I don't think Mum can either. She's hoping you'll tell us how to say them all." Beth handed them plates and slid the cutlery across the table as Charlie's parents came in. Her father was holding two plates filled with slices of some sort of cake in different colours, and her mother was juggling five glass bowls of creamy-looking sweetness.

"Wow. Where did you get these?" Hazaar grinned broadly.

Charlie's father put the plates down and helped her mother with the bowls.

"I made them all. The Internet is a wonderful thing."

"You made them?" Hazaar looked at the goodies on the table. "All of them?" Sarah nodded. "That must have taken hours. *Kheer*, *barfi*, and *balushahi*." She pointed at each item as she said them. Everyone sat down and started helping themselves.

"And what exactly are they?" Charlie's father started filling his plate even as he asked, looking curiously at each treat as he did so.

"Well, *barfi* is like a little sweet cake. It's made from condensed milk and lots of sugar, then flavoured with almonds, or pistachio nuts, sometimes spiced with cardamom too."

"Good for the diabetics then." Andy bit into one of the slices.

"Absolutely. *Balushahi* are pretty similar to doughnuts."

"It's really nice," Beth said around a mouthful.

"Elizabeth Porter, don't talk with your mouth full."

"And what's this one?" Charlie pointed at the glass bowl.

"This is *kheer*. It's like rice pudding but with nuts and fruit and saffron."

"Do they taste like they are supposed to?" Charlie's mother asked.

Hazaar nodded, swallowing quickly before she spoke. "They taste perfect. I'll have to get the recipes from you. These are better than the ones I make."

"Do you have a big family, Hazaar?"

"Not really. Well, not by Pakistani standards, anyway. There are four girls and one boy. My father was determined to have a son, and once my brother was born, he was satisfied."

"Charlie said that your name means nightingale. Is that right?" Beth asked.

"Yes. My father picked all our names with specific meanings. My brother's name is Hatim, which means judge. My older sister's names all have meanings too."

"Such as?"

"My oldest sister is called Nadia. In Arabic that means first. My second sister is Yamha, which means dove. My dad likes birds. My next sister is Badra, which means full moon. Coincidentally, she was born on the full moon."

"Do you know what our names mean, Mum?" Beth asked.

"I do. Charlotte means free, and Elizabeth means—"

"God's promise. Hebrew in origin and has very strong religious ties. As does Sarah, which means princess." Hazaar flushed. "I'm sorry for interrupting you."

"So what do your parents do for a living, Hazaar?"

"My dad is a business man. He does something to do with importing and exporting goods. I'm afraid I can't tell you more than that because I don't know. My brother is being trained to follow him into the business. My mother is a housewife, and my sisters are now all married. My sisters have seven children between them so far, with another on the way, and two of them have moved to Pakistan with their husbands."

"Your parents must miss them terribly. Do you get to see them often?"

Hazaar shook her head. "My oldest sister moved to Pakistan six years ago now. My father sees her when he goes there on business. But the rest of us haven't seen her since then. We get letters and pictures of the children sometimes. My sister Badra also went to Pakistan, but she's in a different part from Nadia. I don't think they've seen each other since she moved there."

"It must be very hard for your mum, not to see her daughters," Charlie's mother said as a frown creased her brow.

"If it is, she's never said so. Neither do my sisters. They do as they're told." Hazaar's voice faltered a little. "My brother is due to get married next year. His bride is going to come to England for the first time three days before she marries him."

"How often does he go to Pakistan to see her?" Beth ate the last spoonful of her *kheer* and licked the spoon.

"He hasn't met her yet. My father arranged it all. He works closely with her father, and it will be good for both of them."

Charlie's mother and father exchanged glances.

"Why's he going to marry someone he hasn't met? Is it one of those arranged marriage things?" Beth leaned forward, obviously fascinated.

"Yes, it's an arranged marriage. It's very often the way in my culture. My parents' marriage was arranged and so were all of my sisters' marriages. My brother has always known his marriage would be arranged for him too. But because he's my father's only son, he knows it will be a good match."

"But they haven't gotten to choose who they get married to!" Beth said.

"No, but that's not unusual."

"I wouldn't let them choose my husband for me!"

"And I'm sure your mum and dad wouldn't want to choose your husband for you. But that isn't how things happen in my culture."

Charlie felt the tension rising. Every answered question cemented in her mind the certainty that Hazaar would have to answer to her parents sooner rather than later. That she would have to decide not only between disappointing them to be who she really was, but between everything she had been taught since birth. *How can anyone fight that?*

"So you're different because you play the piano?" Beth asked.

"Yes. I haven't had a marriage arranged because my studies and my music have brought honour and prestige to my family. They've been content to allow me to continue with that."

"So if you didn't play the piano they would have made you get married?"

"They would have arranged a marriage for me, yes."

Charlie watched her parents exchange glances and tried to think of a way to stop the questions from Beth and allay some of the mounting concerns she could see written on their faces, that most likely mirrored her own.

"But you don't want to get married to a man, do you?" Beth asked.

"Elizabeth Porter, that's enough," Charlie's mother said.

"What? What did I say?"

"It's rude to ask something like that."

"No, it's okay. You're right. I don't want to marry a man. It wouldn't be my choice." Hazaar slowly put her fork down on her plate and smiled at Charlie's mother. "This was wonderful. Thank you for going to so much trouble for me."

"It's my pleasure," Charlie's mother said, easily picking up the change of subject. "Would anyone like some coffee?" Nods around the table followed quickly as Charlie's parents grabbed some plates. Her mother tugged Beth's collar and pushed her gently toward the kitchen.

"But I don't want coffee," Beth said.

"Shush. Get in there."

Charlie watched the door swing shut behind them and took a few moments to collect her thoughts before she spoke. "Are you okay?"

Hazaar nodded. "Are you?"

Charlie tried to smile. "Of course. You'd told me that you were expecting your parents to arrange a marriage for you. It makes sense that they'd done so for your other siblings."

"And do you think it's as barbaric as your sister does?"

She shrugged. "It would be for me, and I don't like the thought of someone being forced to marry against their will, but I don't think your siblings feel the same way about it as you do. I may find the idea of marrying someone I don't know hard to cope with, but you all grew up expecting that, didn't you?"

Hazaar fiddled with a spoon, avoiding Charlie's eyes. "Yes."

"So I guess it comes down to expectations. Flipper and I both expect to grow up and make our own choices about the person we'll spend our lives with. The idea of having that choice taken away is terrifying to us. Things that scare us make us wary, sometimes angry. If I was put in that situation with the mindset that I have, yes, it would be unacceptable for me. In your situation, though?" Charlie wiped her hand across her face, searching for the right thing to say without sounding judgmental, which she'd promised not to be. "I don't really know how I'd feel because I can't be inside your head. I guess the only thing I can be sure of is that I'd feel confused. The desire to conform and rebel would be equally strong, and not knowing from one day to the next which one would win out would be exhausting."

"And how does that make you feel about being with me?"

"Honestly?"

Hazaar nodded and held her breath.

"Scared. Frustrated. Confused. I don't know what's going to happen down the road. But in many ways that's just like every other relationship I know of. With you, at least we know where the trouble is likely to come from, and what we're expecting it to be."

"Maybe we shouldn't continue to see each other."

Charlie stared at her, unable to comprehend what she was hearing. After everything she had told Hazaar, trusted her with, she couldn't believe that Hazaar had even uttered the words. "Is that what you want?" She watched Hazaar swallow hard. "Is it?"

"No." Her voice sounded thick, heavy.

"Then why say it?"

"I don't want you to be scared when you're with me. I don't want to hurt you or let you down. I don't want you to be frustrated with me, either."

"Sweetheart, I'm not. Only when I think about the uncertainty of the future, and some of that fear comes from my own past experiences with Gail. When we're together, when we talk, and laugh, it's everything it should be. Two people getting to know each other. Maybe even—I don't know—maybe even starting to fall in love."

Hazaar took hold of Charlie's hand again and brought it to her lips, joy clear in her eyes.

"I know it's really quick—"

Hazaar silenced her with her mouth. "I think I am too."

Charlie pushed her fingers into her hair and pulled her hard against her lips, the kiss bruising in its intensity. Their tongues battled as Charlie tried to convey the depth of her growing feelings.

"They aren't upset, Mum; they're kissing." The popping sound as they broke apart was audible.

"Oh, God," Charlie said.

Hazaar stroked her cheek lightly. "No, it was definitely your sister."

"I'm going to kill her." She started to stand but was halted by her mother's hand on her shoulder.

"Not while we've got company, darling. I'll help you clear up the mess when we get her later."

She sat back down and they spent the rest of the evening laughing and teasing one another. Charlie enjoyed all of it, but deep down a kernel of fear had taken root. Hazaar saying they shouldn't date made her wonder if, at some point, she might run from the situation before there was a real decision to be made. She tightened her grip on Hazaar's hand, wondering when it would slip from her grasp.

# CHAPTER ELEVEN

*Pakistan, today*

Charlie twisted the cap off her water bottle and swallowed half before she sat at her desk. She opened the file in front of her and studied the pages, poring over the details of yet another case. The sharp sound of knuckles rapping against the doorframe to her office caught her attention. She looked up to see Kenzie smiling at her.

"Liam said you wanted to see me."

"Come in." Charlie pointed at the chair on the opposite side of the desk. "Take a seat."

"Thanks." Kenzie sat down and crossed her legs. She appeared relaxed, confident, and seemingly ready for anything.

"I thought it might be a good idea to know a little bit more about your background before we get started. So I have a better idea of why you're here and what your skill set is."

"You have my file, don't you?"

"Yes." Charlie nodded at the file on the edge of the desk. "And very impressive it is too. Graduated top of your class, fast-tracked through the ranks. I'm guessing Abu Ghraib was their first test for you. After that, they really started to specialise your services. There's an extensive profiling background in there. They used you to profile their most wanted terror suspects. Correct?"

Kenzie nodded but otherwise didn't move. Charlie wondered for a brief moment if she was really as hard as she seemed.

"Were you in the office only, or out in the field?"

"Ma'am, I'm not sure—"

"Charlie, C, Maverick, whatever. But don't call me ma'am. And one thing you can be certain of is that my security clearance is higher than yours. There's nothing you can't tell me." She stared at her across the table. "Understood?"

A flicker of a smile twitched at the corner of Kenzie's mouth. "Understood."

"So?"

"I was out in the field. I'd profile the suspects, then join the recovery team to reanalyze intel as it came in and then adjust if need be."

"Were you part of recovery teams?"

"Yes."

"You know that isn't part of the brief here?"

"I do." She switched her legs. "This is a negotiation task force, not a forceful recovery team."

"Good."

"I aim to please."

"I'm sure you do." Charlie chuckled. "So, all that being said." She picked up the file. "What isn't in here that I should know about?"

"Ma'am—"

"Do you have cotton between your ears, soldier?"

"I'm sorry?"

"Don't call me ma'am."

"I'm sorry. Charlie, I don't understand the question."

"Well, it's pretty simple. What do I need to know about you that isn't in here?" She waved the file.

"I'm sure the file is complete."

"I'm sure it isn't."

"Are you making an accusation?"

"Nope. But I know that something happened to derail you from this path," she dropped the file back onto her desk, "and put you smack bang in the middle of mine. I'd like to know what that is before we head out there and it comes back to bite us both in the arse."

"I was tracking a Taliban general. Nasty piece of fucking work. Oh, sorry—"

"I've heard the term before, Kenzie."

"Anyway, I profiled this guy, knew he had certain…tastes…that would help us to locate him."

"Tastes?" Charlie felt a little queasy. Kenzie's recalcitrance in stating what she was talking about was only leading her to think the worst.

"Yes."

"Children?"

"Yes. We staked out an orphanage in Mehtar Lam, just the other side of the Khyber Pass in Afghanistan. He had to be getting them from somewhere. Turned out he was actually buying them from the guy who ran the orphanage. He used the money to buy food and clothes for the other kids. He figured the needs of the many outweighed the one or two that were sacrificed."

Charlie understood the rationale, but the necessity of it enraged her. Poverty and disease were a way of life in such war-ravaged areas, and people did what they had to do in order to survive.

"When we found him there we followed him back to his compound. We believed he had weapons in his charge that were worth confiscating."

"Did he?"

"No. But what we found was far worse. He was acting as a brokerage. The children were sold on if they survived his induction. His words, not mine. He told us he was preparing them for their futures, for the destinies that Allah had seen fit to grant them."

"Oh, God."

"No, he had nothing to do with this guy. He honestly thought that he was doing these kids a favour."

"Sick bastard."

"Yeah. After that, my focus changed. I didn't care as much about terrorists anymore. I wanted to help those kids."

"And if you can't?"

Kenzie's face reddened and Charlie could see the rage that burned so close to the surface.

"We can't save them all, Kenzie. As hard as we try, you have to be prepared for those times when this process fails. Because it will."

"It doesn't have to."

"Sometimes it does."

"No. I can't accept that. They deserve better."

"Yes, they do. But remember that of the children we are going to help here, the vast majority aren't abused. Very few occasions have I suspected anything had ever happened to the children I've rescued. They're with fathers, usually, who do care for them in their own way."

"It's not enough."

"For us, no. But for them, it isn't bad either. This isn't a game of black and white, Kenzie. This is all about the grey in between and the shades along the human spectrum. Very little is good or evil. We're all just people, after all." Charlie held up the file she'd been looking at before Kenzie arrived. "This is a pretty standard case that we deal with." She smiled wryly. "Well, on paper anyway. You can never be sure of the reality until you're in the middle of it." She handed Kenzie the file. "Hillary has located an address for the father of these two boys. Their mother was awarded custody in 2010 after the divorce was finalised in late 2009. The father was granted visitation rights. Two nights a week and every other weekend."

"The father snatched them on a visitation weekend?"

"Yes. Very common means of taking kids."

"Makes sense. Customs would never think anything was wrong because the kids would be excited about going on a holiday with their dad." She scowled. "It'd be really easy."

"Unfortunately, yes. The kids generally don't have any idea there's anything wrong until they're already in Pakistan and they start asking when they're going to see their mum again."

"These boys have been with their father for a while now. Won't they have adapted?" Kenzie scanned the file quickly.

"To some extent, sure. And there's no reason to think they don't have good lives with a father who loves them. But the fact remains that he's kidnapped these boys. Legally, they belong with their mother. If he were on English soil, we could arrest him and have the police question him to reveal the location of the children and return them to their mother."

"But we aren't."

"No, we aren't. Here, their father has all the rights and the power. And if he wants to keep them, as long as he, and they, remain in Pakistan, we can't do anything about it."

"Surely the Pakistani authorities recognize legal rights of the mothers."

"They do recognize international law in theory, but in practice Pakistani law and Sharia law grant all parental rights to the father. There is no extradition between the UK and Pakistan, so we have no other choice but to negotiate with the men who have kidnapped their own children."

Kenzie snorted. "We can't just go and take the kids when we find where they are?"

"No. Like I said, we aren't a rescue team, Kenzie. Doing that would make us the kidnappers, and we aren't criminals. We can't just barge in and snatch them. We have to get them to hand the children over to us. It's about diplomacy."

"And how do you do that?"

"Depends on the situation. Take a look at the case there for example. When sons are involved, it's much more difficult to get the fathers to surrender the children. We need to find out more about his current circumstances. Has he remarried? Does he have work? Where is he living? And so on. When we have that information, we can start to form a strategy for first contact." The phone rang, interrupting her train of thought. "Let me just get this." Kenzie nodded as she picked up the handset. "Hello."

"Hi, Charlie, it's Pam on reception. I've got a woman on line one who wants to speak to someone about leaving Pakistan to go home to England."

"You didn't give her the number for the travel agent?"

"Seems like there's more to the story than that."

"One second." She covered the mouthpiece and looked at Kenzie. "Are you clear about the background you're looking for on the case?" She nodded at the file.

"I've got it." Kenzie threw a mock salute at her and closed the door behind her.

"Okay, Pam. Put her through."

"Thanks, Charlie."

She heard the telltale click that signalled Pam hanging up and the transfer of the outside line. "Hello, my name's Charlotte Porter. Who am I speaking to?"

There was a gasp down the line, then silence.

Charlie waited a beat before continuing. "Hello?" She could hear breathing down the line. "I'd like to help if I can."

"I can't tell you my name." The woman's voice was barely a whisper, and Charlie strained to make out the words.

Charlie was a little disappointed but not surprised. She understood the fear that always seemed to accompany calls like this. Simple enquiries were rarely simple. "Okay, that's okay. Do you have a name I can call you by while we talk?"

The woman laughed softly. "Call me Maya."

"Maya?" Charlie smiled, hoping she had correctly interpreted the woman's little joke. "Do you like to read, Maya?"

"Yes. I mean no." A sad laugh echoed down the line. "I used to read a lot. Not so much anymore."

"Are you a caged bird, then, Maya? Do you seek freedom?" Charlie referred to Maya Angelou's book, *I Know Why the Caged Bird Sings*.

"Yes."

Charlie was struggling to hear, the whisper was so quiet. "I'm sorry. I can barely hear you."

"I said yes. For both myself and my daughter."

Charlie grabbed a pen and started to make some notes. "How long have you been in Pakistan?"

"Two and a half years."

"Where are you?"

"Peshawar. The old city."

"Okay, and did you marry here?"

"No, we married in England. We were supposed to stay there."

"Why did you come to Pakistan?"

The lengthy pause told Charlie that Maya was weighing her words carefully before she spoke.

"My husband made the choice when he discovered I was pregnant. He wanted his children to be born here."

"So your daughter was born in Pakistan?" Charlie closed her eyes and turned her face to the ceiling, knowing two things for certain. That Maya's explanation was an exceptionally condensed version of events, and that getting her daughter out of Pakistan would be very difficult indeed.

"Yes."

Charlie bit off the groan, knowing how much more difficult this would be now. "Do you have any of her documentation?"

"No. My husband keeps it locked away in a safe."

There were times that Charlie hated being right, and this was one of them. "That you don't have access to." Charlie set her elbow on the desk and rested her head in her hand.

"That is correct."

"Do you have your passport?" Charlie knew the answer, but she had to ask every question.

"No. I tried to leave him once before." Maya's whispered voice faltered. "I am not trusted to even go to market to buy food. I have no access to money, and the doors are locked when my father-in-law and husband go to work or to mosque."

Charlie's heart bled as she pictured the prison the woman was living in. "As your daughter wasn't born in the UK, I can't issue her a British passport outright."

"But she is my daughter." Maya's voice rose to almost normal level and something in the tone tickled at the back of Charlie's memory. "I have a British passport."

"I know. And because of that we can grant her dual nationality and get her a passport after that. But to do so we need several things that I think you will find very difficult to get hold of."

"Such as?"

Charlie heard the frustration and despair in Maya's voice and had to close her eyes. The tone reminded her so much of Hazaar's, but Charlie pushed away the memories of her lost love and tried to focus on the woman talking to her, the woman she could help—or at least try to help—rather than the one who was beyond her reach. "You'll need her birth certificate, your passport, and if possible, your birth certificate too." Charlie listened and heard Maya swallow, undoubtedly contemplating everything she'd have to go through in order to get the necessary paperwork, things that Charlie couldn't even contemplate.

"And if I get those things? Can you come and get us?"

Charlie wanted to cry. She wanted to tell her yes, they would come for them. That she and her team would ride in with tanks, and planes, and helicopters, and anything else that might be needed and free Maya from her prison. But it couldn't be. Legally, they could do no such thing. "I'm sorry, Maya. It isn't quite that simple. We can't break you out of your home. You must come to the British Embassy and present yourself, then we can help you."

"You don't understand. He has the key!"

"I do understand, Maya. I wish I could change it, but—"

"He has the key. I can't get out of the house."

"Does the family live with you too?"

"Yes. My husband's father and his sister-in-law live here."

"He has a brother too?"

"Yes, but he is…" Maya's voice trailed away.

"He's where?"

"Away. He's just away."

Alarm bells sounded in Charlie's head. The population of Peshawar had swollen over the past several years with an influx of people moving out of the mountains and deserts. People from the Pashtun tribe had found a particularly convenient home in Peshawar with its proximity to the Khyber Pass, routes through to Afghanistan, and there was significant evidence to link members of the Pashtun tribe to the Taliban. "Away" sounded suspicious to Charlie.

"Please, you have to help me, Charlie. Please."

"I will do everything I can, Maya. But the British and Pakistani governments have certain protocols in place that we have to follow."

"How am I supposed to get out?"

Charlie looked around the office. "How about a window?"

"A window? Are you serious?"

"How would you get out if there was a fire?"

"I'd probably burn to death. The windows have bars."

"Oh, right."

"Oh, no." Maya's breathing quickened and her whispered voice rose to a shrill pitch. "I have to go."

"Please call back when you can, Maya. We can work something out."

"I have to go, Charlie. I'll call back—"

Charlie stared at the handset as the dial tone continued to sound and she frowned.

*She called me Charlie. I told her my name was Charlotte.*

# Chapter Twelve

*The North of England, then*

Hazaar ran her tongue along the ridge of Charlie's ear, tugged the lobe between her teeth, and sucked hard. Her hand wandered slowly toward her firm breast as Charlie tried to read the pages of information in front of her.

"Baby, you're really not conducive to me getting this done." Charlie turned her head and kissed Hazaar before she continued to fill out the forms for her room in the halls of residence in September.

"I'm not trying to be conducive." She smiled as Charlie shivered against her body. "I'm trying to distract you so you miss the deadline." She trailed slow kisses down Charlie's neck and tugged the collar of her shirt away so she could reach the juncture of her neck and shoulder.

"And why do you want me to miss the deadline? I love my parents, but I'm totally ready to move out of there."

"Move in here. Stay with me." The words were out of her mouth before she even thought about them, and she slowly squeezed Charlie's breast as she used her tongue and lips continued to explore Charlie's tender throat. Charlie swatted her head with pages in her hand.

"Be serious. Just give me five minutes and I'll be done, sweetheart." Charlie clicked the top of her pen and filled in the final few boxes, scribbled her signature across the page, folded the paper, and slid it into the envelope.

"I am being serious." Hazaar grabbed the envelope from her and tossed it onto the coffee table. "I'm being perfectly serious." She shifted, straddled Charlie's legs, and threaded their fingers together as she bent to kiss her lips. "Stay here with me, baby." She trailed her fingers slowly along the hem of Charlie's shirt, and brushed them across her hips and belly before she slipped them inside the fabric and traced a gentle random pattern across her silken skin. Charlie's eyes closed as her head rested against the back of the couch. The buttons of Charlie's shorts quickly gave way beneath her nimble fingers and bared her flesh for more intimate exploration. All Hazaar could think about was exposing Charlie's body. She needed to touch her, kiss her, and possess her. She barely thought about the offer she'd made to Charlie. She was beyond thinking. She was sensation and want personified, her desire to please all consuming.

Hazaar pushed aside the scant lacy fabric of Charlie's bra and lifted each breast from its confines with a reverence that verged on sacred. She stared down at them—at Charlie—with wonder, amazed that she was here with her, that they were together. And she never wanted it to end. She pressed her breasts as close together as she could and suckled each rapidly in turn. Charlie gasped and wrapped her hands in Hazaar's hair.

"Oh, no you don't." Hazaar released Charlie's breasts and grabbed her wrists, pinning them above her head. "Keep them there." Her eyes twinkled as Charlie curled her fingers around the back of the sofa, her eyes glazed with lust, her cheeks flushed. "You are so beautiful, Charlie."

Charlie smiled the slow grin of a woman who knew satisfaction wasn't far away. "I'm very glad you think so, baby."

"I always will." She bent over and brought her hands back to Charlie's breasts, moulding them with her hands so that she could suck them again, marvelling at the wonderful feel of the twin peaks of pebbled flesh that welcomed her tongue in turn. Charlie writhed beneath her, searching for more contact. Hazaar stood quickly and tugged her toward the bedroom.

"Take your clothes off and lie down." She watched Charlie's body quiver at her command, and she knew Charlie loved it when she took charge of their lovemaking. The loss of control, the surrender, made the sex hotter than she thought possible, for both of them. Charlie stripped quickly and lay in the centre of the bed, her gaze on Hazaar as she approached with a selection of silk scarves between her hands. "Do you trust me, baby?"

Charlie wet her lips, and her voice crawled tremulously from her them. "Yes."

"Good. Put your hands on the headboard and hold on."

She did as she was told and gasped as Hazaar wrapped the silk around her wrists and tied it to the spindles. The kiss that followed was deep and wet and left her trying to pull free to wrap her arms about her. Hazaar smiled when Charlie gasped as she traced a tantalizing path from her knee, up over her hip and higher, the silk warm to the touch, and so very soft across Charlie's flawless skin. They moaned in unison as she let the silk flow across Charlie's nipple, soft as a whisper.

"Close your eyes, baby." Hazaar kissed her gently, teasing her lips with the tip of her tongue before covering Charlie's eyes with the silk blindfold. "Can you see?"

"No." Charlie was breathing hard; her breasts rose and fell with each panted breath.

"You are so beautiful, baby." She ran the tip of her finger over each rib, fascinated with the rash of goose bumps that erupted in her wake. "So beautiful."

She climbed off the bed slowly, the moan from Charlie telling her that her presence was missed as soon as their skin parted. "I'm still here, baby. Just relax."

She crossed the room and pulled open the drawer. The black leather harness and dildo stared back at her. It was a fantasy she'd entertained for so long that she had almost given up hope of finding someone to share it with. She thought she'd run out of time first. She looked at the bed again. Charlie's waiting body called to her, enthralled her, and gave her the confidence to fulfil the longings she knew they both harboured.

She buckled up as quickly and quietly as she could because she wanted to surprise Charlie, and she could see her body tremble with anticipation.

She knelt on the edge of the bed and ran her finger from the arch of Charlie's foot along her calf, memorizing every millimetre of skin along the way. Charlie writhed and opened her legs as she travelled higher. She kissed and licked her belly, dipped her tongue inside the shallow navel and smiled as Charlie cried out and squirmed and pulled hard against her restraints.

"You don't like that?"

"No." Charlie panted. "Tickles."

"And that's not good?"

"Not right now."

Hazaar caressed Charlie's body with her fingers and tongue until they both clung to the edge of sanity, the need for release so deep it was her soul rather than her body that craved it.

"Hazaar, please. Please let me come."

She covered Charlie's body with her own and kissed her deeply as she let the dildo brush against Charlie's skin for the first time. Charlie stilled beneath her.

"Is this okay, baby?" She rocked her hips to emphasize her point.

"I've never—"

"I know, baby. Neither have I, but I've always wanted to." She kissed Charlie's throat. "With the right person." She nipped on her earlobe. "I'll take it slow and stop if you don't like it. I promise."

"It's okay." Charlie licked her lips. "I trust you."

Hazaar swallowed around the lump in her throat and the need to see Charlie's eyes, to see the trust in them, burned through her. She pulled off the blindfold. Charlie blinked rapidly to refocus, then stared up at her, and Hazaar felt her heart swell to the point of bursting. There was more than trust radiating from Charlie's eyes. She saw everything she had ever wanted, dreamed of, and wished for, shining up at her. She saw her future reflected from within Charlie's soul, and she knew without doubt that Charlie loved her.

It was the easiest and most natural thing she'd ever done as she slid slowly inside Charlie's body. She waited until Charlie was ready and slowly stroked them both higher, the pressure building in her lower belly, screaming for release as Charlie wrapped her legs around her hips, her lips parted, but her gaze never faltering.

"You are so beautiful," Hazaar whispered as she pumped faster.

"Hazaar." Charlie's voice was hoarse, cracking with emotion, desire, and need. "Please."

Hazaar drove harder, pushing them to the precipice before she whispered the words she never thought she'd say. "I love you."

It was enough.

The admission toppled them both and cast Hazaar adrift on an ocean of orgasmic pleasure that rippled and tossed her upon the waves. Tears rolled slowly down Charlie's face as their bodies bucked, wringing every last drop of pleasure from them.

When Hazaar's body stopped trembling, she wiped the moisture from Charlie's face. "Did I hurt you?" She reached up and released the ties at Charlie's wrists before slowly pulling out of her and discarding the harness over the side of the bed.

Charlie shook her head and pulled Hazaar into a tight embrace. "Not really, no."

"Then why are you crying?"

"I love you too."

Hazaar's heart soared. "Move in with me, baby." She felt Charlie take a deep breath and slowly release it before she answered.

"I don't think that's the best thing to do, sweetheart."

"Why not?" All she wanted was for Charlie to be with her every day. She wanted to wake up beside her after having held her and made love with her all through the night. She wanted familiar evenings in the kitchen, cooking together, laughing, watching TV, or finishing their schoolwork. She wanted a life with Charlie. She loved her—they loved each other—why shouldn't they have those things? Was it too much to ask?

"Well, we've only been together for a few months now. In September, we'll still only be talking about eight months. That's pretty quick to be moving in together."

"But if it's what we both want, then what's wrong with that? I love you, Charlie. I want you to be here with me. I thought you'd want the same thing."

"You think I don't want to be with you?"

"That's what it sounds like."

"Okay, tell me this then, Hazaar, what about your family? How do you see that working out? Me sliding down the drainpipe when they turn up is one thing when all I've got to do is take the clothes I arrived in. But living here means a lot more stuff around than I can carry with me." She shook her head sadly. "Exactly what did you think you'd say to them?"

*Fuck! I didn't even think about them.* "I don't know."

"Well, don't you think that's something we'd need to cover before we take a huge step like this?"

Hazaar's mind whirled. Charlie was right. They would need a reason for Charlie to be there, to stay there, when her family showed up. "Maybe if I told them I was thinking of taking in a lodger, and we used the wardrobe in the spare room for most stuff. I know it would be a little inconvenient, but it would be kind of like having your own personal dressing room too."

"And what would you tell them when they asked why you were taking in a lodger? You told me your dad gives you plenty of money so you couldn't use the excuse of struggling financially."

"I could just say that you were my friend and that you needed somewhere to stay."

"Would they accept that?"

Hazaar shrugged. "I don't know. As far as I know, they've never suspected anything about my sexuality. So a girl moving in shouldn't immediately set off alarm bells. But I don't really know."

"Is it something you're willing to risk at this point?"

She captured her lips again. "I love you. Yes, I'm willing to risk it." Hazaar looked at her, wishing that Charlie didn't have cause to doubt her, but even as she spoke the words her heart demanded she say, her head was already waging a war about the consequences of her desires. "I know I've sprung this on you, so just think about it. You don't need to make your mind up now. The offer is open-ended. Send in your application for halls. You can always change your mind later. Just promise me you'll think about it. Please?"

She knew she should let the subject drop. Just let the words and the request melt into the ether and forget they were ever mentioned, but she couldn't. She was playing with fire.

"I promise I'll think about it."

And as she kissed the sweet smile upon Charlie's face, she knew she was going to get burned.

# Chapter Thirteen

*Pakistan, today*

Hazaar hung up the phone and held a hand over her wildly beating heart. Why now? After all this time, why did fate tease her so mercilessly? For the past three years, she had dreamed of Charlie, of hearing her voice again.

She could hear footsteps in the courtyard and knew it was Amira returning from the market. She had hoped for a little longer because there was so much more she needed to ask, to know. And now she only had more questions. What was Charlie doing in Pakistan? How had she ended up here? Was she looking for her? Hazaar laughed to herself. *Don't be a fool. She'll have forgotten all about you by now, and for that you only have yourself to blame.*

She shook her head as emotions ransacked her and memories filled her mind. She pictured Charlie's face and her beautiful smile. She heard her song and the sweetest laugh, and the tears she'd held back on the telephone ran down her cheeks. She wiped at them quickly and turned to leave the room, still in shock that the door to the office had been left unlocked and the telephone unattended.

As she turned, she came face-to-face with Tazim. The tall, thin man was made even taller by the turban wound about his head, and his eyes burned fierce with hatred, anger, and malevolence.

Her heart pounded in her chest, and her mouth went dry. "Abu." Her voice cracked on the simple word. She cleared her throat and prayed that he had not been in the room long enough to have seen her emotional outburst. There would be too many questions to avoid and too many answers that she couldn't give. She wished she could run, hide, but her mind didn't seem to be working fast enough.

"Abu, I saw the door was open, and I was making sure there was nothing—"

She didn't see him move, but the blow to her face spun her into the wall. Adrenaline surged through her body, and every muscle in her body prepared to run, but there was nowhere to run. There was no escape.

"You lying whore." He grabbed her hair and pulled her to face him. "I heard you, *Maya*." The fist to her gut knocked the wind from her, and she struggled not to vomit. "Do you think I'm stupid?"

She shook her head quickly. "No, Abu. No, I don't."

"Shut up." He dragged her out of the room and down the corridor. "You ungrateful bitch, we have given you everything."

She stumbled as he continued to drag her, and she fell to the ground and curled into a foetal position. He kicked her, the blow landing on her chest.

"Please, Abu, I'm sorry—"

"Sorry is not good enough." He grabbed her hair again and dragged her along the tiled floor. She curled her fingers around his wrists to try to ease some of the pressure searing through her scalp. She tried to walk, to lift herself to her feet, but she couldn't get any traction. She heard a door being opened and knew it was the door to the cellar. "You are lucky, Hazaar." He yanked her to her feet and punched her in the face. She felt her lip split and blood filled her mouth. "I have business to attend to or I would deal with you now."

"Please, Abu, I didn't—"

He turned her toward the open door and pushed her down the steep stairs. She tried to grab for the rail, but it gave way beneath the force of her descent and she crashed down to the hard concrete floor. She tasted the rich iron tang of blood covering her tongue before darkness claimed her.

# CHAPTER FOURTEEN

*The North of England, then*

Music reverberated from the huge speakers that were on either side of the small stage at the front of the hall. A swarm of bodies moved together with a mass of arms, legs, and heads all dancing to the beat beneath the celebratory birthday banner stretched tight across the front of the room.

"I can't believe she's eighteen." Charlie's mother wiped her eyes.

"Time flies, doesn't it?" Charlie grinned as she repeated the phrase her mother had said to her on many occasions.

"Yes, it does." Her mother sat back in her chair. "This is okay, isn't it? She's not too embarrassed?"

Charlie looked around the hall her parents had rented for the party. It had been well decorated, and the DJ was good. There was a buffet table along the far wall, and the caterers had kept it well stocked throughout the evening. The bar was busy, and everyone was having a good time. She smiled and reached for her mother's hand. "It's a great party. And the only thing Flipper has to be embarrassed about is her dancing."

Her mother laughed with her as she pointed to Beth. The jerky style of jumping around that Beth was a fan of looked more like some kind of seizure to Charlie, but she wasn't the only one on the dance floor doing it, so she sat back and enjoyed the entertainment.

Her mother wrapped an arm around her shoulders. "Are you looking forward to going back to uni?"

"Yeah. I've got some good classes this year, and I'm looking forward to working with Professor Swallen. He's got really good connections to the Halle choir, so I'm hoping he might recommend me for an audition this year."

"Very nice. I'll look for my tickets in the post." Her mother laughed and hugged her close. "I'm so proud of you."

Charlie pulled back and frowned a little. "Why? I haven't even talked him into getting me the audition yet."

"You will, and you'll get a place. But I didn't mean just that. I meant everything."

Charlie continued to frown, confused.

"Getting yourself back on track after Gail. Getting into uni, learning to love again. Everything. You're an amazing woman, Charlie, and I'm so proud of you."

Charlie didn't want to tell her mum that most days she felt like a fraud. That she was terrified that the life she was building would come crashing down around her. Instead, she pulled her mum into a powerful hug and willed the tears to stay away. "I love you, Mum."

"I love you too, sweetheart."

Hazaar approached from the bar and held a drink out for Charlie. She motioned toward the dance floor. "I can't believe that's the same gawky sixteen-year-old I met when you first took me home to meet your parents."

"I know." Charlie smiled. "Whoever would have thought you'd have put up with me this long?" She sipped her drink, and the need to dance, to forget her conversation with her mother and the doubts that lingered in her mind, overtook her. "Dance with me?"

Hazaar allowed Charlie to pull her to the dance floor, and their bodies began to move together with the comfort of established lovers. Charlie twirled and turned, and the freedom of the music helped her to relax and enjoy the occasion more than the vodka in her drink. Hazaar's body felt so good against hers, and her perfume danced along her senses until Charlie was drunk on the scent and feel of Hazaar moving in time with her. They were surrounded by Charlie's family, their friends, and Charlie felt complete in a way she hadn't experienced with Hazaar before. She felt like she was part of a couple, just like any other couple there.

She leaned in and kissed Hazaar's lips, then giggled when Hazaar blushed. "Sorry. I couldn't resist."

"You're a brazen woman, Charlie Porter." Hazaar stole a quick peck. "But I love you anyway."

"Good, because you're stuck with me." Immediately afterward, Charlie wished she could pull the words back into her mouth, lock them up, and throw away the key. But she couldn't. They were out there, hanging in the ether between them. A throwaway comment that belied the truth, a truth that had lingered between them for so long it was growing into a barrier between them. It was a wall that she was erecting in the hopes of protecting herself, but she knew she was a shoddy bricklayer, and there were gaps that were big enough for a whole army to walk through, let alone one woman who already owned her body, heart, and soul.

"We never talk about the future, do we?" Hazaar tugged at her hand and led her out of the hall and into the cooling evening air. August had been warm, a barbeque summer that had turned green grass golden and scorched the earth bare, but the cloudless night brought a chill as Charlie stared at the stars and wished she hadn't opened her mouth.

"I'm sorry. It was a joke. A silly, stupid throwaway joke." She gave a fake little smile and tried to walk past Hazaar. "Let's just go back inside and enjoy the party, okay?"

"Charlie, can we talk for a minute?" When Charlie didn't look at her, Hazaar added, "Please?"

"Look, it's okay. Just forget I said anything." She shrugged. "It was a stupid joke."

"Shut up." Hazaar placed her finger to Charlie's lips and smiled to soften the words. "Just listen."

Charlie folded her arms across her chest. She waited, well aware that she looked like a sulky teenager, but not even slightly tempted to give up her stubborn attitude.

"You're such a brat sometimes." Hazaar snorted a tiny laugh. "Why do you never ask about the future?"

Charlie felt the glare melt from her face as the pain settled in her gut once again. She couldn't answer that question without breaking a promise she'd vowed to keep.

"When we met, you were full of dreams and hopes and plans. You never talk about them anymore."

"Yes, I do," Charlie said.

"Not with me you don't. Why do you never tell me your dreams, Charlie?"

She closed her eyes. "This is a party, Hazaar. Beth's eighteenth. This isn't the time or the place for this."

"Why do you never ask about my dreams or plans or hopes?"

"I'm going back into that room, and I'm going to enjoy the party."

"Just tell me."

"Hazaar, I really don't want to talk about this now."

"Don't you want to know? Don't you love me anymore?"

The plaintive note in Hazaar's voice fractured something inside Charlie. The box she'd tried to keep fears in splintered, and they poured out. "I don't ask because I don't want to hear from your own lips that I might not be a part of your future." She dropped her hands to her sides, her fists clenched tight. "I don't allow myself to dream about our future because I'm scared we don't have one. I love you more than I ever thought I could love someone. Especially after Gail. But because of Gail I won't allow myself to picture a future for myself. Because it hurts too much to picture a future without you in it."

Hazaar gently took hold of her fists. "Why are you so sure that our future won't be together?"

Charlie threw her head back and laughed bitterly as she yanked her hands away from Hazaar's. "Because we're almost two years down the line, Hazaar, and nothing has changed." She turned away from her and tried to control the burning anger that scorched through her blood. She wanted to scream and shout. She wanted to put her fist through a wall at how unfair it all was, at how scared Hazaar still was, but it wouldn't change anything. "Nothing." She pulled in a deep breath and tried to hear over the blood pounding in her ears. "I love you, but I can't ask for your future, Hazaar."

"And what if I want to give it to you?"

"Is it yours to give?"

"It is if I'm brave enough to take it."

"I guess that's the million-dollar question then, isn't it?" Charlie turned to face her again, and the sadness in Hazaar's eyes tore at her, shredding her resolve. She crossed the distance between them and pulled her into her arms. "I'm sorry. I promised I'd never put pressure on you. I'm sorry." She kissed her forehead and backed away. "I'm going to go back inside to the party. Are you coming?"

Hazaar nodded. "Yeah, I just need a minute."

Charlie squeezed her hand and pulled the door to the club open. She went straight to the bar. *Fucking pathetic. You promise not to push, to let her make her own decisions, and then you try to pressure her into making promises that you need to hear. Nice.*

She swallowed the shot of vodka and ordered another. *So fucking selfish. You know where that path leads.*

She was swallowing her third shot when Hazaar wrapped her fingers around her arm and tugged until they were face to face.

"I need time to figure everything out with my parents. And that isn't going to be easy."

Charlie turned back to the bar and signalled for another drink. "Look, forget it. I said I'm sorry. It doesn't matter."

"Yes, it does." Hazaar pulled her back to face her again. "I need you to know that I love you, Charlie. And as difficult as I know it's going to be, I can't see my life, my future, without you in it."

"Hazaar, you don't have to say this."

"Yes, I do. I asked you once before, and I meant it then, but you were right. We weren't ready, but I am—we are—ready now. We need to know. If we're to stand a chance, if we're going to build this future together, then we have to start somewhere. Move in with me?"

Charlie shook her head. "I can't."

"Why not?"

Charlie stared at her incredulously. She knew her mouth was hanging open, but she couldn't help it? "Your parents."

"It won't be the easiest issue to get around, no. But there is a way."

"That doesn't have me sliding down the drainpipe every time they pay a visit? Do tell."

"Sarcasm's the best you can do right now?"

"Yes."

Hazaar sighed heavily. "Fine."

Charlie downed her next shot and ordered another.

"Are you just going to get drunk, or are you going to listen to me?"

"How about both? I'm multitasking."

"Jesus, Charlie. I'm being serious here."

"And I'm here for a party." She picked up the glass, then glared at Hazaar when she took it away from her and handed it back to the bartender.

"Move in with me."

"That didn't sound like a question. More like a demand."

"Whatever it takes to get it through your head. I love you and I want you in my life. For now." She cupped Charlie's cheeks to make sure she was looking in her eyes. "Forever. Do you hear me?"

"Well, since you took my drink, it looks like I'm listening to you." The angry chill in Charlie's heart thawed, just a little. But it was enough, and she knew Hazaar was going to convince her to go along with whatever crazy plan she had conceived.

"Please."

Charlie swallowed and closed her eyes. "So what's this grand plan of yours?"

"It's actually the same plan I had before."

Charlie thought for a minute. "Tell your parents I'm the lodger and stick all my stuff in the spare room."

"I wouldn't put it quite like that, but in essence, yes."

"So I'd be your lodger?"

"Yes."

"Paying you rent?"

"Well, no. We'd split stuff like you do in normal relationships."

"Uh-huh." Charlie felt herself swaying a little as the vodka took a hold. "And since Daddy pays all the bills now, how are you going to explain that to him?"

"I'll ask him to give me more control."

"And will he?"

"If I explain it right. He's been complaining about money lately, so maybe having a little financial pressure relieved will be a good thing for him."

"And what about me?"

Hazaar frowned. "What do you mean? Isn't this what you want? A future together?"

"Is that what you think this little plan is?"

"Well, yes."

Charlie stared at her and knew in her heart that as much as she knew it was a bad idea, she wanted it. She wanted to go to sleep next to her every night, and wake up with her each morning. She wanted to argue with her about what crappy TV show they watched, and whose turn it was to cook. She wanted to see her clothes hanging next to Hazaar's in their wardrobe and their toothbrushes sharing the same glass in the bathroom. She wanted to share the bills and chores, and the decorating, the shopping, and everything else that made up a life together. She wanted everything Hazaar could give her. Or, at least, what she thought she could give her, for the moment.

"Will you?" Hazaar whispered. "Will you move in with me?"

*Yes! Oh hell, yes!* "On one condition."

"Anything."

"Your father has to agree to me living in the apartment."

Hazaar paled and swallowed heavily. "You mean…you want me to tell him…" She blinked rapidly. "You want me to tell him about…" She waved her hand between them.

"What? Are you crazy? No."

Hazaar's knees gave out, and Charlie helped her sit on one of the bar stools. "I'm sorry. I thought you meant you wanted me to come out."

"No. I want him to agree to me living in the apartment as your friend, your lodger, school mate, whatever you want to call it. But I don't want to have to flee in fear every time they arrive. I can't live like that." Charlie could hear the voice at the back of her head screaming at her, telling her how weak she was. But at the same time, she yelled back with the one argument that she felt could justify her actions. That living with Hazaar and loving her the very best she could would give her the best chance she had at keeping her when the time came for Hazaar to make her choice. Because whether Hazaar wanted to admit it or not, eventually, she would have to choose.

"And if he does, you'll move in with me?"

Charlie took a deep breath and entwined their fingers. "Yes."

"And if he doesn't?"

"Then I won't."

"But—"

"No buts. If he doesn't agree, then I won't. It's disrespectful and it would cause you a world of trouble."

"But I—"

"I'm sorry, no. I couldn't do it. I couldn't live under that shadow. Even with his permission, don't you think it will be hard enough to live in a way that will cause no suspicion? That it won't make your life with your family harder?"

Hazaar stared at her a long time, nervous, playing with the button on Charlie's shirt. She wouldn't back down. She couldn't. She had to believe, to know, that she meant enough to Hazaar to take this chance, or there was no way she would ever be able to take a bigger one down the line.

"Okay." Hazaar whispered the word, and Charlie knew she would have missed it if she hadn't been staring at her lips.

"Okay?" Charlie repeated, unable to actually believe that Hazaar had agreed, but a grin tugged at her lips.

"Yes, okay."

"You're going to ask him?"

Hazaar relaxed a little and laughed. "That's what I said."

"Okay, now can we go and enjoy the party?" Charlie pushed away from the bar and cursed when the room spun. Hazaar laughed.

"Sure. If you can stay on your feet, we can even dance some more."

Charlie leaned back against the bar. "In just a minute."

Hazaar leaned into her and wrapped her arms about her waist. "Take as long as you want, baby. We've got all the time in the world."

Charlie rested her head on top of Hazaar's. *I hope so.* She kissed her hair. *I truly hope so.*

## CHAPTER FIFTEEN

*The North of England, then*

Hazaar parked her car and grabbed her handbag, fishing out change for the ticket machine. She paid the fee and stuck the square on her dashboard before hurrying to the train station. She had five minutes before the train was due to leave. She glanced at the notice board to check which platform she needed to get to. *Always the farthest one away when you're running late. Damn it.*

When she got there the train was already at the platform and people were filing into the carriages. She joined the back of the nearest queue and picked a seat close to the toilets. She hated being so close, hated that she was going to have to go in there, but she hadn't changed before she got on the train, and she knew her brother would be picking her up when she got to Bradford. While her mother tolerated her wearing Western clothes while she was at university, she didn't when she returned home. In Bradford, her father was a strong, devout, upstanding member of the local community, and she was expected to behave in a manner that befitted his position, which meant wearing the proper attire. Or her mother would never let her live it down.

The change at Piccadilly station was an all-out run from one end of the station to the other, and Huddersfield was no better, just with slightly less time. At some point, she was going to have to get changed in one of those stinking bathrooms and hope she could do so while holding her breath.

She went over and over in her head how she was going to approach her father. What she was going to say. How she expected him to respond. And every time, the conversation played out differently, even though her words remained the same. Every justification wasn't enough for him to allow someone else into her home. She rubbed the back of her neck and tried to twist out the knots as the train left Huddersfield. She ducked into the toilet and pulled the loose-fitting pants and tunic of deep purple over her skinny jeans and fitted T-shirt. It was far easier to keep her Western clothes concealed this way than to try to hide them in her bag. Her lovely brother, Hatim, had a penchant for going through her things at every opportunity, and the last thing she wanted was him parading her Western clothing in front of everyone.

She went back to her seat and sent a text message to Charlie, letting her know she was almost there and that she'd call her when she got back to the train station on her way home. She double-checked the pass code feature was operating and turned the phone off. There was no reason to think anyone would snoop, but it didn't hurt to be extra careful.

She pulled her head scarf out of her bag and wrapped it around her hair and neck, making sure she was appropriately covered for a young woman out with her brother. She hated playing games, hated lying, but felt that it was all she ever seemed to do anymore. It had become her greatest skill, and much more vital to her survival than playing the piano had ever been.

The train jerked to a stop, and the motion caused her to tear at the cuticle she'd been picking at. She cursed and stuck her finger in her mouth as she got off the train. Hatim was waiting at the main doors for her. He smiled and took her bag, slinging it over his shoulder and ushering her out the door to his car. She smiled. Sometimes he wasn't so bad.

She settled into the car and fastened her seatbelt. "So how's married life, Hatim?"

"It's good." He adjusted his beanie cap in the mirror and tugged up the collar of his jacket before he pulled the car out of the car park and turned toward their parents' house. It was a ten-minute drive across the city of Bradford, and the closer they got to her childhood home, the more she felt it was a mistake to come back. Sweat trickled down her back and her leg twitched uncomfortably.

"School is good for you, sister?"

She smiled, grateful for the attempt at small talk. Maybe married life was good for him after all. "Yes. I have a lot of hard work this year, but perhaps you would like to come to one of my concerts?"

Hatim glanced at her, then back at the road. "We'll see. I might be busy. Baba keeps me pretty busy at work now I've got a family to support."

"I understand." She hadn't expected him to say yes, but at least she'd made the offer. He hadn't come to a concert since he'd stopped playing himself, which was more than ten years ago.

"Besides, I have to go to Pakistan with Baba soon."

"Really?" She could see the pride in Hatim's face as his shoulders straightened and his chest puffed up a little.

"Yeah." He smiled. "He's training me in more sides of the business, giving me more responsibility and all that. It's important I meet his contacts over there."

"I'm pleased for you, Hatim. Baba must be very proud of you, and the business must be doing very well."

He shrugged a little, and Hazaar wanted to laugh. Modesty had never been Hatim's strong suit, and his sense of self-importance bled through the false humility. "It's doing okay. It's tough times, you know, sister. Damn government taxes are so high on imports and all that, they're killing business, you know what I mean? They've got to listen to people who know, the people on the street, but them *kafirs,* they're too full of themselves, right?" He shook his head and drummed his hands on the steering wheel.

"Baba doesn't like that word, Hatim."

"What? *Kafir*?" He shrugged. "But it's what they are. Nonbelievers."

"But you know how he feels about these things. That there's no point in alienating people by flinging insults. It's bad for business." Hazaar had yet to figure out if her father actually harboured animosity and held it in check, or if he was accepting. She guessed that she'd find out today, one way or another.

"But anyway, I've made some suggestions that Baba thinks are good and they're making a big difference."

*I just bet they are. Not.* "I'm pleased for you both."

He pulled into the driveway of the large house overlooking the park. The driveway was steep, and as a child, it had always reminded her of the way medieval castles and fortresses were built at the top of hills to give them better defences in case of attack. The look of the house had only added to that impression, as it had a round, tower-like room at each side of the main building, and the pointed conical roof over each one made her think of fairy tales. She'd pictured herself as

Rapunzel many times when she was a girl sitting in her room, waiting to be rescued. *So much for my handsome prince!*

The front door opened, and her mother pulled her into a hug. "You're not eating enough." She pinched Hazaar's cheek and laughed. Once again, Hazaar was reminded of how much she looked like her mother, with her large eyes, high cheekbones, and full lips, and Hazaar hoped she looked as good as her mother did when she reached the same age. "I made some of your favourite, *aloo gosht* and fresh *peshawari naan* bread for lunch. I like this outfit on you. The colour is good."

Hazaar's mouth watered at the mention of her favourite treats: mutton and potato curry and bread stuffed with sultanas, pistachio nuts, and spice. "Thank you, Maa Jee." She kissed her mother's cheek and stepped into her father's warm embrace. The long whiskers of his beard scratched her cheek as he squeezed her tightly and planted a tender kiss on top of her hair.

"It's good to see you, *Jugnu*."

"And you, Baba." She nodded a greeting to Fatima, Hatim's wife, and smiled as the shy young woman almost hid behind her brother.

"Come, let's go and do this spread of your mother's justice." He wrapped his arm around her shoulder and ushered her into the house. It didn't matter how long she spent away from the family home, as soon as she stepped through the door, she felt as trapped as she had always felt. The weight of their love and expectation settled heavily on her shoulders.

The meal passed by fairly quickly as her father and brother discussed plans for the business, and the upcoming trip to Pakistan. It was easy to see how excited they both were about it, and her father appeared more animated than he had about anything since Hatim's wedding. Hazaar picked at her food, her stomach in knots as she tried to decide when would be the best time to broach the subject of Charlie moving in with her.

"You are not eating, *Beti*. Are you sick?" Her father pointed at her plate.

"No, Baba, it's delicious." She smiled and lifted a forkful to her mouth.

"So what do you think?" her father asked.

"I think it sounds wonderful." She hoped that was the correct response, as she had lost track of the conversation, but from the frown that marred her father's forehead she knew it wasn't.

"*Beti*, you were not listening to me."

"I'm sorry, Baba. I was distracted, thinking about my classes. I'm sorry."

He shook his head. "We were talking about the new mosque that is being built at Horton Park." The mosque was huge, and upon completion would easily accommodate eight thousand worshipers to prayer. It wasn't just a centre of worship, but also included information, education, and a gathering place for the community. It was to become the new heart of the Islamic community in Bradford, and her father was proud of the work he had done to help in its creation.

"Is it nearly finished?" She put her fork down and sipped some tea.

He frowned. "Not quite, *Beti*. They have had some delays and are now running low on funding."

"Oh, that's terrible news. What are the problems?"

"There were protests at the planning offices, so getting planning permission took longer than expected."

"Bloody *kafirs*." Hatim plunged his fork violently into his food.

Her father cuffed him across the back of the head, knocking his beanie cap askew. "You will show some respect in my house, boy. You use language like that in front of my wife or my daughter again in my presence and I will remind you what manners are. Do you understand me?"

Hatim straightened his hat and stared at his plate. The flush of humiliation coloured his cheeks, anger and shame emanated from him like a shockwave, and Fatima paled and visibly cringed. Whether in sympathy for her husband's embarrassment or in fear of its consequences, Hazaar didn't know. She hoped for the former, but knowing Hatim as she did, she suspected the latter.

"I asked you a question, boy."

"I understand, Father."

"Good." Her father sipped his tea. "Now apologize to your mother and sister for your lack of control."

Hatim looked up so quickly Hazaar worried that he would hurt himself. The look in his eyes as he stared at their father was nothing short of incredulous, and Hazaar was shocked at the display of power her father was demonstrating. Normally, he wouldn't go to such lengths to teach a lesson for such a slight infraction, and she wondered what else was going on. How else had Hatim disgraced himself to justify her father's attitude? To apologize to his mother in private was one thing. To be made to apologize in front of other people, even if only his own wife and sister, was massively embarrassing, and called into question his honour as a Muslim, as well as a man trying to establish his own household.

"I told you to apologize."

Hatim ducked his head and turned away from their father. "I am sorry for my outburst, Maa Jee. You deserve better from your son and I ask your forgiveness."

"Of course." She nodded her head but kept her gaze on her plate.

"Good. Now as I was saying, because of the delay in getting planning approval, by the time we broke ground, the costs of the project had escalated from around five and a half million pounds to closer to seven."

"Why such an increase, Baba?" Hazaar's voice croaked a little as she tried to give them all the chance to get back to normal.

"The economic climate, increased cost of materials, labour. More bureaucracy. You name it. Anything that has to be paid for, the price has gone up."

"I see." And she did. She sensed an opening and forged ahead. "Baba, you give me a great deal of money each year to support me."

"It is necessary, *Beti*, while you study. You need a good place to stay."

"I know, but perhaps there is a way to reduce what you need to give me in support so that you can help our brothers complete the mosque." Hazaar kept her voice light and schooled her face into a contemplative look. The same as she had adopted as a child when she had tried to figure out puzzles.

"Hazaar, the money I give you is not in the same league as the sums we are talking about to complete this project."

Hatim sniggered and threw her a look that told her how stupid he thought she was.

"I understand that, Baba, but it is a start, and perhaps if you are able to be a little more generous it will make others in the community think about ways they could possibly contribute a little more."

Her father nodded and smiled at her. She knew that he often felt others in the community should contribute far more than they did and that their greed was a major character flaw. "It is a good thought, but if I reduce what I give you, and give it instead to our brothers for the mosque, what will you do about the shortfall?"

"Well, I may be able to find someone to share the expenses of living in the apartment. A girl at university I study with has a problem with the place she was going to live for the upcoming year, and because it's so late she's struggling to find another suitable place to stay. I could ask if she would like to share with me."

"Hmm. She is a friend of yours? This girl?"

"We worked together on several projects last year. She's going into her second year now, but she's a more mature student and we've worked well together. I would class her as a friend, yes."

"And is she Muslim?"

"No, Baba, she is not."

"Then I don't think it would be a good idea."

Hazaar felt nauseous, and at that moment, she wished she was anywhere else in the world, but she had made a promise. She knew that Charlie felt at times as though she didn't matter to Hazaar, that she was still a fleeting affair, and she needed to show her that wasn't the case. She closed her eyes momentarily and gathered her courage. "Baba, over the past year Charlotte has demonstrated good morals and an understanding of our culture when we have talked outside of class. Whilst she is not Muslim, she is not prejudiced or disrespectful either. I believe she would provide a good solution to this issue." She placed a subtle emphasis on the phrase "she is not prejudiced" and hoped that it would play on her father's conscience. She wanted to believe that all his talk of acceptance and not insulting non-Muslims was about more than his own business prospects.

"And when she gets a boyfriend and wants to bring him home? Or drinking? Will she bring alcohol into your home?"

"I suggest we discuss with her strict rules about what is and is not acceptable. If she agrees to abide by them, then I think we should give it a chance."

"Hazaar—"

"Baba, the community needs the mosque. It is our duty to do everything we can. This is a small price for me to pay to support our brothers and sisters."

Her father tore off a piece of naan and chewed on it slowly. "Have you spoken to her about this?"

"No, Baba." She rubbed her hands along her thighs, a feeble attempt at drying her sweaty palms. "I only thought of it when you spoke of the mosque's needs." Hazaar prayed that her face looked as innocent as she hoped and that no one else could hear her heart as it pounded in her chest.

"How do you know she is still looking for somewhere to live?"

"I spoke to her only a couple of days ago about her situation. She was still struggling then. I assume the situation hasn't changed."

He tore some more bread, obviously considering her suggestion, and Hazaar tried to keep her expression neutral. She felt bad manipulating her father's good intentions, but she could see they would all win out of this arrangement. *Is that really such a bad thing?*

"But, Baba, she is talking about living with a *kafir*. That is not acceptable." Hatim's voice rose in pitch with each word.

"Enough, Hatim." Her father slammed his hands down on the table. "I have already spoken to you about your use of language. That word is not acceptable in my house."

"But it is not acceptable for her to live with them. They will corrupt her." Hatim pointed his finger at Hazaar, and she willed herself not to move.

"Your sister is talking about bringing one girl into her home, for both of their benefits." Her father stared at the defiant Hatim, and Hazaar could see his beard trembling and she knew the muscles in his jaw were clenching tightly as he controlled the anger he undoubtedly felt. "Am I correct, Hazaar?"

"Yes, Baba." She couldn't help but wonder if Hatim's objections would work in her favour.

"She is talking about letting a *kafir* into her house. She will be tainted. No man will want her for his wife."

"That is enough. This is my house. If you cannot control yourself in front of your mother and sister, how do you expect me to trust you to control yourself in business? You will leave now, and you will not be accompanying me to Pakistan on my next trip. You will not be accompanying me anywhere until you prove that I can trust you to behave in a respectful, honourable way."

"But, Father—"

"Go." He turned away from Hatim and threw his bread back onto his plate. "Now."

Hatim stood quickly and kicked his chair away so violently it clattered to the floor. Hazaar flinched as he stormed out of the room and slammed the door behind him. Fatima was quick to follow him, mumbling her apologies as she went. Hazaar stared at the closed door, not knowing what to say or do next. The room was silent a long time, and Hazaar took her cue from her mother. She stayed still and silent as stone while they waited for her father to decide what would happen next. She chewed on her lip and picked at nonexistent fluff on her pants.

She heard raised voices outside, the ringing slap of a hand against flesh, a sharp cry, and then a whimper as car doors slammed and tires squealed as the car drove away.

Her heart sank the longer they sat in silence, and she was certain her father would want nothing further to do with her suggestion. She had to fight back tears as she realized just how much she wanted Charlie to move in with her, and now she feared it would never happen while she remained tied to her family.

Her father cleared his throat and reached for his tea, sipping gingerly before he smiled sadly, first at her mother and then at her. "Your brother forgets his place. He thinks now that he is married that he deserves respect. He has yet to realize that respect is earned, not given, and that his lack of respect is dishonouring us all."

"I'm sorry, Baba."

"It isn't for you to be sorry for your brother's failings in this matter, *Beti*."

"I didn't mean to provoke him." She couldn't look up from her plate.

"You didn't. He has been spoiling for a fight for some time now. If not this matter, it would be some other. His intolerance and prejudice is causing problems in my business, and it must end. It isn't what the Quran teaches us, it isn't what I've taught you all, and it isn't good for business."

"You're right, Baba. Still, I'm sorry for the pain it causes you."

"You're a good daughter." He got up from the table and kissed the top of her head as he passed. "Perhaps we should discuss this plan of yours further. If I am to agree to this, I think I should meet the young lady in question. If she is suitable and will agree to the rules that must be adhered to, I don't see why it couldn't work."

Hazaar was trapped between elation and terror. *Meet her? Oh fuck!*

## CHAPTER SIXTEEN

*The North of England, then*

Charlie smoothed clammy palms over her long black skirt and checked herself in the mirror, hoping she'd pass the inspection. She adjusted the frilly edge of the collar on her blouse and flattened a wrinkle she spotted. She wanted to look respectful but casual. *And instead you look like some sort of school mistress from a Charles Dickens novel.* She shook her head, accepting that it was too late to rethink the wardrobe choice now. Part of her regretted insisting that Hazaar get her father's approval, but another part of her was intensely curious to get a glimpse of this part of Hazaar's life.

She smoothed her hair down and walked out of the bathroom. Hazaar was dusting the living room for the third time that morning. Charlie could see her hands shaking as she held the cloth and moved around the room aimlessly, muttering to herself in Urdu, and Charlie strained to make out the words. Charlie had convinced her to teach her the language as something else for them to share, to bridge a bit more of the gap between them. She could make out the words "crazy" and "idiotic plan" and "why won't my damn hands stop shaking." The fact that Hazaar was so nervous actually helped to calm her own nerves a little.

"Can I do anything to help?" Charlie asked.

"No." Hazaar swiped the cloth over the TV. "No, it's fine."

"You sure? I can put the kettle on for tea or something?"

"Oh, yeah. Actually—" The door buzzer sounded, and Hazaar jumped, dropping the cloth and can of furniture polish. "Shit." She picked the stuff up and tossed them at Charlie. "Can you put them away, please? I'll get the door."

Charlie shrugged and took them to the kitchen, putting the kettle on to boil while she was there. When she came out of the kitchen, Hazaar's father was walking into the living room. Charlie was a little surprised at how tall he was, and guessed he was easily six feet tall, with broad shoulders and a full beard. He wore a traditional *shalwar kameez,* and although his smile was welcoming, his eyes looked wary.

"Baba, this is Charlotte Porter." Hazaar motioned in Charlie's direction. "Charlotte, this is my father."

"Good morning, Mr. Alim." Her stomach knotted as she held out her hand. "It's an honour to meet you, sir."

"And you, Miss Porter." He shook her hand and indicated the chair. "Shall we sit?"

Charlie sat where he indicated, crossed her ankles, and folded her hands in her lap. She smiled and waited, knowing that the questions were going to come. He sat in the chair opposite and waited for Hazaar to bring tea. He sipped slowly, and every second he delayed intensified the urge Charlie had to speak and to get the interrogation under way. But Hazaar had warned her how much of a mistake that would be. *Let him lead. Don't try to push him or you'll push him into saying no.* Hazaar's words played over and over in her head, and she studied the elaborately decorated teapot to distract herself from her nerves.

"Hazaar tells me that you are a singer."

"Yes, that's correct."

"And what kind of music do you sing?"

"Almost anything. But I particularly love to sing blues and jazz, and choral music."

"I take it that like Hazaar, you have studied for many years?"

"Yes, sir."

"It takes much dedication and love for the music to devote oneself to it so completely."

Charlie nodded and waited for him to continue. Hazaar sat on the sofa, wringing her hands, her eyes wide.

"So why did you not enroll straight from school as most students do?"

*Shit.* "I had a few issues to deal with."

He nodded. "I see." He sipped his tea. "Please forgive me, but I must ensure that your issues do not cause problems for my daughter."

"I understand. When I was a child, I had a close friend. We grew up together and were more like sisters." *Well, we were closer than friends, but not in a way I can tell you.* "When we were in college, she and her father had a disagreement and he beat her very badly, and while she was in hospital it was discovered that he had abused her. After that, she came to live with me and my family, but my friend was unable to recover physically and mentally. We, my family and I, tried to help her, but we weren't able to get through to her." Charlie couldn't hold his gaze any longer and stared at her hands as she held back the tears that threatened. She felt conflicted. She didn't like hiding any part of herself, but the situation between Hazaar and her family was between them. It was Hazaar's decision and not one she was going to push. But she felt like she was dishonouring Gail's memory by not admitting the true nature of their relationship.

"She took her own life?" His voice was gentle, and when Charlie looked up she could see sympathy in them.

"Yes."

He nodded. "That must have been very difficult for you."

Charlie looked down again. "Yes, it was."

"Our religion does not condone suicide in any way. Despite the wider world view of us, the Quran tells us that it is a sin to take any life given by Allah, especially our own. And it will have grave consequences for our spiritual journey." He leaned forward and rested his elbows on his knees. "But for a child of Allah to feel she has no other choice is the greater sin. Children should be protected and cared for. It is a great shame, and I can see how deeply this has troubled you. Thank you for telling me the truth about a difficult matter. You've set my mind at ease that this situation is not something that I need worry for Hazaar's welfare in, and that you are a young woman who cares deeply and takes care of her friends and family to the best of her ability. That your family was willing to try to help a child not their own also pleases me." He leaned back. "These are admirable qualities."

"Thank you, sir."

He smiled. "Are you still interested in staying here with Hazaar while you continue your studies?"

"Yes, sir, I am."

"You understand that there would be certain stipulations I must insist upon in order to make this an acceptable proposition?"

"I understand that there are certain things that I wouldn't be able to bring in here."

He pulled a piece of paper from the pocket of his coat and handed it to Charlie. "This is a list of food and beverages that are not allowed in a Muslim household. Please read through it and tell me if you think you can adhere to this list."

Charlie read through quickly, finding nothing on it that Hazaar hadn't already prepared her for. "That's fine, sir." She held the paper out to him, but he waved his hands.

"You may keep it for reference."

She glanced quickly at Hazaar, to gauge her reaction to the comment, and was pleased to see her smiling. "Thank you."

"There is one other very big point that must be agreed upon." He cleared his throat. "Boys."

Charlie nodded. She'd been expecting this one. Hazaar had quizzed her on pretty much any question she could think of her father might ask, and this one was a biggie.

"There can be no male visitors to the apartment unless Hazaar has an appropriate chaperone here also. There can never be overnight male guests."

"You have my word, Mr. Alim. I will not bring any man into the apartment save my own father."

"He cannot be here alone."

"Is it acceptable if I'm here, or my mother?"

"Yes, that will be fine." He smiled.

"Thank you."

"Then I am agreeable to this proposal. Shall I contact your father to make the financial agreement?"

"I fund my education myself, so I'll make whatever payments we agree on."

"Very well." They spent a few minutes agreeing to the rent and utility payments before he stood to leave and shook her hand again. "I am trusting you with my daughter, Miss Porter. Look after her."

Charlie swallowed hard, deeply conflicted. She was glad he had given his consent, but she was bitterly angry at having to lie to him. He was a good man, a good father, and he deserved to be treated better than this. In her heart she questioned Hazaar's belief that he would cast her aside if he knew the truth. *Yeah, but you knew Gail's dad for years and look how that turned out, fool.* She smiled, forcing herself to ignore the acid that churned in her stomach.

"You have my word, Mr. Alim."

# CHAPTER SEVENTEEN

*Pakistan, today*

Watery sunlight shone off Charlie's curls and her smile lit up her beautiful blue eyes. Hazaar could smell freshly cut grass and meadow flowers, hear the sound of water as it lapped gently at a pebble-covered beach, and see the stone walls of the ruined castle stood sentry over them. Bowmen in kilts stood atop the ramparts, their arrows all pointing in the same direction, but their target was beyond her view. No doubt some evil foe was aligned against them ready to storm the castle and do battle, to slaughter the cattle, women, and children, to burn fields of crops, sow them with salt, and leave them as barren as their hearts.

"Hey, gorgeous, I missed you." Charlie's voice sounded strange—distorted and far away. There was a tinny vibrato to it, like it was being carried over an old-fashioned telephone line. The faint beep in the background sounded like water dripping into a puddle. The sound was repetitive, rhythmically hypnotic, and tugged at her concentration, drawing her focus away from her beautiful Charlie.

"Charlie?" She reached up to touch her face. She needed to be sure she was real, to make sure she was really there with her, to touch her once again, but she couldn't lift her arm because it hurt too much. The pain made Charlie's face foggy and blur around the edges. She faded in and out of focus. Hazaar didn't want that to happen, so decided the pain didn't matter, she would just keep still. All that mattered was that Charlie was there with her, helping her, touching her, and hope blossomed in her chest, eclipsing the pain that had woken her. "I've missed you so much, baby."

"Try to stay still." Charlie pressed a cool cloth to her cheek.

"Okay. What are we doing here?" She looked around, noting the warmth of the sun shining down on them, but the stars and moon filled the sky. The arrows of the bowmen were aimed at Charlie's head, all focused on a single point. The promise of a spring day rapidly filled with fear, dying hope, and a growing sense of inevitability. *Good-bye* hung in the air like a cloud of mustard gas over the trenches and the sour, bitter scent coated her tongue. *What the hell?* "I don't understand, Charlie. What's going on? What's wrong?"

"Hazaar, try to be still. You are hurt."

It was as though Charlie's words suddenly brought to mind all the pain she should have been feeling since she woke up. She groaned and closed her eyes. "I don't remember what happened. How did I get hurt?" *Has the battle already happened? Did I miss it? Who won?*

She could feel Charlie dabbing at the corner of her eye, wiping and rubbing gently at various patches of her skin, and Hazaar knew she was cleaning away dried blood. *Well, apparently, it wasn't me who won.* Hazaar gasped at a particularly sore spot on her arm.

"I'm sorry."

Hazaar tried to shake her head, but the movement hurt. "No, I'm sorry. It's been so long and now you're here looking after me." She laughed sadly. "Not the reunion I imagined, my love." Hazaar tried to reach for her again, but her hand gently held her down.

"Be still now, Hazaar. You must rest." Charlie's lips moved, but the voice was wrong. Her accent, her words, even her tone was all wrong. It didn't sound like Charlie in any way. In fact, it sounded more like Amira with every syllable she spoke.

"Charlie, I'm so glad you came for me." But even as she said the words, Charlie's face changed before her eyes, fading, blurring, receding, as though she were moving farther and farther away into the fog. Hazaar's heart raced, and the feeling of calm and tranquillity faded. She tried to focus on Charlie's face, to bring her closer again, to keep Charlie with her. Always.

"Charlie, I love you, please don't go." She tried to reach for her again, but the pain in her shoulder made her cry out. "Please don't leave me. I'm sorry I hurt you. I'm so sorry." She lifted her head and opened her eyes.

"Try to lie still," Amira said, as she pressed her back to the ground. The thin woollen blanket she was on did little to insulate her body from the cold, hard concrete beneath her, but it was better than nothing. She closed her eyes again and pushed aside the disappointment at seeing Amira's face instead of Charlie's. The cellar was dark, lit with only a single bulb in the centre of the dank room. The smell of rotten wood, earth, and blood overrode the memory of cut grass. The soothing sound of the waves was replaced by the constant drip of water from a leaking pipe somewhere in the room.

She slowly catalogued every ache in her body, trying to assess the damage that her fall had caused. Her shoulder ached with every breath, and she couldn't move her arm at all, each attempt making her feel ill. Her head ached and her chest hurt, but otherwise she thought she was doing okay.

"Your shoulder needs to be pulled back into place, Hazaar." Amira grimaced as she spoke and pointed at her right shoulder.

Hazaar nodded. "Go ahead."

Amira put a wooden stick between Hazaar's teeth and nodded.

Tazim stepped out of the shadows behind Amira and squatted beside her, a cruel smile twisting his face. He clasped her forearm with one hand and placed the other on her upper chest.

"Who's Charlie?"

"I don't know what—"

"Don't lie to me. Who is this man?"

Hazaar laughed bitterly. "There is no man."

"I heard you, you filthy little whore." He squeezed her hand and she realized there was something wrong with her fingers. The knuckles didn't line up properly and they didn't lie comfortably next to each other. Each squeeze rippled waves of pain down the length of her arm. He lifted her hand a little higher and wiggled her arm. Fire shot through her shoulder and she couldn't stop the scream.

"You don't know what you're talking about."

"I know what I heard, you said 'Charlie, my love.' Who is this man?"

"I don't know a man called Charlie." Tears ran down her cheeks as she tried in vain to pull her injured arm from his grasp, but he wouldn't let go.

"Liar!" He yanked her arm. The sickening crunch echoed in the chilly room as her shoulder slid back into place, and her consciousness fled, letting her fall back into blessed oblivion.

# CHAPTER EIGHTEEN

*The North of England, then*

Hazaar let the final notes from the piano fade and Charlie's voice ring out. She closed her eyes and tried to hold back the tears she could feel welling up at the purity of the sound.

"You sing so beautifully, I could listen to you forever." She smiled as Charlie bent down and kissed her cheek.

"And I could listen to you play forever." Charlie ran her fingers over the back of Hazaar's hand, tracing the veins and tendons. "Such talented hands."

"You say that a lot." Hazaar tugged her onto her lap.

"I do?" Charlie wrapped her arms around her neck. "Well, it must be true if I say it a lot."

"Yes." She leaned in for a kiss and let it linger. Charlie's lips were soft and moved beneath her own with growing passion. "You usually say it when I've just made you come."

Charlie laughed. "You're such a shit."

"Yeah, but you love me anyway."

Charlie kissed her again. "It's a good job. I wouldn't have put up with you this long if I didn't."

"You're a saint."

"I'm so glad you noticed." Charlie glanced at her watch. "I have to get going soon."

"What time's your meeting?"

"Three."

"Are you ready?"

"I think so. Swallen's gonna be a huge pain in the arse though."

"What makes you say that?" Hazaar stroked her hands down Charlie's back, enjoying the way her muscles tensed as she spoke.

"Well," she said, scratching her head in mock confusion. "It's my third and final year. It's my honours thesis. And I've heard rumours." She rested her head on Hazaar's shoulder.

"You shouldn't believe everything you hear, baby."

"Really?"

"Nope."

"You're the one who told me."

Hazaar laughed. "Then you should totally believe everything you hear." She squeezed Charlie's backside, just to make her squirm. "Want me to make dinner while you're out?"

"That would be wonderful." Charlie kissed her quickly before getting up. "I'll catch you later, sweetheart."

"Love you."

"Love you too."

She hated how quiet the house was after Charlie left. She hated that she couldn't hear her moving around the apartment, or just look up and see her working on her laptop, tapping away at some paper or other. She let her fingers find the piano keys just to fill in the silence, and the music began to pour out of her soul.

The doorbell ringing shocked her out of her musical escape, and she shook her head as she walked to the intercom.

"Forget something?"

"Hazaar?"

"Baba?"

"Yes. Are you going to open the door or should your brother and I wait out here?" He laughed a little and she buzzed the door open, quickly putting on her head scarf. He gave her a quick hug when she opened the door to the apartment, and she couldn't help but notice how much older he looked. His beard was almost entirely grey now, and his shoulders looked a little slumped. There were more lines around his eyes than she remembered and the hair she could see from under his *topi* was silver too. She nodded at Hatim as their father left for the bathroom, his gait slow as he favoured his left leg.

"So where's blondie?" Hatim sat down and scowled at her, almost daring her to challenge him.

"Charlotte is at university. She has a meeting with her tutor about her third-year thesis."

"I still can't believe the old man lets you get away with living with that." His lip curled and his nostrils flared as though he smelled something rotten.

"Are you brave enough to ask him about it, Hatim?" She smiled slyly and enjoyed the flash of humiliation that skittered across his face. They both knew the answer to that question.

"You'll be laughing on the other side of your face later." His smile was cruel, just as it always had been.

"What's that supposed to mean?" She didn't expect him to answer, but she couldn't stop herself from asking anyway.

"You'll see, dear sister." He stared at her without saying anything more.

She adjusted the scarf over her head and swung the tail over her shoulder, fidgeting with the corner that had rested over her chest. It didn't matter how many times she told herself not to listen to him, not to let him get the better of her, sometimes he managed to get under her skin like a splinter, a worrisome, irritating splinter that just wouldn't come out, no matter how much she squeezed or picked at it.

She shrugged and tried to play it off. "So how is Fatima?"

Hatim's face clouded again, the smug smile replaced by a grimace. "She is cursed."

Hazaar laughed. "What?"

Hatim jumped to his feet and slapped her across the face. "Do not laugh at my misfortune, sister." His voice dripped venom as he spat the words down at her.

She covered her cheek with her hand and stared at him. They had fought as children, but as a grown man he had never struck her. She was shocked into silence as he ranted, her cheek on fire.

"My wife's curse is not a joke."

"Hatim, not getting pregnant is not caused by a curse. It's a medical condition, or just bad timing. There are many reasons, and being cursed is not one of them."

"You think you're so smart, sister, so well educated." Spittle flew from his lips and landed on her cheeks. "You know nothing of the real world."

"I know enough to know that believing in curses is superstitious nonsense."

"And I know that in our world there is something wrong with you. And our father. He should have stopped this nonsense long ago, not let you go on with this ridiculous studying. He should have arranged your marriage, and I would be rid of you by now. I wouldn't have to live in the shadow of the wonderful Hazaar and the honour she brings to the family. The great, soon-to-be Dr. Hazaar Alim. It's a *kafir* instrument. Not even a proper Muslim instrument. It shouldn't be allowed."

"Says who?"

"Me. The imam, the Holy Quran, our culture, our laws—"

"We don't live in Pakistan, Hatim. We live in England. It's the twenty-first century, and we don't have to live by a set of antiquated rules that are inapplicable to the society we live in and aren't even enforced by half of the Muslims we grew up with."

"You don't know anything."

"I know that I can walk down the street our parents live on and pass half a dozen Pakistani women. Half of them will be in Western clothing, just like everyone else. They won't even be wearing a head scarf. Two will wear a scarf with a pair of jeans, or a skirt, or some other style of Western clothing, and the last one would be your wife. Wearing a full burqa and cursing your name. The only curse your wife suffers from is being married to you and your ridiculously conservative views of Islam and what it means to be a good Muslim."

He lifted his hand to strike her again.

"Do not do that, Hatim." Her father's voice was little more than a growl as he entered the room.

"Father, she was disrespecting me. She is laughing at Fatima's curse."

"She was doing no such thing."

"You were not here. You did not hear her."

"I heard enough. No one laughs at Fatima's curse. Because there is no curse. They laugh at you for believing and repeating such nonsense. That is not disrespect, boy, it is education." He grabbed Hatim's shoulder and pulled him away from Hazaar. "Your wife is not yet pregnant. That is not a curse. That is a medical issue, and it may be you that is the cause, just as easily as it could be your wife."

"Father, how can you say such a thing?"

"Because it's the truth. We aren't some backward, uneducated tribal folk who know no better. I paid a lot of money for the education you threw away. Had you half your sister's brain we would not have the problems in business that we do now."

"You cannot blame me for the business failing."

"Yes, I can, and I do. And you know exactly why."

Hazaar watched the verbal volley and wondered why her father was allowing her to see him berating Hatim.

"If I ever see you hit a woman again, any woman, Hatim, I will transfer you to the packing floor in the warehouse, and you can give up the hope of ever leaving that position in my company."

"Father, you wouldn't do that to me. I'm your only son."

"Try me, boy." He stared at Hatim, and Hazaar could feel the resolve from where she sat.

Hazaar wished she could be anywhere else. She didn't want to witness Hatim's humiliation, certain that she would pay some sort of price for it later, but there was no way to escape the scene.

"Get out. Wait for me in the car while I sort out your mess. Again."

"But I—"

"Now."

Hatim glared at him and then Hazaar before he stormed out of the room. Her father's shoulders slumped as the door slammed, and he let himself fall into the chair behind him. He closed his eyes and she could see his lips moving, but she couldn't make out the words. Was he praying? She didn't know. Her father's pain was obvious, and she wanted to help him, to take it away if she could.

"Baba?"

"A moment, *Jugnu*." He rubbed his hands over his face. "Perhaps some more tea."

"Of course, Baba." She hurried to the kitchen and arranged the tray. So many questions ran through her head that she felt dizzy, but she wasn't sure she wanted to know the answers. Her father hadn't moved when she entered the room and put the tray on the coffee table. She poured the tea in silence and knelt beside him. He covered her hand as he took the tea cup from her. His eyes were damp as he looked down at her.

"This world cannot always be what we want it to be. We are delivered blessings and hardships, sometimes in equal measure and sometimes not. There are dreams we can achieve and others we must learn to let go of. I had dreamt that my son would be a good man, a better man than I. Now I hope he will at least be a decent husband and father, but I don't expect it."

"Baba, he is young. He'll learn."

"You do not need to defend him to me, Hazaar. I know his heart, and it is a black and withered thing that wishes for more than he can achieve, wealth he has not earned, and respect he will never secure." He looked at his teacup and placed it on the table untouched. "But still, he is my son."

"It's not your fault, Baba."

"No?" He smiled sadly as she shook her head. "If not my fault, then whose?"

"You were away so much when we were younger. He simply didn't learn."

"Exactly. I shouldn't have been. The boy needed me. But enough of that. It is the past and it cannot be changed. Now I must do what I can and I must ask you to forgive me, *Beti,* because I cannot give you the life you had hoped for."

Hazaar's pulse raced. She struggled to pull air into her lungs as it felt thick, wet, and dense, like she was trying to breathe through water. *No. This can't be happening. Not yet. I'm not ready to lose them all. I'm not ready to let go of my family.* The muscles in her jaw tightened and clenched as she tried to think of something to say. She wanted to run. She couldn't face what she knew was coming.

"Since you were a little girl, I knew that the music was your love, your passion. And you wanted a life where you could play. You have brought me nothing but joy and pride, *Beti.* You have been a good girl, and I was hoping to allow you a life with your music."

"You have been very good about my studies, Baba."

He smiled sadly. "Yes, but I know you wanted more. A future playing in front of audiences, no?"

"I don't know what to say, Baba."

"You don't need to say anything. I know you. I know all my children. The good and the bad and all those wonderful colours in between. Your sisters were happy enough to marry, to become wives and mothers. You never wanted that life. I know this."

"I'm sorry, Baba."

"There is no need to be sorry, *Beti.* I understand your passion, and the position you will be in with a husband to care for. As much as it goes against our traditions, I had hoped to give you your dreams. I wasn't looking for a husband for you."

"You weren't?" Was he saying what she thought he was? Did he know? "I'm confused. I thought that was always the plan?"

"I know. I felt it best to keep your mother happy for a little while longer, to at least let you finish school before we told her that you were going to be a concert pianist." He smiled widely, wistfully. "I wanted to see you play on the grand stages of the world. To wave at you and smile and tell all the world who you were, my *beti,* my daughter Hazaar Erina Alim. Sorry, *Dr.* Hazaar Erina Alim. My child." Pride and pleasure radiated from his eyes.

"You are my greatest achievement, and I'm proud to have had a hand in shaping the woman you have become. And I wanted to see you happy and smiling and to hear all the wonderful music you would make. That beautiful music comes from your heart, from the passion in your soul. And from the pain you try to hide. The one you think I don't see." He patted her cheek. "I see. And I love you still." He whispered the words. "I have seen everything you have done for your family. The sacrifices you've made for us all. And I love you more. You, my *Beti,* my wonderful daughter, have made me so proud."

"I love you, Baba." He knew and it didn't matter to him. He might not know she was a lesbian, but he knew she didn't want a husband, that she didn't want to follow tradition. And he still loved her. Relief and shame waged a war inside her. Relief that she need not fear him any longer, and shame that she had ever doubted him. He believed in the Holy Quran—peace, acceptance, equality, and understanding. These were the qualities he had embodied all her life, the qualities he had tried to teach them all. And it pained her that she had ever expected anything less of him. "I only ever wanted you to love me, to be proud of me."

"I know, I know." He pulled her into his arms and held her tight. She couldn't remember the last time he had pulled her into such an embrace. He took a deep breath, and whispered against her hair, "But I cannot give you this life you wanted."

Hazaar pulled away from him and sat back on her heels. "What are you saying?"

He took hold of her hand. "Things aren't going well in the business. Hatim has caused many issues. I wish it weren't so, but the boy has no head for business and an attitude that is insulting. I've put measures in place to minimize any future problems, but damage—a great deal of damage—has already occurred. Without help, the business will be bankrupt."

"Baba, why are you telling me this? Surely this is between you and Hatim?"

"It should be. But because of this I have to make you give up your dreams. I think you deserve to understand why I ask this of you."

"You want me to marry. For business." Hazaar's stomach rolled and chills chased up and down her spine. She thought she might vomit.

"You know what that means to me, Baba, and you still want me to marry? I can't."

"*Beti,* I don't want you to. I need you to."

Hazaar pulled her hand from his and got up. She wasn't sure how her legs supported her across the room, but she had to put some distance between them. Her head was spinning. Fear had morphed into dread, into elation, and back again in the space of two heartbeats. "What do you mean?"

"I've been to the bank. They won't loan me the money required to keep the business going. Hatim has made some very unwise investments and they have, well, it doesn't matter now."

*Fuck, he's selling me because Hatim's an idiot.* She looked at him and saw beyond the tired slump of his shoulders and the defeated look in his eyes, and saw fear. Fear of what, she didn't know, and she truly didn't care right now. For one brief, beautiful moment she had believed she could have it all. Her family, Charlie, her music, all of it. But that was just a lie, and her father's words burned holes in every dream she had. She would not—could not—debase herself so that the community wouldn't find out her brother was a wife-beating, idiotic bully and that her father was broke. She had more self-esteem than that. She had more self-respect than to let the petty concerns of a community who wouldn't tolerate her dictate the future she would live. She started to shake her head even as her father started to speak.

"There is a man in Pakistan, Mr. Siddiqi. He has a business similar to ours." He laughed bitterly. "On paper, anyway." He rubbed his hand over his face. "Anyway, he is looking to break into the British market. Hatim thought it would be good to get involved with him to increase our business. Now it's all such a mess."

"I don't understand. If you have this increase in business, then why are you in danger of losing everything?" She held up her hand. "Forget that. I don't care. I won't marry a man because Hatim's an idiot. I can't do it."

He carried on as though she hadn't spoken, as though he had to get out the words before he lost them. "Because I would have never, ever gotten involved with the evil business these people are peddling." His anger bubbled over as he spat out the word business.

*What?* His tone brought her up short. "You said their business was similar to yours."

"On paper, it would appear so." He shook his head. "It doesn't matter now. It is too late to go back to the way things were. And even if I tried, it couldn't work. Hatim…"

He looked up at the ceiling and Hazaar knew he was holding back. The way he held his head, chin resting on his chest, and the way his hands shook, convinced her how bad the situation was that they was facing, and she didn't want any part in it. "We have a deal that can be agreed upon, but he doesn't like the idea of dealing with people who aren't family. He has two sons. The older is already married. They have a strong business, strong connections. Strong enough to get us out of the mess we're in. But we must be family for him to work with us."

Hazaar stared at her hands. She wanted to walk out, or tell him to get out, but she knew she'd regret it if she did. There was more she needed to know. The fact that her father was being so open about the situation told her there was so much more at stake, and she couldn't in good conscience leave the conversation without knowing all of the facts. "What will happen if I, if you, don't agree to the wedding?"

"No other family is in a position to enter into a partnership with us. And If I alienate Siddiqi, the families in Pakistan will stop dealing with me. Business will dry up altogether. I will be bankrupt within a few weeks. We will lose the house." He looked around. "This apartment. Cars. Everything. It is all on the line, *Beti*. I will have nothing. Your mother and I will lose our home and have nowhere to go, nothing to fall back on. And there is no other solution. You have my word, I have tried. I only wanted to do my best for you."

She didn't believe him. There were too many indications that there was more to this than money. She knew Hatim's material need, but her father wasn't a greedy man. "Is that all?"

"Isn't that enough?"

She shrugged. "I guess it is. It just sounded like there was more to it."

He stared at her and his eyes watered again. "You are such a good girl, *Beti*. There are many things in this situation that I wish were different."

"Baba, you always taught us that there were more important things than money."

"Oh, child. I wish your brother had learned that lesson too."

She'd thought about this moment for so long it seemed unreal, like she was watching it happen on TV, and instead of the anger she expected to feel, she felt numb. She rubbed her hands up her arms, then stared at them, shocked by how cold her fingers felt.

"I came from Pakistan with nothing, *Jugnu*. I worked so hard to create a good life for you all. To give you a father, a heritage, you could all be proud of and a legacy to pass on that would help you all." He dropped his head into his hands and she knew he was weeping. "I have failed you."

"How have you failed, Baba, if this is because of Hatim's mistakes?"

"I knew I couldn't trust him. That he wasn't ready yet. I knew but I still allowed him to take too much on and gave him too much freedom. Now we all must pay the price for his stupidity and greed. Without the Siddiqis' backing, financially, and in other ways, your brother and I will end up in prison." He wiped his eyes.

*I knew it.* "Why?"

"Their business. It is drugs, *Jugnu*. Drugs. For money and status, Hatim has gambled the business, his freedom, his reputation." He closed his eyes again. "And mine."

She fought back the urge to throw up and rubbed her chest, where the ache was becoming unbearable. The tightness made it difficult to breathe, and her vision narrowed. The room faded away, and all she could see was the music at her piano, the piece she had played with Charlie lying neatly on the music stand. The clock on the wall was shaped like a metronome, a gift from Beth last Christmas, and the second hand seemed to slow down. Between the passing of one second and the next, she relived every moment of her life with Charlie. Their three years together, loving each other, passed in the blink of an eye. Over and over, she saw the way Charlie looked at her when she said the three simple words that meant everything to her. And the way her heart ached with the pure beauty of it when she told her in return, I love you too.

The memories of Charlie bringing her tea in bed on a Sunday morning, how she would run her a bubble bath after gigs on a Friday night, the heat of which made her skin tingle. She replayed every moment they had touched, kissed, and held each other before the first tear slipped down her cheek. The afternoons out shopping, walking along the canal hand in hand and stealing kisses along the empty towpath. It wasn't enough. It could never be enough. She mourned each new memory they had yet to create, all of them forming in her mind's eye. Graduation, performances, arguments, making up, moving into a house, getting married, having children, watching them grow, their first steps, first tooth, first day at school, and every single day between now and growing old together. Everything life had to offer, she saw, she lived, in that single moment.

"You are our only chance, *Beti*. If we go to prison, they will make sure we cannot talk. They will kill us there behind bars." He looked at her and she felt her future washed away in the tears that fell down his cheeks.

*This is the family you want me to marry into? Men who would have my father and brother murdered. Men who peddle drugs across borders. Fuck!* The realization of where those drugs were coming from and exactly what they were supposedly a part of dawned on her. *Oh, Hatim, what have you done?*

She wanted to ask, but the words died in the back of her throat. She wanted to know, but the mere possibility terrified her. Horror stories that had formed part of her nightmares were coming true. She didn't want to think about the word that instilled such terror into her, and prayed she was wrong, that her fears were an overreaction to finally facing the future she had dreamed of escaping. But the look in her father's eyes told her she wasn't, and the terror blossomed in her chest like a mushroom cloud. Taliban.

"I'm sorry. I'm so, so sorry, Hazaar."

"It'll be okay, Baba. I won't let you go to jail for Hatim's stupidity."

Her breath was shallow as he pulled her into his arms and held her tight. "You are such a good girl, *Beti*. You make me so proud. His father wants him to learn English here and to know the business from this side. You will be staying here."

The promise didn't give her any hope. She felt stuck, like a song track that was jumping and kept on repeating the same few seconds over and over again.

She didn't have the strength to lift her arms and return the hug. She wanted to lie down. She wanted to put her head on Charlie's pillow and smell her shampoo, the face cream she put on each night, and finally the smell underneath it all that was her Charlie. She wanted to feel her in her arms again and never let go.

"It will be a good marriage, *Jugnu*. You will see." He pulled back and kissed her head.

She stared at him with unseeing eyes. How could he even think that? After everything he had just told her, after everything they both knew, how could he possibly believe that it could be a good marriage, a good life for her? She tried to focus on his face, and she saw that it wasn't her that he was trying to convince. It was himself. His body trembled as he held her and he repeated his lines over and over, the new mantra that he would use to persuade himself into believing, a prayer he cast to the heavens in the hope it would become reality. For them both.

"It'll be okay, Baba." *After lying to him for so long, why does that feel like the biggest lie I've ever told him?*

# CHAPTER NINETEEN

*The North of England, then*

Hazaar lay on her bed and pulled Charlie's pillow to her face. Her cheek stung from Hatim's blow where the cotton scratched the sensitive skin. She'd forgotten about it when her father had started to talk. Had it only been a couple of hours since she had cradled Charlie in her arms and felt the warmth of her skin under her fingertips? It felt like a lifetime ago. She didn't feel like she was even the same person. She had expected this day her whole life, and she had fully anticipated that this would be the end of her relationship with her family, that her refusal to agree would put them in such a position that their only option would be to disown her. She knew there were other more drastic courses of action out there, but her father loved her, and she knew he could never hurt her like that.

It was something she had thought about many times. Would her family kill her to restore their honour if she disgraced them? It had plagued her until she had watched the news reports of a seventeen-year-old girl, Shafilea Ahmed, being murdered by her parents for refusing an arranged marriage. Her father had been part of the council group who had pledged their aid in bringing the murderers to justice, and his reaction had instilled in her the confidence that her life would never be forfeit for her choices. Just the life she knew, the one she would choose for herself. *If not for Hatim, I wouldn't even have to give up that. Fucking idiot!*

She let the tears fall. She couldn't make that choice now. It was no longer about a decision to stay with Charlie and live a happy life with her, at the cost of her family connections and the faith and culture she had grown up in. Now it was about keeping her father and brother out of prison—keeping them alive. Could she trade their lives for her own happiness?

She knew, and had always known, that living the life of wife and mother to a man she had never even met would kill her a little every day, slowly bleeding her soul dry until there was nothing left of her. Everything that made her unique would be swallowed up by tradition, propriety, and duty.

She reached into the drawer beside her bed and pulled out a picture. She and Charlie faced each other with huge smiles on their faces, Charlie's dimples prominent, and she traced the line of Charlie's cheek. Beth had taken the picture at Charlie's birthday last year. They had all gone out to a restaurant, and Beth had even brought her new boyfriend.

Hazaar cried harder, great, body-wracking sobs. *Fuck, it's not supposed to be this way.* She hugged the picture to her chest. Charlie was meant to be her future. This was what she'd prepared herself for. Charlie's family were the family she expected to move forward with. It was their laughter she expected to get her through when she missed her father. Beth was the sister she would be closer to than she had ever been with her own, Sarah the mother who loved her children exactly as they were, without condition or expectation. But with one action, her father had taken all of that away from her.

"Happy ever after." She laughed through her tears. "Load of fucking shit."

She wanted to wrap her hands around Hatim's throat and squeeze. She wanted to see him grovel. *The little bastard knew exactly what was going on and he had the gall to hit me. He should have been crawling on his fucking belly begging me to save his worthless fucking life.*

She threw the picture across the bed, but it wasn't enough. She punched the pillow, flailed at the mattress, and then punched again, and again, and again. Over and over until the bed covers twisted around her body and trapped her legs. Her anger morphed, and fear took hold of her.

There was nothing she could do. Nothing. Hatim had condemned them all. Drugs. Taliban. Money. Prison. Death. Hers or theirs. That was her only choice. Hers or theirs.

She saw her hand touching the picture again, but she didn't remember picking it up. She couldn't feel it beneath her fingertips. She held Charlie's pillow to her face; she couldn't smell her anymore.

*How can I tell her? How the fuck do I tell the woman I love that I'm going to marry someone else?*

Hazaar tried to picture Charlie's face when she said the words, and the look of betrayal she saw in Charlie's eyes made her blood run cold. Her fingers felt like ice and she thought she'd never feel warm again.

*She won't stay. As soon as I tell her, she'll leave me.*

Hazaar knew the wedding would be several months away, and the thought of losing time with Charlie, any single moment that they could have together, hurt more than she thought possible. She didn't want to miss out on an hour of holding her, or one more night to kiss her, touch her, and make love to her. There was more than enough time for good-byes in the future. They had just six weeks left to the end of the academic year. Charlie's final assessments were coming up; she had to defend her doctorate thesis in two weeks. Her own future no longer mattered, but Charlie's did. Charlie was all that mattered.

*For fuck's sake, hasn't she been through enough?*

Hazaar cried for the pain Charlie had yet to suffer at her hands and wished she could spare her the tears she was sure to cry, the heartache she would endure. But for herself, Hazaar wouldn't have changed a thing. She would do it all again, suffer every pain, for the time they'd spent together.

She trailed a fingertip down the photograph again, decision made. She felt like she'd been told she only had a few months left to live, and she planned to enjoy every second. Just until after graduation. That was all she wanted, just a few more weeks. Was it too much to ask? With everything else she knew she'd have to face, was a little more time too much to ask for?

She looked at the ceiling. *Is this a good time to start praying?*

"Hey, baby, I'm heading home. I'll be there shortly. Do you want me to bring anything with me?" Charlie held the phone to her ear and pressed her finger to the other to drown out the street noises.

"No, baby, I just need you."

"Hazaar, are you all right? You sound really quiet."

"My dad and Hatim came for a visit."

"You okay?"

Hazaar laughed, but it sounded a little sad to Charlie. "I will be when I get to hold you again."

"Smooth talker. I'm on my way." She hung up and headed for the bus stop, dodging people coming up the steps at the university library.

She was home within twenty minutes and found the front room empty, so she headed for the kitchen, before finally finding Hazaar in the bedroom. She was curled on the bed with a pillow pressed to her face.

"Sweetheart, what's wrong?" Charlie climbed on the bed behind her, spooned herself against her back, and wrapped an arm around her waist. "What happened?"

"Hatim can't take a joke, it seems." She pulled the pillow away from her face to show Charlie the bruise across her cheek and the puffy eye already a deep blue. "My dad told him to leave. Dad told me that the business is in trouble and that they're both stressed."

Charlie softly probed the puffy cheek. "Let me get you some ice for that."

Hazaar grabbed her hand and kept her close. "In a minute."

"What else did your dad have to say then?"

"Nothing, why?"

"Well, it's a long way to go just to tell you that."

"Oh, well," she said, "they'd been to a meeting not far away so they just popped in."

Charlie stared at her. The words made sense, but Charlie felt there was something missing. "Nothing else you want to tell me?"

Hazaar smiled sadly. "No, baby."

She hated to think Hazaar was keeping something from her, but she refused to pry into Hazaar's family business.

"I'll go and get that ice now." She quickly gathered the supplies from the kitchen and went back to the bedroom. "I brought some painkillers too, sweetheart. I can't believe he hit you. What gives him the right—" She dropped everything on the bed when she saw Hazaar crying. "Oh, baby, I know it hurts." She wrapped her arms around Hazaar's shoulders. "Here, take these." She handed her the pills and a glass of water while she wrapped an ice bag with a towel and gently held it against her cheek.

"Thanks."

"I can't believe he did this to you. Little bastard."

"Charlie—"

"I know. I'm sorry." Charlie sighed. "I just hate that you're hurt. It's not fair." She moved the ice pack slightly and grimaced as Hazaar winced. "I'm sorry, sweetheart. I love you."

"I love you too, baby, with all my heart. So much it hurts sometimes."

"That's not good. I don't ever want to hurt you." Charlie smiled and shifted the pack on her cheek. Hazaar pushed the ice pack away and pulled her into a deep kiss.

"I love you so much." Hazaar's voice was thick and husky, and Charlie couldn't tell if it was desire or emotion that caused it.

Charlie frowned. "Hazaar, baby, what's wrong?"

Hazaar tugged at Charlie's clothes, her hands clumsy with desperation. "I love you so much, baby. I need you. Please. Please, just let me touch you."

She couldn't understand what was driving Hazaar or the speed with which Hazaar was moving, but her body responded effortlessly. Hazaar's passion pushed them both quickly toward climax, as their frantic hands caressed every inch of skin they could find while hungry mouths devoured pleas for release. Charlie shouted Hazaar's name as she came and stared into Hazaar's eyes, and the image of a deer popped into her head; a wounded deer, caught in a trap, eyes so soft and soulful that it made your soul bleed.

"I love you so much, Charlie. You are my life, my hope, and I need you to know that there is nothing—absolutely nothing—that I want more than to spend the rest of my life with you."

"I love you too, baby." *Why does this feel like good-bye?*

# CHAPTER TWENTY

*Pakistan, today*

"Charlie, do you have a minute?"

Charlie looked up and smiled at Kenzie. "Sure, take a seat." She pointed at the chair. "What's up?"

She waved a file. "I was looking into the case you gave me."

"The Atkin Chutani case?"

"That's the one. I've got some questions."

"Shoot."

Kenzie laughed. "That's not an invitation you should make to someone with a military background."

"Ha. Funny girl." Charlie held her hand out for the file. "Let me try that again. What are your questions?"

"Okay, I've got an address for this guy in Peshawar, but I can't find the boys registered at any school in the city. Would they be homeschooled?"

"Unlikely. Has the father remarried?"

"I can't find any record if he has."

"Check the newspapers. You may have more luck trying to find an announcement of the joyous occasion than an official registration."

"That's how you found information in your last case?"

"Yeah, it's a very useful way of finding information."

"Guess I'm gonna have to brush up on my Arabic reading skills then."

"Well, it won't hurt, but none of us have the time to pore over everything. Hillary set up a database of all the newspapers digitally." She twisted her laptop around so that Kenzie could see the screen and opened the search field. "Chutani isn't a common name, but you may still have a ton of records to go through." She clicked a few more buttons. "I've routed the results to your terminal. You can thank Hillary later for setting up the translation program that's embedded in this little beauty."

"I will. The woman's a genius."

"That she is." Charlie rearranged her computer and closed the program, a little uncomfortable under Kenzie's stare. "Do you have some more questions?"

"Tons of 'em."

Charlie laughed at the cocky grin on Kenzie's face. "Well, go ahead then."

"How long have you been doing this?"

"Almost three years now."

"How many cases have you worked on?"

"Actively?"

"Yeah."

"Last count was over three hundred."

"How many cases have you closed?"

"Personally, I've closed forty-three."

Kenzie looked baffled.

"I never consider a case closed unless the woman or child is back on English soil, regardless of how many times the husband or father refuses to listen. It only matters when it works."

"Don't you find that frustrating?"

Charlie laughed. "Oh, hell yeah. But things don't always change quickly, and I've learned that patience can be the greatest asset we have in this job." She leaned back in her chair and crossed her hands over her belly. "It may not sound like we have much success, but every single one makes me hungry for the next one. The little girl I brought home to her mother just yesterday, Horia? Just knowing that she'll grow up with a mother who loves her and has the chance at a future where she can be anything she wants to be makes every day that I spend frustrated more than worth it."

"How did you end up here?"

"In Pakistan or doing this job?"

"They aren't the same thing?"

"No. I started in Pakistan working as a visa coordinator."

"Doing what exactly?"

"Making decisions on visa applications. Granting or denying people access to the UK."

Kenzie frowned and shook her head. "Were you in negotiation before that or something?"

"Nope. I was a music student before that." She couldn't help but laugh at the look of confusion on Kenzie's face. "It was pretty much my first job out of university."

"So how did you go from music student, to working for the embassy on visas, to being the top negotiator in Pakistan?"

"Would you believe me if I told you it was a long story?"

"Erm, probably." Kenzie laughed. "I can't imagine it being a quick story."

"So, that being the case, it's probably not best covered on work time."

"Okay. How about dinner tonight then? I'll pick you up and we can go to the Ambassador Hotel." Kenzie winked, her smile spreading to a grin.

*Is she flirting with me?* "I don't think that's a good idea."

"Why not? Two colleagues grabbing a bite to eat, you telling me your long story, maybe a drink or two. What's wrong with that?"

"Well, when you put it like that, nothing, I guess."

"So where do I pick you up from?"

"Why don't we go straight from here? I've still got a little digging I want to do on this case." She pointed at the notes she was making on Maya's phone call. A niggling voice at the back of her head was badgering her about it. *Badgering? Hell, it's downright screaming at me.*

Kenzie shrugged. "Sure." She glanced at the clock on the wall and laughed. "A metronome clock. I should have guessed you were a musician."

Charlie shrugged. "It was a gift from my sister years ago."

"It's cute. So it's almost five now. Another hour? Or do you need more time?"

"That should do it."

"Okay, catch ya in a bit, boss lady." Kenzie stood with a fluidity and grace that made Charlie take a second glance.

"I'm not your boss. I'm just Charlie."

Kenzie turned at the door. "That's even better then." Kenzie's voice dropped in pitch and she smiled a crooked little grin. "Catch ya later, just Charlie."

*Flirting. Definitely flirting. Fuck.*

Charlie grabbed the phone and punched the number for Luke's

desk, pushing the thoughts of Kenzie out of her mind. In the past three years, she had learned to trust her intuition. It had kept her working cases long after others had told her to give up, and instead she'd gotten results. They'd also saved her life, so she trusted that gnawing feeling in her gut.

"Odoze's desk."

"Luke, it's Charlie."

"Hey, C, what's cooking?"

"Need a favour."

"Hit me."

Charlie laughed down the line. "You'll be shocked when I take you up on that, one day, Luke."

"Yeah, yeah. What do you want?"

"I had a call about an hour ago. It came through reception and the woman called herself Maya."

"You want the recording?"

"Yeah. And anything else you can get on the call. If you can get me the number and location, I'll love you forever."

"You do anyway, C." Luke laughed. "I'm on it. Is this a rush?"

"Quick as you can."

"Is this an open case?"

Charlie punched a few buttons on her computer. "It is now. Reference number MA2013."

"Got it."

Charlie hung up and started typing up her notes, including her suspicions that Maya wasn't the woman's real name, the fact that she said she was locked in the house, and that her daughter had been born in Pakistan. Her email pinged, and she opened the file attachment of the recording from Luke. She listened to the call, noting each pause in the woman's dialogue, every time she had started to speak normally and then reverted to a whisper. She heard the gasp at the beginning when Charlie had said her name.

*It can't be.*

She played it again, listening carefully to those whispered tones. She pulled her wallet from her pocket and fished out a picture that had been folded in half, worn down by the number of times it had been opened and closed over the years. She smoothed out the crease as she placed it on her desk. They faced each other, smiling, their foreheads touching, and their happiness and love for each other unmistakable.

"What are the chances of that happening, sweetheart?" she

whispered to the photograph. "What are the chances? Million to one? Maybe a billion."

The phone rang. "You're gonna love me, C."

"Already do, Luke, now spill it."

"I've got a number and an address on that landline. I'm emailing it over to you now. It's in the old city of Peshawar."

"Just like she said."

"Yeah."

Charlie waited for him to elaborate, tapping the edge of the picture against the wooden desk as she did so. "And?"

"I'm emailing the address to you now with a street map. It's totally in the maze, C. Anything else you need?"

"Not right now, thanks."

She looked at the picture again. Was she hearing what she wanted to hear? After almost four years, was she imagining that it was Hazaar's voice? A pause here and there could be caused by her listening for her husband coming home. It didn't mean that she was pausing because she recognized Charlie's name. Did it?

"Knock, knock." Kenzie leaned against the door frame. "You ready to go, just Charlie?" She smiled and her eyes lit up.

"I don't know—"

"Oh, come on. You can't just stay in here all night."

"I'm working on a case."

Kenzie threw her hands in the air. "Well, bring the file with you. We'll make it a working dinner. You are my mentor, after all."

"Yes, I am. That's why this isn't a good idea." Charlie slipped the photograph back into her wallet.

"What isn't?"

Charlie looked her in the eye and cocked an eyebrow. "You know exactly what I mean."

"Okay, I get it. You've made it clear. This is just a friendly dinner, Charlie. You have my word. Now can we please go and get some food?"

Charlie laughed. "Fine. You're buying."

"Yes, ma'am."

"Oh, God, you're going to be really annoying, aren't you?" Charlie pushed her chair away from the desk and grabbed the file as she stood.

"I have been told that on more than one occasion."

"Why am I not surprised?" She pushed Kenzie out the door. "I have a very long story to tell you. You want to drive?" She tossed her keys to Kenzie and pointed to the car. "I'll direct you."

"Direct me? The Ambassador Hotel is two minutes away in pretty much a straight line from here."

"Exactly." Charlie grinned as she got in the car. When they arrived, the waiter seated them and took their order for drinks before leaving them to look over the menu.

"So, you were going to tell me how you ended up in this job?" Kenzie sipped her beer.

"Well, I started working for the embassy straight out of university."

"How? I mean, how do you get to the embassy by doing music?"

"I guess you don't, really. I mean, they do try to recruit from a wide selection of the populous, but it isn't the usual route. I get that. But I speak Urdu and read Arabic. I started out translating documents after I graduated, and when I saw the internal advertisement for visa coordinator here in Pakistan, I applied."

"So you wanted to be in Pakistan?"

"Yeah."

"Why?"

Charlie laughed. "That's a whole other long story. Why don't I finish this one first?"

Kenzie shrugged. "Sure."

"I was working in the Karachi office. We'd deal with literally dozens of applications a day. Sometimes it was the same people applying again and again. Nothing on the form would change and the answer was always the same. We couldn't give them visas for perseverance alone, and I understand that it was frustrating for them. I do. All they wanted to do was go to the UK and work. They wanted a chance to earn a decent living, a chance at a better life. I do understand. But there has to be a line somewhere, and the rules are what they are. I was just putting them into practice."

She waited until the waiter put their plates down before she carried on. "One day, a man walked in. He'd been through the application system six times in the ten weeks I'd been there. He'd escalated his complaint higher up the chain, and he still wasn't having any luck. So he thought he'd try the sledgehammer approach."

"I hope you don't mean literally."

Charlie laughed. "Almost, but not quite. How's your steak?"

"Pretty good, thanks."

"So, he was at the security gate and he refused to walk through the metal detector. But instead of asking him to leave, the security guard was arguing with him." She shook her head remembering the smell of the wet paint that hung in the air from the overnight decorating the maintenance crew had done. The heat that was still oppressive, and she was drinking water like it was going out of fashion. "In the end, the guy pulled a gun from under his robe and shot the security guard."

"Shit. Did he make it?"

Charlie shook her head. "He killed three other people too, and then locked all the doors and windows. Some people had run out screaming already, but there were twelve of us in there with him."

She could see him just as clearly as if he was standing there with them now. Thin and wiry, not an ounce of fat on him, his turban wound around his head and his robes loose about his thin shoulders. The machine gun had looked so big in his hands. The air was filled with the scent of iron as blood pooled on the floor, and the sound of crying echoed off the bare walls. It wasn't until later that she realized that she'd been crying too.

"Were you hurt?"

"No, I wasn't, but my boss was. I had my hands over the wound in his chest and he kept telling me to just let him go."

"I take it all he wanted was his visa? Did you sign it to get rid of him?"

Charlie shook her head. "I talked to him. He didn't speak any English and no one else seemed to be able to understand him." She laughed. "They usually spoke better Urdu than me, but I think in the chaos they stopped thinking."

"Happens."

"Yeah. You must have seen that a lot."

Kenzie shrugged. "I saw a lot of things while I was with the army, but we're talking about you here. I'm sure we'll get round to me later."

"Nice deflection."

"Not that nice. You saw it. So you talked to him?"

Charlie laughed and took a sip of her drink. "Yeah, I talked to him. I couldn't really tell you what I said. We talked about his family, about his work. He was a blacksmith. He loved it too. When he talked about it, you could really see the pride and the love of it in his eyes."

"You got to know him."

"Yes. His daughter was sick. He wanted to go to the UK for medical treatment. By refusing the visa, we signed her death warrant. He couldn't afford treatment for her here." He had wept when he'd told her about his Jasmina, how she cried in pain and all she wanted was to sleep without the hurt waking her in the night. "He was desperate. That's all. In the end, I told him that he would get to see his little girl one last time if he gave up his gun and let everyone else go. I told him he could say good-bye to her." Charlie wiped the tear from the corner of her eye.

"What happened?"

"He put the gun down and opened the door. We'd been in there for three hours by that time. My boss, Mark, had passed away, and the others were in varying states of shock and distress." She sipped her drink again. "They took him into custody and dragged him off."

"Did he see his daughter again?"

"In a way."

Kenzie frowned. "What do you mean?"

"The little girl was too sick to go to the prison, and the police refused to let him go to the hospital. They said they couldn't maintain security there with all those people around. So I went to the hospital and took a picture of the little girl. The police were right, there was no way they could have done it safely, but I had to keep my promise. I had to stand by the agreement I'd made with him."

"And that's how you ended up here?"

"Jasper saw the security video of the negotiation." She laughed. "It wasn't really much of a negotiation, but he thought I had potential. He offered me a chance to train with the task force and teamed me up with Liam."

"It must have been pretty scary for you."

Charlie shrugged. "You know, it actually wasn't all that scary. I didn't really feel like he was going to shoot me at any point. I don't know why."

"You religious?"

"Nope."

"You believe in fate?"

She was about to laugh, but the thought stopped her. Did she? Was it fate that had put her in the right place at the right time to get that phone call this afternoon? Had everything been leading up to that moment?

"I didn't think so, but now I'm not so sure. Do you?"

"Fate, destiny, yeah, I believe in that. Sometimes I don't think there's any other way to explain some of the things I've seen. People surviving things that just don't seem possible, and people dying when it really looks like they should live." She finished her beer and signalled for another drink. Charlie could see the sadness in her eyes. There was a deep-seated sorrow that was built upon the scars of loss and pain. Charlie knew the look well. She saw it in the mirror each morning.

"So how does your story connect to this case?" Kenzie pointed to the file that Charlie had beside her.

"I'm not sure it does yet. It might, or I might just be hearing ghosts. But that's another long story for another night."

"But you said they were connected."

She shrugged. "I'm not sure yet. I need some more information. Besides, it's your turn now. How'd you end up here?"

"I signed up for the army at eighteen, passed the leadership test, and went to Sandhurst. I'd expressed an interest in intelligence. The various tests they put us through showed I had an aptitude for being persuasive and getting information out of people. They decided to train me to harness that knack."

"I bet you were good. How old are you?"

"Twenty-nine, and I'm very good." She grinned.

"You said you believe in fate, so you think you're supposed to be here?" Charlie saw the shadow pass over Kenzie's face.

"I saw a lot of things in Iraq and Afghanistan. But most of what I saw I can live with. Men killing each other for war's sake, casualties on both sides. I don't like it. I wish it didn't happen, but it does, and everyone fighting is a part of it. They've chosen to fight. What I can't live with, the part I can't get my head around, are the people who don't have a choice. The innocents who are harmed, not just through war, but through regimes like the Taliban that bring nothing but oppression and abuse to people. I think I'm here, or wherever I end up, to do something about that in whatever way I can."

"We all wish we could end those things, but what we're doing here isn't bringing an end to the suffering of innocents in war, or trying to change a regime that we don't like."

"No, I know that. But we're doing something. We're liberating some of the women and children to give them an escape from Islam, getting them out from under the bloody veil."

"Kenzie, Islam isn't to blame for the abuses you've witnessed. And if you think it is, then we have a problem here. Islam, the Quran, is like any other religion, twisted and warped by the men with the power to do so. But it's not bad in and of itself."

"So why do they make the women wear the *burqa*? That's oppression, plain and simple."

"To us. To us it's oppressive, damn straight it is. But not to many of the women who wear it. They wear it as a sign of respect, to their husbands, their culture, and their religion. Like many women in the West who wear a hat to church on a Sunday and men who wear a suit and tie. The Quran doesn't say that women are inferior to men. It preaches equality to a greater extent than the Bible does. Religion isn't the issue; it isn't to blame. It's used as an excuse and a justification, just like every other religion has been at different points throughout history. The real blame lies with the people in power. Parts of this country are progressive, forward thinking, and inclusive. Hell, they even had a female prime minister a few years ago. But outside the big cities, this country is run on tribal laws and customs that have been practiced for millennia. Women follow these conditions because they know only what they're told. Religion isn't the enemy. Ignorance is. And if you don't understand that, then you won't be able to work in this job."

"Is that how you excuse it? How can you sleep at night?"

"I don't excuse it, Kenzie, but neither am I deluded enough to think that one person is going to change a cultural mindset that spans the globe or the second largest religion in the world. As for sleeping at night?" She swallowed her drink. "What makes you think I do?"

"Women are stoned to death in the name of Islam. Hung from the goalposts in football fields because they weren't virgins when they married. It didn't matter that they'd been raped."

"I know all the horror stories, Kenzie. I've seen more than a few of them myself. But I will tell you again, the men doing that may have stated that it was in the name of Islam, but it wasn't. Think back on your Western history. How many women were burned at the stake as witches in the name of God? How many men and women were tortured by the Spanish Inquisition in the name of God? Does the Bible tell them to do that?" She shook her head. "No. It didn't stop pious men from taking what they found in there and twisting it to suit their own agenda. What's happening here is no different."

"That doesn't make it any better."

"I know that. But it doesn't make it any worse, either. There is no us and them. We're all just people, with different beliefs and different ideas. You need to work to understand the beliefs held by the people you're going to be working with if you want to be successful in this job."

"So you understand them?"

Charlie laughed bitterly. "Not always, but I try. I don't always get it right. I don't always get the results I want. I am a Western woman operating in a male-dominated Islamic society, which means I have to learn the meaning of the word *failure*. And so will you. But I don't think they're bad people just because they follow a religion I don't like."

"But how can you say they aren't bad? They beat women, kill them in the name of honour, kill them for adultery—"

"And you don't think we do that in the Western world?"

"No, we don't!"

"Think again. We just give it a different name. How many women in the West suffer from domestic abuse? How many men beat women simply because they're drunk?"

"I don't know. A lot, I guess. But it isn't sanctioned by the government."

"UK figures estimate around one point two million women suffered domestic violence in 2012. Approximately one in every four women."

"I'll bet it's higher in Pakistan."

"And you'll probably be right. But their government doesn't sanction that violence, either. They just don't work very hard to stop it. I'm not saying that Pakistan or Islam is better than what we come from. What I'm saying is that we aren't superior just because we put a different name on the abuses we visit upon people. What's the old saying about glasses houses and stones?"

Kenzie laughed. "Okay, okay. I get your point."

"Do you? Because if you don't, you aren't going to be able to do this job. Men here won't negotiate with a woman who looks down on them."

"Hey, I can't help being tall."

"I'm being serious."

"I know. I get it. How do you suggest I adjust my thinking?"

"Honestly?" Charlie sipped her drink while Kenzie nodded. "Read the Quran and talk to people."

"Read the Quran? Have you seen how thick it is?"

"Then get the *Reader's Digest* version, *York Notes*, *Islam for Dummies*, whatever. I don't care. But get to know where they're coming from. And talk to people. Get out there on the streets and ask questions. Ask women how they feel about wearing a veil. I guarantee their answers will surprise you."

"Yes, boss."

Charlie snorted a quick laugh. "And on that note, I think it's time for me to call it a night." Kenzie fished her card out of her wallet and wished her good night.

Charlie stepped out of the hotel. The smell of roses and jasmine hung in the air from the gardens across the street. She closed her eyes and breathed in deeply as she thought about fate and destiny. Did she believe? Did she dare? She tucked the file under her arm and climbed into the car, ready to see what fate had planned for her now.

# CHAPTER TWENTY-ONE

*The North of England, then*

Charlie rolled over and snuggled into Hazaar's arms. They'd spent the previous day travelling. Hazaar's surprise gift for their third anniversary was a getaway at a cottage in Drumnadrochit on the shores of Loch Ness, deep in the heart of Scotland.

"Baby, wake up." Hazaar shook Charlie's shoulder. "Come on, sleepyhead, the day's a wasting." Hazaar moved close and whispered in her ear. "Come on, baby. I have plans for this weekend."

Charlie finally opened her eyes. "You do, huh? Are you going to fill me in?"

"I thought we'd go and visit Urquhart Castle. Then I thought we could go and watch the sunset over the loch."

Charlie couldn't think of anything that sounded more romantic and decided it was the perfect setting for her to give Hazaar her anniversary gift. She couldn't resist the desire to have some fun with her, though. "But they have a Loch Ness Monster museum. Can we go? Please?"

"You're joking, right?" Hazaar's eyes opened wide as Charlie shook her head. "You really want to go and see a museum about a fictional creature?"

"They can't prove it's fictional."

"They can't prove it's real either."

"Come on. It could be fun."

"And if it isn't, that's hours of my life that I'll never get back."

Charlie squeezed her. "If that's the case, I promise to make it up to you."

"And how will you do that, baby?"

Charlie kissed her chest. "Any way you like." Hazaar's lips were hungry as they covered Charlie's.

"That's the kind of deal I can live with." She squeezed Charlie's arse as she kissed her again. "Come on then. If you want to go to this museum and make it to the castle for sunset, we don't have that much time."

❖

It was cold, but the day was clear and crisp. The chilly wind pinched their cheeks and noses even as the sun shone overhead on the short walk to the car.

"Are you sure about this? It's going to be really cold with the wind coming off the water."

Charlie wrapped her gloved fingers around the velvet box in her pocket and smiled. "I'm sure."

Hazaar shrugged. "I'm blaming you if I get hypothermia."

"I'll warm you up. Besides, this was your idea in the first place." She winked as Hazaar turned on the engine and drove them to the ruined remains of Urquhart Castle. Its profile stood in stark contrast to the infamous inky black waters of Loch Ness. The onetime stronghold of Scottish noblemen throughout the ages was now visited by millions of tourists marvelling at the histories of Robert the Bruce and Bonnie Prince Charlie. The eerie quality as the light faded and the sun set added to the ethereal sensation as they approached the ruins and walked around large fallen stones and grassy mounds hiding their secrets. The sheer beauty staring back at her as she looked across the lake made Charlie's breath catch in her throat.

"It's so beautiful."

Hazaar took hold of her hand and pulled her away from the stones toward the edge of the loch and spread a blanket out. Charlie sat and pulled Hazaar to her body, wrapping her arms around her. There was no one else around, and she luxuriated in being able to hold her lover on a whim, enjoying the simple freedom of not having to watch their every move. She reached into her pocket and pulled out the box.

"Happy anniversary, sweetheart."

Hazaar took the black box from her and slowly pulled it open. Resting on the small pillow was a beautiful silver nightingale pendant, its wings spread in flight and its mouth open in song. The detail of the feathers had mesmerized Charlie when she had first seen it, and she could see the same amazement on Hazaar's face now. She watched the emotions play across Hazaar's face. Surprise melted into elation before the shadow of something darker crossed her beautiful face.

"Sweetheart, what's wrong?"

The smile returned and tears tumbled down her cheeks. "Nothing. It's beautiful."

Charlie wiped the tears away and whispered, "It's okay. You don't have to wear it. I don't want you to get into trouble."

"No." Hazaar held it out to her. "Please put it on for me."

Charlie lifted the delicate bird from its pillow and unclasped the lock as Hazaar turned around and lifted her hair out of her collar. She draped the fine chain around her neck, closed the clasp, and gently brushed her fingers over the sensitive skin. "It's on a pretty long chain so you can keep it under your clothes if you need to."

Hazaar turned back to face Charlie, her fingers wrapped around the pendant as it sat on her chest. Hazaar's tears flowed down her cheeks even as she pulled Charlie to her.

The kiss bound their souls together as the sun kissed the water and disappeared for the day. But there was a sense of desperation in the kiss that was becoming familiar to Charlie, a sense that Hazaar was trying to remember and experience everything she could.

"I love you, Hazaar. You mean everything to me. I want you to know that I'm always here for you. If you need something, just tell me. If you want something, just ask. You are my world, sweetheart. My heart and my soul, they're yours."

"Take me home, sweetheart. I need to love you." Hazaar kissed her again before she led them up the hill to the car park as the last rays of the sun disappeared beneath the gentle waves of the loch. The air around them crackled as Hazaar drove them back to the cottage without ever letting go of Charlie's hand. She pushed the door closed behind them and tugged Charlie through the hall and into the bedroom before pushing her to sit on the edge of the bed.

Slowly, Hazaar undressed until she stood before Charlie wearing only the pendant. The silver metal gleamed in the light as she moved. The first kiss was gentle and slow, a tender expression of love.

"You are so beautiful, Charlie. I love you so much."

Hazaar's tongue fluttered across her lips and Charlie's breath caught in her throat tearing a deep moan from her. She could feel Hazaar smile against her lips at the wanton sound and she worked to quickly strip Charlie of her clothes, pressed her back to the bed, and covered her body with her own. Charlie wrapped her legs around Hazaar's hips, threaded her fingers through her hair, and pulled her down for another kiss. The cool metal touched her chest as it hung from Hazaar's neck.

Their bodies rocked together, their hands exploring, touching, and teasing each other.

"Look at me." Hazaar lifted slightly and stared at Charlie's face. "Baby, look at me. I need to see your eyes."

Charlie had lost count of the number of times Hazaar had whispered those words to her, and as ever, it took all she had at that moment to open her eyes. Hazaar was staring straight at her. Her pupils were wide, desire and love reflected in equal measure.

"Keep looking at me. I want to see your eyes when I make you mine, baby."

She slid her hand between their bodies and slipped her fingers slowly into Charlie's sex. Charlie groaned and fought to keep her eyelids from closing.

"I'll always be yours."

Hazaar looked away for a second and wiped her face against her arm.

"What's wrong? Please tell me," Charlie asked.

Hazaar moved her arm again, pumping her fingers into Charlie. "Nothing's wrong, baby, just a hair in my eye." She licked Charlie's nipple, then pulled it between her lips. "Now, keep looking at me, baby." She twisted her hand so that her thumb connected with Charlie's clit on each stroke.

Charlie felt her body tighten and the tendrils of pleasure burned through her until she couldn't keep her eyes open any longer and her orgasm claimed her.

"Baby, I love you so much. I can't lose you."

Charlie wrapped her arms tighter about Hazaar and tried to catch her breath. "I love you too, sweetheart. You aren't going to lose me. I told you. I'm yours." She looked up and saw the tears in Hazaar's eyes. "I'm not going anywhere."

"Charlie—"

"I love you. I plan to be with you always."

"Charlie, stop."

"Marry me?" She hadn't planned to ask. Not now, not ever, but as the words left her lips, she knew she had been holding them back for so long that they had been eating at her. She wanted to make a plan for their relationship after they finished university, to figure out how they would stay together when their convenient excuse was no longer available. The future had been so shaky that she couldn't see it as she looked forward, but voicing the question had set her free. She knew this was exactly what she needed. It was the commitment that she craved to go forward.

Hazaar froze. "What?"

"You heard me. Marry me? I love you, Hazaar. I want you to be in my life. Now, tomorrow, forever. Whatever. Just be with me. Be my wife."

"I can't." The tears fell from her eyes and dripped onto Charlie's skin. Hazaar dropped her head to Charlie's shoulder. "I'm so sorry. I can't."

Charlie wiped her tears away, but Hazaar could see that she was battling to hold her own at bay. "I'm sorry. Forget I said that." Her voice caught in her throat, and even though she smiled, Hazaar could see how much she had hurt her. She knew she needed to give Charlie an explanation, she owed her that much, but she didn't know how to say the words. She didn't know how to tell her that her future had been decided and that Charlie had no place in it. She pulled a deep breath into her lungs and tried to calm her racing heart. She knew she had no choice anymore. She had to tell Charlie and let her make the decision on the amount of time they would have left together.

"It's my father…" Hazaar started, and the words deserted her.

"What about your father?" Charlie frowned.

"He's set a date."

"Sweetheart, I don't understand." Charlie stroked her back and waited patiently for her to calm enough for her to speak. "What are you talking about?"

Hazaar licked her lips, trying to wet them enough to be able to say the words. She couldn't look at Charlie. She didn't want to see her own pain reflected in those blue eyes. It was too much. "My father has picked my husband."

Charlie's hands stilled, and Hazaar felt time stand still. The racing heart that had thundered in her ears seemed to stop beating.

"When?" Charlie's voice was little more than a croak.

"As soon as graduation is over."

"I meant, when did you find out?"

Hazaar sucked in a deep breath. "The day my dad and Hatim came to visit—"

"The day Hatim hit you?"

"Yes."

"Why didn't you tell me then?" The anger was evident in her voice, and Hazaar's fear grew.

"I wanted to spend the rest of the time I have left, with you."

"The rest of the time you have left? Don't be so melodramatic. You make it sound like you're dying, not getting married."

"I'm sorry. I just wanted to be with you for as long as possible."

"So why are you telling me now?"

"What do you mean?"

"It's been a month, Hazaar, and we've still got another couple of weeks until finals. So why are you telling me now?"

"When you asked me to marry you, I couldn't…"

Charlie wiggled out from underneath Hazaar and climbed out of the bed. She grabbed a shirt from the drawer and pulled it over her head.

"Baby, please don't go." Hazaar knelt on the bed and let the covers pool around her body.

"Go?" Charlie turned around quickly and she stared at her. "Go? Where would I go, Hazaar? We're in the middle of fucking nowhere!" Hazaar faltered under the anger that emanated from Charlie's normally calm and unshakeable demeanour. She fell back and leaned heavily against the headboard. "Is that why you brought me here? Why you decided to tell me here? So that I've got nowhere else to go to?"

"I didn't plan to tell you here."

"Oh, so you were going to continue to keep this from me."

"No. I was always going to tell you. I was. I just didn't know when. I didn't know the best way to do it. I just didn't know how."

"Am I so hard to talk to?"

"No. I just didn't know the best way to do this." Hazaar's voice faded. She knew that everything she said sounded cowardly, a lame excuse and a terrible way to treat the woman she loved, and she knew that nothing she could say would undo the hurt she had caused by maintaining her silence as she had.

"Best way? You think there's a good way to tell someone something like this?"

Hazaar shook her head. "No."

"Then why wait? Why didn't you tell me?"

"I didn't want to hurt you."

Charlie's laugh was bitter and hollow sounding in her ears. "You think this doesn't hurt?"

Hazaar shook her head and let it fall to her chest as tears rolled down her cheeks and down onto her bare breasts. "I'm so sorry, baby. I just couldn't get the words out. I just wanted to ignore it and let it all go away."

"This isn't going to go away, Hazaar."

"I know."

"You've been running away from this your whole life. Now you're out of time." She shook her head, her blond curls bouncing about her shoulders as she sat heavily at the foot of the bed. "There's nowhere left to run." She stood and paced around the room.

"It wasn't going to be like that."

"No?" Charlie stared at her, and the twisted look of disbelief felt like a knife through Hazaar's gut.

"No."

"You're going to stay with me? Is that what you're saying?"

"That's what I wanted. I saw the future with you and me growing old together." She longed for Charlie to reach out and hold her, comfort her and try to make it all go away.

"Then why did you say you won't marry me?"

"Because I can't."

Charlie slammed her hands against the wardrobe door. The loud bang made Hazaar jump.

"Fuck." Charlie took a deep breath and visibly tried to calm herself down. "We both knew this was coming. You tried to warn me from day one. This isn't a surprise." She pushed her fingers through her hair. "The one thing I asked you to do was to be honest with me. To keep me in the loop with what was going on." Charlie swiped angrily at her tears. "Why couldn't you do that for me?"

"It wasn't going to be like that. This last year, living with you, I knew that was the future I wanted. I was going to tell them no. I was going to refuse the marriage when he told me."

"Then why didn't you?"

Hazaar paused. Could she tell her the truth? Could she tell her all the sordid details she knew and watch Charlie beat herself up over it all again? She knew the guilt Charlie still carried over Gail's death, and she knew that Charlie blamed herself for something that wasn't her fault. She couldn't burden her with more worries. The pain of leaving her was more than enough. She shook her head and went with the only truth she knew. "I'm scared."

"Of what?"

*Everything.* Hazaar opened her mouth to speak, but the words didn't come.

"What are you scared of?"

*Losing the only person who's ever loved me for who I truly am.* Hazaar still couldn't get the words out of her mouth.

"Of your father? Your brother?"

"No."

"Then what?"

"You don't understand. My family have—"

"What? Expectations? Traditions? Will disown you if they find out? Will they be mean to you? Will your family be as cruel as Gail's father was? Will your father beat me? Will he try to kill you?" They both shook as Charlie's raised voice echoed through the room. Her fists shook at her sides, and Hazaar knew she was fighting back the memories.

Hazaar shook her head. "No."

"Do you want to know what I think, Hazaar?"

"What?" Hazaar's voice cracked.

"I think you're scared for yourself. You're terrified to tell them the truth and see what the consequences will be. And you know what?"

Hazaar started to shake her head and then stopped. Charlie needed a reason. She needed some sort of explanation, and the truth would only make her want to save her. Charlie would do whatever was necessary to ensure her safety, and Hazaar couldn't let her do it. She couldn't keep her tethered any longer. So instead she kept quiet. *Better she believes I'm a coward and that I won't fight for her, for us. Let her blame me.*

"It's okay to be scared. It's okay to worry about how they'll react. It's okay to be scared that you'll lose your family, that they won't speak to you again." Charlie sat on the bed and slowly reached for her hand. "I understand being afraid of all of that. But what you choose to do now, that's your decision. Yours. Not your father's, not your brother's, not mine. It's yours. I will support you in any way I can, in any way you want me to. But you have to make your peace with this decision in a way that you can live with for the rest of your life."

"I know." *Oh, Charlie, baby, that's what I'm trying to do.*

"You know me, Hazaar. You know I love you and that I will spend every moment of every day for the rest of my life proving that to you.

I want you to stay with me. I want to marry you. I'll be everything for you. But you have to want that too, you have to choose me. Here and now, Hazaar. Here and now, you have to tell me that you want me too. That you love me just as much. If you can't, if you choose to do what your father wants and marry this man, I will cherish every moment we've had and wish you happiness…" Her tears fell, her voice cracked and trailed away. "I love you so much, Hazaar. So much that I love you enough to let you go." She wiped the tears from her cheeks and held Hazaar's face in her hands. "If that's what you want." She kissed her lips softly. "But I love you enough to stay with you for the rest of my life, if you want me." She pulled Hazaar into her arms and held her tight. "I love you."

"I don't want to lose you."

"Then choose me."

"It's not that easy."

"It really can be, Hazaar. It really can be that easy. Just tell me you love me."

"I do love you."

"And that you want to be with me."

"I do. But this isn't my choice."

"It *is* your choice, Hazaar. I belong to you."

"I'm sorry." She kissed Charlie's lips, memorizing the softness of them, revelling in the way they parted beneath her own. She seared each microsecond into her brain as she held Charlie in her arms for what she knew would be the last time. When Charlie finally pulled away she traced her fingertips over Hazaar's eyebrows.

"You can choose me, Hazaar. I'll never let you down."

"I can't. I wish it could be any other way."

"Please don't throw me away. Don't give up on us." She stroked Hazaar's cheek. "Please." Charlie kissed her gently. "I can't beg forever. I just can't."

"I don't want you to beg."

"Then I'll ask, one last time." She knelt in front of Hazaar on one knee and brought her hand to her lips. "Would you please make me the happiest woman in the world, and be my wife?"

One word. One single word would change her future. Everything in her screamed at her to say yes. To kiss Charlie, and make love to her, and live happily ever after. One single word. Three little letters would make it all possible. One single word she couldn't live with herself if she spoke. She couldn't condemn her father to death. Not for the sake of her own happiness.

"No."

Charlie looked away, and it was obvious she was holding back more tears. "Then I can't stay."

"Charlie, we're in the middle of nowhere."

"I don't care." Charlie threw her belongings into her bag, pulled on clothes, and was out the door within minutes.

Hazaar didn't blame her, and as much as she wanted to go after her, she knew that letting her go was the best thing for them both. She curled into a ball in the middle of the bed. She had no tears left to cry; the pain was too great. And all she had left to keep her warm were her memories.

# CHAPTER TWENTY-TWO

*Pakistan, today*

Hazaar shivered on the cold concrete. She ignored it and closed her eyes, desperate for a little sleep, but the infernal dripping was driving her mad. She wished she knew where it was; she was thirsty, and every drip reinforced the need for water. She licked her lips and shouted, "Amira." Her voice cracked, and the raspy call didn't sound like her own. "Amira, please." She coughed. "I need water."

She heard footsteps and voices outside the door, but she couldn't make out what they were saying. She coughed and licked her lips again. Her tongue felt swollen, stuck to the roof of her mouth, and coated in the coppery tang of dried blood.

"Amira, I need some water, please."

The door handle rattled, like someone was trying to make it turn. She tried to roll onto her side to see who was coming in, but the pain in her shoulder reminded her it wasn't a good idea.

The rattling stopped and footsteps headed away from the door.

"Amira, please, no. Don't leave. I just need some water." She stretched her hand out toward the door. "Please come back."

She stared at her hand. Her nails were chipped and broken from her fall, the skin was torn, and the fingers were badly misshapen, whether from the fall or from Tazim's manhandling, she didn't know, and she didn't really care. She wished she had something for the pain. And some water to drink. She was lying against the wall farthest from the door. The door was at the top of a flight of stairs, and she was at least twelve feet from the base of the stairs. It may as well have been miles, for all that she could consider moving.

She laughed at herself. *I'm losing it.* She laughed harder. "Nope.

I've already lost it, never mind losing it." She laughed harder and grimaced as the pain in her shoulder and ribs doubled her over and brought fresh tears to her eyes.

She placed a hand to her chest and felt her pendant lying above her heart. "I miss you." Tears welled in her eyes, but she refused to let them fall. She'd cried enough for the mistakes she'd made, and right now she needed to think.

The door handle rattled again.

"Amira, please, I just need some water."

"Water? Is that all you want, Hazaar?" It wasn't Amira who spoke.

"Abu, please?"

"Please, what?"

Hazaar didn't know what to say. She didn't know what would anger him further and chose silence as her best option.

He carried a chair down the stairs with him and placed it in the middle of the small, dark room. "Sit."

"I can't. Please, Abu. It hurts too much to move. I need a doctor."

"I said sit." He grabbed her injured arm and yanked her to her feet, throwing her against the chair in one fluid, excruciating movement. Hazaar couldn't stop the scream that was ripped from her throat, and she fought to stay conscious. Black spots swam before her eyes, and bile rose in her throat.

"We shall talk now, you and I, Hazaar. I am going to ask you some questions. Do you understand me?" It was all she could do to nod her agreement as he paced around her in a circle. She tried to focus on him, but it was too much. The circling reminded her of vultures circling a dying animal, waiting, watching, biding their time before they swooped upon the carcass to feast with cruel talons and savage beaks. "And you will answer every question. Do you understand me?"

She nodded and a blow caught the back of her head, and her dizziness increased.

"I said, do you understand me?"

"Yes." She let her head fall to her chest.

"On the phone at lunch time, who were you talking to?"

"I wasn't—"

The blow to her shoulder caused her to vomit as the pain shot through her body. "Who were you talking to?"

"I don't know what you're talking about."

"It was only a few hours ago, Hazaar. Just this lunch time, and

I know you pride yourself on what a clever girl you are. So let's not pretend. Once more, who were you talking to, and before you lie to me again, I want to tell you that I have checked who the call was made to. I rang the number myself."

"Then why are you even bothering to ask?"

"So that I know just how much of a lying whore you really are."

She looked up at him, and she knew there was no way he was going to let her out of the cellar alive. Her answers, no matter what they were, wouldn't change that. She had no chance of convincing him that she was innocent, because she wasn't and they both knew it. The only thing her answers could affect was her daughter's future. She needed to give her the chance at the best possible future she could have. And if there was any way possible to hasten the end of her own misery, well, that would be a bonus.

"I was calling the British Embassy, my wonderful Abu." She sneered at him.

"Insolent bitch." He slapped her hard across the face and her eyes watered. "Did they tell you that they can do nothing for you? Did they tell you that you are his wife and there is nothing, not one single thing, that they can or will do about it?"

She licked the split on her lip and spat the blood onto the floor beside her. That didn't exactly match what Charlie had said, but for the time being it amounted to the same thing. They couldn't help her until she could get out of here and make a formal request for help. "That's what they told me."

The spreading grin on his face told her she had said the right thing. She wanted to laugh. *There's a first time for everything after all.*

"And so now you are stuck here. With my son. With me."

She watched the grin on his face turn to a leer and her skin crawled. She had always hated the way he watched her. It made her feel dirty, and today was no exception. She wanted to ask where Yasar was. If it had been hours since she had been in the cellar, why wasn't he home?

"You are truly a filthy whore, aren't you? Charlie, my love." He mimicked her voice. "The idea, the thoughts, those words put into the heads of good men. Putting temptation in the paths of good Muslim men with your Western, bastardized ideas of what a good Muslim woman should be." He squatted in front of her and lifted the hem of her dress till it rested on her knees. "My boy should have been the only man to see these legs." She tried to push him away as he stroked her calf. "He should have been the only man to touch this skin."

"Stop it." She slapped at his hand as he caressed her knee. "Until this very second, no man but your son has ever touched me."

He grabbed her hand and squeezed. The bones in her broken fingers grated together and the nerves burned. Fire spread through her hand and up her arm, and she couldn't think anymore. She may have begged, pleaded, bartered for mercy; she had no idea. The tears she had tried to hold back ran freely down her cheeks, and she didn't care.

"You tell me there was no man before my boy, yet you call out for Charlie. You love Charlie. I heard you with my own ears." He let go of her hand and she pulled it to her chest, trying to cradle her mangled hand, but her injured shoulder only added to her pain. When she looked down, she could see bones sticking out of thin flesh of her middle and index fingers.

"I have known no man but Yasar."

"You are a liar."

"I'm telling the truth." He grabbed the hair on top of her head and yanked back sharply, wrapping his hand about her throat and squeezing, slowly applying pressure to her windpipe and cutting off the flow of blood to her brain.

"You're getting boring now. So I'm only going to give you one last chance, Hazaar." He increased the pressure a little more. "If you don't tell me about this Charlie of yours I am going to tighten my fist." He flexed his fingers to emphasize his point. "I am going to do it slowly. Very slowly. I'm going to squeeze until all the blood vessels in those pretty eyes of yours burst and the whites turn blood red." He leaned in closer to her, and she could make out the spittle gathered at the corner of his mouth, the smell of garlic on his breath from the curry he had eaten at dinner making her stomach churn. "I'm going to keep squeezing until you pass out." He tightened his fingers. "Just." They tightened a little more and the spots swam in front of Hazaar's eyes. "Like." Her vision blurred, and she could feel the pulse pounding in her neck against his obstructing fingers. "This." Her pulse pounded as death came calling. The black of his pupils began to spread, eclipsing first the dark brown irises, then the whites of his eyes and quickly spreading until black was all she could see.

❖

"Wake up."

The water was cold and shocked her back to awareness for the third time. Her dress was drenched and clung to her body. She was shivering; she could see it in her hands, hear it when her teeth chattered, but she couldn't feel the cold. All she felt was disappointment to be awake and facing him once again.

"Tell me about your man Charlie."

"There was no man."

"Don't make me do this again, Hazaar." He wrapped his hand around her throat again. She could feel the bruises under his fingers, tender and aching as he began to press. "Soon even this added entertainment will become boring."

"I'm telling you the truth, Abu. There was no man." He started to squeeze. "I always knew you were a truly evil bastard." Her throat closed beneath his fist, and she almost wished that this time she wouldn't wake up. She smiled as the blackness began to envelop her.

"No." He let go of her neck. "Oh no, you don't get what you want, Hazaar." He tapped her cheek as she automatically sucked a great lungful of air into her body. "No, you will answer my questions. You will tell me what I need to know." He threw some old rags into a pile on the dirt floor and grinned as he set them alight. She stared at him as he crouched on the other side of the flames. His face twisted in a lopsided sneer shadowed evilly by the licking flames.

"You think you're some sort of avenging messiah, Abu, torturing me, for what? The honour of your family? Pride?" She laughed. "You are a devil. Sitting there across the fires of hell. And that's where you think you'll send me? Is that right, Abu? You want to send me to hell?"

"It's the only place you deserve to be, you filthy whore." He grabbed hold of her ankle and pulled her foot toward the fire. "Who is Charlie?"

"No, no. Please, don't do this. Please. Please."

"Tell me who he is!"

There was no way out. There was no escape, no release, no second chance. She could continue to deny Charlie and go to her grave with the heaviest weight she could imagine burdening her soul, or she could finally set it free. Time seemed to slow down as she fought him trying to hold her foot over the growing flames. She could smell the acrid odour of burnt hair and knew that the tiny hairs on her skin and his hands were being sacrificed. She closed her eyes and imagined her greatest fantasy as the flames kissed the sole of her foot. She pictured her daughter laughing as she ran down the grassy bank to the edge of the water at Loch Ness. She watched as Charlie scooped her into her arms and spun her in the air as the odour of burning flesh began to overpower the damp smell of the cellar. She saw Afia put her little chubby baby hands on Charlie's cheeks and plant wet kisses on her face. She heard herself scream as the heat on her foot went cold and spread across her flesh. It felt as though the only choices she'd had up to now had been trying to decide between the lesser of two evils.

"If this is the way it's going to be, then I will be true to myself. There is no sin in who I love. I love Charlie. There is no evil in this room but you, Abu." She yanked her foot from him and the chair fell backward to the ground, making her scream as her shoulder hit the concrete. "I have known no man but Yasar—"

"Still you lie." He towered over her.

"Charlie isn't a man." She struggled to her knees and faced him. "Charlie is a woman. She was my lover, my best friend, and the love of my life." She pulled the nightingale pendant from beneath her clothes. "I was ready to give up my family for her. Just to be with her. Then Hatim got involved with you." She laughed in his face. "I had to choose to save my father and brother, or stay with Charlie. I chose wrongly."

"A woman? Charlie was a woman?"

Hazaar sniggered. "Yes, Charlie's a woman. Short for Charlotte." He stared at her incredulously.

"An amazing, incredible woman, in fact."

Abu stared at her, then at his hands. "You have lived in my house. You have touched my son. Touched me. You are an abomination." He stared at her and then back at his hands. "You have brought shame to my family."

"What shame have I brought, Abu? No one knows."

"Allah knows."

"And you think he cares?"

"Yes!" His face was red and blotchy. "You have disgraced me. My son. All of us. You…you…you…whore!"

She laughed at him. "Is that the best you can do? Whore?"

He grabbed the pendant at her neck and tore it from her. "The best I can do is reclaim my family's honour. You will pay for the crimes you have committed."

"The only crime I have committed was to give up Charlie. That was my crime. And my punishment has been the prison you have held me captive in for all these years."

"You and your perversion will be cleansed from this earth." He held the silver bird in his fist and shook it in front of her face. "I will send you to the fires of hell." A smile spread over his face as he said it. "I will even start the fire for you myself." He opened his palm and held the bird by his fingertips. "A nightingale, no?" He tossed the pendant into the remains of the fire smouldering on the dirt floor.

　　She didn't speak. She didn't have to. They both knew.

# CHAPTER TWENTY-THREE

*The North of England, then*

"For God's sake, smile," Charlie's mother said. "Contrary to popular belief, Charlie, it won't crack your face. It's your graduation, remember? You know, the big day you've been working toward for the past three years." She tugged on the shoulder of the black dress robe and adjusted the hood slightly.

Charlie tried to shrug her off. "Mum, stop fussing. It's fine."

"Mum, whatever you do, don't lick your handkerchief and wipe her face." Beth bumped shoulders with Sarah and grinned.

"I'd never do that," her mother said as she stuffed the cotton-and-lace square back into her pocket.

Charlie chuckled. "Old habits die hard, hey, Mum?"

"Yup." She wrapped her arms about Charlie's shoulders. "I am so proud of you."

"Thanks, Mum."

"Now, go join your class and get your diploma. Your dad's already found us seats. I love you."

"Love you too."

"Hey, Charlie." Beth pulled her into a tight hug. "Will she be there?"

Charlie shrugged. "Probably."

"Well, if she is, remember one thing for me, okay?"

"What?"

"Regardless of the decision she made, she loves you."

"Well, she's got a funny way of showing it."

"Charlie, I know you're angry, and you have every right to be, but you know as well as I do that she loves you. She will always love you, and one day she's going to realize that she made a huge mistake. All we can do is hope that she realizes it sooner rather than later."

Charlie tried to pull away.

"No. Remember she loves you, and she's going to be hurting too. If you see her, if you have to talk to her or anything, remember that and don't do anything to make the hurt worse. For either of you."

"Thanks for the pep talk, Flipper." Charlie pulled away.

"Go ahead, mock. It won't make you feel any better if you do."

Their mother took hold of Beth's hand. "Come on."

Charlie watched them go and realized she was seeing Beth in a new way. Gone was the gangly, awkward teenager, and in her place was a beautiful young woman of whom Charlie was immensely proud. As much as she joked, she knew Beth was right, and as angry and hurt as she felt, she knew that doing anything to hurt Hazaar would only make her feel worse. She turned around and tried to avoid looking at anyone, because the only face she saw on campus was Hazaar's. It didn't matter who she was talking to, her professors, classmates, even the woman in the cafeteria, all she saw was Hazaar.

She'd loved her time at university. Loved the classes, her friends, the sense of freedom she'd found in the music, but now all she wanted to do was be away from the buildings that reminded her of everything she had lost.

The woman who had mended her heart, only to shatter it against the pillars of faith, duty, honour, and expectation would be in the auditorium; she had no doubt about it. It was Hazaar's graduation too. *One of her last days of freedom.*

Charlie shook her head. *It was her choice.*

She drifted through being lined up and led into the auditorium. She fidgeted on the uncomfortable seat through speeches she didn't hear, and the procession of students crossing the stage and receiving their scrolls. Hands were shaken, photographs taken, and smiles spread across every proud face. Charlie was at the edge of the stage when she finally saw her sitting on the front row. She was so surprised that she missed the first step and almost fell. She caught herself in time, but the motion had drawn attention to her. Hazaar looked at her and their gazes locked.

Hazaar's eyes glistened with unshed tears, and Charlie wanted desperately to wipe them away and comfort her. She wanted to run from the stage, take her in her arms, and make everything right again. It was a fantasy, and she knew it. It was a dream she could never have again, and it cleaved her heart in two when she saw the tears track down Hazaar's cheeks.

Charlie knew she was moving across the stage; she could feel her body moving, but she couldn't tear her gaze from Hazaar's. She didn't want to. If this was the last moment they were to have together, she didn't want it to end. She didn't ever want to have to say good-bye or admit it was truly over. She didn't think she could do that. She didn't think she was strong enough to survive losing her heart again.

But she could see it. It was there in Hazaar's beautiful, weeping, chocolate brown eyes. Love. It was still there, shining like a beacon, calling her to safety, calling her home.

"Charlotte Porter, congratulations." The dean held the scroll out to her with one hand, and the other waited for her to shake as he pulled her attention from Hazaar.

"Thank you." She shook quickly, smiled for Beth's camera, and fled the stage as quickly as she could. When she reached the foot of the stairs, she looked back to see Hazaar, to look into her eyes again, to feel alive again.

The chair was empty.

## CHAPTER TWENTY-FOUR

*The North of England, then*

"Do you know the young man's name yet, Hazaar?"

"I'm sorry, what was that, Auntie?" Hazaar smiled at the older rotund woman. Hana Shallam had been her mother's best friend for as long as Hazaar could remember.

"Keep your arms up, child." She pushed Hazaar's arms higher and tucked a pin into the fabric at her wrist. "I asked if you knew his name yet."

"Oh, yes." Hazaar frowned and faced front as her mother twisted her head.

"Keep still," her mother said.

"Ow." She arched her back as the pin her mother wielded dug into the skin between her shoulder blades.

"I told you to keep still."

"Sorry, Maa Jee."

"So? Who is he?" Hana finished tacking the sleeve and moved to the other side. "I go away for a few weeks, I come back, and she is being married off." She shook her head slightly, and Hazaar knew what she was thinking. She smiled. It normally took around twelve months to make all the proper preparations for a good wedding, and trying to do so in the few weeks they had usually meant that the bride-to-be was in trouble. Hazaar wanted to laugh at the thought. *I am in trouble, just not the I'm-pregnant-so-I-have-to-marry-the-stupid-bastard kind of trouble.*

"Yasar Siddiqi. He and his parents flew in from Peshawar yesterday."

"Hmm." She tucked some pins between her lips and spoke around them. "Not a local family then, Nisrin."

"No. They are a good Pakistani family, Hana. It is a good match and good for the business. It will bring good things for Hatim's future as well as Hazaar's."

Hazaar let the conversation revolve around her, moving as they directed, holding her arms up, straight out, to the sides while they adjusted the wedding dress her mother had made for her over the past weeks. The rich red silk and gold trim wrapped around her body like a boa constrictor moving in for the kill. She feared one wrong move would cause it to crush her.

"Ay, ay, ay. No." Hana rubbed a scrap of cloth over Hazaar's face. "No crying. You will stain the silk."

Hazaar hadn't even noticed the tears. "I'm sorry."

Hana smiled gently at her. "Don't worry. All brides are a little nervous. It's natural, but don't worry. Everything will be fine."

Hazaar nodded and let them continue with their task, barely noticing when they pricked her with a needle on occasion, so deeply was she immersed in her own thoughts. As much as she tried, she couldn't stop herself from thinking about Charlie. She couldn't focus on the fast-paced wedding preparations. She knew that the marriage contract had been drawn up and agreed to by the fathers of both the groom and the bride, which meant that the bride price had already been negotiated and agreed upon. She wanted to laugh. *I wonder how they're going to discreetly present me with bribed officials and heroin?*

So much of the normal buildup had been forsaken in the speedy preparations. The proposal party and the official engagement party had both been sacrificed. And rather than months, they had but a few weeks. A few weeks that were almost over. In two days, she would have to sign the contract and sit through the celebrations that would go on around her. She would have to endure all that came after that. In just two more days.

"Are you ready for tonight, child?"

Hazaar turned to Hana. "I'm sorry. What was that, Auntie?"

Her mother slapped her lightly on the shoulder. "Pay attention, *Beti*. Anyone would think the plans for your wedding were boring you." She laughed gently.

"I'm sorry. Daydreaming, I guess."

"I said are you ready for tonight? For the Mehndi?"

"Oh." Hazaar shrugged, then flinched as her mother's pin found the tender skin of her lower back. "Ow."

"Keep still. I wouldn't have to make such adjustments if you hadn't lost so much weight, *Beti*."

"I'm sorry, Maa Jee."

"So what time are they arriving?" Hana smiled.

"The Siddiqis are arriving at six." Her mother pulled the zipper down on the dress. "Step out, Hazaar."

Hazaar did as she was bidden and wrapped the robe Hana passed her around her body.

"Is it a large party attending with her, Nisrin? Would you like some help with the preparations?"

"Hana, my friend, I would, but the party will not be a large one. I would be honoured if you would also attend to help with the henna ceremony tonight."

Hana beamed with pride. "It would be my pleasure and an honour." She took the dress from her mother's hands. "This will take me barely a few minutes to adjust, then we can make our preparations." She turned to Hazaar and kissed her cheek. "We will make you proud, child."

"I have no doubt, Auntie." And she didn't. Despite the rush and the small number of people attending, she knew that her mother and her friends would create a celebration that would show the Siddiqis what a good family they were joining with. Tonight was just another part of that.

Hana pinched her cheek. "Now, go get ready." She nodded in the direction of the bathroom. "You have much preparation to do, and now is not a time for a bride to be rushing." She laughed. "There will be many years of that to come, so enjoy the peace and quiet while you still have it." She chuckled as she left the room, and Hazaar turned toward the bathroom.

"*Beti*," her mother said, "I know you are nervous. I understand."

Hazaar turned to her mother, her head cocked. "You do?"

She nodded and smiled gently. "All brides worry as the big day approaches. It is natural. You worry about being a good wife, and eventually, a good mother. Every woman does."

"I'm fine. I promise."

"I know you think I'm old-fashioned and that your progressive new thinking is so much better than traditional values. You've seen your *kafir* friends—"

"Mother, you know father doesn't like you to use that word."

"How dare you tell me what to do or say in my own house?" The gentle smile was replaced by the icy look of determination. "Your *kafir* friends have turned your head, Hazaar. You've never been satisfied with your place in our world. I know this. You always wanted to be more, to be better than everyone else. To be better than your brother. Well, that is not the way we work. A woman's place is to look after her husband, not go off playing a piano. A woman's place is to raise her husband's children to be proper Muslims, not to daydream and waste years and a small fortune of her father's wealth. It is a woman's place to please her husband, not to lust after a life that is sinful and unholy. My father arranged my marriage to your father, and it has been a good marriage. He is a good man and I grew to love him very much. I have had a happy life taking care of him and our children. It will be good for you too. It is how we do things."

Hazaar had to bite her tongue to prevent the words she really wanted to say from slipping past her lips, but she knew her mother was waiting for a response—the proper response. "I know."

"Your friends have told you, no doubt, that you should be in love with the man you marry. But that is not important. It will come later. It will grow from the life you share together, from the children you will create together, and from the memories and happiness you will share with each other. These things you cannot get from music and a life of loneliness, *Beti*. Pianos do not love you in return."

"I know that."

"When I was approaching my wedding day, I too was nervous. I asked the questions that you are no doubt asking. What if my husband does not like me? What if I do not like him? What am I supposed to do on my wedding night?"

*Oh fuck, no.* Hazaar pulled back slightly, and her mother smiled comfortingly around the look of discomfort that pained her features.

"Yes, I thought this was what might be bothering you, but do not worry."

"Maa, it is fine."

"Your husband will know what to do, and he will guide you."

"It's okay. I'm fine."

"Do not be embarrassed, *Beti*. It is the duty of every married woman to please her husband."

*Holy hell, how did this end up being a talk about sex with my mother?* "Maa, honestly, I understand. I'll be fine."

"It may be painful at first."

*Please make her shut up now.*

"But your husband will have been told how to make it less painful for you. He will know what to do."

*If I stick my fingers in my ears do you think she'll notice?*

"Your father has told me that he's made sure Yasar is a good man. He comes from a good family."

*You have no idea, Maa Jee. None at all.*

"So his father will have spoken to him about the correct way to—"

"Maa, it's okay. I promise, I'll be fine."

"But—"

"Like you said, his father will have spoken to him." She smiled, trying to convince her mother that she could let the subject go. "I'm fine, and I know how busy you are. You have so much to do for the ceremony tonight." *So please let this go and leave me alone.*

"You are sure?"

"Yes. Positive. I'm twenty-eight years old, Maa. I am well aware of what to expect on my wedding night."

"Okay."

*Thank you.*

"But you know where I am if you want to ask me any questions."

"I do." *Not a cat in hell's chance.*

Her mother smiled and hugged her. "It will not be as bad as you expect, *Beti.*" She pulled the door closed behind her.

Hazaar closed her eyes and let the tears fall. No, it could be so much worse.

❖

The green of her dress reminded her of the grass at Urquhart Castle. She ran her hand over the cloth covering her chest, satisfied when she felt the slight bump of the pendant that lay against her skin. Hatim was standing on the landing when she left the room.

"Nice dress, sis." He smiled at her. "Almost makes you look like a proper Muslim woman."

"Don't start, Hatim."

"Start what? I paid you a compliment."

"That was meant to be a compliment?" She shook her head. "You should try looking up what that word means. It might help you in the future."

He closed the distance between them, his face darkened with anger. "It might help you in the future to watch your mouth. Not everyone is as forgiving as I am."

She laughed. "Forgiving? You? Now you want to make jokes?"

"You might be my older sister, Hazaar, but I am a man. You will show me the respect I deserve."

"I am showing you the respect you deserve." She stepped closer to him. Her own anger had been burning and boiling toward him since she had learned what his stupidity was going to cost her, and there was no way she could take any more needling from him. "I know exactly why I'm being married off, Hatim. I know what you've done, what you are. You're a bully, little brother. A fool who thought he could play in the big leagues and come out on top, but instead you lost everything and all you can do about it is go home to beat your wife because you can't accept you're a failure." She stepped closer again as his eyes widened and his face paled. "You got yourself in so deep that the only way out for you was prison or death." She laughed. "Maybe both." She pointed at his chest. "Were you scared to share your cell with the big boys, Hatim? Worried they might take a liking to you?" She sneered at him. "Worried they might treat you the same way you treat Fatima?"

"You don't know what you're saying."

"Yes, I do. I know exactly what I'm saying. And so does everyone else. You play at being a man, with your business and your wife and your home, but in reality you would be nothing without Baba to keep bailing you out. He gave you a job and you almost destroyed the business. He gave you a house he has to pay the mortgage on because you gamble the money away. He found you a good wife." She sneered. "Does he have to take care of things for you there too?"

"How dare you?" He pulled his hand back to strike her.

"I wouldn't do that if I were you, Hatim."

He stopped, his face blood red, his eyes bulging, and his fist pulled back, ready, poised. "You need to be taught a lesson."

"Maybe she does, but not by you."

They both turned at the new voice. "Who are you?" Hatim didn't drop his hand but stared at the man. He was tall, with powerful, broad shoulders, a neatly trimmed beard, and slicked-back hair. The *topi* on his head was elaborately embroidered, and the waistcoat was a rich forest green with gold trim on the edges.

"Yasar Siddiqi. Please forgive me, Miss Alim. I know I should not be here while you are uncovered, but I could not stand by while I heard your disagreement from the bathroom."

"This is a private family matter, Siddiqi. And like you said, you shouldn't be here."

"I believe in this matter, the breaking of the customs can be forgiven a little." He smiled at Hazaar. "After all, we are suitably chaperoned, are we not?"

"Mr. Siddiqi, I'm sorry you overheard something of our disagreement. It's fine now. Isn't it, Hatim?"

Hatim didn't say anything. He stared at Hazaar, his hand still poised to strike her.

"She's right, Hatim. You really shouldn't do that." Yasar stepped closer to him and whispered so quietly that Hazaar had to strain to hear. "Your big sister is saving your life. And you wish to repay her by beating her?" He wrapped his hand around Hatim's bicep, and Hazaar watched his knuckles turn white as he squeezed and Hatim flinched. "She was right about everything she said to you, boy. How does it feel to be bested by a woman? Because that is what she's doing. By saving your life, she has bested you, put you forever in her debt. You know this, do you not?"

Hatim dropped his hand and wrapped it around Yasar's fingers where they still dug painfully into his arm, trying to loosen Yasar's grip.

"She is to be my wife." The word was little more than a growl as his continued to whisper. "And you will show her respect." He shook his arm. "Or you will answer to me. Are we clear, little boy?"

Hatim didn't say anything.

Yasar smiled at him. "I am your boss, boy. I control you. You will answer me. Are we clear?"

Hatim nodded stiffly.

"Good. Now stand by the stairs while I talk to your sister, for propriety's sake." Hatim moved away quickly. Yasar reached for Hazaar's hand and brought it to his lips. "You have my word, Hazaar, for all the days you are my wife, I shall protect you."

Hazaar watched him as he bent over her hand. He was handsome, strong, and masculine. His hand was warm against her skin, but she fought hard to suppress the shudder that ran down her spine. There was no doubting he was a man who was confident, in control of himself, the business he was part of, and those around him. She was equally certain that she would be just another thing he would control. She couldn't help wondering at his flawless English, after her father had said he didn't speak the language.

"Shall we adjourn to our separate parties, my lovely bride-to-be?" He held out his elbow for her to take.

She nodded and allowed him to lead her down the stairs with Hatim trailing sullenly behind them.

"Ay ay ay, no. No, this is not—"

"Mrs. Alim, please forgive me, but we bumped into each other on the landing. We were suitably chaperoned at all times, I assure you. Your son was with us. Were you not, Hatim?"

"I was there, Mother. It's fine." He pushed past them all and skulked into the sitting room.

Yasar smiled at her mother. "You have a wonderful family, Mrs. Alim. You must be so proud."

Her mother grinned and flushed. "Thank you, yes, I am. Very proud." She took Hazaar's hand and pushed her toward the kitchen. "The men are through there." She pointed to the sitting room at the back of the house. Music poured out when the door opened.

"Yasar, this way."

"Coming, Abu." He bowed toward Hazaar and her mother before leaving.

"So handsome, so polite." Hazaar's mother tugged her into the kitchen and sat her at the table. "Your father has picked very well for you, *Beti*. Very well indeed, I think." She was beaming as she and the other women took Hazaar's hands and cleansed them before slowly applying the oil and henna to create the elaborate and intricate temporary tattoos across her hands and wrists. She'd taken part in her sisters' wedding celebrations and always thought the pattern around the wrist had looked like charm bracelets. *But they're not, are they? They're shackles.*

# CHAPTER TWENTY-FIVE

*Pakistan, today*

The drip was annoying. The periodic tiny splash prevented Hazaar from sleeping on the uncomfortable and smelly mattress that had been thrown into the cellar. But it was more annoying that she couldn't do anything about it. Her shoulder hurt each time she moved. Hell, it hurt every time she breathed, so getting up and trying to quiet the drip wasn't going to happen. Instead, she tried to focus on the sounds outside the room. She could make out the sound of wood clattering against ceramic tiles and knew Afia was playing with her animal puzzle in the courtyard. The occasional bubble of baby laughter made her smile. She was grateful her beautiful daughter seemed unaware and unaffected by her mother's predicament.

She lifted her hand and laid her palm on her chest, being as careful as she could be of her twisted and painful fingers while searching for the pendant that should have lain under her clothes. She closed her eyes when she couldn't feel it, remembering instead the hours of the pain, the smell of smoke, and the agony she still felt in her left foot.

She startled when the door opened and the wooden stairs creaked under someone's weight. She turned her head toward the light, but the figure was silhouetted and she couldn't make out who it was, and the pain of the movement lanced through her shoulder. She sucked a breath through her teeth. There was so little left that she had any control over; her own reaction was the one thing that was hers. She refused to show them the fear she felt.

"Why?" Yasar's voice was quiet, soft, almost gentle as he spoke from the foot of the stairs. He set a box of what looked like medical supplies on the floor.

"Your father's crazy."

He laughed a little. "Yes, but that doesn't mean you weren't wrong, Hazaar. Why would you do this?"

"Your father misunderstood. The door was open. I was just trying—"

Yasar laughed louder. "You're a liar, Hazaar." His sandals slapped against the concrete floor. "You're a liar, and not a very good one." He squatted beside her. "You want to leave me. I know this." He stroked a finger gently down her cheek. "I have known this from the beginning, my dear, loving wife." He brushed the hair from her face. "But you were my wife, my responsibility, mine to protect and care for."

"Yasar, I—"

He put a finger over her lips. "Hush now, and listen." He lifted his finger away, and she stared at the man who was her husband. The man who had taken her from her home, from her family, from everything she knew, and delivered her to her own personal hell.

"Was I not a good enough husband for you?"

Hazaar knew it was a rhetorical question and didn't move.

"I have provided for you well, given you a child, a good home. I give you everything you need for a good, comfortable life. Do I not?"

Hazaar wanted to disagree. To tell him that he was her jailor and her tormentor, packaged in a convenient title—her husband, and that every time he touched her she wished she could say no and have it make a difference to the outcome. She wished she could tell him that what she needed for a good comfortable life was the one thing he had denied her since he forced her onto the plane. Her freedom.

"I knew on our marriage night that you were not the virgin you were meant to be, but I protected you. I kept your secret. Do you know why I did that for you, Hazaar?"

She shook her head as he ran his finger along her jaw.

"Because I care for you." He smiled at her. "I could have loved you, Hazaar. All I wanted was to be a good husband to you. For you to be a good wife. Was that too much to ask?" He shook his head sadly. "I could have loved you."

"Then let us go."

"You know I cannot."

"Will not, you mean."

"No, my darling, whatever you may believe of me, there is far more to this than you ever realized. Far more to me than you ever got to know. You judged me before you knew me."

"You're a drug smuggler."

"I'm a business man."

"Your business is death."

"I provide a product that is in demand. Nothing more. I do not force people to use it. I do not even advertise my product. People seek me out for it, and I use the wealth to support you and our daughter to the very best of my ability. What am I doing wrong?"

"It's illegal."

"Alcohol is still illegal in some places in America. Would you think me a monster if I branched out into wine or beer or spirits?"

"That's not the same thing and you know it."

"No? Do people not die from alcohol poisoning? Do they not die from long-term diseases caused by alcohol abuse? If not alcohol, what of tobacco? Should I go into the cigarette business? Would selling cancer be more acceptable to you? Would this stop you from wanting to leave me? Would this make me good husband material for you?"

"No."

"No. Because you never wanted a husband." He sat on the edge of the mattress. "Thank you."

She looked at him. "For what?"

"I had wondered what I did wrong." He picked up her hand and examined it. "This will hurt, but the fingers need to be straightened." She nodded as he gently took hold of one fingertip and pulled. She gritted her teeth and held her breath to stop herself from screaming. "I had worried that I was not a comparable lover for you." He laughed and tugged on the second finger. "I suppose I was right, in a way."

"I'm sorry, Yasar."

He looked at her. "I believe you." He wiped a damp cloth over her fingers, washing away the blood before taping them together. "You used to moan her name in your sleep. Your Charlie. I made the same mistake as my father. I thought you were talking about a man."

"There was no other man. Not ever."

"I know that now. Give me your other hand." She did and gritted her teeth, ready for him to set her fingers. "This hand is not so bad as the other one. Are you ready?"

"Yes."

He tugged and the knuckle slid back into place. "Did you always know?"

"Yes."

He taped two fingers together and gently laid the hand back

against her stomach. He slowly ran his fingertip over her neck, where her necklace had always been. "Where is it?"

"He threw it into the fire."

"She gave it to you?"

"Yes."

He leaned toward the pile of ashes and moved them around until he found the long chain and the twisted, partially melted metal. "She meant a great deal to you? Would you have given up your family for her?"

"Yes."

"I understand why you hate me." He coiled the chain into a spiral in his palm. "Was it her you spoke to today? Abu said you called the person Charlie."

"Yes." She watched him trace the undefined edges of the bird's wing. "I don't know how or why she's here, but yes. That was her on the phone."

"From the embassy?"

"Yes."

His brow furrowed and he seemed lost in thought.

"Yasar?"

He turned to face her.

"What are we going to do now?"

"We?"

"Yes. He said he's going to kill me. He wants to kill me. What are we going do?" She clung to the hope that he would still honour his word and protect her as he had promised. "You promised to protect me as long as I was your wife."

"I did." He held the bird between his thumb and forefinger. "You made me a few promises too. As I recall, there was a promise that you were a virgin. There was another to respect and honour me. Another to obey me. And another to love no other." He held the pendant up. "Have you kept your promises, Hazaar?"

She knew she hadn't, they both did, but surely he could see that this was different. They weren't talking about some trivial little matter. This was about her life. This was about him walking out of this room and allowing his father to kill her. "You said you loved me."

"No. I said I could have loved you. I cared about you. You are beautiful, intelligent, good to talk to. You could have been my equal in this partnership and helped me build a better life for us, for our children. You could have had it all, Hazaar." He placed the necklace on her hands. "Instead, you betrayed me." He leaned forward and kissed her forehead. "You would have kept me from my daughter. You would still keep me from her. My own flesh and blood. My child. That is the one thing I can never forgive you for. Never."

"So you're going to let him kill me? You're going to let him burn me to death because I don't love you?"

"No. I'm going to let him do what he must to satisfy his honour. Then I will do what I must to satisfy the law, my duty as a husband, as a father, and a business man."

Hazaar fought to think clearly through the pain. Was he really saying what she thought he was? "You're going to let him kill me and then let him go to prison?"

"Is that not the correct place for murderers?"

"But I don't understand. You can stop him."

"Yes, I could. But that gains me nothing but an ungrateful, disloyal wife and a father who is running the business to fund his zealot friends and their quest for Jihad. It is a foolish, fruitless, never-ending battle that has no point but to sign the death warrants of many men on both sides. I have bigger plans than that. I have an empire to build for my daughter. I have a legacy to create for her."

"You would let your daughter run it?"

"Yes. If she was able." He laughed. "You know me so little after all this time, Hazaar. I would have had you run it by my side. I have no issue with having my daughter take over from me. I'm not my father."

"But I—"

"You thought I didn't appreciate you? That I couldn't respect you because you were a woman?"

"Yes."

"I couldn't respect you because you betrayed me. Your sex has nothing to do with it."

"Why didn't you tell me that?"

"Respect is earned, Hazaar, not given. And trust is a fragile thing that is so easily destroyed. Tell me what reason you ever gave me to trust you? What did you ever do to earn my respect?"

"I guess I didn't do anything. But has that really earned me an execution?"

He shrugged. "It hasn't earned you an intervention."

"I'm the mother of your child, Yasar. I'm your wife. Don't do this."

"I'm not doing anything, Hazaar. I'm simply letting nature take its course." He stood and walked to the steps.

"Yasar, please don't do this. Please don't leave me to your father."

"I have more important things to worry about now, Hazaar. I will have a daughter to raise, a business to run, and no one to help me do it."

"It doesn't have to be like this."

"Yes, it does." He walked slowly up each step. "You haven't given me any other choice."

"What about Afia? Please let me see her."

"No. Seeing you like this would scare her. She doesn't need that. Not yet."

"Please let me see her."

"No." The light pouring through the opened door blinded her for a moment and she looked away to shield her eyes. When she looked back, he was gone and she could hear the sound of the key in the lock and murmured voices, then footsteps moving away as she was once again left alone in the darkness.

She looked around, slowly studying each wall. There were only two ways out of the cellar. Escape. Or death.

# CHAPTER TWENTY-SIX

*Pakistan, today*

Charlie rubbed her eyes with one hand as she picked up the phone with the other and glanced at the clock. "It's two in the morning. This better be good," she said, her voice rough with sleep.

"I'm sorry to disturb you, Miss Porter. It's Cheryl at the embassy."

She flipped on the light and tried to smother a yawn. "And to what do I owe the pleasure of this late-night chat, Cheryl?"

"I answered a phone call a few minutes ago from a woman asking someone to meet her at the market in the Peshawar old city at six in the morning. I have an address and a specific market stall. She said to make first contact at the Cunningham Clock. Shall I give you the details now?"

Charlie yawned again. "Why are you giving them to me at all?"

"Oh, sorry. The woman was calling from the number that you had flagged this afternoon."

"Maya?" Charlie jumped out of bed and went to the living room.

"No, the woman said her name was Amira."

Charlie frowned. "But it was definitely the same number?"

"Oh, yes. She said that she needed to talk to someone. That her sister-in-law's life was at stake, but she was in danger by using the phone. She also said that there wasn't much time."

"Wait, slow down." Charlie started to scribble notes as she spoke. "I need you to pull the recording of the conversation for me and send it to my terminal."

"Okay." Charlie could hear keys rattling on the other end of the line. "Done."

"Thank you, Cheryl. Now, on the phone, did Amira tell you what the danger was to the other woman?"

"Yes. She said that she was to be executed. That she has shamed the family and that their father-in-law was going to burn her to death to reclaim the family's honour."

"Fuck." Charlie wedged the phone under her chin, grabbed some clothes, and started getting dressed. "Did she give us a time frame? If she's calling now, it means we aren't too late. We can still help this woman. Whoever Maya is, no one deserves to die like that."

"Amira said that he had plans to make, and that she had been instructed to give her sister-in-law water in the meantime, no food."

"Got it." She dropped the phone on the bed while she pulled on her shirt. "Listen," she said, "I need you to call the rest of my team and get them in." She picked up the handset again. "Tell them it's an emergency and that I'll give them the full story as soon as I get there, but we don't have much time. It's at least a two-hour drive to Peshawar."

"I can do that, Miss Porter."

"Thank you." She began running through the checklist of all the things she'd need to do before briefing the team. "Except Luke. I'll call him myself now."

"No problem."

Charlie couldn't help but smile at the slightly deflated sound of Cheryl's voice. Everyone knew she had a crush on Luke, except Luke. "I'll be there in twenty minutes."

She hung up, punched another button, and frowned when it went to voice mail. She tried again and again, each time refusing to leave a message. "Wake up, you lazy bastard, or I'm gonna come round there and drag you out of bed myself." She put her phone in the cradle in her car and turned on the engine, punching the button and hanging up over and over again until she was greeted by a grunt at the other end of line.

"Get your lazy arse out of bed, Luke. I need you in the office, now."

"I'll be there first thing in the morning."

"No, Luke, I need you there now. We got another call from Maya's address. They're gonna kill her."

"What? 'S'okay, I got it." She could hear the bedclothes rustling. "I'm up. I take it you need the full works?"

"Yeah. I need everything you can find on the address, the people who live there, absolutely everything, Luke."

"I'm on it."

"And, Luke?"

"Yeah?"

"Make it fast. I'm gonna have to be in Peshawar by five thirty. She wants to meet at six."

"Don't you need Jasper to give the okay on that?"

"I need to be in Peshawar by five thirty, Luke. This woman isn't dying if I can do anything about it."

"Understood."

She turned in to the diplomatic conclave and stopped before the security guards to show her ID.

"Another late night, Miss Porter?"

She smiled at the tall soldier. "Yeah, looks like it, Sarge." He pushed the button and moved out of the way. She parked and hurried into the building, her hands shaking as she grabbed the door handle. Kenzie was passing through the metal detector as she walked in. "Bloody hell, you got here fast."

Kenzie shrugged. "I don't sleep much."

Charlie emptied her pockets and walked through the detector before retrieving her stuff on the other side. "You speed." Charlie grinned.

"Yeah," Kenzie said, "that helps too." She grinned. "So what's going on?"

"You remember that phone call I got yesterday? While you were in my office?"

"Yup."

"We got another call from the same address. I'm going to listen to the recording now."

"Want some company?"

"Yeah." She nodded at Cheryl. "Thanks for the call."

"You're welcome, Miss Porter. The rest of your team are on their way."

Charlie led Kenzie to her office and booted up her computer.

"You gonna tell me about the first call?"

"A woman who called herself Maya phoned. She said she was a British citizen and wanted to return home with her daughter."

"You don't think Maya was her real name?"

"No, I don't. I think it was a name she felt comfortable giving me. That's all."

"So she wanted information?"

Charlie grimaced. "I think she was hoping for more, but that was all I could give her." Kenzie cocked her head in question. "Her daughter was born in Pakistan, she lives with her husband and his family, and she said she isn't allowed out of the house. She doesn't have her passport or any official papers for her or her child, and unless she could actually get to the embassy to ask for help, there's nothing I can do."

"So what's changed now?"

"Let's listen to the tape and see." She hit the play button on her computer and turned up the volume on the slightly crackly call.

"Hello, British Embassy."

"You need help her." The woman's English was broken and heavily accented. Charlie frowned as she worked to understand the heavily accented whispers and turned the volume up as high as she could.

"We need to help who?"

"Sister-in-law is to killed. She dishonour family name. He must to kill her."

"I understand. My name is Cheryl. What's your name?"

"Amira."

"Okay, Amira, Who is going to kill your sister-in-law?"

"Abu."

"Your father?"

"No. Husband's father."

"Your husband's father?"

"Yes. He say must to kill her for family honour."

"Okay. Where is he now?"

"He sleep."

"And your sister-in-law?"

"She lock in room. Under floor."

Cheryl gasped. "Can you let her out? So she can go to the police station?"

"No. No key. He sleep with key. Please you must to help her. She come from England before baby born. Send her back. Please to send her back."

"Jesus." Kenzie leaned forward and shook her head. "They make it sound like she's on a sale or return policy or something."

"Where are you, Amira?"

"I…" Her voice trailed away as though she was listening to noises outside the room.

"Amira, please tell me where you are?"

"I must go. I cannot call again. Please to have someone meet with me in market tomorrow. I go to market at early. Get bread. Peshawar old city clock tower. I will be there at six o'clock. Must to follow me to buy bread."

"Amira, what's your address?"

"Must go. Very dangerous. Please to save her."

The line went dead and the recording ended. They both sat in silence for a moment, taking in the enormity of the call.

"She didn't give her address."

"No, but that doesn't matter."

"Why not?"

"I had Luke pull it after the last call. He got the number and address then. That's how I flagged it."

"So if you already have the address, why did Cheryl try so hard to get it?"

"She didn't know we already had it, and you can't help someone if you don't know where they are."

"Fair point."

Charlie smiled. "You're so gracious."

"I do try. So what next?"

"Next, I brief the rest of the team on the first call and this one and then I drive to Peshawar."

"And when we get there?"

"That depends on what Amira has to tell us about her sister-in-law."

"Knock, knock." Luke peeked around the door. "I've got everything you need. JJ's in the conference room with everyone else."

"Good. Thanks, Luke."

"No worries." They followed him into the room and took seats. Charlie sat next to Liam and nodded.

"So who's going to tell me why I'm out of bed and in the office before three in the goddamn morning?" Jasper stretched his arms over his head and leaned back in his chair.

Charlie quickly told them all about the two phone calls, watching them as they got a handle on the nuances of the case so far.

"Okay, so we have a woman who's looking for help, claims to be a British national, unsubstantiated, and another woman who claims she's now going to be killed. No details on why, when, how, where, just the who." JJ frowned. "What am I missing here?"

"After Charlie told me about the second call, I gathered everything

I could about the address and the people in there. The house belongs to Tazim Siddiqi."

Charlie was stunned. She closed her eyes and held her hand to her chest, her heart racing. She felt the air rush out of her lungs. It had been years since she had heard that name, and every day since, she prayed that she would hear it again, yet feared that she would in equal measure. She closed her eyes and forced the memories away. *Not now. I don't have time for this now.* She knew they would have to be dealt with. She knew she would have to reconcile each and every feeling of rage and terror that buffeted her as she realized exactly what was now facing them. And exactly whose life was on the line. *Oh, Hazaar, why couldn't you just tell me?*

"Okay." Jasper waited.

Luke glanced at the page in his hands. "Tazim Siddiqi owns a business that exports spices to the UK. He has a partnership with Alim and Son out of—"

"Bradford." Charlie felt her lips moving and all eyes turn to her.

"Yeah." Luke frowned at her. "How'd you know that?"

Charlie shook her head. "Doesn't matter. Sorry. Go on." She clasped her hands in her lap and tried to keep them from shaking. She knew it was a lost cause, but it gave her something to focus on as she listened to Luke.

"Okay, so this dude Siddiqi has been on the watch list for quite a while. But the authorities can't get anything on him."

"Watch list for what?" Al asked.

"Drugs. They think all those spice containers are stuffed with heroin. They moved into the house in Peshawar about eight years ago from the Khyber region. Siddiqi was supposed to be way up there in the Pashtun tribe before then, and we all know what that means."

"Taliban." Hillary shook her head. "Siddiqi? The name rings a bell." She pulled out her notebook and tapped on some keys while Luke continued.

"He's got two boys. The oldest, Rafi, is supposedly away. To me that means one of two things." He held up his index finger.

"He's tending the poppy fields," Liam said, "or he's in one of the training camps."

Charlie shook her head slowly. Every detail she heard was one more thing she knew would haunt her for the rest of her life. *Why the hell didn't I fight harder? Why the hell did I just let you walk away?*

*Every sacrifice you made was for nothing, and you probably don't even know it.*

"There's a third option," Al said.

"And that would be?" JJ looked at him.

"He's dead. Lot of that goes on in these tribal thingies, never mind the drug thingies."

Jasper nodded. "True. Not great, whichever is the truth, but it does explain why Amira was able to be out of bed to make the call. Increases her credibility." He turned back to Luke. "And the younger son?"

Hillary hit a button on her computer and a picture filled the screen on the far wall. "Yasar Siddiqi. According to all the reports, he's the business man of the family. Squeaky clean reputation and a powerful business man. He deals with the spice companies, the officials. Trained as a lawyer, makes everything nice and official. It would appear he's the face of the company. And he's good. Very good. For the past eight years, the authorities haven't been able to confirm anything."

"For the past eight years. What about before that?" Liam leaned a little closer to Charlie as he spoke. She could feel the heat radiating off him, and she tried to latch on to it, to let it ground her and keep her from spinning out of control as her world sped up and threatened to cast her off into the cold emptiness of her own growing despair.

"They had someone in custody, a couple of people actually. Girls who were caught at customs smuggling heroin through into the UK."

"What happened?"

Charlie swallowed hard and focused on her breathing. She was determined not to throw up.

Hillary looked at her notes and clicked her keyboard. Two mug shots filled the screen. "Poojah Ahmed and Shala Ahmed. Sisters. They were mules, bought tickets for cash at the airport just in time to check in and go through security. It raised red flags at customs so they were stopped as a routine. The younger one, Shala, broke down as soon as they were stopped and customs officers had them x-rayed. They were carrying twenty pellets each with an estimated street value in the region of fifty grand each. Once the younger sister started talking, they both let fly about everything they knew and they were prepared to testify. But they died in prison before they could testify."

"How?" Liam asked.

Hilary pounded the keyboard. "Death certificate records heart failure due to blood loss from stab wounds."

"Shit." Jasper rubbed his hands over his face.

"Want me to find the official reports of the incidents?"

"Do we need them?" Luke shook his head and slumped in his chair.

Jasper scowled. "We deal with facts, Luke. Not suspicion. Find me everything you can, Hilary, thanks."

"Okay." She tapped at the keys again. "Well, since then they haven't been able to get them on anything."

"So we've got a drug family with Taliban connections," Al said.

"Yup." Hilary nodded without looking up from the screen.

"They could be running the drugs out through Afghanistan rather than Pakistan."

"Al, they could be doing a whole lot of things. None of which we are in any position to do anything about. We aren't drug enforcement." Jasper held up a hand to forestall argument. "Our priority is as it has always been. The women and children."

"Ever get the feeling it isn't enough?" Liam asked with his eyes closed.

Jasper stared at him for a long time before he nodded. "Far too often, my friend. But I have to focus on the things I can change and know when I can't make a difference." He looked down at his hands as they rested on the table. "I have to make a decision here, people, and given what we know about this family, I have to think this may be one of those occasions where we have to show caution. We don't have definite confirmation that the original contact was from a British citizen. And getting involved with this family will be bad news all round."

Charlie couldn't believe what she was hearing. She didn't want to believe the words coming out of Jasper's mouth. "You can't do this, JJ. She is. We have to help her."

"Based on everything we have—the tapes, the background info on the family at that address—I think we're asking for trouble in a place we don't need to go."

"Yes, we do. We can't walk away from this. She's British. She needs our help."

"We don't know that."

"They're going to kill her." Panic formed a knot in her stomach, and she knew she was going to be sick if she wasn't careful.

"Unfortunately, Charlie, people die every day. We can't save them all."

"Not her. We can save her." All eyes in the room were on her. "Please, Jasper, please don't turn this one down."

He shook his head. "I'm sorry."

"At least let me go and meet with Amira. See what she has to say."

Jasper stared at her. "What do you know?"

She shook her head. "Nothing."

"Bullshit. Tell me what you know or I'm shutting this down right now."

She knew that if she told him her involvement with Hazaar, he'd pull her from the case and there was no one else in the room who was able to deal with the situation the way she could. Liam was a skilled negotiator, but he couldn't work in the field. Flashbacks and anxiety attacks out of the office made it impossible for him to be effective out there, and Kenzie was on her second day. She wouldn't put Hazaar's life in their hands.

"I'm waiting, Charlie."

But she had to tell him. She had no other choice. If she didn't, she would be leaving Hazaar there to die, to burn to death as her final sacrifice for the lives of her father and brother.

"Fine, then I guess we're done here."

"Wait." *I'll just have to convince you that I'm capable of doing my job anyway.* "Yasar Siddiqi married Hazaar Alim just over three years ago. Hazaar Alim is the youngest daughter of Isam Alim, owner of Alim and Son. The marriage was the cornerstone of Alim and Son joining forces with Siddiqi Exports. Hazaar is a British citizen. She was born in Bradford, raised there until she went to Manchester to study music. She got her bachelor's degree, master's, and her doctorate at the Royal Northern College of Music."

"You were classmates?" Liam put his hand on hers.

"She was already studying for her master's when I started there." She smiled at him.

"You knew her?" Jasper scowled at her. "Why the fuck didn't you say that to begin with?"

"I wasn't sure until Luke said it was Siddiqi's house."

"Thought you went a bit pale then, C." Luke smiled at her.

"I'm sorry, JJ. It was something of a shock."

His expression softened a little. "I get that." He took a deep breath and sighed heavily. "So just how well did you know this woman?"

She turned her hand in Liam's and squeezed. "We lived together for two years."

"Lived together as in flat mates?" Kenzie cocked her eyebrow, a crooked little grin on her face. "Or lived together in the biblical sense?"

Charlie swallowed. "It was while we were in university."

"Don't give me that crap, Porter. I got you less than six months after you graduated. She was your girlfriend. Correct?"

"Yes." Liam squeezed her hand.

"Fuck." Jasper slammed his hands on the table. Water glasses shook, and Hilary's notebook bounced into the air. He stood up, forcing his chair back to the wall. "You're gonna go whether I sanction this or not and every one of us knows it." He turned back to face her. "Aren't you?"

"Yes."

He snorted and shook his head. "Well, at least you didn't lie to me."

"I've never lied to you, JJ."

"No, but you've never told me the whole truth before, have you?"

"Only about this." She dropped her head. "I'm sorry. I couldn't. And I really didn't think I'd ever see her again."

He scrubbed his hands over his face, obviously still pissed. "Liam, what's your situation? Can you go out there?"

"No, you can't ask him that!" Charlie shouted.

"You haven't given me much choice and you damn well know it. Kenzie's untrained. No offense."

"None taken," Kenzie said.

"And your judgment is compromised," Jasper said.

"No, it isn't. I can do this."

"Like hell you can."

"Liam isn't ready to go back in the field. That's why you wanted me to train Kenzie in the first place. I'm the only one who can do this, Jasper."

"Look at you. You're still in love with her." He waved his hand at her. "You think you can go in there and negotiate for her release against a man who wants to kill the woman you love?"

"I'll do what I have to do."

"That's the part I have a problem with."

"Jasper, you and I both know I'm the best chance she has."

He looked around the room. Everyone was staring at the table.

"You know what, Charlie? The damndest part of this is that you *are* the best chance she has at the moment. But you want to know what I'm looking at right now? If I send you in there and this falls apart, what happens then, Charlie?"

"It won't."

"This meeting could be a setup."

"I'll wear a wire, a vest, a video camera, whatever you want. Luke can have it all set up and ready to go, right?" She looked over at him and watched him nod quickly. "Please, JJ, whatever you want…just let me do this."

"If this goes bad, Charlie…if you fail—"

"I won't fail." Her voice sounded strange in her own ears, like steel ringing. "I can't afford to fail her this time."

Jasper shook his head and mumbled. "That's what I'm afraid of." He sat back in his chair. "Get her set up with the full works, Luke, and get the van rigged too. Hillary, Liam, you're working out of here with me. Al, you're in charge on the road. Kenzie?"

"Yup?"

"How are you behind the wheel?"

She grinned as Charlie groaned. "I feel the need." She winked at Luke. "The need for speed."

Everyone looked at each other then burst out laughing. Luke clapped her on the back. "Oh my God, I can't believe you just went there. *Top Gun*? Seriously?"

"It's a classic film."

"It's something all right." Jasper clapped his hands. "Okay, if we're doing this, you better get going or you'll need jets to get there by six." He pointed to the door. "Go on, get."

They all moved to their tasks.

"Charlie."

She turned to face JJ.

"Be careful out there, okay? This has the potential to turn into a shit storm, and I don't want to lose you."

"You won't."

## CHAPTER TWENTY-SEVEN

*The North of England, then*

Hazaar drew in a deep breath and concentrated on steadying her hand. *Maybe I shouldn't bother. He might not want to marry me if I poke my eye out with a mascara brush.* She chuckled to herself and started to apply the black liquid to her lashes, the pattern on her hand catching her eye with every movement. The intricate combination of dots, spirals, and lines made up images of the sun, moon, and stars, flower buds, and paisleys. The images were hypnotic, and she could feel herself being pulled into the pattern. She shook her head and concentrated on the application of her makeup. They were symbolic of new life, passion between new loves, and fertility for her new marriage. *Let's hope they're nothing but old wives' tales.*

"You look beautiful, *Beti*."

"Maa Jee, I didn't hear you come in." She looked at her mother in the mirror.

"Too busy concentrating on making yourself beautiful." She laughed. "He will be proud to be your husband." She squeezed Hazaar's shoulder. "It is time for us to go downstairs."

"The guests for the procession have arrived already?"

"Oh yes. And you should have seen the cars that Yasar and his family arrived in. There may not be many people coming to this wedding, Hazar, but the way those cars were decorated for the procession," her mother said, "they will be talking about this wedding procession for years to come, all over Bradford." She smiled widely, her chest puffed out, the look of pride and contentment obvious on her face.

Hazaar tidied away her makeup and walked back into her bedroom. Tonight would be the last night she would spend in here.

They had opted for a traditional styled ceremony, as so much of the preparation had been rushed, her father had insisted that they follow as many of the proper traditions as possible. So tonight, she and her new husband would spend the night in separate rooms in her father's home. Tomorrow, her father would take them both to her husband's home and bid her good-bye. He would say farewell to her and pass on the responsibility of her welfare to her husband. From that day on, she would share her life with Yasar. Her bed would be his and her body his to share. She shuddered. *I can't think about that. I just can't.*

She picked the red scarf up off the edge of her bed and ran it through her hands. The gold beads, sequins, and heavy trim would keep it weighted and her face covered throughout the whole ninety-minute service, and already Hazaar could feel the ache in her neck muscles. The weight of the fabric was nothing, little more than the weight of her long, thick hair, in reality. It was everything it represented that weighed on her. Each sequin represented a dream she would never have the chance to make a reality, every bead was an expectation she would have to fulfil to maintain the charade her life was to become, and the weight of the trim holding it all down was the weight of the lives she knew she was saving. The only good thing she could see about living under the veil was how easy it would be to hide her tears.

Her mother adjusted the length at the back as she placed it on her own head and let it hang.

"It is perfect, *Beti*. You make me so proud." Her mother wiped tears from her face and clasped her hands under her chin.

Her father had set up a massive marquee in the garden. Tables and chairs lined the walls, and at each end of the tent there were raised platforms with decorated chairs; one for him and one for her. Her father's influence in the community had also allowed him to arrange for the imam of the mosque to perform the ceremony, despite the last-minute nature of the wedding.

Her mother, Hana, and some of the other women led her into the marquee and onto her little platform, arranging the veil about her as she sat down. Ninety minutes. That was all the ceremony would take. Ninety minutes, then her life would be over.

Yasar was already sitting on his chair. Hazaar shook her head slightly. *No, Yasar is already sitting on his throne.* He looked like a prince waiting for the coronation that would make him king. His pristinely white suit almost gleamed in the light. His hair was slicked back under his white turban, and his beard was neatly trimmed to a goatee and a thin line along the edge of his jaw. It made his face look chiselled, sharp, and handsome. The distance between them didn't allow her to make out his features clearly, other than the wide smile that graced his full lips.

The imam began the ceremony, and Hazaar stopped listening as he recited the first chapter of the Quran, the opening, the beginning, the start, the foundation of everything that comes afterward. All the things the ceremony was meant to represent for them both. People nodded and smiled. Some raised their hands to the heavens and praised Allah for giving them the holy sanctuary of marriage. Hazaar stared at her hands and the shackle-like henna tattoos at her wrists and prayed it wouldn't be the prison she feared. Her mother had told her that she had found herself in marriage, that it was when she came to realize her own worth and her own power. Hazaar feared that in her marriage, she would only lose any sense of self she had ever had.

They were presented with the *nikah,* and Hazaar's hands shook as she signed the marriage contract and she felt like she was watching everything happen as opposed to taking part herself. She could see hands touching her body, leading her this way and that, but she couldn't feel them. She could see people talking to her, see herself looking at them, but she felt like she was watching them on a screen, listening to them through headphones; her own eyes and ears didn't seem to be working. The nerves in her body seemed to have deserted her as she picked up the pen and looked at the paper on the table.

One single piece of paper.

The signatures of two male witnesses, as well as Yasar's and her own on a single sheet of paper bound them together in every way, for the rest of her life. There would be no divorce in this marriage. At least not one she could choose. To do so would negate the business partnership too, and she knew where that left her family. There would be no separation from him, no end to this *nikah,* unless he chose it.

She poised her hand over the page, pen at the ready.

*What choice do I have?* She looked at her father, the smile on his face seemed frozen rather than happy, the look in his eyes a mixture of regret, fear, and a tiny, tiny flicker of hope. To not sign her name would be signing his death warrant. This man who had given her life, given her the education he never had, the opportunities he never dreamed possible, and loved her from the moment she was born. There was pride in his posture as he watched her, and fear in his trembling hands as he raised them slightly to her in question.

*I do this for you, Baba. Not for Hatim, or any of the others would I give up my life.*

The pen scratched the paper as she pulled it across the page. She felt a rush as though she was finally returned to her own body and the sound of the pen on the paper was too loud in her ears, but it was done. She was married.

As the final prayer was offered up to Allah for them, she was led to her husband's platform. Her father and his joined their hands, and she was seated on a chair next to him, a smaller, less ornately decorated chair, next to his throne. Hatim and another man carried a huge, heavy mirror and stood before them. Hazaar drew a deep breath as an elaborately decorated green scarf was draped over both of their heads, and her mother stepped forward to uncover her face. This was supposed to be the first time her new husband would see her face, through her reflection in the mirror, and to the rest of the world, it was. Only her mother, Hatim, and they themselves knew otherwise.

As she looked at her husband through the glass, she knew nothing of her mother's feeling of power in her marriage. She felt powerless. There was no way out now.

The feast began, music played, and people enjoyed themselves. Yasar clasped her hand and squeezed. "Hello, Mrs. Siddiqi." He smiled at her.

It hit her like a fist to the gut and she fought to keep the bile from rising. She was his wife. She was Mrs. Yasar Siddiqi and not Hazaar Alim anymore. The longer she stared into the mirror, the smaller she felt, like her own image was receding and his was filling the glass, taking over hers.

*What the fuck have I done?*

# CHAPTER TWENTY-EIGHT

*Pakistan, today*

Charlie covered her hair with a long black scarf and climbed out of the van. She checked her watch as she pulled the door closed behind her. Five fifty-five. She walked past stalls that were setting up, shops that were opening, and toward the clock tower. Built in 1900 to commemorate the diamond jubilee of Queen Victoria, it was a major tourist attraction in the area, and it wasn't unusual for tourists to be seen staring at it. She pulled out a camera to further clarify her purpose for hanging around and began taking pictures in the early morning light. The red clay façade covered the whole of the four-tiered building, but at least half was covered with banners advertising local music bands and new shops. The slumbering city was being chased into activity as the faithful were called to prayer and the shops and market stalls surrounding the clock tower set up for the day's trading.

She got close and squatted to get a different angle and noticed a woman heading toward the building. She was dressed in a blue burqa, only her eyes visible as she approached and met Charlie's gaze. Her nod was slight, and if Charlie hadn't been looking for it, she would have missed it completely. She pulled the camera to her face again and pretended to click off another shot.

"Contact made. Please confirm GPS tracker is working."

"Tracker is pinging, C. You following the blue lady?" Luke's voice crackled in her ear.

"Yup."

"Don't see too many full burqas these days," Luke said.

"What's that mean?" Kenzie's voice came over the radio.

"A greater chance of these guys being the extremists we think they might be," Luke said.

"And that's not good for our girl, right?" Kenzie said.

"Nope. Not good at all."

"I thought all burqas were black," Kenzie said.

"No, there are four colours, black, white, yellow, and blue. The blue is common to the Afghanistan Muslims, but the Pashtun tribe covered the northern regions of Afghanistan and Pakistan. So it's not uncommon here."

"Do the colours mean anything?"

"The blue is supposed to be about hope and heavenly paradise, and it's supposed to ward off the evil eye."

"Are you serious?" Kenzie laughed.

"Totally serious."

"Christ."

Charlie tuned out Kenzie's incredulity and followed the woman, snapping photographs as she went. She followed her through the bazaar and stood next to her as she purchased roti bread and went to the grocery stall. She filled the basket she was carrying with fresh fruit and vegetables before leading Charlie to an alley around the back.

"You are from embassy?"

"Yes. Amira?" The woman nodded. "My name's Charlotte."

"You have come to help Hazaar?"

The casual mention of her name made Charlie shiver. "I will do everything I can."

"I do not have long. If Abu suspects I have done this…" She let her voice trail away, but Charlie didn't need her to fill in the blanks. She knew that Amira was risking her own life. Amira pulled an envelope from under her tunic and handed it to Charlie. "You will need address."

"I have that already. Who is going to kill her?"

"Abu." She shook her head. "Father-in-law. He say burn to cleanse family name."

"How badly is she hurt?"

"She need doctor. Shoulder not right, bleeding from head. She breathe badly, hurt here." She pointed to her ribs. "Her hands not good. Bones sticking out of skin. He burn feet too."

Charlie felt sick. How could anyone do that to another person? "What about Hazaar's husband? What does he say?"

"He very angry at his father for hurting Hazaar. Say he should not have touched, that it his place to speak to own wife. Not for someone else to decide."

"Is he going along with the honour killing? Do you know when they're planning on doing it?"

Amira shrugged. "I not hear and I not see before I leave this morning."

"I understand." The news that Yasar had confronted his father about his treatment of Hazaar confused Charlie. Why stand up for her but not get her medical attention? Why pretend like you care and then not take care of such basic needs? What was going on? She wished she had time to drill down with Amira into the family dynamics, not only to try to understand what Hazaar's life had been like these past three years, but also to figure out the best way to negotiate with these men. She needed to understand what was in their heads and the best way to use that to save Hazaar's life.

"You come get her now?"

"I wish it was that simple." Charlie tucked the envelope into her pocket.

"But they will to kill her."

"I will do all I can. Who should I talk to about her release?"

"Talk? You cannot talk to them. They will know." Amira's voice became shrill and she clutched at Charlie's arm. "Please."

"I have to try and talk to them, or at least one of them, to negotiate for her release."

"If you talk to them, they will know I am speaking to you."

"Amira, this is how we work."

"And this is how he work." She held her hand out, fingers curled into a fist. Charlie held her hand out and caught the small item Amira dropped. "You talk, not do, this happen to both of us." She turned and walked away.

Charlie opened her hand and stared at the twisted hunk of blackened, melted metal. It was difficult to make out the shape or the details, but Charlie didn't need to. She knew what it was. She saw the details exactly as they had been in the shop when she bought it. She saw the way the fading sunlight had bounced off the metal as she'd fastened it to Hazaar's neck. She saw the chain intact rather than the broken, twisted, and melted string that hung from the edges of the warped wings.

Charlie hurried to catch up with her. "How did you get this? I mean, how did it end up like this? You said she was still alive?" *Please don't let me be too late. Please. Not after all this time.*

"She is. He threw in fire after he burn feet." She looked over her shoulder. "I go in to give water and she beg me take this. She beg me give to bring you to help."

"Why are you helping her? You know that by doing so you are risking your own life, so why?"

Amira straightened her shoulders. "She have little girl. She need mother." She frowned as though she was trying to find the right words. "When I little my mother to kill by her father. She bad wife and shame family. Should make all good when dead, but they not like me after this. It was difficult time, bad time, and it not good for girl child. Hazaar love child. She good mother. Baby deserve good life."

"I understand."

"You save them both."

"I will." Charlie slid what was left of the pendant into her pocket. "You have my word, Amira. I will help." She watched Amira walk out of the alley.

"You don't know that you're going to be able to do that, Charlie. You know better than making promises you might not be able to keep." Al's voice was gruff over the comm line.

"I know my job, Al."

"Yeah? Then act like it."

She pulled the bud out of her ear and walked toward the van. She went over everything that Amira had said, and the only thing that was unexpected had been the information about Yasar and how he had responded to his father's assault of Hazaar. She wished she'd asked Amira if he been violent toward Hazaar. The answer would have been very revealing, but she had an inclination that he wouldn't have touched her like that. That he would consider it beneath him to lose control in this way. She didn't know how she knew; she just did.

She pulled open the door to the van and climbed inside. "I need everything on Yasar Siddiqi. And I do mean everything. I want college records, dissertations, public speeches, the works. I want to know how this guy thinks, and I need it yesterday."

"I'm on it." Luke was already on the line to Hillary.

"Kenzie?"

"Boss?"

"Just how good a profiler are you?"

She turned in the front seat and grinned over her shoulder. "I'm very good."

"Just what I needed to hear. Go over everything Luke digs up and tell me everything you can about this guy. Why did he confront his father about him beating her? Something tells me this is pivotal."

"On it."

"Al, do we have a map of the area?"

"We do. How accurate it is, well, that's a whole other story." He tossed a roll of paper at her. "Take a look. The alleyway that you disappeared into isn't even marked on here."

"Right. Looks like we need a recon of the area then."

"Charlie, we aren't sanctioned to do that."

"I just want to be prepared, Al." She glanced up at his scowling face. "All I'm talking about is taking a little walk around the area. See what it's like. That's it."

"Yeah, and I'm Mother Teresa." Luke and Kenzie sniggered. "I know you."

"I'll be good. I promise." His scowl deepened. "I swear." She crossed her fingers over her chest. "Want me to pinkie swear too?"

"Funny."

"Look, Al—"

"I get it. Just don't get us killed, and I'd like to keep my job too, if you can manage it."

"Working on it."

# CHAPTER TWENTY-NINE

*The North of England, then*

Hazaar stared at the stick resting on the bathroom counter. Two pink dye lines showed clearly in the tiny window and the instruction paper shook in her hand. *Six months. I've only been married six fucking months and I'm pregnant already.* She shook her head and tried to focus. *I haven't even finished decorating the house yet.* She tossed the instruction pamphlet in the bin and leaned against the counter. She ran the tap and splashed water over her face.

Stupid questions ran through her mind repeatedly despite the fact that she knew the answers. Questions like, "why me," "how the hell did this happen," and "what the fuck am I going to do now?" plagued her. Her legs felt weak, like they wouldn't support her, so she dropped the lid on the toilet and sat down. She put one hand across her lower abdomen and tried to remember the details of her sisters' pregnancies. How big would it be now? She'd missed one period and put it down to the stress of the wedding, the house move, losing Charlie, and getting used to her new life, but being late for the second month in a row wasn't something she could ignore. *Two months, baby, how big would you be? Are you a boy or a girl?*

She tried to picture what her child would look like, something her mother had talked about over and over since first seeing Yasar. Her mother was certain he would give her beautiful children who were tall, strong, handsome boys and beautiful girls for her to raise. Hazaar had ignored her ramblings, not wanting to think about it in any way. She wanted to forget his touch, not linger on the thoughts of what it would create. Now she had no choice. She hadn't wanted to admit that it was only a matter of time before it would happen.

Yasar was a strong, virile man. He wanted a family and he was looking forward to it. Now she tried to picture the baby's face, the little fingers and toes. Would it have hair when it was born, or would it be bald? She rubbed her stomach slowly, soothingly, like she was stroking the child's back as it slept soundly and waited for birth.

*What will you be like, baby? Will you love music as I do? Will you want to choose your own life or will you be content with the life you'll be given? One chosen for you by your father.*

She pictured the son that he could be, growing strong in his father's image. She had learned in the past six months that Yasar had his own code, his own set of rules that he lived by, and he was comfortable with that. He was sure of himself and he would protect what was his, no matter what. His business was simply that, business. He would raise his son to follow in his footsteps and teach him his trade, to live the same life that he was happy and content with. Smuggling drugs and being a part of a family dynasty that would order the execution of people who knew information about his business would be normal for her son as it was normal to Yasar. Just like any other day at the office.

She rubbed her stomach again, this time higher up. She moved quickly and managed to get the lid of the toilet seat up before she vomited. She hung her head over the bowl and waited until the room stopped spinning.

"Are you okay?"

She twisted her head to the side and looked up at Yasar as he stood in the doorway. "I'm sorry. I didn't hear you come in."

"I'm not surprised. I could hear you downstairs." He squatted beside her to rub her back. "Something you ate, maybe?"

"Is my cooking that bad?"

He laughed. "No, my darling, it isn't." He reached for some tissues and handed them to her.

"Thank you." She wiped her mouth.

"Let me get you some water." He stood and paused over the sink. *Shit, I didn't throw away that damn test stick.*

"Hazaar?" He held it up, his eyes wide, a smile starting on his lips. "You are pregnant?"

She nodded as he pulled her up off the floor and spun her around in his arms. "Oh no, don't. I'll be sick again."

"Sorry." He put her down and crushed her in his arms. "I'm so happy. You have made me so happy." He kissed her head. "A father." He cupped her face in his hands and kissed her forehead. "I'm going to be a father." He lifted her into his arms and carried her to their bedroom, where he laid her gently on their bed. "Let me get you that water, my darling." He went back to the bathroom. "How long?" he asked as he came back to the side of the bed.

She took the glass he handed to her. "I don't know."

"I'll call the doctor and make an appointment." He pulled out his phone and clicked a button, and within minutes he had an appointment set up for her and had cancelled a meeting for the afternoon. "I'll take you."

"You don't have to do that. I know how busy you are."

"I want to. I'm your husband. I swore to look after you, to protect you, and you're pregnant with my child. It's my honour." He looked so happy and so sincere, so proud of himself, and of her. He put his hand on her belly. "Our child."

"Yes." She sipped her water with her eyes closed.

"If it's a boy I'll name him in honour of our fathers. Perhaps Isam Tazim Siddiqi?" He kissed her hand. "And a daughter will be yours to name."

She looked at him, surprised by the unexpected concession. It was traditional for the first son to be named after their grandfathers, either entirely or their second names, but allowing Hazaar total freedom in the naming of their daughter wasn't something she had expected. She had thought he might take her choice into account, but not like this.

"Do you have a name in mind for a daughter?"

"I haven't really thought about it." She hadn't considered giving birth to a daughter. She hadn't considered giving birth at all. She didn't want to think about it, but now she couldn't stop. Should the child be a daughter, she had no doubt that Yasar would be devoted to her, that he would love her and care for her. He would teach her, and eventually, he would marry her into the same life that Hazaar had. Her daughter would have few, if any, choices in the world she would be born into. She looked down where his hand rested on her belly, possessing not only her but her unborn child too, and she knew she couldn't do this anymore.

In a choice between the life of her unborn child and her father's, there really was no contest.

# Chapter Thirty

*Pakistan, today*

"Kenzie, tell me good things about this guy." Charlie stared at the picture, the image of Yasar and Hazaar on their wedding day. He was smiling broadly into the camera, one arm around Hazaar's waist and the other holding a piece of fruit to her lips. Hazaar's smile didn't reach her eyes.

"How long do I have?"

Charlie raised her eyebrow and closed the folder she was holding.

"Not long, got it." She tossed Charlie a cheeky grin. "Okay, this guy is complicated, smart, and dedicated." She pointed at the tablet in front of her. "He wrote papers during college about a huge variety of things, but his way of thinking is very clear."

"Kenzie, give me bullet points."

"Bullet points. He's well educated and has a well-developed code of ethics that he lives by."

"Ethics? The guy's a drug smuggler."

"I know. He wrote a paper on the Atlantic trade routes of the sixteen and seventeen hundreds, where he posited the opinion that they weren't just slave traders but also the drug traffickers of their day, supplying sugar and tea around the Empire to the addicted Brits and reinforcing the slave labour workforce as they did so, to continue to supply their habits. That they're condemned as slave traders when all they were doing was supplying a product that was in demand. That they were business men and sought only to earn a living and provide for their families to the best of their abilities."

"Sick," Luke said.

"Well, not really, no. He makes some very valid points, and while I don't agree with slavery or condone it in any way, he's right. Had there been no demand for slaves, there would have been no trade. They were men who filled a need that society at the time had called for. Business men."

"Surely you can't agree with that?" Luke was staring at Kenzie.

"Agree with slavery? No. Never. I already said that. But I do agree with the point he made. It wasn't the traders who created the societal culture that allowed slavery to flourish. They merely made the most of the opportunities they had."

"Luke, Kenzie, we could debate this till the cows come home, I'm sure, but I don't quite see what this is telling us about Yasar." Charlie tapped her fingers on her leg.

"It tells me that he sees himself as a business man who is vilified for reasons that he feels are unjust. It has made him angry and all the more determined to succeed and be the best he can be."

"The best drug dealer, you mean?"

"Yes. But it also tells me more about his motivations."

"Such as?"

"This is how he provides for his family. He is competitive and wants to provide for them the best way he can. He wants the world to see how well he is doing for himself, and for his family. He is also loyal, resolute, and intractable. He is a man who would be devoted to his family, take his responsibilities toward them seriously, and as such, he would expect complete loyalty in return."

"Complete loyalty?" Charlie didn't like the sound of that.

"Yes. Any betrayal would incur his wrath."

"Such as?"

"Well, with a man like this, obviously sexual betrayal would be one way, but also anything he saw as a betrayal of what he held dear."

"Like his marriage?"

Kenzie frowned. "Well, yes, I already said that sexual betrayal would—"

"Sex isn't the only way to betray a marriage. When you say wrath, do you mean he would be violent toward Hazaar?"

Kenzie shook her head, obviously considering the question carefully. "Very doubtful."

"Why?"

"Because he values strength and control. To strike out at someone weaker than he is would shame him. He views domestic abuse as a coward's choice."

Charlie leaned forward in her seat and rested her elbows on her knees. "How do you know that?"

"Because he said as much when he testified against one Hatim Alim when he was jailed for beating his wife Fatima and causing her to have a miscarriage with their first child. Yasar was the prosecution's main witness, and from the transcript, he was very clear. He testified to a pattern of abuse and also to intervening when Hatim had tried to strike Hazaar on one occasion. He says very clearly that he believes men who show such little control, respect, and honour deserve to discover for themselves how such treatment feels at the hands of others stronger than themselves."

"Wow." Charlie felt her spirit lift a little. She remembered so clearly the bruises Hatim had left on Hazaar when he'd hit her. It felt good to know that not only was Yasar not like him, but that he had stood up for Hazaar against him, protected her, and kept her from harm. Charlie felt a stab of emotion, but she couldn't decide if it was guilt or jealousy. Guilt that she hadn't been able to stand up for Hazaar in any way, that she had never been given the chance, and jealous that it was his right, his privilege, to do so.

"Yeah. His final words to Hatim were to wish him luck in prison."

"When was this?"

"A little over three years ago."

"I take it Hatim has been released now?"

"Unfortunately, he was killed in prison."

Charlie cocked her head in question and Kenzie shrugged. "The report says a prison brawl got out of hand, and Hatim was found at the bottom of a pile with a shiv in his throat." She glanced at her tablet. "He'd only been in there two days."

"Fast work, Yasar." Luke had a look of grudging respect on his face.

"Maybe," Kenzie said and Luke gave her an incredulous look. "Okay, more than maybe, but it was never proved. Hell, they didn't even convict anyone. There were no prints on the shiv except Hatim's and of course, no one saw anything."

"Dude's ruthless."

"Yeah." Charlie frowned and ran her fingers through her hair. "So where does this put him on the side of honour killings?"

"Probably publically disagrees, but honour is a vital part of his personal code. We can't rule out that if he was backed into a corner he may go along with it. Sources indicate that the brother isn't away, but has in fact, been dealt with in a more permanent way after bringing disgrace to the family."

"He killed his own brother?" Al spoke from the front seat.

Kenzie shook her head. "No, the brother was causing a multitude of problems because he got a taste for the product, so the father ordered him to be taken care of."

"Where does this intelligence come from?" Al turned to look at them all from the driver's seat.

"It was in the statement made by the Ahmed sisters to the police in the UK before they were killed."

"Okay." Charlie tapped her fingers against her lips. "From everything you've read, how open is he to negotiation?"

Kenzie shrugged. "In business, he has to be. Personally, he's obstinate. Once he's made his mind up, it would be almost impossible to change it."

"Almost?"

"This isn't an exact science. Just a pretty fucking close one."

"Got ya." Charlie gave her a quick smile and turned to look out the window, considering her options.

She played back over everything she knew of the situation from what Hazaar had said on the phone, from her conversation with Amira, and everything Kenzie had said. "I still think we have a better chance approaching him than Tazim. Tazim's an extremist, pure and simple, and one who had his own son killed. There's no negotiating with him, only measuring up for coffins."

Kenzie nodded. "Definitely looks that way from everything I've seen."

"Right. You have a number for Yasar in that file of yours?" Charlie held her hand out as Kenzie passed her a piece of paper. "Thanks. Luke, how are we doing on getting eyes and ears in there?"

"Ears was a piece of cake. I've got a trace on the line. No one's making any calls, though. At least not off the landline."

"Are there mobile numbers?"

"Yeah, I got a first ping a couple of minutes ago. It's in Urdu."

"Play it. I'll translate for you."

Luke cued the recording and hit the button. Charlie listened to the short recording of the quiet, muffled voice.

"Again." She frowned as she concentrated on the slightly gravelly tone of the voice. "I think it's Tazim."

"Makes sense. The number we found for Yasar is different."

"Right. He's ordering someone, I think the guy's name is Hani, to bring a car to the back of the house after dark. And to fill the jerry cans with diesel. He says they're heading for the mountains."

No one spoke. The only sounds in the van were the whirring and beeping of the electronic equipment. Charlie's heart thundered in her ears, and she felt stifled in the sweltering heat of the muggy van. She pulled at the neck of her shirt and wished it was all over.

"So we have our time frame, people," Al said. "Charlie, you ready to make this call, or do you need a minute?" He held the headset out to her.

"We don't have much time." She put the earpiece in place and nodded to Luke. "Put me through to him."

"You got it, C."

The phone rang three times before it was answered.

"Who is this?" The man spoke in Urdu and Charlie had never been more grateful for the hours Hazaar had spent teaching her the language, and she answered him back fluently.

"Is this Yasar Siddiqi?"

"Yes."

"My name is Charlotte. I work for the British Embassy."

"I have nothing to do with the embassy."

She knew he was about to hang up. "I know about Hazaar, Yasar."

"What did you say?" His voice dropped dangerously.

"I said I know about Hazaar. I know what your father plans to do to her."

"I don't know what you're talking about."

"We intercepted a call from him, ordering a car and diesel fuel to take her to the mountains, where he plans to burn her to death."

"You're lying." His voice was little more than a growl in her ear.

"No, I'm not." She could feel the calm she always felt descend upon her when she was negotiating. The peace she felt came from knowing that she was doing the absolute right thing, that she had someone's life in her hands and right this second, it was her job to make sure that she didn't lose that life. And it had never been more important than it was right now.

"Yes, you are."

"If I was lying, how would I know about the nightingale pendant that he threw into the fire last night?" She blocked the memories of giving the necklace to Hazaar. She couldn't let herself see the way she had looked as she wrapped it around her neck, the way her kiss had felt, or the way they had made love afterward.

"But she—"

"She isn't wearing it. Check. See that I'm telling the truth."

"No. I won't listen to this."

"If you don't, he will kill her."

"No, she is under my protection. He knows this and will not touch her."

"Was she under your protection last night when he beat her? When he burned her feet to stop her from running away?" She curled her toes in her shoes at the thought.

"He will not touch her. I don't believe you."

"I can prove everything I've said to you." There was silence on the other end of the line. "I'm not looking to prosecute anyone. I'm not the police."

"Meet me in one hour."

*Yes!* She wanted to run and shout and scream and dance, but there wasn't time, and this wasn't the place. "Where?"

"Outside the Peshawar Museum. You know what I look like?"

"Yes."

He grunted. "Come alone. Follow me. When I am certain you are alone, we will talk. You will show me your proof."

"One hour."

The line went dead.

# CHAPTER THIRTY-ONE

*The North of England, then*

Hazaar took a deep breath as Yasar turned off the engine and quickly ran around the car to open the door for her. He took her hand and helped her out. He kissed the back of her hand as he led her to her father's door, his smile wide. Hazaar wished she felt the same way.

"Yasar, I'm really not sure about this."

"Nonsense, my darling, the doctor said you're two months pregnant and that everything looks perfect."

"Yes, but she also said that most people wait until after the first trimester before telling people, as the risk of miscarriage is greatly reduced." She wanted to buy herself some time, time to think, to decide, to plan, but she knew he wouldn't give her that, and there was no way she could explain to him why she wanted that without making him suspicious of her motives. Throughout the appointment with the doctor, all she'd been able to think about was her unborn child and the future she was condemning it to. If she stayed with Yasar, their child would be well looked after, without question. He or she would want for nothing, except the freedom to choose their own future. If she left Yasar, she had no way of knowing how she would provide basics such as food and a place to live for herself and her child. Could she earn enough playing or teaching piano? Possibly. Could she do so while she was raising a child alone? She didn't know.

"There's no need to worry, Hazaar. I'll take care of you and our baby. Everything will be fine. I promise."

Hazaar wanted to point out that there was no way he could keep that promise, that as much as he could control most things in his world, nature wasn't one of them.

"I want to tell your father." He winked at her. "I want to tell the whole world. I'll call my own father tomorrow. It's too late now to wake him, even for such wonderful news." He rang the doorbell and they waited. "Everyone will be so excited. They've been waiting to hear this news."

"My mother will be pleased that I'll gain weight."

Yasar laughed. "It will make her happy on many levels, my darling." He wrapped an arm around her shoulders. "As you've made me happy."

"Yasar, *Beti,* it's so good to see you, come in, come in." Her father pulled the door open and waved them in. "To what do I owe this unexpected pleasure? I would have thought you'd be at work on a Wednesday afternoon."

Yasar held her hand and tried to help her sit down, but she waved his hands away. "I'm fine. I can sit down by myself." Her father looked at her, a strange frown on his face, then glanced back to Yasar.

"We have some exceptional news to tell you."

Her mother opened the door and carried in a tray of tea. This was the future she would give to her child. She looked at her father. He sat in his chair, and the proud set of his shoulders was gone. She hadn't seen it since he'd given her away. Before that, if she were being truly honest with herself. But Hatim's imprisonment and subsequent death had aged him. He looked gaunt in a way she had never seen before. His shoulders slumped, his hair was greyer than before, and the dark circles under his eyes were testament to a lack of sleep. Regret wasn't a kind mistress.

"Uncle, Auntie, I, we, have great news." Yasar sat on the edge of his seat, elbows resting on his knees and his hands clasped around his cup. He put the cup down and took her hand in his. Her mother smiled broadly at the gesture. "We are going to have a baby."

Hazaar kept her gaze locked on her father. His eyes widened and his jaw slackened slightly as her mother jumped from her chair and pulled her into a hug. He shook Yasar's hand and kissed his cheeks before Hazaar found herself in front of him. He cupped her face in his hands, and she could see the questions in his eyes. He kissed her forehead and pulled her into a tight embrace.

"You have made me the proudest father in the world, *Jugnu.* Never could I have asked for more from a daughter and still you make me even more proud."

"Thank you, Baba."

"She is a wonderful woman, Uncle. You have every reason to be proud of her." Yasar beamed at her and kissed her hand again. The action made her cringe. It made her feel possessed, owned, controlled, rather than cared for in the way she had felt when Charlie had done the same thing.

She heard them talking around her, Yasar asking after her mother's health and her state of mind after Hatim's recent death. She'd been surprised when her mother had continued to be cordial toward Yasar after he testified against Hatim in court. There was no denying that Yasar's testimony had been the most damaging, and had effectively sealed her son's fate. The son she had doted on, spoiled to the point where he believed the world and all the women in it were his to command, and given in to every temper tantrum so that he believed he should always get his own way. But Yasar was a different story. He had quickly shown them all why his own father held him in such high esteem. He was shrewd, quick-witted, and ruthless. It was easy to see that he would rule his father's empire, probably sooner rather than later, and this was why she was certain her mother had continued to support him despite his testimony. Hatim's shame was more than enough reason for her mother to publicly distance herself and align herself with Yasar. After all, public appearance was really all she was concerned with.

Hazaar glanced over at her father again, noting the sad smile on his face. *If only you had been able to undo the damage Maa Jee caused. We might have all had a chance.*

Yasar's phone rang. "My apologies, Auntie, Uncle. I must take this call." He left the room.

"Why so quiet, *Beti*? You should be jumping for joy." Her mother pointed at her and wiggled her finger. "You've lost weight again. You need to take better care of yourself. Especially now you have a child on the way."

"I've been looking after myself, Maa Jee."

"And that man of yours. He's a good man. So sweet to you, taking time off work to go to the doctor's with you. Such a lovely boy." She clapped her hands together and held them beside her face. She had done it for as long as Hazaar could remember, whenever she was excited and happy, and Hazaar had always thought she looked like a little girl when she did so.

"Yes, I'm looking after him too."

"Well, see that you do. You don't want to lose a man like that."

"She has no fear of that, Auntie. You have raised her to be a perfect wife." Yasar walked back into the room and leaned over to kiss the top of Hazaar's head. "I am sorry, but I have to go to work. There is a problem I must take care of. I'll take you home."

"If you're going to be out for a while, I could stay here for a little bit."

He shook his head. "I don't know what time I'll be able to come and pick you up later."

"That's okay. I'm sure Baba will take me home," she said, "won't you, Baba?"

"Of course."

"We don't want to put your father out of his way, Hazaar." Yasar tugged gently on her hand.

"It's no trouble, Yasar. We see so little of Hazaar. It's a pleasure to spend time with her. I'll make sure she's home safely before you get there."

Yasar frowned. "You're sure, Uncle?"

"Certain."

"Very well." He stood and tugged on the waistcoat he wore. "I'll be home by eight at the latest."

"I'll have your supper waiting for you," Hazaar said. He nodded, kissed her mother's cheek, and left.

Her mother shook her head. "Why did you do that?"

"Do what?" Hazaar looked at her, hoping the mask of innocence would work.

"Don't look at me like that. I know you, Hazaar. You could have gone with him. Why upset him when he's been so nice to you?"

"I wasn't trying to upset him. I wanted to spend some time with you and Baba, that's all."

"Pff. Do I look like I was born yesterday?"

Hazaar laughed. "No, Maa Jee, but it isn't every day I find out I'm pregnant for the first time either. There are things I want to talk to you about."

Tears welled in her mother's eyes. "Of course, how silly of me. You have always been so different from the other girls—it didn't occur to me that you would have the same questions they did. I'm sorry."

"It's okay."

"Come, we'll go to the kitchen and talk. This isn't for men's ears, *Beti*."

Hazaar shrugged and followed her into the kitchen, where her mother went into detail about her own five pregnancies, how she suffered with morning sickness every day for nine months while she was pregnant with Hatim, but only for a few weeks with each of her girls. She told her about her cravings, her mood swings, the crying, everything that Hazaar should expect in the next few months. And every second, Hazaar was thinking about getting away from her, about talking to her father, about making the plans she needed to make. She feigned a yawn and stretched her arms over her head.

"Already with the sleepiness?" her mother asked.

"No, it's just been a big day. I'm going to go see Baba for a little while before I go home." She found him in the garage, sorting through various pieces of wood. He smiled when he saw her.

"For your sisters and Fatima, I made the crib for the baby when they first found out they were pregnant. I will do the same for you." He pointed at the wood. "What colour would you like?"

"Baba, it doesn't matter."

"I made it for them. I'll make it for you too." He smiled sadly. "It's expected."

"Baba, I don't expect it."

"No, *Jugnu,* not by you. But by the eyes that will watch." She cocked her head to one side. "Your mother, *Beti.* She'll ask questions if I don't do the same for you as I did for them. Even though I know you won't need this crib."

"Baba—"

He put his finger to her lips. "There is no need. I know. I understand."

"What do you understand?"

"That you're going to make me even more proud of you. You're going to do what I wasn't strong enough to do, aren't you?" He put the pieces of wood down and dropped his hands to the workbench. "You're going to do what is right for your baby."

Hazaar let out a breath and quickly wrapped her arms around his waist, tucked her head under his chin, and held him. "Please don't cry, Baba."

He chuckled and wiped his eyes. "It's not good for a man to cry before his daughter, *Beti.* You deserve better."

"You're my father. I love you. There is no better."

"Hazaar, I made you marry that man to save my own life."

"No, that was the reason I agreed. It wasn't the only reason you asked." She wiped his cheek with her thumb. "If it hadn't been your life I was saving, though, Baba, I wouldn't have agreed."

"I know. But now the other reasons I asked don't matter. Your brother is gone. Shamed by his disgraceful behaviour and killed in prison. Slaughtered like a pig with its throat cut. There's no reason to continue the charade."

"That's not true. When I do this, they'll come for you."

He cupped her face in his hands. "Let them come."

"Baba, they'll kill you." Hazaar almost choked on the words as she forced them from her lips.

"Then let them kill me. I have learned my lesson, *Jugnu,* and I will live—or die—with it. You and your child are more important than the days I have left on this earth. To die protecting you will be my honour." He kissed her forehead. "I only pray that it will be enough to atone for putting you in danger to begin with. I should never have asked this of you. The price for me hasn't changed, nor had it for your brother. I could have spared you this pain."

"You were trying to do the best you could. You didn't know Hatim would end up in prison."

"No, I didn't know your brother would end up in prison, but I did know the kind of man he had become, and the kind of woman you were."

"I can't stay. I can't let my children be sucked into the world he lives in. If I have a son, he's being born to be a drug dealer, and a daughter of Yasar's is nothing but a bargaining chip in business. Yes, he would love them. He would care well for them. But that isn't a life I can condemn my child to. I'm sorry."

"No need to apologize." He squeezed her again, then turned and crossed the room. He pulled out two folding chairs and pointed for her to sit down. "If you give me a few days, I'll see what I can do. I'll get some cash, perhaps a car, if I can. Maybe I'll be able to find you somewhere to go."

"You don't have to do that."

"I know. But I'll do everything I can. You're my daughter. You're carrying my grandchild, and I'll do everything in my power to take care of you as I should have done before."

She didn't know what to say or what to think. Her father wasn't only accepting that she was going to run away and put his life on the line, but actually planning to help her do so.

"I won't forget this, Baba."

He nodded. "Will you go back to her?"

Hazaar stared at him. Was he really asking what she thought he was? Was he asking about Charlie? Did he mean something else? He nodded as she continued to stare at him. She didn't know she was crying until her dress was soaked though. He put his fingers to her lips again when she tried to speak. "No. No apologies, no explanations. You're my daughter and I love you. I want you to be happy, no matter the cost to me. I was too blind, too weak to do this for you before. I failed you, and I beg your forgiveness, *Jugnu*. You have nothing to be sorry for. Go to her and be happy."A noise outside the door startled them both. He opened the door to find the hallway empty. He shrugged as he sat down again. "Perhaps it was the wind."

Hazaar wiped her eyes. "Are you sure, Baba?"

"About the wind, no, but there—"

"I meant about helping me."

"Oh, yes." His face set into stubborn lines. "More certain than I have been about anything in my life."

"But why?"

"You are my daughter. I love you. It's that simple."

"I love you too, Baba."

"Three days, *Beti*." He smiled and squeezed her hand. "And we will set you free."

# CHAPTER THIRTY-TWO

*Pakistan, today*

"Here."

Charlie caught the black bundle that Al threw to her. "Thanks." She unravelled the package and ripped open the Velcro tabs on the tactical vest before slipping it over her head and slapping the tabs in place across her chest and stomach. She nodded her thanks to Kenzie when she handed her a loose black shirt to wear over it.

"This," Luke said, "has a GPS device built in. It's also your microphone." He handed her a watch.

Charlie shook her head. "That won't work. I can't be talking into my wrist all the time."

"You don't need to. The mic is omnidirectional. If you can, keep your hand on a table or across your chest, like this." He held his arm across his midsection.

"Luke, if I walk around like that, I need a sling to carry my arm, or I'm going to look suspicious."

"Use this." Kenzie passed her a messenger style bag that she could wear across her body. "Keeping hold of the strap while you walk or talk won't look suspicious."

"Good thinking." Charlie eyed her. "Covert ops?"

Kenzie winked. "On occasion."

"Do we have video?" Charlie turned back to Luke.

He handed her a pair of black-rimmed glasses. "They have those tinted lenses that get darker outside in the sun so you can keep them on at all times."

"Nice." She turned them in her hands as she opened the stems. "I'll look like Buddy Holly in these things."

"Nah, rims like that are all the rage, Charlie."

Charlie laughed and put them on. "How do I look?"

"Very sexy." Kenzie wiggled her eyebrows jokingly and Luke sniggered.

"All right, enough. Are we ready?" Al turned around again.

"Yup." Charlie slipped the bag over her head and shook out her head scarf.

"Right, then we'll let you out here and find somewhere to park near the museum. You make your way there on foot. We're a two-minute walk away here. Just stay on this road and keep going."

"I know, Al. I've been here before you know."

"Yeah, but this is different, Charlie. This is personal."

"All the more reason to make sure I do this properly." She checked her watch. "Five minutes."

"I put the recording on the MP3 player in your bag. Also copies of the statements made by the girls in the UK."

Charlie frowned. "The ones who said Tazim had the older brother killed?"

"Yeah. Just in case you need a little extra ammunition."

"Thanks." She gripped the handle of the door. "Okay, see you all afterward."

"Charlie." Al called her and she looked over her shoulder at him. "Be careful. This guy's dangerous."

"I will be." She climbed out of the van and tugged the door shut behind her. It was almost nine thirty in the morning and the heat of the day was already climbing. Sweat trickled down her spine and soaked the waistband of her jeans. She tried to focus on the uncomfortable feeling at the small of her back, the way her shoes pinched the back of her ankles, the way the strap of the messenger bag felt against her palm, anything to keep from thinking about who she was going to meet. Every time she thought of him, the anger and jealousy that smouldered in the pit of her stomach flared to life and burned through her blood. Right now she needed to stay calm, focused, and do the job she needed to do. To save the lives she knew were at stake.

The museum was built in 1907. The brick building was surrounded by beautiful gardens and stretched out before her. It reminded her of a garrison with its three double doors at the entrance, brick columns and archways, and huge terra-cotta domes that decorated the balustrades and rooftops that loomed above her as she approached.

She'd seen his picture. In fact, she'd spent most of the morning staring at the image of him with his arm wrapped around Hazaar's waist, but she wasn't quite prepared to see the man himself as he waited outside the entrance. She wasn't sure what it was that threw her. She shook her head and slowly walked toward him, careful to keep her gaze on him, waiting for him to notice her. She took in every detail as she neared and allowed the practice to calm the last of her nerves. The cut of his hair, the precisely trimmed beard around his mouth and jawline, the pristine white of his *shalwar kemeeze* all suggested he was a man in control. He stood perfectly at ease, looking as though he were simply enjoying the delights of the garden, the beautiful day, perhaps even the sound of the birds chirping in the trees. There was nothing to indicate that he was anything but an ordinary man on an ordinary day. Charlie chewed on the inside of her lip and tried again to find that calm within herself. She needed to focus, to concentrate, and to let go of the emotion she felt. *Yeah, like that's going to happen.*

She was so busy berating herself that she almost missed the moment he finally made eye contact with her. The nod was barely perceptible, but he deliberately turned and walked through the doors. She followed, keeping a distance of around fifteen feet. There were very few people around as she watched him wander through the exhibits, apparently reading some of the information cards, looking at the statues, coins, paintings, early weapons, and jewellery, even an early version of the Quran was displayed amongst the collection. There were wooden benches in each hall, and when he sat down she slowly made her way to sit beside him.

The room housed a collection of Buddhist stone sculptures and terra-cotta figurines, but no people. She smiled and crossed her legs, resting her clasped hands around her knees.

"Good morning, Charlotte."

"Mr. Siddiqi." He smiled, obviously pleased at her show of respect. "Thank you for meeting with me."

"You have information for me." He held out his hand.

She reached into the bag and pulled out the MP3 player and ear buds. He handled them carefully and put the bud to his ear without placing it against his skin. She pressed play and watched his face darken whilst it seemed he didn't move a muscle. The energy around him changed, and the mild-mannered man she had witnessed for the past twenty minutes vanished. He hadn't moved, but his demeanour, the energy that crackled off him, now felt aggressive, enraged, and dangerous. She had to suppress a shiver as he handed the device back to her.

"I could point out to you that you have broken the law by recording my father's conversation, but we both know that doing so would also mean that I am admitting to that line belonging to myself or someone in my household. And since I'm not doing that, I cannot comment on the legalities of you possessing that recording."

"I'm not here to discuss the legalities of the recording any more than I am here to discuss other activities that we may or may not have become privy to since monitoring began." She paused to let the subtle threat sink in. They had no other recordings, no other evidence to his illegal activities, but he didn't know that. She was hoping it would be enough to make him at least pause, to consider her request, to buy them some time. "Those things are not my concern, nor do I need to worry about those possible recordings, or where they might end up once I complete my investigation."

"But your concern, Charlotte, is my wife?"

She nodded. "My concern is for any British national living in Pakistan. My concern is to help them to the best of my abilities."

"And my wife has asked for your help?"

Charlie swallowed. "Yes."

"How?"

"She called."

"Liar."

"No, I'm not—"

"If she was in the situation you described, Charlotte, how could she call you? How could she reach out and solicit your help?"

"Yesterday lunchtime I received a call from a woman who called herself Maya. She was enquiring about leaving the country with her daughter, but didn't have their passports."

"And this is your call for help? A woman who wishes to leave?"

"No, that alone wouldn't be enough." Charlie knew that her explanation would be putting Amira's life in just as much danger as Hazaar's. It didn't matter that Amira already knew the risk she was running and had willingly accepted it. It mattered to Charlie that her actions here and now were going to put another woman at risk, one she stood little chance of being able to save. She shook her head. "We received another call. Late last night, the call came from the same number but a different person. This person told us that the woman was in grave danger and asked us to save her."

"How do you know this is not a hoax?"

"You mean besides the fact that you met me this morning?"

He smiled and inclined his head. "Aside from that."

She was taking a chance. Everything Kenzie had profiled told her that Amira was not in danger from the man sitting in front of her, and that to engage his help, she had to gain his trust. Only the truth would do that. The subtly veiled threats and suggestions of rewards weren't going to work with this man. *Please let me be right about this, or they're both dead.*

"I met with Amira this morning. She told me that Hazaar was injured. That she needs medical attention and that your father has promised her a coffin rather than a doctor."

"Hazaar is my wife. I will protect her."

"From your own father?"

"If need be." He growled the word. "She is my wife. Mine. Not his or anyone else's. It is for me to protect her, discipline her, and teach her."

"Then protect her. I can take them away from here."

"No."

"Mr. Siddiqi, in your business you have bigger concerns than a disobedient wife and a father who interferes." The acid in her stomach roiled and rolled, each word concentrating it further and making it stronger; strong enough to eat her from the inside out. Hazaar was his wife. Those hands had touched her, those lips had kissed her. *No! Stop it. Now is not the time for this.* She breathed in and watched him frown at her.

"What are you talking about? I am a simple business man. What other concerns could I possibly have?"

"I believed that you had interests in more high-value products than spices, Mr. Siddiqi, and it occurred to me that a man in such a business would have some concerns about his...reputation...if it were to become common knowledge that he couldn't control things at home. I'm sure his rivals would think him weak and ripe for attack. Perhaps, even those in his own organization would think he didn't deserve to head up such an outfit, if this were the case." She smiled a tiny smile. "But obviously I was mistaken, as you are a simple spice man, after all." She pointed to the MP3 player. "You heard the recording. He has it all planned. If you want to protect her, let me help."

He stared at her, eyes narrowed to slits. "She is mine to protect, Charlotte. Mine." He stood up. "They both are."

He walked away. She could hear his shoes clicking on the parquet floor, the rustle of linen from the crisp, perfectly pressed loose-fitting pants. She knew he had left and that she was alone in the room filled with terra-cotta figurines and marble sculptures. She felt as hollow as the moulded clay, and as heavy and cold as the crystalline stone.

She waited until the black spots faded from her vision, but her knees still didn't feel strong enough to support her weight, so she sat on the bench and breathed. She glanced at her watch again. It wasn't even ten o'clock yet. It had been less than twenty-four hours since the first phone call from Hazaar, and her whole world had shifted. Was it really going to end like this? Was this the closure she would get after so many years of dreaming about Hazaar?

# CHAPTER THIRTY-THREE

*The North of England, then*

Hazaar waved to Yasar as he reversed out of the driveway, and then she ran up the stairs to their bedroom. She pulled a bag from the wardrobe and stuffed her clothes in as fast as she could. The past three days had crawled by, and now that it was time to leave, there wasn't a second to waste. Her taxi was due any moment to take her to the train station, where her father had a car waiting for her. He said he'd put cash in the spare tire well and a map with directions to an apartment he'd arranged for her. He said it wasn't much. In truth, she didn't care. She just needed somewhere to go while she got herself sorted out.

"Going somewhere, my darling?"

Hazaar whirled to face the door, one hand at her chest, the other over her mouth to stop the scream that threatened. "Yasar." She panted, her heart raced beneath her palm, and all she wanted to do was run. There was a look in his eye she hadn't seen before, and it scared her. "Did you forget something?"

"Perhaps I did." He closed the door and leaned against it. There was no other way out of the room. "I asked you a question, Hazaar."

"I'm sorry, I didn't catch it."

He pointed at the bag. "Are you going somewhere?"

She looked at the bag, and wanted to come up with a quick, plausible explanation, but fear dulled her mind. "I…" *Think, damn it. Think.*

"Yes?"

"I was going to take them to wash."

"In a backpack?"

*Stupid fucking idiot.* "Yes."

"To the washing machine downstairs?"

She closed her eyes as she nodded. She knew he didn't believe her. He wasn't a fool.

"Is there something wrong with the laundry basket?"

*Maybe he'll buy that baby brain syndrome thing my sisters talked about.* "I got a little confused. Couldn't remember where it was. Hormones or something."

"You couldn't remember that the laundry basket was in the laundry hamper? In the bathroom? Where you put your clothes every night?"

She sat on the edge of the bed and let the tears of frustration fall.

"Your mother warned me about this, you know."

Hazaar looked up, shocked that her mother had been speaking to Yasar about such intimate things as pregnancy, but she was grateful. She smiled, wishing she would see her mother again to thank her. "She did?"

He nodded and sat next to her. "Yes. She called me on Wednesday. While your father was bringing you home."

"That was nice of her. It must have been an awkward conversation." She remembered the uncomfortable conversation just before her wedding when her mother had tried to discuss the events of the wedding night. She could scarcely imagine her mother talking to him about her pregnancy and what to expect from her throughout it.

"Yes, it was. But I am very pleased that she had the courage to do so. It takes a strong person to do the right thing for one's family, no matter how awkward you may feel about it. Don't you think?"

The hairs on the back of her neck stood on end. "Yes, she's a very good mother."

He nodded and took hold of her hand. "Yes, you were blessed when Allah granted you Nisrin as your mother."

"Yes."

"She talked to me for a long time on Wednesday. Told me many things. She is a very…knowledgeable woman, your mother."

There was a strange look in his eye as he said it and something registered in Hazaar's mind. She remembered the noise outside the garage door on Wednesday afternoon and her pulse rocketed. "And exactly how knowledgeable is my mother, Yasar?"

His grip on her hand tightened. "She was knowledgeable enough to tell me that you were planning to take my child from me, Hazaar."

*Fuck.*

"She was knowledgeable enough to know what a poor decision

this would be for you." He squeezed her hand tighter. "And that your father was planning to help you." He pushed the sleeve of her blouse up her arm. "She knows how much shame you were going to bring to the family, Hazaar."

"No, Yasar, she's wrong."

"You call your own mother a liar?" He pulled a syringe from his pocket and pulled the needle cap off with his teeth.

"No, never. She must have misunderstood." She tried to pull her arm away, but his grip on her wrist was too strong.

He shook his head sadly. "I don't think so." He shook the syringe and she watched in morbid curiosity as the bubbles rose to the top. "She told me that today is the day you planned to leave this house, my darling, and not return."

"It must have been some kind of mistake. My father and I talked about the baby crib he's making. We were going to look at paint for it today. That's where we're going. That's what we were talking about." She sprang to her feet and tried to pull her arm from his grasp.

"If you keep still, I can make this less painful for you."

She twisted and turned in his grasp, and hoped that every movement prevented him from being able to inject whatever was in the syringe into her body. She didn't know what it was. She didn't want to; she didn't need to. All she knew was that whatever it was would render her unable to escape, and that was all the motivation she needed to utilize everything at her disposal to ensure she got away from him.

She couldn't pull free of his grip, so she tried to run, hoping that the momentum would shock him enough to loosen his grasp. Instead, he allowed it to haul him to his feet and then he caged her against the wall.

"Don't hurt the baby, please."

"I have no intention of hurting my child. Hold still and I won't hurt you either."

"No." She landed a knee to his groin. She curled her fingers and gouged at his face.

Yasar howled, wrapped his arms around her waist, and pushed her onto the bed. She lay trapped beneath his body weight, her wrists pinned above her head in one of his large hands, while he cupped himself with the other. His eyes watered and his face was scarlet as she struggled beneath him. She kicked at his shins, twisted her body trying to buck him off, and even tried to bite his shoulder in desperation, but he didn't move. He kept her pinned to the bed and let her wear herself out. There was no escape.

He leaned in close and whispered, "You are mine. You are my wife. You are carrying my baby, and I will look after you." He lifted up enough that she could see his face clearly. "I vowed to protect you and to take responsibility for you for the rest of our lives. And I will do that. No matter what." He stretched over to the nightstand and grabbed the syringe. She hadn't seen him put it there before, but it didn't matter. "I wanted to love you, Hazaar." He held the syringe up and squirted out the bubbles. "We could have been happy. I cared for you. I would have given you everything you could have wanted in a husband." He gripped the syringe barrel between his teeth and ripped the blouse sleeve to expose her upper arm. "We could have lived here and been happy, and perhaps in time you could have taught your music. Maybe you could have learned to love me. Was I not good to you?"

"Yes, you were, Yasar."

"Did I not try to please you?"

"Yes, you did. You tried very hard."

"Then why could you not give us a chance? Why must you betray me like this? I would have given you the world." His gaze shifted from her face to her arm. He looked genuinely puzzled.

"Please don't do this."

"I didn't do this, Hazaar. You did. All you had to do was be a good wife, a good mother, and I would have taken care of everything else for you. I would have shared my world with you."

"I didn't want you to take care of everything for me, Yasar."

"You wanted to do it for yourself, is that it? That is why you were going to betray me? To steal my child? To be independent?"

"No." She tried to pull her arms free again. "I wanted to be away from you for our child. To save my baby from all this."

"I don't understand, Hazaar, from all what? A father who will love the very ground they walk upon? Who will give them everything they could ever desire? Who will teach them to be strong, good Muslims—"

"And drug smugglers or bartering tools to grow your business for yourself and your sons."

He stared at her, his head cocked to one side. "You think I'm not good enough for you? For our children? That our culture, our religion, is beneath you and your Westernized bastardized idea of Islam?" He sneered at her. "You have no idea what it is to be a good Muslim wife. You have no idea what we have come from, my family and I." He jabbed the syringe into her upper arm and she cried out. "But you will learn. Intramuscular injection, my darling." He spat the words in her face. "I didn't need a vein." He pushed the plunger. "Just bare skin."

"The baby…" Her arm felt heavy and a warm feeling spread from the injection site.

"Will be just fine." He pulled the needle from her arm and dropped it back on the bedside table. "I will be here to protect my baby. Always."

The heavy feeling in her arm spread on the wings of the soothing warmth that suffused her body. She felt like she'd been submerged in warm water, floating peacefully along the current as he moved her and dressed her.

She knew she was drifting in and out of consciousness, for each time she opened her eyes the landscape was something new and unexpected. Her bedroom morphed to Yasar's car in the blink of an eye, and in the next she was at the airport. Her brain felt sluggish, unable to keep up with the way events were changing around her, and she knew it was the drug. She just hoped that he would have to let it wear off a little so that she could walk through the security gates. Even just a little less of the drug in her system and she would call for help, scream, anything to call attention to herself.

She hadn't realized that she was in a wheelchair until he pushed her toward the check in desk and the woman stood up to look at her, rather than expecting her to stand so she could check her passport. Yasar was smiling at the woman as he handed her a piece of paper.

"The doctor has said that she is fit to fly, as you can see." He pointed at the page as she read it. "Unfortunately, the pain of her condition means she isn't always very communicative due to the amount of painkillers she has to take."

"And what is her condition, sir?"

*Very good question, lady. I don't have a medical condition. It's a fake. Call the practice. Call the doctor.* She wanted to shout. In her head, she was screaming every word, but nothing came out. Her mouth refused to move, and her arms were too heavy to lift.

"She has cancer." He smiled sadly. "She wants to go home for her final days."

*Home? Where the fuck is he taking me?*

"That's so beautiful." Hazaar could hear her fingers flying over the keyboard and a printer spitting out boarding cards and luggage tags.

*Check the passport, you stupid woman. You'll see I'm from England.*

"Here are your tickets, sir. Flight PKA96 to Islamabad will be departing at two p.m. from gate number twelve. If you try to get there about one o'clock, the girls on the door will get you and your wife on before the rush."

"That's wonderful. Thank you for your help."

"No problem, sir. If you keep that letter handy when you're going through security, they'll help you there."

"Excellent. You've been most helpful." He put his bag over his shoulder and wheeled her away from the desk and toward the security gate. He leaned over her as if to adjust her clothing and whispered in her ear. "It didn't have to be like this, Hazaar. If you hadn't betrayed me, it could have been so different." She felt the sting of another needle in her upper arm and she couldn't believe his audacity. "I know what you're thinking. That anyone could see me do that to you here, right?" He squatted and tucked a blanket around her legs. He slid a small box behind her back. "It's an insulin pen filled with my own special mixture. Even if they saw, no one would question me giving my sick wife her medicine. I have the doctor's note to prove it." He patted his pocket. "It's good to have connections in my business. You never know when you might need a new passport." He waved a new Pakistani passport in front of her face, her picture showing clearly. "A new birth certificate." Another piece of paper. "And a doctor's medical notice." He smiled and slipped them all back in his pocket.

Her eyelids grew heavy as she looked at him, and she could feel her head sinking onto her chest.

"Sleep, my darling. When you wake, you'll be at your new home."

Her eyelids closed and the heavy slumber claimed her before the tears had dried on her cheeks.

# CHAPTER THIRTY-FOUR

*Pakistan, today*

Charlie jumped and turned as a hand touched her shoulder.

"Sorry. You stopped responding, so Al sent me to come and see what's wrong." Kenzie sat on the bench beside her, the spot where Yasar had sat only a few minutes earlier.

"I didn't hear him."

Kenzie pointed at the earpiece on her lap. "Well, I know his voice carries, but you'll still need that to hear him while you're in here."

"Damn it, is he pissed?"

"A bit."

"Shit." She started to push up off the bench, but Kenzie took hold of her shoulder.

"Just give it a second. I can see how pale you are."

"We don't have time. We only have nine hours until sunset and—"

"And rushing a man like Yasar won't get him to agree to your position."

"It's all the time we have. You heard that phone call. He said just after sunset. That's seven p.m., Kenzie."

"I know. But nine hours may not be long enough to get him to agree to let her go. You know that, don't you?"

Charlie didn't want to admit it, but she couldn't deny it either.

"What's your backup plan?"

"Backup?"

"Yes. You know, the one you try when the other one fails." Kenzie smiled the crooked little sarcastic smile she had.

"I know what you mean, but we don't have time to form another negotiation strategy. We agreed this was the only way that we could make it work."

"True. If this fails, there is no other negotiation. So what are you planning to do next?"

Charlie closed her eyes and leaned against the bench. She knew what Kenzie was hinting at, but what she didn't know was whether Al had sent her in to find out if she would go in to try to save Hazaar without sanction and have her taken off the case. She sighed heavily and decided there was only one way to find out.

"Did Al send you in to try to profile me, Kenzie?"

She laughed. "Nope." She dropped a small bag on her lap. "He sent me in to tell you that he's working on plan B."

"What's this?" She pointed to the bag.

"New earpiece." She took the old one and deactivated it. "Luke was concerned that Yasar may have been able to get a reverse trace on your line. He did explain it, but it sounded like mumbo jumbo to me so I chose to forget it all. He'll enjoy being able to explain it all to you himself later."

Charlie laughed. "You have a way with people, Kenzie."

"I know." She sighed. "It's a curse."

She followed Kenzie out of the museum and across the road to the van. Al was in the back, pointing to a map on one of the terminals as Luke watched him intently.

"We need to switch this van for a couple of Jeeps. If he goes off-road, we're gonna need to be able to follow him. This thing can't handle that terrain." He flipped to another screen. "Luke, can you get two equipped and ready to follow a GPS tracker? We'll find a way to get them on the van."

"No problem. If you can get me the Jeeps, I'll need an hour, tops."

"You're going to follow the van and try to get her from Tazim?" Charlie stared at him. "That's your plan B?"

"No. That's plan C." Luke grinned.

"Plan B is where we try to get into the house while Yasar and Tazim are out and then we can make sure that we have all of them safe, Amira included," Al said.

"Is there a safe house for her?"

"I've got Hillary looking for one." He pointed to another screen. "This is a satellite image of the house. And the overlay is the layout, as far as we can tell."

The two-story building was centred around a courtyard. The kitchen and bathrooms were easy to see on the schematic, but the layout of the other rooms was open to suggestion.

"Where'd you get all this?"

"Between Hillary and the boy wonder over there, all I had to do was ask." He shrugged. "Seems they already had it waiting for me to say the word."

"JJ sanctioned this?"

Al laughed. "JJ's exact words were, 'I don't know anything about you going in the house to help those women, or failing that, heading out toward the mountains to help anyone stranded when the tires on their van blow out.'"

Charlie laughed. "It's his plan?"

"This isn't official, Charlie. We have no jurisdiction and no government backup. We can try the old diplomatic immunity, but honestly," he said, "if this goes wrong, we could all go to a Pakistani prison."

Charlie shuddered and shook her head. "No. I can't let you take that chance."

"You aren't letting us, Charlie. You aren't asking. We're doing this because it's the right thing to do." He put his hand on her shoulder. "I can't speak for everyone else's reason in this, kiddo, but I can tell you that there have been too many times I've had to sit back and let too many women suffer when I could have done more."

"It's not as simple as that, Al." They were her friends, and together they had saved lives and given hope to so many. Now they were offering the same to her, and to Hazaar.

"No, it isn't. But maybe it should be." She didn't realize she was crying until he wiped his thumbs across her cheeks. "This one time, it can be."

"You're risking your lives."

"Only if we get caught, and Wonder Woman over there assures me she could do this on her own, in her sleep, and still get away with it. So we should be laughing."

"Al, I've got that thermal imaging layer you wanted," Luke said.

"Nice. Can you overlay it on the schematic?"

"Your wish is my command, Master." The screen flickered, and the new image came up. The house now had five multicoloured blobs of differing sizes in varying parts of the house, moving at different speeds and in different directions. There was one that didn't move at all, and the colours were more subdued than the others, varying shades of blue, green, and yellow.

"How can we tell who's who?"

"We can take a couple of educated guesses based on what we know of the family unit living in this place." Al pointed to the smallest spot. "This is likely to be the little girl. We know she's about two and would need to be cared for, so the heat signature with her is most likely to be Amira, and these other two are probably Yasar and Tazim." He pointed to the blue-green shape. "Based on what Amira said about Hazaar being kept in the cellar, her feet being burned, and the other injuries, it's very likely that this is her. This person hasn't moved, and the fact that she's below ground level could account for the lower thermal reading."

"Could?"

"Yes, could."

"And what else could account for it?" She stared at him, but Al looked away. "What else?"

"The early stages of hypothermia or death," Luke said, and Charlie felt her chest tighten. "I've magnified it, though, and there are small movements, more like undulations really, so I think she's breathing."

"Okay. So what do you need me to do?"

"Honestly?" She nodded, unable to look away from the screen. "I need you to contact Yasar again."

She was about to ask why when they had all these plans, but she knew it was a silly question. If they could rescue Hazaar without having to execute either of these plans, then it would make life much simpler for everyone involved. It also meant that none of them were risking their lives. She grimaced as the other option crossed her mind. Prison. She wasn't sure which would be worse, death or prison.

She glanced at the monitor again. She wasn't sure if it was her imagination or not, but she thought the blue looked a little cooler, the yellow more faded, and the green seemed to have shrunk. Her hands felt so cold, she wondered for a moment if it was possible that she was feeling what Hazaar was, absorbing the chill from her body. She laughed at her own silly thoughts and wished she could reach through the monitor and touch her, wrap a blanket around, and just tell her that it would be okay. Just a few more hours and it would all be over. One way or another.

# CHAPTER THIRTY-FIVE

*The North of England, then*

"All right, I'm coming," Charlie shouted as the bell rang again. "I said, I'm coming." She pulled open the front door, ready to shout at whatever door-to-door salesman or canvasser had dared to disturb her. She closed her mouth quickly when she saw Hazaar's father wringing his hands and frowning.

"Mr. Alim, what are you doing here?" She shook her head. "I'm sorry. Please forgive my rudeness. I wasn't expecting to see you. Please come in." She ushered him into the sitting room where Charlie's mother stood and shook his hand.

"Mr. Alim, I'm Mrs. Porter. It's a pleasure to finally meet you."

"And you, Mrs. Porter."

"Can I get you something to drink? Some tea, perhaps?"

"A glass of water would be welcome."

Charlie's mother excused herself to the kitchen and Charlie pointed to the chair. "Won't you sit down, Mr. Alim?"

"Yes, thank you." He sat on the edge of the seat. His elbows rested on his knees, his hands shook as he clenched them in his lap. He was nothing like the man she had met over the years. She hadn't had a great deal of contact with him, but it was more than enough to see how distressed he was. She could have sworn he was ready to cry as she watched him fidget, tugging at his cuffs, his collar, adjusting his *topi*, seemingly unable to keep still at all.

"Mr. Alim, how can I help you?"

"Is she here? Hazaar. Is she here?"

Charlie's mother looked at her as she walked across the room and handed him a glass, clearly wondering what he was talking about.

"No."

"You don't need to hide her from me. I'm not here to make her return."

"I'm not hiding her."

"Please." He put his glass on the coffee table in the centre of the room. "Please, I beg you. Just tell me she's safe and pass on a message for me."

"Mr. Alim, I haven't seen her since graduation. The last time I spoke to her was weeks before that, when she said she was getting married."

"Please, Charlotte." He clasped his hands as though offering her a prayer. "Please, just tell me she's okay. As long as I know that she is safe, I will leave both of you alone. No one will ever learn from me where you are. You have my word."

"What do you mean you need to know she's safe? Why wouldn't she be safe?"

"She wanted to run away. She was going to come back here." He swallowed hard. "To you." He looked into her eyes, imploring her. "She truly isn't here?"

Charlie looked at her mother and saw her own shock mirrored on her face. She wasn't sure if she was more shocked that he knew about Hazaar's relationship with her or that he was sitting here, talking to her, despite the fact that he knew.

"No. I haven't had any contact with her, Mr. Alim."

He looked like he was about to crumble before her eyes. His skin paled, and the sheen of a sickly-smelling sweat made his face look waxy. The shadows beneath his eyes grew darker, deeper, and the profound sadness in his gaze was something she knew would haunt her for the rest of her life. She'd seen it before. The fathomless stare of someone whose sorrow knew no end.

"Then I've condemned her."

"Condemned her? To what? Mr. Alim, I don't understand, but you're frightening me." She sat next to him on the sofa and wrapped her hand around his. "What are you talking about?"

"Did Hazaar tell you?"

"Tell me what?"

"Why she agreed to the marriage?"

"She told me that she wasn't as strong as she had hoped she would be, and that she couldn't bring shame on you. She wanted you to be proud of her, to love her. So she was going to do what you wanted her to do."

He cried. He buried his face in his hands and sobbed. Charlie couldn't ignore the piteous sound and wrapped her arm around his shoulder, as her mother passed her a box of tissues.

"She was always my pride and joy. Always." He took the tissue she held out for him. "She married him because her stupid brother got us in trouble. If she hadn't, it would have cost us our lives—mine and Hatim's. She did it for me. Not to save my pride. But to save my life."

"What? How? What trouble could have put you in such danger?"

"Hatim was involved with drugs. They were going to have us killed. They were prepared to help us with the authorities, to go into business with us, to pay off the debts and the problems Hatim had caused. But they needed assurances from us that we wouldn't betray them."

"And Hazaar was the price they demanded?"

"Yes."

"She never told me." The sorrow that had been inside her touched the edges of the red sky and consumed it, devoured the energy of the rage and despair and fear, and made it her own. She let it fuel her and erupted.

"You sold her."

"Charlie!" Her mother stood and grabbed hold of Charlie's arm. "Don't."

Charlie was beyond hearing. "You sold her to fucking drug dealers to save your worthless boy's arse." She edged forward, towering over him as he sat in his seat. "You took her dreams, her life, and you sacrificed her for that worthless fucking scumbag."

"Charlie, stop." Her mother wrapped her around about her. "This isn't helping."

"It's helping me."

"No, it isn't." She grasped Charlie's face. "Look at him. Look at him and tell me you don't think he's suffering enough."

"He sacrificed his own daughter."

"Yes. He did, and he knows it. Look at him."

Charlie stared at her mother and slowly looked back at him. The man she'd met in Hazaar's apartment didn't exist anymore. He was dead, and in his place was this shell of an old man who had given up. Her rage left her as quickly as it had come.

"I made a mistake. I thought I could control where she would be and the man she was marrying. I thought, 'He is a young man. He will take my counsel and be good to my daughter.' That is what I thought. I thought I would still be able to look after her." He wiped the tears from his eyes. "I thought I could control her world for her. So I asked her to give up the most valuable thing to her because I was selfish. I put myself before my daughter and I asked her to give up her heart." He looked Charlie in the eye. "I asked her to give up her relationship with you."

"She would never have made any other decision. Not when she knew your life was at risk. She just couldn't. But why didn't she tell me?"

"I don't know." He shrugged. "Perhaps to protect you. To discourage you from trying to change her mind and making it more difficult for her."

"I wouldn't have done that. I'm not a monster, Mr. Alim. I wouldn't put my own happiness before your life."

"Then I don't know. Perhaps she was scared she wouldn't be able to leave you."

Could that be the case? Could that be the reason? That she was scared? It didn't matter now. It was done. She was married.

"What did you mean? When you said you've condemned her?"

"We made an arrangement. Today, this afternoon, she was going to run away from her husband."

"What?"

He nodded and leaned back. "Yes. I arranged a small flat not too far from here, a car at the train station, and money. All arranged."

"You were helping her?"

"Yes. I couldn't watch the light in her die any longer. As soon as she was ready, I agreed to help her."

"Are you no longer in danger, Mr. Alim?"

"The danger hasn't changed. But I no longer care, Charlotte."

"If it was all arranged, why are you here?"

"Because the car is still waiting at the train station. The money hasn't been touched, and the flat is empty." He drew in a long, shuddering breath. "I fear I wasn't fast enough in my preparations for her. Her home was empty when I went to check on her. Her bag sat on the bed half-packed. I hoped with everything in me that she had been interrupted and come here instead. That she had found a way back to you, Charlotte, to her happiness."

"She isn't here."

"I know, child. I know."

"Where else could she be?" Charlie's mother asked the question Charlie couldn't bring herself to voice. "Any other friends or relatives?"

He shook his head. "No, Mrs. Porter. Yasar hasn't been seen all day. It's this news that made me suspicious."

Sarah frowned. "Yasar?"

"Yasar Siddiqi, Hazaar's husband. He works with me."

"Ah, I see."

"Yes." He inched his way to the edge of the seat and scrubbed his hands over his face. "Please forgive me. I must go now."

"Where are you going?" Charlie gripped his arm. "I'll help you look for her."

He patted her hand and shook his head sadly. "No, child, that is not for us to do now. I'm going to the police station."

"Police. But why? I don't understand." Charlie watched as her mother and Mr. Alim exchanged glances, certain she was missing something, but her brain just didn't seem to want to focus, to grasp the threads that were unravelling before her. She didn't want to look at the picture he was leading her to.

"I must report Hazaar missing, Charlotte. If I am fast enough and he has not yet left the country, they may be able to stop him if he is trying to take her to Pakistan."

"You think he's kidnapping her?"

"I would rather think that he is taking her to live in Pakistan, than anything else."

"Would you like us to come with you, Mr. Alim?" her mother asked quietly as she tugged Charlie to her and wrapped an arm around her.

"No, thank you for your kind offer. But this is something I must do alone."

Her mother held Charlie tighter to her as he closed the door behind himself.

"Mum, what did he mean that he'd rather she was living in Pakistan than anything else? What did he mean?"

Her mother pulled her down onto the sofa. "You know what he meant, Charlie."

"No. No, no, no, no, no." She tried to push her mother away. "No. She is not dead." She pushed harder. "No. She isn't."

"Charlie, we don't know."

Charlie pushed her away and backed toward the door. "I know." She placed her hand over her heart. "I know. I can feel her."

"Oh, sweetheart."

"No, don't. She isn't dead. The bastard's taken her. He's taken her somewhere, but she's okay." Her mother reached out to her, but she slapped her hand away. "I know she is."

"Okay. I believe you." The look on her mother's face told her that she was humouring Charlie. That she didn't truly believe her, but it didn't matter. Charlie believed it.

She played every decision over and over in her mind as she paced the room. Could she have done anything differently? Could she, should she, have fought to keep Hazaar from marrying him? Would it have been better? Would Hazaar have been able to live with that decision, knowing it would have cost her father his life? What had been the final catalyst for Hazaar? That moment when she decided enough was enough, and that her life away from her husband was more important than saving her father? Would she ever know?

She was realistic enough to understand that maybe she would never get the answers to all her questions, and that some were better off not answered anyway. But maybe there were one or two answers she could find. If she could find Hazaar. If she could find a way to start looking for her. Mr. Alim said that he'd probably take her to Pakistan, which meant that was where Charlie needed to go.

She closed her eyes and tried to feel her, to feel Hazaar's heart beat inside her own. *Are you still out there, Hazaar?*

# CHAPTER THIRTY-SIX

*Pakistan, today*

Something moved in the cellar and Hazaar opened her eyes in time to see the long tail of a rat as it scurried away under a storage rack. She wondered just how close the disgusting little creature had been to her and trembled as she imagined that tail brushing against her skin, or those little claws scratching at the fabric of her clothes while cruel teeth gnawed at her flesh. She couldn't feel her left foot anymore, and the burnt sole could have been the rodent's meal, for all she knew. She hated rats. She had never seen them before coming to Pakistan, and now they seemed to be everywhere. She saw them in the street when she'd looked out from her window, in the house, and it had made her afraid to leave Afia alone for even a minute. She was terrified that she would walk into Afia's room to find one of the vile creatures nibbling on her beautiful face.

*Oh, my darling Afia, I'm so sorry.* She could feel the tears running from the corners of her eyes and into her hair, but she couldn't wipe them away. Even if she'd had the energy, her fingers were so broken and twisted that she couldn't have controlled them to wipe the small streams of moisture. Since the day she'd held Afia in her arms, she'd dreamed of teaching her to play the piano, of teaching her to read and write and take passion in learning. She'd dreamed of finding some way to take her away from this family and give her a different life. She swallowed the sour taste of failure and accepted that it had been her pursuit of these dreams that had brought her to this. Her desire for more, for better, was going to destroy her. No, it *had* destroyed her. There was no hope left. She couldn't remember where she'd heard it, maybe she'd read it somewhere, but a line haunted her, teased and taunted the edges of her brain. *Hope. That is the last refuge of madmen and dreamers.* The only hope she had left was for her child, her sweet, innocent little girl. It was the only dream she would allow herself, and it was driving her mad.

She knew Amira would love Afia, care for her, and teach her how to be a good Muslim woman, but Amira would never teach Afia how to be herself. She would never allow her the freedom to choose her own life, to make her own choices, or even teach her that there was a different way out there. It was repugnant to her and it broke her heart. Afia was the only good thing that had come out of this whole mess.

The drip from across the room disturbed her. It was her measure of time, her reference point in a world that was black and riddled with pain. She no longer counted seconds or minutes or days. Time existed only from one drop to the next, and inside those moments, she lived and relived a lifetime. Hers and Afia's and more. There was one image that plagued her more than any other. It filled her mind and pretended it was real. It told her that it could be, had been, and would always be. Afia's little hands explored a face Hazaar knew better than her own. Her cherubic little mouth pouted, then smiled when Charlie's lips curled into a smile that could reignite a dying star. It was her dream, to see Charlie with Afia in her arms. She longed to see them smiling, laughing, loving each other. It was the image that she knew would haunt her as she breathed her last breath, the beautiful picture of her past and her future together. They were the two threads in the tapestry of her life that created the image of her happiness. Slowly, between one drip and the next, they shifted, changed, aged. Afia grew older, lived her life as they watched her grow. She blew out the candles on a birthday cake and put on her school uniform for the first time, a little book bag over her small shoulders, her fingers wrapped around Charlie's hand while she smiled up at her and giggled. Charlie's face was a little different from how she remembered it. There were a few lines at the sides of her eyes, a crease on her brow that had only deepened with age, and there was a smattering of grey that was barely visible in those blond curls. And she had never looked lovelier.

But it was only an illusion, a trick of the light, a misfiring of neurons in her brain. And as the tears fell again from one drop to the next, she knew it was the picture that could never be. They turned their backs on her, those beautiful laughing faces, hands still clasped, their feet striking the concrete to the beat of the falling water.

"Please don't go."

Just one more smile was all she wanted. One more to remember, when she was all alone again. She choked back her sobs as they faded away.

"Please don't leave me alone."

But her dream family never even looked back.

# CHAPTER THIRTY-SEVEN

*Pakistan, today*

Charlie stared at the screen and watched each shape, each person, going about their day. Only the child and Amira had any contact with anyone else, and the spot in the middle of the screen grew darker, smaller, and colder. She watched one shape leave the building and hoped it was Yasar, but in truth it didn't matter if it was Tazim. As long as Yasar was away from his father, she would use the opportunity to speak to him. She picked up her earpiece and slipped it into place as she waited for it to connect.

"Hello."

"Did you think about my proposal?"

"I don't recall you making one, Charlotte."

"Let me take them away for you. Put an end to your problems."

"You think that makes it all okay, Miss Porter?"

Charlie froze. *I never told him my surname.*

"Yes, that's right," he said. "You see, you aren't the only one who can find information."

"Does my surname change the situation with your wife and your father, Mr. Siddiqi?"

"The situation? No. Your part in it? Considerably. Don't you think, Charlie?"

*Fuck.* She looked up and saw Kenzie staring at her. "I'm not sure I know what you mean." So many questions ran through her mind, she had problems picking which one to focus on. Was he simply letting her know that he could find out who she was? Or was he hinting that he knew more about her? And if so, how much more did he know? Did he have her history spread out in front of him? Was he reading her life story as she'd read his? Had he stared at pictures of her, read her dissertation from university? *Fuck.* The realization hit her hard. Did he know that she had been at university with Hazaar? Did he know that they knew each other? Did he know how they had known each other?

He laughed, tearing her from the rollercoaster of unanswered questions clamouring for her voice. "Oh, you do. You know exactly what I mean. So let's not play games. Not now. Time is of the essence, is it not?"

The simple inquiry banished all others from Charlie's mind, and the exodus left her with a single focal point. Save Hazaar. Nothing else mattered.

"Agreed." She wiped her palms on her jeans, but they still felt damp, clammy. "Time is short. Your father has seen to that. The question now is what you intend to do about it?"

"I don't have to do anything about it."

"You'll go to jail if you do nothing."

"No. My father would. And considering his justification, I would be shocked if he was sentenced to more than a year."

"I can prove that you knew about his plan. That you're an accomplice."

"No, I am a husband betrayed, in shock, and under the duress of my father, should I have to explain myself. But we both know how likely that is to happen, don't we, Charlie?"

She knew he was right. There wasn't a court in the land that would try him as an accomplice in the murder of his wife, not in this situation. "So you're just going to sit back and let your father do all the dirty work for you and then reap the rewards. Find another woman to raise your child and warm your bed, is that it?"

He laughed at her. "Perhaps."

"What happened to the man I met earlier who said he was going to protect what was his?"

"I am, so please don't insult me and try your lying and scheming tactics at manipulation."

"I didn't lie to you."

"No, but you were hardly honest either."

"Touché."

"So what is it that you want, Miss Porter? For me to open the door and let you come and take my wife?"

"And her daughter."

"My daughter. She is mine."

"And what life will you offer her without Hazaar? What abuse will she suffer at your father's hands because of who her mother is? How is that fair to her?"

"She is my daughter and I *will* protect her."

"Like you protected Hazaar? She was yours to protect too, wasn't she? You were supposed to protect her, and what state is she in now? How badly injured is she, Mr. Siddiqi? Can she walk? Can she move? Will she live long enough to make it to her execution?" Kenzie grabbed her arm and shook her head, eyes narrowed as she mouthed the word *stop* to Charlie.

"Enough," Yasar said.

She shrugged off Kenzie's hand. "No. No, it isn't enough, Mr. Siddiqi. Is that what your protection amounts to? Is that what you'll allow to happen to your daughter too? Where will you draw the line? When will you say stop for her? When you dig her grave too?"

The line went dead and silence hung heavy in the small space of the van. *Holy fuck, what did I just do?*

"So," Luke said, "that should probably be considered a lesson in how not to carry out a negotiation, Kenzie."

"Yeah, I got that." Kenzie covered Charlie's hand with her own. "You okay?"

"No."

"He isn't going to change the plan. He's happy to let his father take the fall for this. Who knows, maybe he plans for him to have an accident like Hatim did and take over the business while he has the opportunity."

"Maybe."

"He's a chess player, Charlie. His end game is already in play."

Kenzie was right, and Charlie couldn't believe her own foolishness. Why hadn't she seen it? Why hadn't she recognized the tactics? She had spent so many years reading, studying, and playing game after game, moving her pieces around the chequered board, winning and losing, but always learning. And the first thing she had learned was to leave emotion at the door, or logic was always her sacrifice. Now, when the game was at its most important, she had forgotten her most precious lesson. She had surrendered logic and reason to fear. She bent forward and rested her face in her hands. "The queen sacrifice. He's playing the queen sacrifice."

"What are you to talking about?" Luke stared at her.

"The queen sacrifice is a chess strategy where you let your

opponent take your queen for a good position on the board. It's a risky move because you're giving up the most powerful piece on the board for a strategic position. You have to be absolutely sure of the advantage it will achieve, or it can cost you the game."

"So Yasar is going to let his dad do this to get rid of him?"

"In essence, yes." Charlie pictured the chess board, trying to figure out the next move.

"Slimy bastard."

"Yup," Kenzie said. "It's a clever move and practically risk free for him."

Charlie didn't know if Yasar cared for Hazaar, now or ever, but it didn't matter. He hadn't brought emotion to the board, and she had no doubt he was lining his pieces up for the final move, and she had to figure out what that move was going to be and how to counter it. She needed to align her pieces, organize her defences, and strategize her counterattack. If she didn't, they were all in far greater danger than just ending up in a Pakistani prison.

# CHAPTER THIRTY-EIGHT

*Pakistan, today*

Charlie looked out the window as the sun dipped behind the buildings and the sky accumulated the pink, orange, and purple hues as it ushered out the day. She checked her watch and keyed the radio mic on the console.

"Any movement?"

"Nothing." Al was sitting in a tea shop across the street from the Siddiqi house. Kenzie was shopping at one of the local bazaars, ready to play her part. Charlie fidgeted in her seat. She wanted to be out there. She wanted to be the one taking the risks, but Siddiqi knew her face, and they couldn't risk compromising the operation to satisfy her desire to be involved in every aspect of the plan. There were people on the team with far more expertise in this kind of thing than she had.

"Okay, keep me informed."

"I will." She heard a page turn on the newspaper he was reading. "Just like I told you I would five minutes ago."

"Right. Sorry." She chewed viciously on her gum and drummed on the steering wheel of the Jeep that Luke had outfitted with a huge array of toys. Kenzie had practically drooled when he had gone over it all with her. GPS, radios, satellite tracking. Charlie had asked if it would let them follow and keep up with the vehicle they planned on following. When he said yes, she stopped listening and went back to poring over the information on Yasar, looking for anything that would confirm or refute her suspicions about his motives and intentions.

"We have a van approaching. Coming down the main street from the east." She could hear Al folding his newspaper over the mic. "He's slowing down and turning into the alleyway."

"Okay, everyone, you know what to do." Charlie gripped the steering wheel so tightly her knuckles turned white.

"We have movement inside the house," Luke said.

"Are we still missing Yasar?" Charlie hadn't liked the fact that he had left the house earlier in the afternoon and still hadn't returned. Each time she had called, he had refused to answer, and it made her nervous.

"Still no sign of him, C."

"Confirm it's not Yasar getting out of the van. Repeat, it is not Yasar in the van." She could hear Al's breathing over the line as he walked. "The driver has exited the van and is now entering the building."

"Luke?"

"Confirm new heat signature in the house. Two signatures are now moving around. Everyone else in the same positions as before."

"Al, can you hear any conversation between them?"

"Negative. Door's closed again."

"Shit." She slapped the steering wheel. "Kenzie, how are you doing?"

"Device is attached and on now."

"Christ, that was fast." Charlie was a little surprised at how quickly Kenzie had gotten from the bazaar more than two hundred yards away to the back of the small alley at the side of the Siddiqi house. The wall on the eastern side was eight feet high and had to be scaled to enter the passageway unseen. Kenzie told them earlier that she would enter that way to attach the GPS tracker to the underside of the van. She also said that she only needed ten seconds to get the job done. It had only been seven.

"I've got the van online. Nice work, Kenzie."

"Thanks."

"Yeah, yeah, now hurry up and get out of there before they come out." Al grumbled. "I don't wanna be stood out here all fucking day, you know."

"I've got movement inside the house," Luke said.

"Tell me." Charlie visualized the layout of the house. The square courtyard in the centre with the cellar underneath it, the rooms of the two-story building wrapped around the central square and fitted together in smooth blocks.

"Tazim and his new friend have just dropped in temp. They must have gone into the cellar, and it looks like they're approaching the one we assume is Hazaar."

*Oh God, please let her be okay.*

"The three signatures have converged. There looks to be some agitation upstairs."

"What do you mean?"

"The smallest signature ran for the door. If I had to guess I'd say that the kid heard Hazaar scream and bolted to her mum. Amira's got her again. The signatures have converged there too."

Charlie wiped the sweat from her brow.

"I can confirm screaming," Al whispered. "I can only make out what sounds like a child's voice, though."

"Understood," Charlie said.

"The three signatures from the cellar just got warmer, and a hell of a lot bigger. Looks like Daddio is carrying Hazaar out to the van, and Al just arrived, ready to follow. C, we're good to go as soon as these bozos move out."

"Still waiting on Kenzie."

"You called." Kenzie pulled open the passenger door and climbed inside.

"Check that. She's here." She watched Kenzie check her weapon and tuck it into her shoulder holster, then quickly arrange the laptop in front of her. When she was satisfied, she nodded. "We're good to go."

"Looks like Hazaar is now in the van and one of the two is in the back with her. The other one is going back into the house."

"Why?"

"Don't know. Maybe he forgot his lighter or something."

"Not even fucking funny, Odoze."

"Sorry, just trying to alleviate a little—fuck. No, no, no, no, no. Don't even—"

"Luke, talk to me."

"I...oh God, no."

"Luke?"

"I'm pulling up the thermal imaging, Charlie," Kenzie said next to her. "Let's see what's got him so—holy fuck. The bastard."

Charlie looked over her shoulder at the screen. There was one thermal signature lying still, completely unmoving on the floor of what they had presumed was the nursery. It was too large to be the two-year-old child. "Amira?"

Kenzie nodded, but her eyes never left the screen as the largest figure moved through the house. It was clear to see that his temperature had risen from his exertions and the white, red, and orange hues were even visible down the length of his extended arm as he dragged a small, warm shape behind him.

Charlie didn't want to think about what it meant when the two heat signatures merged again and exited the house. She swallowed when she saw Tazim move away from the back of the van alone, and she imagined the terrified child now huddled beside her badly injured mother. She didn't want to think about it, but she couldn't stop herself either. She could only think of one reason why he would take the little girl with them. The van pulled out and she turned on the engine.

There was no way she was letting him do this. None.

"Al, can we get someone in there to tend to Amira?"

"Al's already heading in. You follow them and we'll catch up."

"Got it, Luke. Thanks."

"No need. Be careful, and don't do anything stupid. Just don't let him out of your sight."

She pulled out of her parking spot and hit the gas. "Not a fucking chance."

## Chapter Thirty-Nine

*Pakistan, today*

"This whole fucking place is nothing but rocks and dirt."

"We're heading for the Khyber Pass, Kenzie. What did you expect?"

"A water bungalow over a crystal blue sea, bikini-clad babes, and a coconut drink with a straw and one of those little umbrella thingies."

"You're twisted."

"Yup. But not as twisted as that fucker." She pointed to the van ahead of them.

"Very true."

"C, make sure you keep at least eighty feet back, but within one hundred, okay?"

"Okay. Why?" She glanced over and Kenzie wiggled a small black box. "What's that?"

"I didn't tag them with just a GPS device earlier."

Charlie bounced in her seat as she hit a pothole in the road and did a double take on the gadget in Kenzie's hand. "What the hell? You put a bomb on the van?"

Kenzie grinned. "Just a small one. That way we can make sure they stop before we cross the border into Afghanistan. Dealing with the Pakistanis is a breeze compared to those guys."

"But she's in there with her kid now."

"I know. The charge is only big enough to blow the rear axle. They won't be able to drive, but it won't do anything else."

"What if it catches the fuel tank or something and blows them all to kingdom come? What then, genius?"

"Oh gee, I didn't think of that." She tucked the box in her pocket.

"In case you missed it, that was sarcasm. I've done this before. I know what I'm doing, Charlie, and I wouldn't put lives in danger for a little firework display. This will work. Trust me."

"Does Al know about this?"

"His idea."

"Fuck."

"Not right now, thanks. But I'll keep it in mind for later."

"Why do you always make a joke of everything? Can't you ever be serious?"

"This situation, and you, are plenty serious enough, C. A little levity will help keep me relaxed. That's when I operate best. And today you want me at my best."

She glanced at Kenzie, and the resolute set to her face under the dim glow of the moonlight told her that Kenzie was deadly serious. "You do know that this is supposed to be a negotiation team, don't you? It isn't usually all this action stuff. Think you can handle that too?"

"Sweetie, I have many skills." Kenzie winked and turned back to her laptop. Charlie fought with the wheel as she hit another pothole. "Damn, woman, you need me to drive this thing too?"

"Funny. Stop distracting me."

"Yeah, yeah, blame me. Two days into the job and it's already all my fault."

Charlie kept her eyes locked on the back of the van, carefully maintaining her distance. "Any news from Al or Luke?"

"Yeah. Amira had been knocked unconscious but was otherwise fine. They've got her in the Jeep with them. There wasn't enough time to get her to the safe house. So she's still with them."

"They're sure she's okay?"

"Yeah. Split lip, shook up, probably more scared of being around those two than anything else right now. What'll happen to her at this safe house?"

"Depends on what kind of place Hillary managed to find. Some of them are really good. They help the woman find work, start a new life, that kind of thing."

"And the others?"

"If there are no safe houses, the only way the authorities can keep the women safe is to put them in prison."

"Prison? Are you joking?"

"No. I wish I was." Charlie followed as the van turned right off the main Khyber road. "And then it gets worse. They can only be released into the custody of a male relative who signs to assure their safety." She pointed ahead of her. "What the hell is this road?"

Kenzie studied the topographical map on the laptop. "Shit, unmarked. Kill the lights and get closer to them. Try to follow close enough that we can see by their lights."

"Won't they hear us then?"

"Not over that ancient piece of crap they're driving."

"That means you can't use your bomb." Charlie killed the lights and pushed harder on the accelerator.

"Wanna bet?" She grinned, her even white teeth sparkling in the eerie light from the laptop on her knees. "We just have to make a few adjustments to the plan, C."

"Are you at any point going to tell me what this plan is now?"

"Where would be the fun in that?"

"Let me think." She didn't take her eyes off the taillights she was gaining on. "Survival."

"Well, the plan was to get a little closer to the checkpoint at the pass, blow the axle, swoop in, and save the girl. Now I'm thinking we need to blow this sooner rather than later. The only reason I can think of coming off here would be to head for a rendezvous up in those mountains." She pointed to the mountain range looming ahead of them. "There's probably a network of caves in there where there could be Taliban cells, or they're going to a nomadic village. Here today, gone tomorrow, and never gonna be found again."

"Seriously?"

"Yup." She keyed her radio. "Al, they're off the main road heading straight for the mountains. How far out are you guys?"

"About two minutes, but you have company."

"What are you talking about?"

"You've been tailed all the way out of the city. The driver killed the lights as soon as you left the main thoroughfare."

"Shit. You got an ID on the driver?"

"No, but I know who I'm putting my money on."

"Yeah. How far behind us is he?"

"Just turning off the Khyber road now. I'd say you've got a minute lead on him. Wait."

"What?"

"He's gaining fast."

"Shit. Al, put your foot down and get here. Now." She pulled the black box out of her pocket. "At least eighty."

"I can't see eighty fucking feet."

"Then stop. And when you hear the bang…"

"Yeah?"

"Drive toward the light."

❖

Hazaar felt nauseous and light-headed, but she wasn't sure if it was the pain or the smell of diesel that was causing it. There were several canisters along one wall of the van, and one was clearly leaking. The pain in her soul had an entirely different source. She wrapped her arms around Afia as best she could and cuddled her crying daughter to her chest. She murmured nonsense words into her ear and promised her everything would be okay. She tried to keep her off the cold, rutted steel floor and comfortable enough to allow the motion of the vehicle to lull her to sleep.

It was so unfair, so cruel. She couldn't understand why they needed to punish Afia too. She was just a baby.

"Why are you doing this? Why?" She spoke loudly from where she was lying on the floor, so he could hear her over the rattle of the ancient van.

"You know why. You've shamed us all. You are an aberration of nature and you do not deserve to live. You sully our good name, our people, our religion. Your existence is an insult to Allah himself. What I do, I do to restore balance, order, righteousness to our people. To our family."

"I've done nothing wrong."

"You lie." She heard him move in his seat. "You lie, you cheat, you came to your marriage carrying the impurity of a woman's touch. And you dare to say you've done nothing wrong." He whispered a prayer under his breath. "May the fire burn hot enough to cleanse the stain of you from our family, and the fires of hell scour your soul for all eternity."

"You're mad. You know that, right?"

"What I know is the will of Allah."

"No, the will of Allah was peace, not murder in his name. Not the slaughter of an innocent child."

"She is not innocent. She was fouled by you before she was even born."

"You'd kill a baby because of who her mother is?"

"Spawn of the devil. She too must be purified. The honour of our family will be reclaimed. I will not allow some pitiful woman to destroy what generations of my family have built."

"What? A drug smuggling ring filled with crazy, extremist terrorists? Wow. You must be so proud. You can kill me. It doesn't matter anymore. I've lived more in my short life than you'll ever know. I've loved and was loved. I've known passion and felt the pure, sweet caress of a woman who truly loves me. I've been kissed by an angel and stared into forever when I touched her, watched her sleep, wiped her tears, and listened to her breathe. I've seen my soul reflected back in her eyes." She moaned as they hit a pothole and every agony she felt revisited her. "I will love her forever, and for that, I will never apologize."

A thunderous bang tore through the night and echoed inside the van. Light exploded outside the windows. The floor fell away from her feet, and as she landed on the hard, furrowed steel beneath, for the first time since Tazim had held her legs over the flames, the agony tore through them. She couldn't stop the scream that rose from her chest and spilled over her lips. Afia's terrified cries joined hers as the small puddle of diesel on the floor of the van caught alight.

# CHAPTER FORTY

*Pakistan, today*

"Hit the gas, now."

Charlie didn't need to be told. She was already accelerating hard toward the flickering flames on the underside of the stricken van. Kenzie had her gun out of the holster, cocked and ready. She hoped to God they wouldn't have to use it, but if she had to choose, there was no way she was going to let him kill a child, Hazaar's child. The embassy would understand that. Right?

Kenzie was out of the Jeep before she even stopped. She used one round on the back door as she passed, but she didn't pause. She circled round to the front of the van, arms raised to shoulder height, her head cocked to follow the sight of her gun, then she disappeared from Charlie's sight.

Charlie climbed out of the Jeep and ran to the back of the van. She could smell smoke and burning as she approached, but Kenzie had assured her that the blast wouldn't hit the fuel tank, that it was a safe explosion. The phrase sounded like an oxymoron to her, but what she knew about explosives would fit on the back of a postage stamp. They blew shit up. And something was sure as hell on fire.

"Show me your hands." Kenzie's voice sounded so loud in the darkness, but she couldn't see her. She assumed she was talking to Tazim and his driver. "Now get out of the vehicle, slowly. Keep your hands where I can see 'em."

Charlie reached for the handle on the hanging rear door. She could hear crying inside. A child sobbed, and there was a pained sound of suffering. She wrapped her fingers around the twisted steel that Kenzie's bullet had mangled.

The sharp tinny click of metal at her back caught her attention.

"I wouldn't do that if I were you, Miss Porter." She whirled around to see Yasar's cruel smile glowing under the pale moonlight. "I knew you wouldn't be able to let it go."

"So you followed me to make sure I didn't stop your father."

"Stop him or not, at this point it doesn't matter. I have what I want."

"Your father out of the way."

"Yes. Either he'll be killed by your friend over there, or he'll live and go to prison." He shrugged. "And we all know how easy it is to have accidents in prison, don't we?" He laughed. "So yes, with him out of the way, I will have full control of the business. I won't be held back by some religious zealot beholden to a group of terrorists."

"You don't believe in Islam?"

"I couldn't give a shit about a book written millennia ago. Do you know what religion is, Charlie?"

"Why don't you tell me, Yasar?"

He growled at the use of his first name. "It's a means of controlling a mass population. A set of guidelines in story form that men in their infinite wisdom have twisted and corrupted to mean anything they want it to. They use it to gain and maintain power through fear. Fear for one's immortal soul."

"And you don't fear for your soul, Yasar?" The smell of burning behind her was getting stronger. Kenzie must have been wrong; the fuel tank must have caught on fire. The cries and coughing inside the van were getting louder, increasingly fearful, and Charlie knew she had to get them out of there. Now.

"No. I fear nothing."

"What about the death of an innocent?" She nodded her head in the direction of the van.

"She's no innocent. She tried to leave with my beautiful little girl, to steal what is mine."

"I wasn't talking about Hazaar. Her daughter is in there with her." She could feel the heat coming off the vehicle behind her. She turned and saw that the underside of the van was burning as well, and on one side the paint was bubbling as though it was getting hot from the inside.

"What are you talking about?"

"We saw your father carry your little girl out to the back of the van too."

"You lie."

"No, I don't. Have I lied to you about anything? This van is going to blow up. We need to get them out, now."

"You're an expert in these things?"

"No, but I know it's on fire, and I know that diesel burns and blows up. If I'm wrong, and your little girl isn't in there, what are you going to lose by letting me open the door?" He hesitated and she knew she had him questioning, that the love of his child was the only thing that was going to get him to capitulate. "And if I'm right, then you can make sure your little girl is safe."

"If you're lying to me, I will kill you."

"I'd expect nothing else."

In the dim moonlight, she saw him nod. "Open the door."

She wrapped her hand around the metal and felt the searing sting of her burning flesh as the hot steel branded her. She used every ounce of willpower she possessed to keep hold of it as she tore open the door and let it swing on its hinges. The sudden rush of oxygen into the vehicle increased the burn power, and the flames grew along the draught, kissing the air and eating up anything in its path. Charlie ducked under the back draught and plume of smoke. Driven by instinct alone, blinded by the smoke and heat, she kept as low as she could while she reached into the inferno and grabbed hold of what she thought was a foot.

She knew Hazaar was injured, but there was no time to be cautious. She pulled, praying that Hazaar and the child would be clinging together. The foul stench of burnt hair and flesh filled the air, far more prevalent than the odour of burning fuel, metal, and rubber. She gagged and fought the urge to throw up as she saw that the foot she was holding was charred, the sole blackened and cracked. *Oh God, I'm too late. It took too long.*

She hauled the dead weight as far as she could before she tore her thin shirt from her body and twisted it around her hand to try to beat out the flames that licked at the fabric covering Hazaar's body. The little girl lay on top of Hazaar's body, her small hands clinging to the material across Hazaar's chest and her hair caught in those tiny hands. Hazaar's arms enveloped her and the broken, twisted fingers were covered in soot and blood. They were terribly, horribly still.

*I was too late.* She beat the last of the flames out. The burns to Hazaar's sides, shoulders, and head weren't as bad as she'd thought they were going to be. But in the dim light, it was difficult to tell as they lay still on the rocky ground, neither appearing to breathe. *I'm too late.*

Charlie stared at Hazaar's body. She looked almost peaceful, like she was just holding her baby and sleeping. Wicked hands disturbed the tableau, though. They pulled at Hazaar's arms and tried to rip the child from her embrace. Charlie pushed them away, but everything seemed to be going so slowly. Her arms wouldn't cooperate, and they felt clumsy, like they didn't belong to her as she tried to stop Yasar from separating mother and child.

"Haven't you done enough? Leave them alone."

"This wasn't my doing. Afia wasn't supposed to be here."

"No, but you forgot to account for the religious zealots and how thorough they like to be." She shoved him so hard he fell back in the dirt, her rage giving her strength. "Did you really think your father was going to leave Hazaar's child alone? Were you really so stupid?"

"I told him she was my child. That she was under my protection, and that I would raise her properly!"

Charlie laughed, still unable to tear her gaze from Hazaar and Afia as they lay on the dusty, rocky ground at the side of the Khyber Pass. "I guess you really are that stupid, then."

She heard Yasar roar his indignation as he launched himself from the ground. She prepared herself for the hit, stiffening her back and tensing her muscles, certain he was going to attack her. But he swept past her and kept going. The sickening crunch of bone against bone could be heard even above the creaking of burning metal and the popping of smouldering rubber as the fire raged on. She turned in time to see Tazim hit the ground. He landed on his back and Yasar connected with punch after punch to his father's face. She wondered briefly why Tazim didn't raise his hands to protect himself, then realized she really didn't care. She hoped Yasar beat him to death. She hoped she'd get the chance to tell this all in court and watch as Yasar was led away to prison, poetic justice for the man who thought to make himself king.

Kenzie was standing over them, gun held loosely in one hand, the other wrapped around the arm of a second man. Charlie assumed he was the driver and noted how his arms were fixed with his hands behind his back. She smiled as she realized why Tazim hadn't protected himself under Yasar's onslaught—his hands were cuffed behind him.

Charlie knelt next to Hazaar and Afia. *Do something.* Her first aid training began to kick in, and she started her initial assessment before she even realized what she was doing. She stroked her hand over the baby's head, her hair so soft, like strands of silk between her finger, and she moved under Charlie's hand. A tiny reflexive movement that Charlie didn't even register for a moment. She let her hand drift down the child's back and stared at Hazaar's deformed hands, the same hands that had created the sweetest music Charlie had ever heard, that had drawn from her body unparalleled pleasure. They were bent at odd angles beneath the burnt remnants of tape and gauze. They were warped and misshapen as they trembled in the shadows of the flames.

*Wait.* Charlie stared harder at Hazaar's hands. *Are they? Is that my imagination? Please, please, please, don't be an illusion. It can't be...*

She stroked Afia's hair again and watched as the movement became more noticeable, more definite, and a tiny cough formed in those little lungs. Hazaar's trembling hands were instinctively trying to soothe her child, even though she wasn't conscious. *Smoke. You fucking idiot, they were passed out from the fucking smoke.*

She ran to the Jeep and grabbed the first aid kit, ignoring the pounding she could still hear going on from the fight behind her. *Where the hell is it?* She pulled up the rear seat and searched the cavity for the small green case. When she saw it, she latched her fingers around the plastic handle and pulled it out. Her fingers shook as she tried to put the oxygen mask together to slip over Afia's head. She was coughing in earnest now, trying to rid her lungs of the black smoke, but Hazaar was barely moving. The breath in and out of her chest rattled, and Charlie wished she had two masks, because having to share the one she had between them was going to be of little effect.

She covered Afia's face and turned on the flow of gas. She coughed and cried and struggled to be rid of the irritating mask, but her breathing grew easier. Charlie smiled gently and began to slip the elastic off her head.

"No, leave it. I've got this one for Mum." Luke knelt on the other side of Hazaar and slipped a matching mask over Hazaar's head and turned the tap on the oxygen bottle beside him.

"Didn't hear you arrive."

"Just pulled up now. Al's with Kenzie. You okay?" Luke looked at her as he pressed his fingers to Hazaar's neck. "Looks like you'll need to get your hair cut. Any other burns I should look at?"

Charlie frowned and put her hands on her head. She could feel that one side was considerably shorter than the other and there was a bald patch on the top too. "I didn't feel it."

"Adrenaline. Any other burns?"

She shrugged. "I don't know."

"Okay. We'll get you taken care of. Hands are usually one of the first places to get burns, so hold 'em out for me."

She did as he asked and was amazed to see how badly burned her right hand was. The palm and fingertips were blistering, and she swore she could make out the impression of a keyhole near her thumb.

"Ouch, that looks nasty." He put a wet gel pad over the seared flesh. "This should help a little till we get to the hospital."

"Don't worry about me. It's Hazaar and Afia we need to take care of."

"And we are. Luke has it all under control." Al squatted next to her, touching her back gently. "Kenzie has Yasar and the driver cuffed. Tazim died under Yasar's assault before we could convince him to stop."

"Shame," Luke said, applying more gel packs to Hazaar and Afia.

"Yeah, I know," Al said. "But we have to decide now what you want to do about that." He looked at Charlie.

She frowned. "I don't understand."

"We're in the middle of nowhere, and given the state of the van, we could easily arrange for the bodies to be put in there and for them to have had an accident. Kenzie still has plenty of explosives left to take care of it, and the driver explained that they were carrying forty gallons of diesel in the back of that thing. That's what caught fire."

"Kill them?"

Al shrugged. "It's one option."

"One they deserve," Luke said.

"No." Charlie was shocked that they had even suggested it. "We didn't come here to kill anyone. We came here to stop the killing."

"Then we have two other options."

"We could just leave them here to fend for themselves. Maybe they get lucky and find a village or a car that can get them back to Peshawar."

"No. It's more likely that they'll die trying to find their way out. I said no killing."

"Technically, that's not killing them."

"And that's just fucking semantics, Al."

"Then the third option is to hand them and Tazim's body over to the police. It's going to mean having to explain to the authorities why we were out here and what happened. It's going to mean us explaining why there are explosives under the van when they examine it, why we didn't take our suspicions to them in the first place, and will probably mean us being prosecuted, losing our jobs, causing a diplomatic incident, and going to a Pakistani prison."

"I'm not keen on that option," Kenzie said as she walked toward them, pushing Yasar and the driver in front of her. "I've got another option for you."

"What's that?" Charlie looked at Hazaar's pale face. "And it better be quick, because we don't have much time. We need to get out of here and get Hazaar and Afia to a hospital."

"We could take them back to Peshawar and let them go."

"What the fuck are you talking about?" Al shouted.

"He killed his father—"

"Hear me out. I just need a second. Mr. Siddiqi here is now the head of a rather large drug cartel operating through Pakistan and Afghanistan and smuggling his wares into the UK. I say we let him continue and pass on the information we have to the relevant people who may be interested in his little operation. His cooperation will help to put a number of terrorists, drug smugglers, and other criminal types behind bars and means he's no longer our problem. We can walk away knowing we have him over a barrel, a lot of other bad guys are going to be brought to justice, and that no one is going to prosecute us."

"You'll be signing my death warrant," Yasar said.

"I kinda think you did that yourself when you beat daddy dearest to a pulp back there." He pulled at his cuffs, obviously wanting to get to Kenzie, but Al held him in place.

"Kenzie, I take it you have a number to call?"

"I can do it while we drive."

"You're a fucking genius." Luke held his hand up to high five her.

"I do believe you're right." Kenzie blew on her nails and buffed them against her shirt.

"Enough of the love fest. Can we get moving now?" Charlie was anxious to be under way. They had at least an hour's drive to the hospital.

"No worries. Kenzie, I want you to drive to the hospital with Hazaar, Charlie, Amira, and the child. When you have an address for me to drop these scumbags at, let me know."

"Got it."

"Luke, help her drop the backseat. We need to keep Hazaar as comfortable as possible while they drive. She's going to be heading into shock, if she isn't already. Get Amira in the front with the baby. Charlie, can you sit in the back with Hazaar? It's not going to be comfortable, and you're injured too."

"I'll be fine. Just get us out of here."

She leaned forward and gently kissed Hazaar's forehead. *It's gonna be okay now, baby. It'll all be okay.*

# CHAPTER FORTY-ONE

*Pakistan, today*

Charlie cradled her hand to her chest and tried to block out the pain. She forced herself not to look at the clock, knowing it had only been a few minutes since the last time she'd looked and that there was still far too long to wait till she could get some more pain relief.

"Knock, knock." Kenzie opened the door to her room and dropped onto the end of Charlie's bed. "You're so gonna love me."

Charlie sighed. "Yeah, and why's that?"

She pulled a pair of scissors and a comb out of her pocket. "'Cos I'm gonna fix you up and make you all pretty again." She snapped the scissors open and closed. "Let's get you in a chair and tidy that mop of yours up a bit."

"Kenzie, don't be ridiculous."

"This is deadly serious. We need to get you ready for your big date." Kenzie swung Charlie's feet off the bed and tugged her until she was sitting in a chair. Charlie didn't argue because every miniscule movement released a throbbing ache in her hands. The burn specialist assured her that this was a good thing and that it meant the nerves were repairing and the skin was healing. As far as Charlie was concerned, it was a fucking nightmare.

"What the hell are you talking about?"

"She's awake. Hazaar is awake."

"You said that yesterday."

"Yeah, but now she's awake properly. She's talking, well, kinda croaking, from what I heard the nurse say. The smoke probably did that, so it should get better pretty soon. The doctors are running a shit load of tests, so we'll just have to wait and see. But you may be able to see her soon, and you shouldn't look like you got into a fight with a fireplace."

It had been four days since they'd come into the hospital, and they were being well cared for. Afia was being treated for an infection in her lungs caused by the smoke inhalation, but Amira was with her most of the time, and she seemed fairly settled. Charlie had been told that her hand would heal and didn't require skin grafts, and that her hair had burnt, but her scalp was okay. She didn't care. It was Hazaar they were all worried about.

They had taken her into surgery as soon as they had arrived at the hospital, and the medical staff had been able to tell them very little about her condition, mostly because it would take time to see how Hazaar would recover from the hypothermia and burns to her foot. The wounds to her right side, back, shoulder, and head were superficial and would heal fully in time, and, like Charlie, her hair had fried, but her scalp was okay.

Her broken fingers had been reset and the nerves in one hand repaired. Again, only time would tell if she would regain full function or not. Between the anaesthetic wearing off, the pain medication they administered constantly, and pure exhaustion, Charlie had yet to see Hazaar open her eyes, even though she sat by her side for as long as they would allow, every day.

Kenzie ran the comb over her head and started to even out the shaggy mess.

"Look, I really don't care about my hair. If she's awake, I want to see her."

"Well, since the doctors are with her right now, and that isn't possible, why not let me do this and then we can head over there?" She cut off a shank and dropped it to the floor. "See if we can't put a smile on that sour puss of yours."

"I'm in pain, you know."

"Yeah, yeah. You *are* a fucking pain, that's what I know."

She settled in her chair and smiled for the first time in days. Hazaar was awake. She was going to see her, talk to her, touch her. *My Hazaar, my love.* She couldn't block out the memories any longer so she let them come, and the tears fell alongside her shorn hair. She remembered Christmas morning, waking up in Hazaar's arms, sitting beside her at the piano, and making dinner together in the apartment. She saw Hazaar's face smiling, laughing, and crying, every emotion playing across those beautiful features as they had lived their lives together.

And the last time she had seen her at their graduation, with that endless sadness in her eyes. *My Hazaar.*

It occurred to her that maybe Hazaar didn't remember their life together the way she had. Maybe it wasn't a life she wanted to go back to. The doubts crept in and burrowed into her heart. What if Hazaar didn't want a life with Charlie after all? Was she really going to walk into Hazaar's room and just say "Hey, it's me. How're you doing? Let's pick up where we left off, shall we?" She laughed at herself. This was Hazaar. Her Hazaar, her nightingale, the woman she had waited and searched for. The woman she had dreamed of, and in the depths of the long, lonely nights, she was the woman Charlie had prayed for. And now, she was going to see her again, to talk to her. Would Hazaar still see the woman, the girl, she had been, the one she'd loved?

When Kenzie finished, she wheeled her through the hospital and into Hazaar's room. "I'll leave you to it. Just buzz when you're ready to go."

"Thanks." She heard the door close and slowly stood up.

Hazaar's eyes were closed. The thin cannula under her nose provided humidified oxygen to help her breath more easily. Bandages covered most of her body, and wires trailed to a heart monitor beside the bed. And sleeping beside her, curled against her body, was Afia. Charlie saw for the first time that the woman in the bed wasn't her Hazaar. Instead of being the woman Charlie had dreamed about, she was a woman who had lived through a nightmare. She was mother to a little girl, had been someone's wife, and lived a life Charlie didn't even want to imagine while they'd been apart.

"Charlie." Hazaar's voice was scratchy and hoarse, so different from the voice she remembered, the voice that had whispered intimately to her in the dead of night as they loved each other. "It's so good to see you."

"It's good to see you too."

Anger at the time stolen from them began to filter into the fear that bubbled in her belly, and the acid bile of resentment grew stronger as she realized exactly how much they had missed. And that life would never be what she had wanted it to be.

"You got hurt."

Charlie waved her uninjured hand. "It's nothing. Just a little burn that'll heal in no time."

"I can't believe you're here." Hazaar's voice cracked. "I've dreamed of seeing you again since Loch Ness. All I ever wanted was to be with you again, and now you're here. In Pakistan. How? Why? I'm sorry. I'm getting ahead of myself. I missed you so much, Charlie. So much." She lifted her hand and groaned. "Damn it, I wish I could touch you. I want to make sure you're real."

Charlie looked away. It was a foolish, childish mistake to think that she could get Hazaar back and everything would be like it had been before. Neither of them were the women they had been before they graduated. She stared at the little girl. Afia. *Her name is Afia, and she's Hazaar's daughter*. The child Hazaar gave birth to, that grew inside her because of Yasar. Jealousy added its distinctive flavour to the bile in her gut, and she knew it was going to eat her alive.

"I should let you get some sleep." She reached for the nurse's buzzer.

"I don't need to sleep, Charlie." Hazaar frowned. "What's wrong?" She paused. "I know I must look an absolute mess. I'm sorry. This really isn't the way I imagined us meeting again." She laughed sadly. "I always imagined some romantic setting, candlelight, music, privacy." She nodded to Afia. "Let me see if Amira will take her back to the nursery. I'm told she hasn't been sleeping well because of the nightmares. She must be terrified after the fire and everything. Hang on."

"No. This was a mistake. I'm sorry. You have to take care of your daughter." She pushed the buzzer and Kenzie came into the room.

"That was quick." Kenzie looked confused.

"I need to go back to my room."

"Charlie, will you come back later? We should talk." Hazaar's eyes were wide, her forehead furrowed.

"There's no need, Hazaar."

"What? I don't understand."

"You're safe. You and Afia can go back to England as soon as you're well enough to travel and everything's as it should be."

"What are you talking about? What about us?"

"What about us, Hazaar?" She let her head fall to her chest. "There is no us. You ended it, remember?"

"Charlie, I made a mistake."

Charlie shrugged. "We all made mistakes. But at least now you're safe, and you can go back home, and you can be happy again."

"Are you crazy? How in the world do you think I'll ever be happy without you, Charlie? I've done nothing but dream of ways to get back to you since the day I had to leave. Yes, I made that choice, but the only choices I had were bad and fucking awful. If I hadn't agreed, terrible things would have happened."

"I know. Your dad told me."

"Everything? Doesn't that tell you something?"

"Yes. But that was also more than three years ago, Hazaar. A lot of things have changed for us both in that time. The fact that you're lying there cuddling your daughter tells us that."

"And the fact that you're here right now, you know what that tells me?"

Charlie stared at her. This was the Hazaar she remembered, the one filled with passion and fire, both of which burned brighter in those chocolate eyes.

"It tells me that you never gave up looking for me, either. I don't know how you knew where I was, but you don't honestly expect me to believe that it's a coincidence, do you? Because I'm not fucking stupid. You're here because I am. You're here because you were looking for me."

"I was looking for what we had. For what we were, Hazaar." Charlie cursed her own stupidity.

"Oh, you silly girl. That can never be, not again."

"I know." She laughed bitterly. "That's why it's best if I go."

"No. That's exactly why it's best for you to stay."

"I don't understand."

"I'm not letting you get away from me again, Charlie. Not now, not ever, and if I have to employ your friend here to keep you in this goddamned room while I talk some sense into you, then so be it."

"I'll work for free on this one, ma'am." Kenzie inclined her head and chuckled, ignoring Charlie's death stare.

"Thank you. What's your name?"

"Steph MacKenzie, but everyone calls me Kenzie. It's lovely to meet you."

"And you, Kenzie." Hazaar tuned back to Charlie. "So are you going to stay here and talk to me, or do I have to ask Kenzie to help me with that?"

"Fine." Charlie slouched in her chair. Kenzie left and closed the door behind her.

"Don't pout. You know how that makes me want to kiss you." Hazaar winked at her, and Charlie burst out laughing.

"How do you do that?"

"What? Make you laugh? It might have been three years, Charlie, but I still know you better than anyone else in the world, and I always will." She fixed her gaze on Charlie's. "You're my soul. You and Afia are the only things that have kept me going all this time."

"I've changed." She waved her hand at Hazaar. "Hell, you've changed beyond all recognition. You're a mum, Hazaar."

Hazaar smiled gently at the sleeping child and leaned forward to kiss her head. "Yes, and I know we'll have a lot to figure out. Probably even more than you realize, sweetheart. But I want to. I want you so much. I don't think I can stand the thought of you not wanting to be a part of our lives. I lost you once."

"I felt like you threw me away. You didn't even explain."

Hazaar stared at her, tears welled in her eyes, and her breath shortened. "Is that what you think?" Her voice caught in her throat. "Is that truly what you believe? That I honestly didn't want you? That I didn't want our life together?"

Charlie didn't speak. She couldn't, so she let her silence answer for her.

"Charlie, I was ready to walk away from my family. I was ready to tell them about us. Hell, my dad already knew about us. He was going to let me off the family obligation before Hatim screwed up. Did he tell you that?"

Charlie shook her head.

"He knew about us, and he was going to let us stay together. We'd have to keep it quiet of course, for the family's sake, but it was going to be okay. We were going to have our future together."

"Was going, were, would have been. They're all past tense, Hazaar. None of it happened."

"I love you. I never stopped loving you."

All the nights she'd dreamed of hearing those words again flooded her brain, and the tears rolled down her cheeks. Nights she'd drunk herself to sleep, nights she'd stayed awake, listening to the clock tick away her dreams, one second at a time, as she imagined holding Hazaar and hearing those words whispered in her ear. She'd longed to feel them against her skin, the way they coloured the air and made the whole world bright, gave her body life like nothing or no one else had before or since. She looked up and held Hazaar's gaze. She wanted to reach out and let go of the pain that was eating her up from the inside out, but fear of the unknown kept her from giving in. "That doesn't make everything all right."

"I know. But that doesn't make it any less true, either."

"What is it that you want, Hazaar?"

"Honestly?"

"Yes."

"I want you and me together again."

"How can that happen? You're right. I always hoped I'd find you. But do you really think we can just pick up where we left off?"

"Well, no. But we have to start somewhere, don't we?"

"You're a mother now."

"Yes, and she's a wonderful little girl, and I'm sure…" She paused and looked at Afia in her arms. "Is that the problem? You don't want to be a parent? We talked about children before, Charlie. You always wanted them."

"Afia isn't the problem."

"Then what is?"

"He is." And there it was. The raging fire of jealousy tore through her as she pictured his hands on Hazaar's body, his lips claiming hers, touching her, loving her, and she felt like she was coming out of her own skin.

"He? He who?"

"Your husband."

"What about him?"

"What about him? Are you serious?" Hazaar's eyes widened as she straightened in her chair. "The fact that you have one isn't enough?"

"Charlie, I didn't have a choice. If I hadn't married him, he would have had my father and brother imprisoned and killed. I wanted to be with you. I was ready to give them all up, my family, my culture—none of it mattered compared to you. None of it. All I wanted was our life together." She took a deep breath. "Charlie, I could sacrifice those things for me. I was willing to pay the price of exile for us, but I couldn't condemn my father and brother to death for my happiness—for our happiness. Do you honestly think that either of us could have lived with that choice?"

Charlie stared at her. Every argument she thought of was flawed, imperfect under the love she still carried for Hazaar.

And there it was. She still loved her. Had always loved her, would always love her, and no amount of jealousy or worry about the future was enough to keep her away. No amount of anger would rip them apart when her whole world had been about finding her again. And no amount of pain would match what she would feel if she walked out of the room without telling Hazaar how she felt. None.

But was that enough to make it work? Could it be enough after all they had been through, all they had suffered with each other, for each other, to find each other again? Could they do anything less than try to make it work? *Don't I owe it to myself to at least try?*

"You hurt me."

"I know." Hazaar's voice cracked again. "I wish with all my heart I could take that back. I wish I could undo it, but I can't."

"You made me so angry. But I still love you. I always have."

"And I love you. With everything there is in me." She swallowed hard. "I guess all that's left is whether you can forgive me?"

Afia stirred in Hazaar's arms, turned over, and startled herself awake. She cried at the sudden shock and sat up in the bed, a movement that caused Hazaar obvious pain. Charlie stood and used her good arm to scoop Afia away and cuddled her close to her body. She rocked and cooed until she settled in her embrace and started to look around. She waved a chubby hand at Hazaar and stared at Charlie, her dark eyes wide, her little mouth hanging open, and her tears drying on her cheeks. She felt the little hands grab a fistful of her hair and examine it with gusto. She rubbed Charlie's cheeks and squished them together until Charlie's lips pursed. She looked back at Hazaar frequently, checking she was okay, and Hazaar smiled and laughed gently through her tears.

"Afia, this is Charlie."

"Charlie." Afia repeated and giggled as she pressed on Charlie's cheeks again.

"Without him, I wouldn't have her. And she is a miracle, Charlie. Please forgive me. Let me make it up to you and prove to you that we can be happy together. That we can be a family, and that we can make this work. Please?"

*One last time, can I take that chance? Can I risk it all again?* Charlie stooped to deposit Afia on the bed, then leaned over and kissed Hazaar's forehead. "Yes. Always, yes."

# CHAPTER FORTY-TWO

*The North of England, today*

Hazaar carefully applied cream to the right side of her neck, shoulder, and upper arm. The skin had healed well from the burns, and only a small amount of scarring was visible now. The pigmentation of the skin was lighter than the surrounding flesh, but that was all. Her hair had grown enough for her to have a stylish cut fashioned for the day. Charlie kept telling her she looked like Halle Berry with the new style, and she had to admit that it did look good, but she missed her long hair and couldn't wait for it to grow out.

"No regrets," she said, "not today." She capped the cream and started to apply her makeup.

"Mama?"

"Yes, sweetie?"

"Pretty dress." Afia pointed at her own pink dress and gave her best ballet turn to show it off.

"It is a very pretty dress, baby girl. You look beautiful." She bent over and kissed the top of her head. "Will you go and tell Charlie I'm nearly ready?"

Afia nodded and ran out of the bedroom. Hazaar picked up her necklace and tried to work the clasp, but her fingers still didn't work properly. The nerve damage to her ring and pinkie finger in her left hand had been irreparable, and even though she was making steady improvement, it was clear she would never be able to play the piano again in the way she had in the past. *No. Not today.* She pushed the maudlin thoughts away. Today was the start of a brand-new life for them all.

"Can I help with that?" Charlie stood in the doorway.

"You aren't supposed to see me."

Charlie laughed. "Baby, we woke up together this morning. I think we've destroyed all the typical wedding traditions."

"You're probably right." She handed the pendant to Charlie, and the light glinted off the polished silver nightingale. Charlie deftly fastened the clasp and let it fall against Hazaar's chest.

"You're so beautiful." She kissed Hazaar's neck, just under her ear, and Hazaar still had to fight with herself not to reject the compliment. The burns had left her with more than just sensitive skin. They had left her self-confidence smouldering in the back of the burnt-out van. But slowly, Charlie's genuine love and desire were proving to her that she was more loved and wanted than she had ever been. "Are you nervous?"

Hazaar laughed softly. "No." She reached above her head and stroked Charlie's cheek. "I'm sure about you and this wedding, baby."

"I meant about seeing your dad." Charlie wrapped her arms around her waist and rested her chin on Hazaar's shoulder. "It's been a long time."

"I never thought he'd be able to do something like this."

"It is pretty incredible. But I happen to think he's a pretty incredible guy. I mean, just look what he did to your mum for everything she did to you."

"I still can't believe he sent her to Pakistan." She shook her head. "Do you know what it'll be like for her, living with my father's brother?"

"You mean it isn't a holiday?" Charlie caught her eye in the mirror and winked.

"I'm being serious."

Charlie kissed her cheek again. "I know, baby. I also know that she's probably being treated little better than a servant by your uncle and his wife. And I think your dad is a very clever man."

Hazaar had to agree. Exiling her mother from her home, her friends, her family, and sending her to Pakistan had been a stroke of genius. While he couldn't stand to have Nisrin around him, he couldn't bring himself to harm her either. Yet setting her free to attempt to rebuild another life for herself didn't seem fair either, after the destruction her treachery had caused. Instead, he had carefully crafted an understandable reason for her exile, under the guise of helping his brother care for his sick wife in Karachi.

Hazaar knew that her mother and aunt had always hated each

other, and that her aunt had taken a singular pleasure in irritating Nisrin in every way possible. When she had read the details in the letter her father had sent her while still in the hospital, it had provided Hazaar with a sense of satisfaction and a true understanding of the phrase "what goes around comes around." She had no doubt that her aunt was driving her mother mad. And she loved her father all the more for it. She had believed her mother had loved her, but in the end, she had put tradition and image before Hazaar's safety and happiness, and that was something she could never forgive.

"So back to my original question, and don't think I didn't notice the change of topic—"

"You changed the topic."

"Are you nervous about seeing your dad?"

"He's coming to my lesbian wedding." Charlie raised her eyebrow and waited. "He hasn't seen my scars, my daughter—his granddaughter—and I haven't seen him since I told him I was going to leave, knowing full well he would likely be killed as a result of that decision." Hazaar closed her eyes. "I'm terrified."

"Don't be, *Jugnu*."

Hazaar turned toward the doorway, gripping Charlie's arms that were still clasped about her waist. "Baba."

"I'm sorry. I know I shouldn't be up here, but I couldn't wait any longer." Her father held his hands out, ready to cup her face. Tears ran down his cheeks. "I am so sorry, *Beti*. I didn't know."

"Baba, it's okay. I'm sorry too."

He touched her cheek gently. She expected him to stare at the scars on her neck, but his eyes locked onto hers and he didn't look away. "Every pain you've suffered, I would gladly have suffered in your place. Every wound, scar, and hardship, I would take from you if I could."

"There's no need to do this, Baba."

"There is every need. As your father, all I've done is fail you."

"No, you haven't. You're here today, and that means more to me than I could ever tell you."

"I would never have been anywhere but by your side on your wedding day, *Jugnu*." He glanced at Charlie then back to Hazaar. "No matter who you were marrying."

"I'm going to ruin my makeup." Tears ran down her face, leaving an inky path in their wake. There was so much still to say, so many questions still to answer, but now they had time.

"Mascara washes off, *Beti*." Her father enveloped her in his trembling arms and held her tight against him. "I must ask you one question."

"What?" Her voice was muffled against his chest.

"How did you convince Yasar to divorce? Are you in more danger, Hazaar?"

"No." She chuckled and pulled out of his embrace. "No, I'm not."

"It's a police matter, national security, all that kind of stuff, Mr. Alim. We really aren't allowed to tell you." Charlie grinned. "Hazaar even had to sign the Official Secrets Act because of all this stuff."

"Oh my." His eye opened wide and Hazaar laughed.

"She makes it sound far more exciting and interesting than it really is, Baba." The doorbell rang, and Afia shouted up the stairs.

"Mama, door."

"Okay, baby. Charlie's coming to get it."

"Would you like to meet your granddaughter, Mr. Alim?"

His eyes welled with tears again. "It would be my honour."

Charlie squeezed Hazaar's hand. "Don't be long. This is probably the registrar."

"Okay."

Charlie led her father to the stairs. "Did you come alone, Mr. Alim?"

"No, Fatima accompanied me. She is waiting for me outside. The girl has been wonderful."

"Fatima?"

"Hatim's widow."

"Of course. I'm very sorry to hear about your son."

He waved her off and followed her down the stairs. "The boy was far too like his mother, and we're all better off without them for company."

His voice faded away under Afia's happy squeal. She imagined Charlie hoisting her up into the air and eliciting those wonderful sounds from her lips. Afia was lucky. Despite the life she had been born into, she had known nothing but love from her father, and now from Charlie. The nightmares she had been plagued with after the fire had dwindled, and it had been weeks since the last one. Hazaar hoped they were gone for good and that Afia would forget the memories of her broken body and the flames that had kissed them that night.

She shuddered and turned back to the mirror, where she quickly fixed her makeup and grabbed hold of her cane. The doctors had worked wonders and managed to save her foot, but there were days when the pain was so bad she almost wished they hadn't. Shoes were still far too painful for her to wear, and Charlie had arranged for the garden path to be carpeted so she could walk barefoot. She didn't like the idea of being the only one at her wedding in bare feet, but there was nothing that could be done about that. She refused to be out of her head on pain medication today. She wanted to remember every detail. She hobbled slowly down the stairs.

"Why didn't you call for my help?" Amira stood at the bottom of the stairs with her hands on her hips. "I would have helped you."

"I know. But I wanted to try myself." She stepped onto the bottom step. "And see? I can do it."

"Do you always have to be so stubborn, Hazaar?"

"Yes." She wrapped her arm around Amira's shoulder and leaned heavily against the walking stick. "You should be used to that by now."

"I am. But I think you will always drive me to despair."

"It's just one of the things you love about me, right?"

Amira smiled. "If you insist."

Hazaar squeezed Amira tightly to her. Thanks to Charlie pulling some strings, Amira had applied for and been granted asylum, which meant she could stay with them in England until she decided what she wanted to do, now that the decision was hers to make.

The sun shone brightly in the back garden, and trains of ivy and white and purple roses decorated the fence posts leading to the beautifully carved pergola at the centre of the garden. Friends and relatives were all seated around the centre piece in a circle, all dressed in their finery, all happy and smiling. Charlie's parents sat at the front, clearly positioned so they would be able to see Charlie's face. Beth leaned against the upright post next to the steps at the pergola and blew kisses to her boyfriend and smirked as he blushed and fidgeted in his seat next to her father. Hazaar smiled, immensely glad that some things never changed. JJ, Kenzie, Liam, Luke, Al, and Hillary sat just behind them. After what they'd all been through in Pakistan, they'd been sent home for a well-deserved break. Smiling broadly when they saw her standing in the doorway, Kenzie and Luke were the first to their feet, applauding as she slowly stepped out onto the rich, thick purple carpet, careful where she placed her cane; the last thing she wanted to do today was humiliate herself by falling over and landing on her face.

She climbed the steps gingerly, too busy concentrating on her feet to notice anything else. When she finally stopped, she looked up and smiled at the registrar, then Charlie. She was grinning so widely that Hazaar couldn't help but return the smile and wonder what it was that was amusing her so much. She held Afia in her arms, and she was smiling too. Charlie had insisted upon Afia being a part of the ceremony. As far as she was concerned, Hazaar and Afia came as a package, and she was marrying them both.

Charlie rocked forward on the balls of her feet and winked.

Hazaar frowned a little. *Is she trying to tell me something?*

Afia kicked her feet against Charlie's tummy and giggled, then kicked her bare little feet again. *The little rascal.* She looked down at Charlie's feet and watched her wiggle her bare toes on the purple carpet.

Hazaar tipped her head back and laughed. "Have I told you recently how much I love you?"

Charlie leaned forward and kissed her. "Not nearly often enough."

"Damn. Guess I better marry you, then."

"Is that your way of saying you love me?"

"Forever." She smiled. "It's my way of saying I love you forever."

# About the Author

Andrea lives in Norfolk with her partner, their two border collies, and two cats, running their campsite and hostel to pay the bills and writing down the stories she dreams up.

Andrea is an avid reader and a keen musician, playing the saxophone and the guitar. She is also a recreational diver and takes any opportunity to head to warmer climes for a spot of diving.

Andrea's first novel, *Ladyfish*, received an Alice B. Lavender Certificate and was runner-up in the 2013 Rainbow Awards Debut Lesbian Novel and Lesbian Novel categories. Andrea's second novel, *Clean Slate*, is a 2014 Lambda Literary Award Finalist in Lesbian Romance.

# Books Available From Bold Strokes Books

**Switchblade** by Carsen Taite. Lines were meant to be crossed. Third in the Luca Bennett Bounty Hunter Series. (978-1-62639-058-4)

**Nightingale** by Andrea Bramhall. Culture, faith, and duty conspire to tear two young lovers apart, yet fate seems to have different plans for them both. (978-1-62639-059-1)

**No Boundaries** by Donna K. Ford. A chance meeting and a nightmare from the past threaten more than Andi Massey's solitude as she and Gwen Palmer struggle to understand the complexity of love without boundaries. (978-1-62639-060-7)

**Sacred Fire** by Tanai Walker. Tinsley Swann is cursed to change into a beast for seven days every seven years. When she meets Leda, she comes face-to-face with her past. (978-1-62639-061-4)

**Timeless** by Rachel Spangler. When Stevie Geller returns to her hometown, will she do things differently the second time around or will she be in such a hurry to leave her past that she misses out on a better future? (978-1-62639-050-8)

**Second to None** by L.T. Marie. Can a physical therapist and a custom motorcycle designer conquer their pasts and build a future with one another? (978-1-62639-051-5)

**Seneca Falls** by Jesse Thoma. Together, two women discover love truly can conquer all evil. (978-1-62639-052-2)

**A Kingdom Lost** by Barbara Ann Wright. Without knowing each other's fates, Princess Katya and her consort Starbride seek to reclaim their kingdom from the magic-wielding madman who seized the throne and is murdering their people. (978-1-62639-053-9)

**Season of the Wolf** by Robin Summers. Two women running from their pasts are thrust together by an unimaginable evil. Can they overcome the horrors that haunt them in time to save each other? (978-1-62639-043-0)

**The Heat of Angels** by Lisa Girolami. Fires burn in more than one place in Los Angeles. (978-1-62639-042-3)

**Desperate Measures** by P. J. Trebelhorn. Homicide detective Kay Griffith and contractor Brenda Jansen meet amidst turmoil neither of them is aware of until murder suspect Tommy Rayne makes his move to exact revenge on Kay. (978-1-62639-044-7)

**The Magic Hunt** by L.L. Raand. With her Pack being hunted by human extremists and beset by enemies masquerading as friends, can Sylvan protect them and her mate, or will she succumb to the feral rage that threatens to turn her rogue, destroying them all? A Midnight Hunters novel. (978-1-62639-045-4)

**Wingspan** by Karis Walsh. Wildlife biologist Bailey Chase is content to live at the wild bird sanctuary she has created on Washington's Olympic Peninsula until she is lured beyond the safety of isolation by architect Kendall Pearson. (978-1-60282-983-1)

**Night Bound** by Winter Pennington. Kass struggles to keep her head, her heart, and her relationships in order. She's still having a difficult time accepting being an Alpha female—but her wolf is certain of what she wants and she's intent on securing her power. (978-1-60282-984-8)

**The Blush Factor** by Gun Brooke. Ice-cold business tycoon Eleanor Ashcroft only cares about the three Ps—Power, Profit, and Prosperity—until young Addison Garr makes her doubt both that and the state of her frostbitten heart. (978-1-60282-985-5)

**Slash and Burn** by Valerie Bronwen. The murder of a roundly despised author at an LGBT writers' conference in New Orleans turns Winter Lovelace's relaxing weekend hobnobbing with her peers into a nightmare of suspense—especially when her ex turns up. (978-1-60282-986-2)

**The Quickening: A Sisters of Spirits novel** by Yvonne Heidt. Ghosts, visions, and demons are all in a day's work for Tiffany. But when Kat asks for help on a serial killer case, life takes on another dimension altogether. (978-1-60282-975-6)

**Windigo Thrall** by Cate Culpepper. Six women trapped in a mountain cabin by a blizzard, stalked by an ancient cannibal demon bent on stealing their sanity—and their lives. (978-1-60282-950-3)

**Smoke and Fire** by Julie Cannon. Oil and water, passion and desire, a combustible combination. Can two women fight the fire that draws them together and threatens to keep them apart? (978-1-60282-977-0)

**Love and Devotion** by Jove Belle. KC Hall trips her way through life, stumbling into an affair with a married bombshell twice her age. Thankfully, her best friend, Emma Reynolds, is there to show her the true meaning of Love and Devotion. (978-1-60282-965-7)

**The Shoal of Time** by J.M. Redmann. It sounded too easy. Micky Knight is reluctant to take the case because the easy ones often turn into the hard ones, and the hard ones turn into the dangerous ones. In this one, easy turns hard without warning. (978-1-60282-967-1)

**In Between** by Jane Hoppen. At the age of fourteen, Sophie Schmidt discovers that she was born an intersexual baby and sets off on a journey to find her place in a world that denies her true existence. (978-1-60282-968-8)

**Under Her Spell** by Maggie Morton. The magic of love brought Terra and Athene together, but now a magical quest stands between them— a quest for Athene's hand in marriage. Will their passion keep them together, or will stronger magic tear them apart? (978-1-60282-973-2)

**Rush** by Carsen Taite. Murder, secrets, and romance combine to create the ultimate rush. (978-1-60282-966-4)

**Scars** by Amy Dunne. While fleeing from her abuser, Nicola Jackson bumps into Jenny O'Connor, and their unlikely friendship quickly develops into a blossoming romance—but when it comes down to a matter of life or death, are they both willing to face their fears? (978-1-60282-970-1)

**Homestead** by Radclyffe. R. Clayton Sutter figures getting NorthAm Fuel's newest refinery operational on a rolling tract of land in upstate New York should take a month or two, but then, she hadn't counted on local resistance in the form of vandalism, petitions, and one furious farmer named Tess Rogers. (978-1-60282-956-5)

**Battle of Forces: Sera Toujours** by Ali Vali. Kendal and Piper return to New Orleans to start the rest of eternity together, but the return of an old enemy makes their peaceful reunion short-lived, especially when they join forces with the new queen of the vampires. (978-1-60282-957-2)

**How Sweet It Is** by Melissa Brayden. Some things are better than chocolate. Molly O'Brien enjoys her quiet life running the bakeshop in a small town. When the beautiful Jordan Tuscana returns home, Molly can't deny the attraction—or the stirrings of something more. (978-1-60282-958-9)

**The Missing Juliet: A Fisher Key Adventure** by Sam Cameron. A teenage detective and her friends search for a kidnapped Hollywood star in the Florida Keys. (978-1-60282-959-6)

**Amor and More: Love Everafter**, edited by Radclyffe and Stacia Seaman. Rediscover favorite couples as Bold Strokes Books authors reveal glimpses of life and love beyond the honeymoon in short stories featuring main characters from favorite BSB novels. (978-1-60282-963-3)

**First Love** by CJ Harte. Finding true love is hard enough, but for Jordan Thompson, daughter of a conservative president, it's challenging, especially when that love is a female rodeo cowgirl. (978-1-60282-949-7)

**Pale Wings Protecting** by Lesley Davis. Posing as a couple to investigate the abduction of infants, Special Agent Blythe Kent and Detective Daryl Chandler find themselves drawn into a battle over the innocents, with demons on one side and the unlikeliest of protectors on the other. (978-1-60282-964-0)

**Tumbledown** by Cari Hunter. After surviving their ordeal in the North Cascades, Alex and Sarah have new identities and a new home, but a chance occurrence threatens everything: their freedom and their lives. (978-1-62639-085-0)